Taking Care
of Business

Also by Lutishia Lovely

Sex in the Sanctuary

Love Like Hallelujah

A Preacher's Passion

Heaven Right Here

Reverend Feelgood

Heaven Forbid

All Up In My Business

Mind Your Own Business

Taking Care
of Business

LUTISHIA LOVELY

Kensington Publishing Corp.
http://www.kensingtonbooks.com

DAFINA BOOKS are published by

Kensington Publishing Corp.
119 West 40th Street
New York, NY 10018

Copyright © 2012 by Lutishia Lovely

All Kensington Titles, Imprints, and Distributed Lines are available at special quantity discounts for bulk purchases for sales promotions, premiums, fundraising, and educational or institutional use. Special book excerpts or customized printings can also be created to fit specific needs. For details, write or phone the office of the Kensington special sales manager: Kensington Publishing Corp., 119 West 40th Street, New York, NY 10018, attn: Special Sales Department, Phone: 1-800-221-2647.

Dafina and the Dafina logo Reg. U.S. Pat. & TM Off.

First trade paperback printing: April 2012

ISBN-13: 978-0-7582-6580-7
ISBN-10: 0-7582-6580-8

10 9 8 7 6 5 4 3 2 1

Printed in the United States of America

For Alpha Valree Hines Westbrook, my extraordinary 95-years-young great aunt, who taught in the Georgia school systems for more than thirty years, and who during Sunday School classes and family reunion legacy presentations . . . teaches still.

ACKNOWLEDGMENTS

Another round of thank-yous...yippee! Why does this make me so happy? Because if I'm writing acknowledgments, that means I've completed another book!

In much the same way each pregnancy is different, birthing each novel is its own unique experience. At times, the process of completing *Taking Care of Business* was challenging, but there was beauty in these moments because that's when I called upon the support of my fellow writers and the sustaining power of friends. Veterans Rochelle Alers and the incomparable Beverly Jenkins were their usual inspiring selves. These ladies have been in the game for decades and have written dozens and dozens of novels. So when they say, "You'll get it done," and "You can do it," you believe them. Talking with and learning from the one and only Walter Mosley was a special honor and joy. He's not only a fantastic writer, but also a great person. Look forward to seeing you at the next event, Mr. Mosley! Other authors and industry friends who inspired me during the TCB journey include Brenda Jackson, Pat Simmons, Kimberly Kaye Terry, Ernessa Carter, J. D. Mason, Dwan Abrams, Sasha Campbell, Trice Hickman, Pat Tucker, Jacqueline Luckett, Naleighna Kai (can we say Chi-town, 2012?!), Karla Brady, J. M. Benjamin, publicist Linda Duggins, Black Expression's Carol Hill Mackey, EDC Creation's Ella Curry, Simply Said Accessories Owner Debra Owsley, Urban Literary Review's Martin Pratt, and NBCC founder Curtis Bunn. I want to take a moment and give special homage to two literary ladies who made their heavenly transition during the completion of this work: P. M. Morris and Leslie Esdaile Banks. These two women impacted my life in different ways for different reasons. I never met Patricia Morris, but her presence in my literary journey dates back to the beginning: before contracts and Kensington. She had various Internet websites and networking groups in which I participated, coming together at a time when we both were working to gain a foothold in the publishing field. Leslie, also known as L.A. Banks, was the consummate writer and an amazingly warm, giving, and loving soul. I last saw her in April at the RT Booklovers Convention. She'd just finished working out on a treadmill and I told her I needed to join her next time, never imagining that "next time" would never come. May these sisters rest in peace and enjoy their new lives on the other side.

Without that wonderfully fabulous, amazingly giving, and voraciously word-hungry sect of society known as readers, we writers wouldn't get to do what we do. Well, we could write books, but trust me, knowing that people are reading and enjoying them takes the experience to another level! Here's a virtual hug to just a few of my ardent supporters: Wanda Williams, Lakanjala Campbell, Shiela Toby, Ryan Ivory, Angelia Menchan, Lesley Wilson, Carmon Blalock, Kimberly Nelson-Jones, Tenesha Mapson, Kenya Bradley, Kimberly Chapman-Spotville, Marsha Kroeger, Monty Parker, Mia Danielle, Mary Fleming, Princess Richardson, Sondra Vereen-Cook, Kimyatta Angola, Lawana Johnson, Vanessa Radden, Yolanda Gore, Stephanie Wilson, Shonna Vance, Meta Anthony, Lorraine Mungo, Deborah Banks-Boyd, Genetta Smith, Genetta Jackson Sloan, Valarie Loduem, Kathy Jones, Erma Clinkscale, LaTina Johnson, Angela Peterson, Angela McLemore, LaWanda Grace, Shon Collins, Calisa Lynk, Kenay Bradley, Arnesha Benjamin, and my ride-or-die put-a-candy-bar-in-the-tank chick—Sherri Roulette-Mosley. Ha! Love you, girl . . .

Book clubs are the heartbeat of this reader community, and discussing my novels with you guys is one of my favorite pastimes. I am especially appreciative of those who've embraced The Business Trilogy and those who have it on their list. These are just a *very* few of the clubs who've contacted me about this series, so if I've left out your club, you know what that means...I have to write another book! Love and hugs to F.A.M.E., Drama Queens, Page 59, WEBB (Women Empowered By Books), RARE Books (hello, Ms. Lovelace), Black Pearls, Beauty Shop, Circle of Color, Sistas of Essence, Sistahs On The Reading Edge, Readers In Motion, Sugar & Spice, Beyond Words, and PWOC (Prominent Women of Color). Book clubs...::waving::...hollah at your girl!

I am blessed to work with an absolutely AMAZING editor, Selena James. Her unwavering faith, support, and keen insight to this project were pivotal to what I consider one of the best storylines I've ever written. Her question, "Who are these people and why are they here?" was a game changer! Thank you, Selena. Love you tons!!! And speaking of Kensington, thanks so much to this publishing house that makes me feel like family: Steven Zacharias, Laurie Parkin, Lesleigh, Alex, Rosanna, Robin, Brian, Paula, Hilary, Mercedes, Adeola, and all of the rest. You guys make me happy to spell my name A-U-T-H-O-R.

My family's support is a big ole hug to the psyche all day long. There are no words to thank my mother, Flora Louise; my sisters, Dee and Cella; my brother, Johnny; and my niece, Tanishia, for being my rowdy and encouraging cheerleading section.

As always, Spirit is my constant companion, my very breath. I am grateful for the You in me.

Now we're getting ready to take care of some business, y'all. Sit back, turn the page, and enjoy the ride!

1

All was quiet on the West Coast front. And all was cozy in Bianca Livingston's world as she lay cuddled up next to Xavier Marquis, her husband and the love of her life. Had it been only seventy-two hours ago when she thought she'd go crazy?

Just three short days before this moment, Bianca had stood in the center of TOSTS—her pride and joy—ready to pull the hair she'd decided to grow long again right back out of her head. The chic, quaint eatery on Los Angeles's west side, formally named Taste of Soul Tapas Style, was two days away from its one-year anniversary celebration. The place had been in chaos. The truffle, caviar, and special champagne shipments had all been backordered, the cleaners had destroyed the new waitstaff uniforms, and the chef had been called away due to a death in his immediate family. The stress had brought on the unexpected arrival of Miss Flo, Bianca's monthly, complete with bloating, cramps, and a pounding headache. What was a sistah to do?

Put on her big-girl panties and make it happen, that's what. What other choice was there?

Forty-eight hours ago, Bianca had huddled with her assistant and the sous-chef, who'd then called all over America until they found last-minute supplies of truffles, caviar, and bubbly. After reaming the cleaners a new a-hole, Xavier had called in a favor from a designer friend and had ten new uniforms whipped up posthaste. Finding a selfless bone in her weary body, Bianca had had flowers delivered to the funeral home that housed her chef's brother and had quieted Miss Flo and Company with some prescription-strength pain pills.

Twenty-four hours ago, Bianca had finished her day at the second L. A. Livingston Corporation establishment, the increasingly popular soul food restaurant, Taste of Soul. She'd spent two hours on a conference call with her brother, Jefferson, and the finance department at corporate headquarters, overseen a fiftieth birthday luncheon for a party of twenty-five, and soothed the soul of a hapless vegetarian who'd been losing her mind because she'd eaten the cabbage and *then* realized that this particular selection was seasoned with smoked turkey legs. Bianca had found it convenient that sistah-girl had eaten the entire plate before making this observation, demanding her money back and threatening lawsuits. Not to mention that she'd somehow missed reading the ingredients to the Chaka Khan Cabbage side dish clearly listed on the menu. Bianca was furious but had too much work and too little time to argue. She'd given the emoting customer a gift certificate for two free dinners and a menu to take home so that she could study it before placing her next order. With a bright smile to hide her frustration, Bianca had asked Ms. I-Haven't-Eaten-Meat-In-Twenty-Years to pay particular attention to the items with a small *v* beside the name, identifying them as vegetarian dishes.

Eight hours ago, Bianca had linked arms with her husband and officially welcomed the guests to TOSTS' one-year anniversary. Tickets for the evening's event had been steep—two thousand dollars—but the price included an all-you-can-eat buffet, a champagne fountain (filled with the double-priced bubbly that had had to be rush-ordered and FedEx'd to the event), and an intimate evening with the night's entertainment, Prince. As if pleasing the palate and the auditory senses weren't enough, the tickets were also tax deductible, with part of the proceeds benefiting a soup kitchen. Following in the footsteps that the Taste of Soul founders Marcus and Marietta Livingston had set, the establishments Bianca managed did their part in making the communities around them a better place.

An hour ago, Bianca had kicked four-inch-high stilettos off her aching feet, slid a Mychael Knight designer original off her shoulders, separated herself from a Victoria's Secret thong, and eased into the master suite's dual-head marble shower. Seconds later, Xavier had joined her.

"*Mon bien-aimé de chocolat*," Xavier murmured as he eased up behind Bianca and wrapped her in his arms. "You are the chocolate on the menu for which my heart beat all night long." He took the sponge from her hand and began soaping her slender body from head to toe.

"Mmm, that feels good," Bianca said. She leaned back against her husband's wide, firm chest. Moments before, she'd been dog tired, but now her husband's ministrations were filling her with new, lusty energy. She wriggled her soapy body against his and was immediately rewarded with a long, thick soldier coming quickly to attention. They made quick work of the cleaning process before Xavier lifted Bianca against the cool marble wall and joined them together in the age-old dance of love. The contrast of the cool marble, hot water, and even hotter desire swirled into a symphony with a melody known by Xavier and Bianca alone. This was their first time together in almost seventy-two hours. Ecstasy came quickly, and then they climbed into bed for an encore.

Five minutes ago, Bianca had screamed in delight as her body shook with the intensity of a seismic climax. Xavier, the quieter of the two lovers, had shifted rhythms from second to third, before picking up speed and heading for his own orgasmic finale. He hissed, moaned, squeezed Bianca tightly, and went over the edge. Too spent to move, Bianca had kissed Xavier on the nose, turned herself to spoon up against him, and vowed to take a shower first thing in the morning. She smiled as Xavier kissed her on the neck. *That man knows how to rock my world,* she thought as she looked at the clock. It was early morning: 4:45.

At 4:50, a shadowy figure crouched along the buildings on Los Angeles's west side. He stopped, looked both ways, and walked purposefully toward a door on the other side of the alley. It was the back door to TOSTS—Taste of Soul Tapas Style. In less than one hour, Bianca Livingston's world would get rocked again.

2

On the other side of the country, near Lithonia, Georgia, Marcus and Marietta Livingston were enjoying their morning ritual. It was 8:30 a.m. and because of hard-dying habits honed over half a century of work, this couple had already been up for more than two hours. Marcus pored over the business and sports sections of the *Atlanta Journal-Constitution* while Marietta watched the *Today* show. Or at least that's what Marcus had thought until he looked over to find her staring off into the distance with the slightest of frowns on her usually placid, still wrinkle-free face.

"What is it, Etta?" he asked, though he already knew the answer.

"Nothing," Marietta replied.

Marcus put down the newspaper. "Uh-huh, I know that *nothing*, which means it's definitely something. You got a feeling, huh?"

Marietta nodded, her eyes narrowed.

"Good one or bad one?"

Glancing at her husband, Marietta responded, "It's got my stomach rumbling a little bit."

Marcus passed a weary hand across his chocolate brown,

still-handsome face. Two years ago when his wife's stomach "got to rumbling," they'd soon received a phone call telling them that one of their twin sons, Adam, had been shot. Last year she could have sworn that something was going on in the company, something that—like now—had given her indigestion. Later, their eyes had been glued to the screen as they watched a man in handcuffs named Quintin Bright get carted off to jail. Turns out he'd somehow hacked his way into a Livingston Corporation bank account and helped himself to hard-earned company funds. To this day, Marcus believed that there was more to that story than the twins had shared. He figured now may be just as good a time as any to get to the bottom of that mystery, along with the one that even now had his wife's face, as beautiful in her seventh decade as it had been in her second, marred with a frown.

"Mama." Bianca paused, trying to hold on to the last vestiges of control she had before breaking down from the pressure of an early morning phone call. "Let me talk to Daddy."

Diane Livingston, who'd been enjoying a cup of coffee with her husband in the family's newly remodeled kitchen, immediately knew something was amiss. She sat up straighter, put down her coffee cup, and asked, "What's wrong?"

"It's business!" Bianca cried. "I need to speak to Ace!"

Ace heard Bianca's raised voice and reached for the phone. A quick look passed between him and Diane. "Ace speaking," he calmly answered. He'd noted the alarm in his daughter's voice yet spoke professionally, the way he always did when discussing work with his children.

This sense of normalcy was exactly what Bianca needed to calm her escalating panic. "Ace," she said, speaking in a strong voice even as tears threatened, "there's been a fire."

Fire, Ace mouthed to Diane, who looked on with deep concern. "Where at, baby?"

"At TOSTS."

Ace frowned, the father in him replacing the businessman. "Bianca, are you okay?"

She, too, segued from businesswoman to daughter. "Yes, Daddy. A little panicked but otherwise I'm fine."

"Where are you?"

"We're on our way to the restaurant."

"Xavier is with you?"

"He's driving."

"Good." It had been a rocky road at first, but Ace had come to both respect and love his fiercely independent son-in-law. "Call me as soon as you get to the site."

"Okay, I will."

"And, Bianca?"

"Yes?"

"We'll be on our way there just as soon as the pilot can gas up."

They said their good-byes and Bianca hung up the phone. Even though she didn't know the extent of the damage, she didn't think for a moment to tell her father not to come. When something happened to one Livingston, it happened to all of them. That's just how they rolled.

Marietta was channel surfing but upon seeing a commercial featuring her grandson, she stopped. "You can barely turn on the TV these days without seeing Toussaint." She tried to add a bit of chagrin to her tone, but it couldn't get past all the pride in her voice. "That child sure loves a camera."

"And the camera loves him," Marcus said, noting how handsome his grandson looked and how natural speaking to millions through a small camera lens came to him. Because of his presence on the Food Network and his brother Malcolm's BBQ Soul Smoker invention, the Taste of Soul brand had witnessed a phenomenal national growth spurt in the last two years. The line of Livingston barbeque sauces was now in every major chain across the country, including Target and Walmart, and was being sold in very large volumes.

"Did you ever see this coming, Marcus? Any of this?"

Marcus shook his head. He knew exactly to what Marietta referred. When they took over managing a small barbeque joint on Atlanta's famed Auburn Avenue at the beginning of the civil rights movement, they had no idea that their tireless efforts would result in a trend-setting food conglomerate that, combined with the entrepreneurial efforts of the third generation of Livingstons, was worth well over a half a billion dollars. "All I wanted to do was get through college and save enough to buy you a ring."

"Oh, so you were that sure of yourself, huh?" Marietta asked, a twinkle in her eye as she remembered the tall, dark, handsome man who'd cut quite a swath across campus. "And all this time I thought you were just looking for a competent waitress."

"Honey, the way you whipped up those baked beans and potato salad, not to mention how those curves of yours filled out that baby blue uniform? Any man would have been a fool not to know you were worth more than a weekly paycheck."

"Ha! Especially when that check barely topped ten dollars."

"C'mon, now. You got to keep the tips."

Marietta fixed him with a look of chagrin, but her eyes were smiling. "We were crazy to do what we did."

"Yeah, well, crazy comes with youth."

These septuagenarians became quiet as they remembered those early days, when Marietta was carrying a full load at Spelman and Marcus was juggling a double major at Morehouse. The days before both of their thick heads of hair turned gray. Marcus's father had inspired in him the love of grilling. Even as a teenager, helping Papa Nash cook vats of his secret barbeque sauce on Saturday afternoons was one of his favorite pastimes. A whole hog would be turning on the spit and Mama Jane would be whipping up cobblers in the kitchen. The next day, he and his brother would jump into their grandfather's jalopy and sell barbeque dinners across Alabama, where Marcus was born, until the foil-wrapped dinners were gone. A whole pig every single Sunday . . . that's what they'd sell.

And that's how Marcus had gotten seriously bit by the barbeque business bug. When a classmate told him that his uncle needed help at his restaurant, Marcus jumped at the chance to run the spot. Later, when the owner decided to sell, Marcus took a look at the ledgers and the long lines of patrons and put his dreams of becoming a doctor on permanent hold. After a handshake sealed the deal, he brought in the woman he'd been eyeing at the Spelman / Morehouse meet-ups to run the front of the house and married her that same year. The next year saw the birth of their twins, Adam and Abram (nicknamed Ace), and the rest is Livingston history.

Both Marcus's and Marietta's attention was pulled back to the television when a "Breaking News" banner filled the screen. Soon thereafter, a reporter came into view, with a smoldering building serving as her backdrop. Marietta reached for the remote and turned up the volume.

"An explosion rocked Sunset Strip early this morning," the reporter intoned in an appropriately serious voice, "sending residents running for cover and causing early morning joggers near the location to flee for their lives. Officials say that TOSTS—"

"Jesus!" Marietta exclaimed.

Marcus leaned forward as a scowl jumped onto his face.

". . . the trendy tapas bar on the city's west side went up in flames around five a.m., totally destroying the building and all its contents. So far it appears that the business was empty. No injuries or missing persons have been reported. Major damage was sustained by the neighboring buildings as well, but at this time, reports remain sketchy as to the cause of this powerful blaze. What is known is that this morning, as the smoke clears, it is to find that this popular new establishment, Taste of Soul Tapas Style, has literally gone up in smoke. For Channel Eleven News, I'm Leslie Myers reporting."

Marcus had already reached for the phone and was speed-dialing his son's number as Marietta muted the television. No words were exchanged. None were needed. Because both knew they'd just heard why Marietta had "got a feeling" that made her stomach rumble.

3

"Toussaint!" Alexis Livingston hefted her eleven-month-old daughter onto her hip as she headed to the master suite, her waist-length locs swinging back and forth with the motion. "Baby, come here!"

Toussaint shut off the water and stepped out of the shower. Ignoring the water pooling off his dark chocolate, six-foot-two-inch frame (not to mention his delectable nine-inch flame), he reached the bathroom door in four long strides. He'd heard the tremor in his wife's voice. Something was wrong.

They reached the bathroom door at the same time—Alexis on one side, Toussaint on the other. He pulled open the door and, seeing his daughter's observant eyes and ready smile, muted his response. "What is it?"

"The news," Alexis said, walking into the suite and turning the television to CNN. "They just broke a story about a fire at TOSTS." CNN had moved on to another story so Alexis kept punching the remote, searching for another station that might be reporting on what she'd just heard.

Still naked, Toussaint walked to his cell phone charging on the nightstand. He punched Bianca's number on speed dial.

The call went to voice mail. "Cuz, it's me. Lexy just saw something about a fire at TOSTS. Call me."

In the time it took for Toussaint to leave the message,
Alexis had gone into the bathroom, retrieved a towel, and
begun to dry off her husband's still-wet body. He reached for
it, carelessly wrapping it around his lean hips while he balanced the cell phone under his chin. The call to his parents'
house went through. His mother answered.

"Good morning, son."

"Mama, have you heard?"

Candace Livingston, who had been working out in the
family's home gym, trying to keep size fourteen from becoming sixteen, turned off the treadmill and reached for her water
bottle. "Heard what?" she said, before stepping down and taking a long swig.

"There's been a fire at TOSTS."

Candace almost choked on the liquid. "What?"

"I was in the shower, but Lexy heard the tail end of a
breaking news story about a fire that happened early this
morning. She's trying to find the story on another news station. I just called Bianca and got voice mail."

Candace immediately went into Livingston mode: everyone informed, everyone involved. "I'll call your father."

"Good. I'll call Ace." Toussaint got ready to call his uncle,
but before he began dialing, his phone rang. "Ace," he said
after checking the caller ID, "I was just calling you about the
fire at TOSTS."

"Bianca called a short while ago."

"She's okay, then?"

"Yes. She and Xavier were on their way to the restaurant
when we talked. She had no idea then how bad it was."

"It looks pretty bad, Ace."

"So you saw the news."

"I'm looking at the picture right now." Toussaint sat on the love seat in the master suite's sitting room, taking in the devastation he viewed with disbelief. "It looks like a war zone."

"Bianca had to have been devastated when she saw it."

"I just tried to reach her before calling you and got voice mail."

"She's tied up with the authorities and reporters. Xavier called to give me an update. I told him we were heading that way within the hour."

"I'll meet you at the airport."

"Adam is going to stay here and hold down the fort, and try and keep Mama and Daddy calmed down."

"The grands know about this already?"

"Yes," Ace said with a sigh. "They were watching television when the story broke."

"Well, so much for keeping GrandMar out of this one." GrandMar was what the family called Marcus after Toussaint's older brother, then two years old, refused to call him *Grandpa* or anything else.

Ace's chuckle held no humor. "We've been fortunate to keep him and Mama unaware of the level of craziness the family has handled these past few years. But he's going to be smack dab in the middle of this situation. He's already on his way to the office. Needless to say, Adam is in for a grilling."

Toussaint smiled in spite of the seriousness of events. "Marcus Livingston . . . my man."

"It's been hard trying to keep Daddy in retirement."

"And out of family drama, especially when the news is all over the TV."

Ace's next thought was verbalized before he could stop it. "I just hope this was an accidental fire that can be handled with a few insurance papers and an efficient construction company."

Toussaint was immediately on alert. "Of course it's an accident. What else could it be?"

"Nothing else," Ace said a bit too quickly.

"Uncle..."

Of the business dynasty's third generation, Toussaint was by far the most volatile. But spilled milk couldn't be put back in the bottle, so Ace tried to make light of what he'd just said. "Don't mind me, boy. You know I watch too many crime shows, always looking for an ulterior motive around every corner."

Toussaint laughed, but an uneasy feeling remained. With all that had happened to the Livingston clan over the past two years, no one would fault them for being paranoid. "I'll meet you at the airport," Toussaint finished.

"I'll call Jefferson so he can meet us there as well." Ace hung up and quickly dialed his son. When Jefferson's home phone went to voice mail, he hung up and dialed his cell. There, too, he was met with a message. "Jeff, it's Ace. Meet me at our private hangar as soon as you get this message. There was an explosion at TOSTS last night. It burned to the ground. Your sister needs us."

On the other side of town, Jefferson Livingston rested his head against the back of his chocolate-brown leather recliner. His television was muted, yet he watched images of firemen scurrying behind his sister, whom he'd earlier heard speak of her sadness at arriving to a business quickly going up in flames. He took a drink, punched the button on his answering machine, and listened once again to his father's request—to meet them at the airport for an emergency flight to Los Angeles. A part of Jefferson knew that he should be off the couch, in the shower, and flying through traffic to board the plane. But the larger part of him—the part that was still smarting over the fact that Bianca had been chosen for the West Coast job over him in the first place, and the part that knew his favorite cousin, Toussaint, had cast his vote for her, and the part that still wrestled with other, more personal events that happened last year—didn't give a damn.

He looked down at his glass and, noting that it was empty, reached beside him. Soon a small trickle of premium cognac was filling the crystal tumbler that for the past few months had rarely left his side when he was home.

It was not yet 10:00 a.m., but for Jefferson, the fact that liquor had replaced coffee as his breakfast drink of choice had stopped being a problem.

4

As news about the TOSTS fire spread across metropolitan Atlanta, Georgia, reaction was mixed.

At the law firm Riley & Company, Cooper Riley, Bianca's ex-fiancé, slowly sipped his coffee as he watched the woman he'd loved for more than half his life being interviewed on the news. His heart clenched in spite of himself as he watched her, looking attractively disheveled in a T-shirt and jeans, her shoulder-length brown hair pulled back in a ponytail, no makeup and beautiful. He tried not to notice the strapping Frenchman by her side, his arm protectively wrapped around her shoulders, a scowl properly displaying both power and concern. Cooper was in love with another woman and happier than he ever thought he'd be without Bianca. But a part of him still ached for her. As he turned off the television and opened the file of the day's cases that were before him, he wondered if it would always be this way.

In downtown Atlanta, near the Bank of America building, Shyla Martin's eyes remained glued to the television set even though she'd seen the newsflash half a dozen times. *Serves those bastards right,* she thought as she absentmindedly stirred her tea.

The ex-marketing director for the Livingston Corporation, who'd once been an integral part of their operations, Shyla had had a rib to pick with this soul-food dynasty ever since she was unceremoniously canned almost two years ago. Selective memory had allowed her to disregard the fact that very specific actions on her part had led to their parting of the ways. Namely that she'd tried to take her and Toussaint's casual intimacy to the next level by inviting herself on a business trip, finagling her way into his hotel suite, and shocking the guest who he *had* invited—and who was now his wife—when she'd returned to their room. Instead of Toussaint, a near-naked Shyla had lounged in the bed.

To call the subsequent chain of events a brouhaha would be putting it mildly. Shyla was asked—translated, forced—to submit her resignation, and an attractive incentive of a $200,000 severance payment had sweetened the deal. She'd left the company and, for a while, the state. Her return last year had not been without its share of drama, and now, with a dwindling savings account and a still-bare ring finger on her left hand, forty-one-year-old Shyla found herself working at a small advertising firm, one she'd snubbed her nose at years ago when they'd tried to entice her away from Taste of Soul and one she'd come crawling back to—head held high and attitude in place, mind you—six months ago.

Shyla flipped through the channels to see if there was another station reporting the fire from another angle. Satisfied that there was not, she turned off the TV and once again focused her attention on her latest project—a campaign for an all-inclusive insurance company. An undertaking that was about as exciting as watching a turtle cross the lawn, Shyla decided. And then, without warning, something else came to mind. Or, more specifically someone. Shyla stood from her desk and walked to a window that looked out onto a nondescript parking lot. Its plainness, however, could not dim the beauty of the warm, spring day with bright blue skies, fluffy cumulus clouds, and sun everywhere. Nor could the concrete crowded with parked cars skew the vision in her mind's eye of a man she hadn't seen in over a year and had seldom thought about . . . a man who at one time could almost cause her to orgasm just by looking at her. "Interesting that I'd think of him," she whispered to herself, even as she returned to her desk to again focus on the insurance campaign. "I wonder if he watched the news today."

He'd watched. And now, in a prison more than five hundred miles away, Quintin Bright settled his back against a narrow bench. He gripped the steel rod above him, the ends of which held one-hundred-pound weights. He balanced his large feet on either side of the bench, planted them firmly on the concrete below him, closed his eyes, and channeled all of his energy into lifting the barbell off of its dock and high above his head. "One," his exercise partner intoned. "Two," he said after Quintin had lowered the bar and raised it again. And on it went until Quintin had successfully completed ten repetitions, his muscled arms glistening with sweat and rippling with power as he lowered the bar a final time and placed it in its holder. And as he lay back on the bench gathering his strength to do ten more, he thought of the newscast he'd heard earlier today. The family he felt was responsible for his present predicament had experienced a setback. Quintin felt the joy of this turnabout. *Those Livingston muthafuckas are getting a little taste of the heat I've been feeling for the past damn year.* Quintin smiled, reached for the bar, and after making quick work of ten more lifts, sauntered over to the basketball court to finish his one hour of exercise in the prison yards.

Joyce Witherspoon ran a hand through her freshly cut curls as she watched the news story being reported on television with more than a mild interest. Just yesterday she'd clicked on the TOSTS Web site, becoming immediately intrigued with the eatery's idea of serving upscale soul-food appetizers and high-end signature drinks. Her mind envisioned such cuisine at her events: being offered to guests by handsome servers in stark-white jackets. Bad blood between them aside, Joyce continued to admire the Livingstons' highly astute business acumen, still desired to marry their successful reputation and stellar food with her rapidly growing business. Reaching for her mouse, she absentmindedly scrolled through the five-page proposal outlining a series of fund-raisers for a political client. But her eyes weren't really seeing what she'd typed for the influential congressman Jon Abernathy. They were focused on another proposal. One she'd sent to the Livingstons about two years ago . . .

She'd just started her event planning business, Loving Spoonful, and had approached Adam Livingston about Taste of Soul and its legendary chef, Oliver Bouvier, becoming her primary catering source. Part of the reason she'd initiated these discussions in the first place was because she'd wanted him to get a little taste too. Of her. He'd initially dismissed her overt flirtations but after a while made it clear that he was not only happy with his wife, Candace, but also faithful to her. At the end of the first round it was Business: 1, Personal: 0.

Then there was his son, Malcolm. This business partnership had started quite by accident, through conversations begun when she'd run into him at FGO, For Gentlemen Only, an exclusive old boys' club recently opened to women. The result had been her very critical participation in the launch of his wildly successful meat smoker. Something else had almost commenced—an affair. His marriage had hit a rough patch, and Joyce had been more than willing to help him smooth things over. She'd even gotten a chance to stroke the Livingston love stick—long, thick, and she imagined quite powerful. But much to her chagrin, she'd discovered that something called the *Livingston legacy* trumped the desire of a Livingston stick, and fondling aside, she'd basically come away empty-handed. Oh, he'd paid her for her participation in presenting his invention, and then he'd politely told her to get the hell on. At the end of the second round: Business: 2, Personal: 0.

Joyce clicked off the presentation and picked up the phone. It had been more than a year since her last dealings with the Livingstons. Perhaps enough time had passed for her to attempt yet another venture with this soul-food dynasty. In short: maybe it was time for round three.

5

Chardonnay Wilson sat in her office at the Taste of Soul Buckhead location, her eyes riveted to the flat screen. It had been that way since the restaurant's assistant manager first arrived at work and heard the news: Bianca Livingston's business baby—Taste of Soul Tapas Style—had burned the hell up. "God don't like ugly," she mumbled under her breath, sitting back in her chair and crossing her arms. *That's what y'all nuckas get for not giving me the paper you promised.* She'd never gotten over what happened last year—that she'd helped put the man who'd stolen from the Livingston Corporation behind bars, only to have them renege on the reward money. They'd promised up to a quarter million. Instead, for her troubles she'd gotten ten lousy grand. That she'd seriously damaged her money-making position with the Livingstons before said man was captured (by trying to blackmail Bianca and when that didn't work, later selling a story about her to the *Atlanta Inquirer*) was—for Chardonnay—beside the point. If she'd had her way, a few more locations would go up in flames, along with some of their houses.

She was tired of seeing wealthy people get over on others without consequences. Now, if you were poor, and hustling, and trying to get over, that was another story. Namely hers. So even though her babies were fed from Livingston paychecks, her bosses' seemingly effortless success (that had actually come through hard work and sheer determination, with a little blood, sweat, and tears thrown in to boot) was a continual stick in her less-than-humble craw. In her opinion, it was time for the high and mighty Livingstons to get brought down a peg or two, find out that the sun didn't rise and set on their barbequing asses. Five feet four inches and about a buck-o-five of pissed off sat stewing, trying to figure out a way to recoup her perceived losses.

A click of the office door sent her hands scurrying toward a stack of papers to pick up and look busy. If she'd been working instead of brooding, she would have had the front of the house schedule mapped out half an hour ago.

"Hey, baby girl." Bobby Wilson, Chardonnay's husband and the sous-chef at Taste of Soul, sauntered into the office. There was a ton of confidence packed into his slight, five-foot-nine-inch frame, and what he lacked in height he more than made up for in what he was packing behind the zipper. His oversized appendage had been one of the things that had most surprised Chardonnay and a large part, pun intended, of the reason why she married him.

"Damn, Bobby. You scared me. What the hell you want?"

Bobby crossed the room and plopped down in one of the two chairs facing her desk. "Okay, what you meant to say was, 'Hey, baby. I'm so glad to see you. I was just thinking about how good some on-the-job dick would be right about now.' Go ahead, I'm waiting."

"Yeah, whatever, okay?" She acted properly bored, but his words had caused a flutter in her va-jay-jay. More than once, she and her husband had taken advantage of the modest privacy afforded in the pantry and maintenance room, and a few times after hours right on the main dining room floor. "What's that, the food order for next week?"

Bobby placed the paper he'd been holding on the desk. "For the next couple weeks, actually. Chef wants to get a jump on the Memorial Day crowd and increase the orders of ribs, chops, chicken, and beef. Last year we came up short with our grass-fed product and had to substitute. He doesn't want to be left hanging this year." He looked up at the muted TV, which was showing scenes from the fire at TOSTS yet again. "That's too bad about the fire in LA, huh? I still can't believe how bad it was, burning down to the ground. The report said it went up in flames in a matter of minutes. That blaze must have been hella strong."

"It was a restaurant, Bobby. Lots of flammable liquids. Plus, the place wasn't that big from what I hear." Chardonnay shrugged. "It don't matter. They have insurance. They'll file a claim, collect a bunch of money, and probably build a couple more restaurants as a result."

"Be careful not to show too much compassion," Bobby sarcastically retorted.

"Okay, I won't."

The two were quiet a moment as Chardonnay shuffled papers and logged times into the computer, and Bobby continued to watch the words scroll across the bottom of the TV screen.

"I wonder who did it."

Chardonnay's head popped up. "What?"

"The fire. I wonder who set it."

"Who set it? You mean like . . . on purpose?"

Bobby nodded.

Chardonnay frowned. That the fire had been set deliberately was something she hadn't considered. "You think this was arson?"

"Maybe," Bobby said with a shrug.

Chardonnay immediately thought about the man she'd helped put behind bars and wondered if he was out. Another squiggle in her va-jay-jay. She and Man-in-Prison-Who-Might-Be-Out-of-Prison had once had quite the fling.

"Don't you think it's weird how it burned like that? Could a grease fire be that strong?"

"It's either that or some fool left a fire under a pot, and if that happened, somebody's getting ready to be a sued, broke-ass chef!"

Bobby's cell phone vibrated against his waist. He pulled it out of the case attached to his belt. "What's up?"

"Did you hear about the fire?"

"Yeah. Me and Chardonnay was just talking about it."

"Still want to put all of your marbles into the Taste of Soul basket? Or are you ready to spread your wings and have your own joint?"

"I already told you, there's too many strings attached to that proposal."

"Only one, really," the caller said. "Me." When Bobby remained silent, the caller continued. "We'll make it well worth your while."

"We?"

"Yes. I've pulled in two more major investors with deep pockets. It can be whatever you want, Bobby. The sky is the limit. In Atlanta, there won't be anyone in the restaurant business badder than you. Will you think about it? Seriously?"

"Yeah, I'll think about it."

"Good. Come by my house later on. I've got someone I want you to meet."

"Bet." Bobby hung up the phone.

"Who was that?" Chardonnay asked.

"Just another restaurant interested in my grilling skills."

"Which one?"

"You ask too many questions, woman," Bobby said, rising from the chair and heading to the door.

"If I'm asking, then I must want an answer."

"I'll see you when you get home. And I'm getting off before you do, so I'll pick up the kids."

Chardonnay's eyes narrowed as she watched Bobby leave. *So you've got secrets, huh? Is that it? You think something is going to go down without me knowing about it?* She reached for the remote and turned off the television, ready to focus on finishing the schedule and getting back on the floor. For now she wouldn't put too much energy into finding out whatever her husband was hiding. Because when it came to secrets, she was carrying a pretty big one herself.

6

In a luxuriously appointed home situated in a gated portion of LA's tony Marina del Rey community, the mood was quiet and the faces were grim. The initial shock had worn off, but everyone present—Bianca, Xavier, Adam, Ace, Toussaint, and Toussaint's brother Malcolm—were still taken aback at the ferociousness of a fire that virtually obliterated a building in less than fifteen minutes. Various scenarios as to the cause had been bandied around: gas leak, unattended lit burner, cigarette flicked on a combustible surface. In the end, it was decided that the best thing to do was wait for the fire chief's initial report. That and try to console a grieving Bianca, devastated at the loss of her baby—more than twelve months of blood, sweat, and tears gone up in smoke. To her credit, she'd remained stoic through that first critical hour, when the lookyloos were swirling and cameras were all up in her face. She'd stayed strong through endless rounds of questioning by newspapers, TV stations, and the police. It wasn't until the authorities had finally allowed her inside the shell that remained and she saw the charred TOSTS sign lying on what had been the eco-friendly bamboo floors that she broke down.

"We can rebuild, baby girl, simple as that," Ace said into

the silence, ignoring his feeling that things weren't this simple. He pushed aside his half-eaten plate of food that had been delivered from the West Coast Taste of Soul location. No one had eaten more than a few bites.

Bianca nodded. "I know it's just a building, Ace," she whispered. "But I gave that place every ounce of energy inside me. We all worked hard to make TOSTS what it was, literally the toast of the town. And for that to be taken away in a matter of minutes is hard to take, you know?"

Ace put an arm around his daughter. "I know."

Xavier, who'd been intently watching the heartfelt exchange, poured a glass of water from the carafe sitting on the table and then walked over to his wife. "Your father is right, *cherie*," he said, handing her the glass and placing a kiss against her temple. "We will build again. And we will spare no expense." Xavier placed a comforting hand on Bianca's shoulders and looked directly at Ace. "Whatever the insurance policy does not cover, I will provide."

Ace simply nodded. He squelched the urge to refuse Xavier's generous offer. When it came to Bianca no longer being his baby girl but somebody's wife, Ace was still learning the ropes. His youngest child's marriage had been unexpected and unapproved by him. So accepting Xavier had come in stages. Helping Ace, however, was the fact that thanks to Xavier's late grandfather, his son-in-law was an extremely wealthy man. "I appreciate that, Xavier," he finally said.

Xavier nodded. "No worries, Ace." He began massaging his wife's shoulders.

Bianca bowed her head as Xavier's strong fingers went from her shoulders to the nape of her neck. "I still can't believe it," she whispered, a fresh tear rolling down her cheek. "Last night was so perfect. The place was packed, standing room only, a line down the block. We had such a good time—"

Her comment was interrupted by a knock on the door.

Toussaint quickly crossed over, looked out the side pane, and opened the door. "Are you the fire chief?" he asked the uniformed gentleman with deep laugh lines framing his hazel eyes and gray streaking his brunette hair.

The stranger nodded. "May I come in?"

Once he entered the home and took a seat in one of two wingback chairs, he dove right in. "Preliminary findings show that a gas leak led to the explosion that caused the fire at your restaurant. It's the only explanation for what substance could generate a heat that strong."

"How does a gas leak happen?" Ace thought that the explanation made sense but given the family drama of the past few years, he couldn't help but feel there might be more to the story.

"Gas leaks can occur in several ways," the fire chief answered. "It can be something as simple as leaving a burner on or something as complicated as a leak in the gas line below the building—one too small to elicit notice through a smell or malfunction, but one that over time could build up enough gas to cause the type of combustion that looks to be at the core of what happened early this morning."

Toussaint, who'd been listening while leaning against the wall, returned to the couch and sat down. "So this was an accident."

The fire chief nodded. "That's what we've concluded."

Malcolm glanced at Ace, saw the trace of doubt in his eyes. "But you're not sure."

"The evidence suggests an explosion caused by a faulty gas line. If the family wants to conduct a more in-depth investigation, that would be a matter for you and the police department."

Everyone remained quiet as Xavier walked the fire chief to the door. Once the chief left and the door closed, Ace spoke. "Everybody in here satisfied with the fire department's findings? That the fire was an accident, nothing more?"

"Makes sense," Malcolm said. "A fire happening at a restaurant is not unusual."

"We've been in business for fifty years," Toussaint countered. "How many buildings have we had burn down?"

No one spoke but everyone knew the answer: none.

Malcolm walked to the dining room and a small but well-stocked bar. He poured two fingers of his favorite cognac. "The fire chief said a gas leak caused the fire," he said, returning to the living room's large picture window and looking out. "So I think the case is closed."

Ace gave Malcolm a look, but said nothing.

Toussaint eyed his uncle. "You don't think this was an accident, do you?"

"I think that considering all the ... interesting situations we've dealt with lately, it's worth having this matter thoroughly checked out so that we can be sure."

Everyone in the room knew exactly what Ace meant. The Livingstons were a wealthy, powerful family who were not without their share of haters. In the past eighteen months alone, they'd dealt with one drama after another. There'd been the task of putting Quintin Bright behind bars—the man who'd shot Adam (oh, and that is *after* he'd had an affair with Adam's wife) and then added insult to injury by using Livingston money to evade authorities for almost a year. Then there'd been Quintin's sister, Keisha, the source for said Livingston money. At Quintin's orchestration, she'd begun a relationship with Bianca's brother, Jefferson, specifically to hack into his bank account and funnel large sums of money to Quintin. Unfortunately, Jefferson had fallen for the girl, and if not for the discovery of her part in the criminal activity, she would have been Mrs. Jefferson Livingston right now. Unlike Adam's earlier fate in the company's parking lot, the Livingstons had dodged this bullet. These situations alone would have been more than the average family could handle. Clearly, the Livingstons were above average.

"I agree with Ace," Toussaint said. "I think we should—"
His vibrating phone interrupted his train of thought. He
looked at the screen. His brow creased with the frown that
marred his model-handsome face. "I think we should—"

"Wait, son," Adam interrupted. "Who was that?"

"Nothing," Toussaint quickly replied.

"Nothing sure put a frown on your face," Ace said.

Adam pressed the issue. "Who was it?"

Toussaint sighed. "Joyce Witherspoon."

Adam stiffened. "What the hell does she want?"

"I don't know," Toussaint replied. "Probably seeing news of
the fire is what has her blowing up my phone."

"You know you need to watch yourself," Adam warned.

"I'm handling my business," Toussaint said, a tad harsher
than he intended. "And right now, that business is this fire. We
need to stay focused and cross off any and all possibilities that
this was anything but an accident."

Bianca nodded. "I agree."

Ace looked around the room. "Is there anyone here who
doesn't think launching our own private investigation is a
good idea?"

Silence.

He pulled out his cell phone. "I'll see if Sterling can meet
with us tomorrow. The quicker we can get him on the case,
the better, before the scene gets too contaminated and poten-
tially telling evidence or clues disappear."

Bianca didn't even want to think about the chance that the
fire was not an accident. Who'd be bold enough, or angry
enough, to blow up her place? She got along well with neighboring businesses: a Chinese restaurant to the left of TOSTS
and an art gallery on its right. Both their owners and their
managers had patronized her establishment and she theirs, and
several area employees stopped in during happy hour or after
they finished work. Bianca had been too busy to meet many

people outside of work and therefore too busy to make new enemies. *Which would leave only the old ones.* Cooper Riley, Chardonnay Wilson, and Shyla Martin immediately came to mind. Bianca didn't think Chardonnay had the resources to pull off a job like this, but then again, she hadn't thought that the money-hungry wench would sell a story to a tabloid either. The family had never been able to prove it, but the story appearing shortly after Chardonnay had witnessed the just-secretly-married Livingston cuddling with her new husband was—for Bianca—more than coincidence.

Cooper was another matter. As a defense attorney, he'd rubbed shoulders with his fair share of criminals. And he had been understandably upset when she called off their engagement. But she'd heard that he was seeing someone. *Is it conceivable that Coop could do something like this?* Finally, there was Shyla Martin. She seemed the least likely to still be harboring a vendetta against them, but word had it that she was working at a small advertising company—which definitely sounded like employment below her pay grade. Could taking this job have rekindled anger at how close she'd been to the brass ring and the lifestyle it could have afforded? Bianca leaned into Xavier's embrace, suddenly feeling a foreboding chill even though the room temperature was set at a cozy seventy-four degrees. Sterling Ross was one of the best private eyes in the country, and a trusted family friend. If there'd been foul play regarding the fire, he would find it. Bianca's unease was replaced with resolve. Let the investigation begin.

7

Diane stepped off the elevator into the plush lobby of the Livingston Corporation. It was the first time she'd visited the offices since Toussaint's interior designer wife, Alexis, had worked her magic. Even Diane's troubled mental state did not detract from observing a job well done. The lobby had always looked good, but now, with its sun-gold silk walls, burnished Brazilian rosewood furnishings, colorful glass blocks, and a large mounted flat screen displaying photos of the business history, there was a sophistication mixed with homeyness that made the atmosphere at once professional yet inviting. She stopped before the screen, smiling at images of a young, apron-wearing Marcus and Marietta standing in front of the first Taste of Soul, Adam and Ace holding up a first-place BBQ cooking contest trophy, and a more recent one of Toussaint doing his thing on the Food Network. *What a great idea,* she thought as she crossed from the sitting area over to the receptionist. The longer she knew Alexis Livingston, the more she understood why she'd been the one to domesticate the once-thought-untamable beast named Toussaint.

"Mrs. Livingston," the receptionist said cheerfully. "What a pleasure it is to see you!"

Diane smiled at the attractive young woman, looking professional and poised in a navy suit. "Thank you. I'm sorry, but I'm so bad with names."

The receptionist laughed. "No worries. I'm sure you meet a lot of people, and it has been a while. My name is Angie, and we met two years ago at the Christmas party."

"I met so many wonderful people that night. It's a pleasure to see you again, Angie."

"Thank you. Is that a new hairstyle?"

"Yes," Diane said, her hand going to the asymmetrically cut bob. The hairdresser had said it worked well for her angular face and that the honey-blond color worked with her butterscotch skin. "What do you think?"

"Very flattering, especially the color."

"Thanks, Angie. I'm still getting used to this straight look, so I appreciate your feedback. Listen, I'm here to see Jefferson. Can you ring him for me, ask if he has a few minutes for his mother?"

Angie frowned slightly as she punched his number on the phone board. "I don't believe he's here, Mrs. Livingston, but I'll be glad to check." She waited and then shook her head. "His direct line went to voice mail. Let me call his assistant. I'm looking for Jefferson," Angie said when his assistant answered. "Is he in the area, or in a meeting perhaps?"

"No, Angie. Jefferson isn't here. He called to say that he was working from home and that in case of an emergency, he could be reached on his cell phone."

"Okay, thanks." Angie ended the call and relayed the information to Diane. "Would you like me to try his cell now?"

"No," Diane answered. "It wasn't important. I was simply in the area and since it had been a while, thought I would stop by. Thanks, Angie. Keep up the good work."

"I will, Mrs. Livingston. Thank you."

Diane squelched the urge to bother her brother-in-law

and decided to call his wife instead. As soon as she was in her car, she dialed Candace.

"Hey, Diane," Candace answered. "I was just thinking about you. Are you at home?"

"No, I'm at company headquarters."

"You're at the Livingston Corporation?" Both women had worked at the company in the early years of their marriages, but aside from the biannual board meetings, neither had been active in decades. "What are you doing there?"

"Looking for my son. Ace called me earlier and said that Jefferson hadn't made the flight to LA. He's called his house and cell phones and keeps getting voice mail. I was hoping that maybe you'd heard from him, or maybe your sons."

"He hasn't called me," Candace answered. "And I haven't talked to either Malcolm or Toussaint since this morning. Do you think everything is all right?"

"I don't know," Diane answered honestly. "But I'm heading over to his place now to find out."

Less than an hour later, Candace opened her front door and hugged her sister. They'd done away with that whole "in-law" madness decades ago. "Come on in, girl. I'm back in the kitchen marinating chops for dinner tonight. You and Ace are welcome to come over."

"Thanks, Can."

Hearing the worry in her voice, Candace looked at Diane more closely. She remained quiet as they reached the kitchen, and Diane took a seat at the large granite-covered kitchen island. Candace went to the fridge, poured them both a glass of sparkling wine, and joined Diane at the counter.

"Talk to me, sis."

Diane took a sip of wine and began. "I went over to Jefferson's house."

"And?"

"No answer."

"Was he there?"

"I think so."

Candace was immediately intrigued. Aside from the fiasco with Keisha Miller, the woman who'd almost successfully duped him into marrying her conniving ass, she viewed Jefferson's life as the calmest of their generation. "If Jefferson was there, he would have answered. He probably wasn't home."

"I thought that, too, which is why I peeked through the window of his garage and saw his car. I went *back* to the door, rang the bell, and waited. When I didn't get an answer, I called his home phone and listened to it ring from outside his door. He was there, Can. He just didn't want to let me in."

Candace thought for a moment about what Diane had said. A slight smile scampered across her face. "Maybe your son was busy, if you know what I mean. He and Divine might be dating again."

Diane sat back in the chair, thought for a moment, and then slowly shook her head. "If they are, we sure haven't seen her. But I don't think so. Call it women's intuition or mother's wit or whatever, but I've been feeling it for a couple months now. Something is going on with my son."

This comment settled around the shoulders of both women like an itchy, ill-fitting wool sweater.

"You think he's still smarting over the breakup? Jefferson loved that girl," Candace offered, before adding, "Scandalous ho that she was."

"True, he took that betrayal hard, and for the first couple of months after it happened, I understood his behavior. Jefferson is an introvert by nature, so his being withdrawn and quiet didn't alarm me. Not at first. But it's been over a year, Can, and I've continued to see a change in him. It's subtle, so much so that y'all haven't noticed. But a mother hen knows when her chick is dealing with something, and I don't care how many times he tries to convince me otherwise, Jefferson is not himself."

"Have you asked him what's the matter?"

"Several times."

"And what does he say?"

"His mouth says he's fine, but his eyes say he's lying." Diane took another sip of wine. "And then, just last month, I suggested that he go see Dan Morgan."

"Who's that?"

"One of Ace's college buddies and a top-notch therapist."

Candace put down her glass. "A shrink, Diane? Do you really think it's that serious?"

"I don't know what to think. All I know is that if Jeff doesn't want to talk to his mama or his family, then he needs to talk to somebody."

"I can't imagine that suggestion went over well."

"Like a lead balloon. He's been avoiding me ever since."

Candace pondered Diane's words for a moment. "Well if not the breakup with Keisha, what else could it be?"

Diane finished her wine, narrowed her eyes. "I don't know. But I'm getting ready to get all up in his business. Believe that."

8

When it came to Jefferson's whereabouts, Diane was wise not to have bothered her brother-in-law. As it were, Adam's hands had been full dealing with someone else very determined to get answers...someone named Marcus.

"Dad, I really wish you'd taken my advice and not come here. I told you this morning that if anything came up, we'd call you!"

Marcus reared back in his seat, partly pissed and partly proud. Proud that his son was a chip off the old block, reminding him of himself in his younger years and pissed because Adam thought that he could be appeased with general answers and half-spoken truths. "Boy, who do you think you're talking to?" he finally asked.

Adam inwardly winced. He knew what this tone meant: Marcus Livingston was done with the bullshit. But still, Adam stalled. If he told him one thing, such as the real reason he'd been shot two years ago, that would open the floodgates to more drama than he felt his father needed to know. There was a reason he and his brother had gently forced his dad's semi-retirement. It was because Marcus had worked his butt off for over fifty years, and the twins wanted their parents' best days to be their last—relaxing, rewarding, and most of all drama-free.

But Adam knew there was no stopping Marcus when he wanted something. His dad's tenacity, perseverance, and determination were the very reasons Adam now ran a multimillion-dollar corporation. Stifling a sigh, he asked, "Dad, what exactly are you asking me?"

"For starters, I'm not asking about the fire," Marcus calmly replied, looking at a set of perfectly buffed nails. "I'm asking about whatever it is that you boys have been withholding from me and your mama, things that have to do with this business, a business that I founded just in case you need reminding!" Marcus surprised himself with the force of this declaration. Obviously, not being in the know was affecting him more than he'd realized. "I might have been born at night, but it wasn't last night."

Adam didn't stifle the sigh this time. "Daddy, you know how it is in business. Things come up, you handle them. Yes, there have been some . . . issues . . . over the past several months, but they've all been resolved. The company's bottom line is strong and our coffers are overflowing." Adam leaned back and clasped his hands over a cognac-induced paunch. "Now . . . is there any way you could do what you promised and let me and Ace run this company while you enjoy your life?"

Marcus eyed his son with affection. "I appreciate what you brothers are trying to do. But can I tell you something? Being retired is overrated, and while I love having the extra time to spend with Etta, other times I'm bored to death. I've worked all my life, son, and quite frankly, I miss it. I miss being in the mix, as you kids say. I miss the excitement. Now, true, whatever's been happening might be too much for your mama to handle, but I want to know. Not because I don't think *you* can handle it, but because it will make me feel as if I still belong, as if I'm still a part of this thing I created, that's grown bigger than I ever dreamed. Do you understand me, son?"

Adam sat back, his chest tight with emotion. He'd never

considered what his father had just explained to him, never thought that in doing what they felt was noble, he and Ace had denied Marcus the thing that brought him joy—work. "I do now, Dad," he said a bit hoarsely. "Wow. I'm sorry. We didn't mean to make you feel that way. We were just trying to—"

"I know what you were trying to do, son, and like I said, I appreciate it. You boys have taken this business farther than I ever dreamed, and the grandkids"—Marcus shook his head, surprised when a tear formed at the corner of his eye—"I couldn't be more proud of what you've done for the Livingston name. Papa Nash is smiling down from heaven, and Papa John, y'all's great-grandfather, is probably toasting us with a glass of white lightning right about now."

The men laughed.

Marcus continued. "You've done the business proud, son, and upheld the legacy."

"Thank you, Dad."

Marcus shifted in his seat and then looked up with a twinkle in his eye. "So now that we've got all that straight, do you want to tell me what the hell has been going on around here?"

9

Later that night, Candace watched her husband remove his robe before climbing into bed. His head had barely hit the pillow before she snuggled up against him. Every day, she thanked her lucky stars that she was still Mrs. Adam Livingston. A lesser man would not have been able to handle what had happened between them in the last two years: A lesser marriage would not have been on the rocks; it would have been over. But Adam Livingston was not a lesser man. He was the epitome of what that word meant: strong, loyal, forgiving, true. The Livingston legacy was well known—not just within the family, but also to some outside it. No infidelity, no divorce. But Candace knew that she and Adam weren't still together because of what Adam's great-grandfather John had started. They were together because of the type of man Adam was.

"Mmm, you smell good," she said, burying her nose in the crook of Adam's neck.

"Smell like I always do after taking a shower," he replied nonchalantly. Yet there was a smile on his face.

Candace settled her head on his shoulder and rubbed her hand across a chest lightly sprinkled with graying hair. "Dinner was nice tonight."

"Woman, I don't think it's in you to fix a bad meal."

"Ah, thanks for the compliment, baby. But I was thinking more about the dinner conversation, and what you guys have planned for Jefferson. From what I've heard, this promotion couldn't come at a better time."

Adam turned to look at her. "How do you figure?"

Candace shared a bit of her earlier conversation with Diane. "She's worried about him."

"Aw, you women worry too much. That boy's all right."

"I'm a little worried about you too. Discussion of Jeff aside, you seemed rather quiet tonight. Any particular reason?"

Adam shrugged.

"Okay, don't talk about it, but don't try and tell me nothing is on your mind." She turned over in a huff, away from the warmth of Adam's stocky body.

Adam connected his phone to its charger before placing it on the nightstand. He turned and took Candace back into his arms. "You know me better than anybody, you know that?" he asked, kissing her temple.

"Everybody except Ace maybe," Candace replied, acknowledging the uncanny bond that often existed between twins, even as she relished the feel of Adam's hardening member against her plump behind.

"Daddy stopped by the office today."

This comment immediately got Candace's attention. She turned to face Adam. "I thought you'd talked him out of that by telling him you'd keep him updated on any news."

"That's just it, baby. He didn't stop by to question me about the fire, although he was obviously concerned about what happened and mostly about whether or not Bianca was okay."

"If not the fire, then what?"

Adam tightened his arms around Candace, settling her more comfortably against his side. "He wanted to know what else we've been keeping from him and Mama. Says she's been getting her *feelings*, and he's long been suspecting things too."

"Oh, Lord. That had to be an awkward conversation."

Adam nodded.

"What did you tell him?"

Adam looked at Candace and answered, "Everything, baby. I told Daddy pretty much what he wanted to know."

Across town, Diane was doing the same with Ace—telling him everything, especially how worried she was about their son and how happy she was about the promotion.

"I don't know, baby," Ace said after listening to the causes for Diane's concern. They were lying in bed. Ace was naked, his body toned with regular exercise, still hard at fifty-six. Diane wore a simple, satin nightgown, her naturally slim body also belying its age. "I admit that he's been quieter than usual, but when it comes to the business, he's still on his game."

"What about the meeting he missed last month?" Diane countered. "The one where you came home pissed off because you had to fill in and do his report?"

"Yeah, there was that. But I talked to him and he assured me that it had just slipped his mind."

"Uh-huh. And how many times in the years you've known him has that happened? I could believe an excuse like that coming out of Bianca's mouth, but Jefferson? He's as responsible as they come."

"It happens, baby. Our boy is genius, but he isn't perfect." Ace shifted Diane so that he could put his arm around her shoulders. She nestled her head into his neck. "Maybe it's a delayed reaction or something, and it's just now hitting him how much he misses that girl. If you think about it, that was the most serious relationship I remember Jefferson having, and even though it was a short courtship, she obviously had his nose open. I think he loved those boys as well. Sometimes it's hard to get used to a quiet household once it's been full of life."

Diane nodded, remembering the withdrawal pains she'd endured once Bianca left home. Without the sounds of the TV blaring or hip-hop blasting, she'd barely known what to do with herself. "I wonder what happened to Divine, that pretty artist with whom we thought more than a friendship might develop? Candace asked about her today."

"I don't know, baby. Maybe that's who was in there when you went over to a grown man's house without calling first." Ace ran his hand along the hem of Diane's gown and pulled it upward. "Maybe he was just trying to get some, like his daddy is doing right now."

"Yes, maybe," she replied, swatting his hand playfully, even as her legs parted of their own volition. That Ace was still as sexually driven at fifty-six as he'd been at twenty-six didn't make sense. Nor did the fact that he still could turn her on like a light switch after thirty-some years. "That promotion will surely help."

"I believe so."

"Too bad about Mark's mother-in-law." The retiring CFO, Mark Stewart, had been with the company for twenty-five years. "But I applaud his wife for not wanting to put her mother in a nursing home."

"It wasn't an easy decision. But Mark's decided to open up a consulting business after they relocate to Florida. We hate to lose him, but I think the move will do him good."

"It will do Jeff even better, give him a new focus."

"A little sooner than we expected but that's the plan."

"Do you think he's ready?"

"He's a Livingston, baby. We're born ready. And speaking of...," Ace whispered, placing Diane's hand on his quickly hardening shaft and then running his hand across her hip before squeezing a cheek. "I'm ready for some of this thick, soft goodness." He pulled his hand back across her hip bone, teasing her skin with his fingernail before gliding his hand between her legs and parting folds already damp with desire. He ran his middle finger down the length of her, flicking her nub once, and again. "Can Daddy get a little bit of this right here?"

Diane answered by rubbing her hand over Ace's bald head, which was lowering to latch on to her large, hard nipple. She continued to stroke his shoulder and run her hand down his strong back and onto his rock-hard buns. He continued to stroke her, fingering her love button, applying pressure and then releasing. She moaned her pleasure, widening her legs when he placed a finger inside her, moaning even deeper when he made it two. Without further ado, Ace shifted, positioned himself over Diane's invitation, and plunged deep inside her to RSVP. For a moment they lay there, their lower bodies still, their heads turning until their mouths connected. Their twirling tongues made words unnecessary; Ace's slow pull and push of his hard, massive shaft and Diane's intermittent tightening of her inner walls became their conversation. This was the kind of dance possible only after years of practice, decades of shared love, loss, tragedies, and triumphs, honed by navigating a journey of twists and turns and in the end having being together be the only thing that mattered. Ace deepened each kiss as he deepened each thrust, until Diane's mouth went slack from the thrill of it all. Ace raised her leg for greater access. Diane showed her thanks by grabbing his booty and pulling him near. They were as connected as possible, as close as two people could be, but she wanted to be closer.

"Who does this belong to, huh?" Ace murmured as he repositioned them side by side and sank in again.

"Ace Livingston," Diane whispered as he continued to murmur in her ear, each sentence nastier than the last. He loved it when she spoke his name like that, while he was pumping inside her as though he were drilling for oil. He told her in explicit terms what he was going to do, and when he lined up his upper lips with her lower ones, he fully made good on the promise. Diane thrashed wildly as an orgasm overtook her before Ace quickly lifted himself and sank in to the hilt. In this moment, Diane thought of that first time, when she'd been seventeen and he a year younger. That night she had been the aggressor, and on this, his first sexual experience, they'd screwed like rabbits. He'd been an eager learner with the right tools for the lesson, and she hadn't thought that night filled with multiple orgasms could get any better. She'd been wrong. "Ace!" she cried as he grabbed a hold of the headboard and deepened his thrusts.

"Give it to me!" he demanded, as he had for thirty-plus years.

And she did just that, gave him what he wanted. And when they'd rested and caught their breaths, she gave it to him again.

10

Ace and Adam sat across from each other in the Livingston Corporation's private dining room. Chef, called only by that name and a mainstay in the TOS restaurant chain for many years, had veered away from the soul-food playbook and prepared a succulent lunch of chateaubriand, basmati rice, and fresh mixed vegetables. The meat was melt-in-your-mouth tender, covered with just the right amount of au jus.

"Twin," Adam began, wiping his mouth after several bites of heaven, "have you gotten a hold of Jeff yet?"

Ace shook his head. "I was going to head over there after work, but I have a meeting with the accountant that can't be postponed. I'll give him one more day before I send out the posse. Sometimes we just need a break, know what I'm saying? That boy hasn't taken a vacation in years."

"So he doesn't even know about Mark yet?"

"Nope, didn't want to leave that in a message." Ace smiled. "Can't wait to see my boy move up to the big office."

"He'll have to get up to speed quickly. There's so much information that Mark needs to transfer, and while he's promised to be available by phone as long as we need him, he and his wife are moving as soon as escrow closes in thirty days."

"Jeff can handle it."

Adam nodded slowly. "No doubt." He took a long swallow of water. "How long do you think it will be before Sterling gets back with us?" Sterling had met with the Livingston men as soon as they arrived back in Atlanta and then accepted their offer of the company jet to fly to LA the following day so that he could personally inspect the site of the fire.

"Hard to say," Ace answered. "Sterling is all about quality; he won't rush his process just because we're chomping at the bit for an answer."

"Can't believe we're back here, man."

"Where? Wondering who it is this time trying to stab us in the back?" Each was silent as they mentally explored the possibilities. "Truth be told, I'm hoping it's a gas leak," Ace continued. "We can put this unfortunate incident behind us and move on."

"But you don't believe that's the case—you haven't from the moment you heard from Bianca, and honestly, I don't understand why."

"I just have a feeling . . ."

Adam laughed. "Now you sound like Mama."

"Hmm, not sure that's a compliment."

"Me either."

"Speaking of our parents, I heard that Daddy paid a visit to the office yesterday."

Adam's smile turned upside down. "Much to my chagrin."

"Ha! Were you able to properly detract and deflect?"

"Not this time," Adam replied, his tone lacking the playfulness that Ace's comment should have elicited.

Ace sobered, reached for his tea, and waited.

"He shared a perspective I hadn't considered before." Adam relayed to Ace what their father had shared. "I saw how much it meant to him to stay intimately connected with us and the business. I told him, Twin," Adam ended.

Ace's arm stopped midway from bringing the glass from the table to his mouth. "Told him what?"

Adam finished a long swig of tea. "Everything."

Ace slowly put down his glass. "What do you mean, everything?"

"Well not about my wife's extramarital fucking, if that's what you're thinking."

"That's exactly where my mind went."

"What I told him is that Quintin Bright had had the nerve to... disrespect Candace by coming on to her. And I'd shut that shit down."

A day late and a dick short, but better late than never, is what Ace thought. "Uh-huh," is what he said.

"I told him how Quintin's business had been shut down and how he'd come after me in the parking lot as a result. Now, Daddy knows that the man who stole hundreds of thousands of dollars from the company also tried to take my wife."

A long moment prefaced Ace's one-word response: "Damn."

A longer moment passed.

"You had to have a good reason, man," Ace said, once he'd come out of shock and could speak again. "But... why? The affair was two years ago, and Quintin is in prison for what he did. So why did you think Daddy had to know?"

"Because Mama has been picking up on stuff anyway, and more than that, he wanted in, Twin. He knew that some serious shit was going down in the family, shit he used to handle. And not having any part in handling it—hell, not even knowing what needed to be handled—was making him feel old and unnecessary. Our father has not been a happy man."

"What did he say when you told him about the real reason behind the theft?"

"His exact words were in the form of a question." Adam adopted Marcus's gruff, deep voice. "Why is that muthafucka in prison... instead of a grave?"

11

Keisha Miller sat on the bench at the foot of her king-sized platform bed, leisurely rubbing shea butter over her smooth, blemish-free legs. Her long, naturally curly hair was wrapped in a towel, the rest of her café-au-lait richness totally exposed. She'd soaked in the tub for a full thirty minutes, had allowed the jets to massage her body until the water turned cool and the neo-soul album she listened to had ended. Sometimes she still had to pinch herself to see if she were dreaming. A couple years ago, she could only imagine this type of lifestyle, and a year ago she thought she'd lost her one chance to experience living in the lap of luxury. But the gods of fate had given her and her boys a second chance, and his name was Cooper Riley Jr. And she didn't intend to blow it.

When her phone rang, she almost didn't answer, but after checking the caller ID, she hurriedly picked up the phone. "Yes," she said to the automated recording asking if she'd accept a collect call. And seconds after that, "Hey, Q!"

"Hey, little sis."

Keisha placed the phone on speaker and reached for her robe. "How are you, brother?"

"As well as I can be for a man in prison."

She sighed. "I hate that you're in there, Q. But all things considered, it could be worse."

"How do you figure?"

Keisha heard the anger in his voice and rolled her eyes. She'd been trying to get him to see reason since getting locked up over a year ago. "Really, Q? We have to do this again? You could have gotten a lot more time for what you did. Instead, because of Cooper, your sentence was reduced."

"Your boy did all right. But my sentence got reduced because your forward-thinking brother had an insurance marker—old girl's bare pussy caught on tape. Ha!"

Keisha laughed. "That was pretty genius."

"Damn straight it was and I wish I had more ammunition. The whole predicament I'm in right now is those muthafuckas' fault."

"You just had a few months left, Q, and you had to go and act crazy. That's your fault!"

"Because a dude stepped to me and I had to knock his ass out? Because he had to feel froggy and leap and shit? You don't know how it goes down in here, sis, and I hope you never have to find out. I'm always going to protect myself, always!"

"I know, Q. I'm sorry. It's just that I'm as frustrated as you are—"

Quintin snorted.

"I am! I miss you, and the boys miss their uncle, especially Dorian. He's been acting out and I know it's because you being in jail bothers him."

"Sounds like Mr. Cooper needs to handle his business."

"He's trying to be a father figure, but it's not the same. He's getting close to Antwan but Dorian just pushes him away."

"Well, if he's going to step in and be stepdaddy, he needs to learn how to rule the roost, know what I'm saying?"

"He's trying," Keisha repeated, taking an exasperated breath as she thought about her softhearted—okay, wimpy—fiancé.

While he was intellectually brilliant and could run rings around most lawyers when trying cases, at home he was a docile lump on the couch, comfortable with letting Keisha be the disciplinarian and wear the pants. Things were different when she'd been with Jefferson. He was quiet but had such an air of authority that the boys did what he told them, no questions asked. Jefferson...she missed him. "Hey, did you hear about the fire?"

Q cracked up. "Yeah, I heard about it, all right."

"It's not funny, Q," Keisha said, though her brother's guffawing put a smile on her face. "Somebody could have been hurt."

"Yeah, well, we're saving that for next time."

Keisha instantly sobered. "Q..."

"What?" he asked, his a voice a study in innocence.

"Please tell me that you had nothing to do with that fire."

"Girl, please. How am I going to have something to do with something on the other side of the country with my ass on lockdown?"

She breathed a sigh of relief. "Of course you couldn't. It's just the way you said that...*we*."

"Just a figure of speech, baby sis. But I'd be lying to act like that shit don't make me happy. Those muthafuckas deserve every rotten piece of luck they get."

Keisha was sorry she'd mentioned the Livingstons. For Q they were a sore spot, to say the least.

"Cooper is working hard to get you out of there. He really loves me, Q, and will do anything to make me happy."

"Oh, yeah? Has he popped the big question, or is he another highfalutin rich nucka who thinks you're to be fucked but not to be married?"

"You're the one who just said that, Q, not Cooper."

"That's because I'm going to keep it real with you, baby sis. Hold on to your heart, that's all I'm saying. And while he's doing anything to make you happy, as you say, make sure he's keeping the paper flowing. And make sure you're putting some of that shit back on the low just in case the day gets rainy. You feel me?"

"I feel you, big brother." Keisha couldn't help but smile. Q had been her protector and most dependable provider from the day she was born: from beating up boys who wouldn't take no for an answer to stealing food for dinner when Mama was too drunk. He'd always had her back. Which is why no matter what, she'd always have his. "Believe it or not, Cooper has brought up the M-word. But right now, I'm the one who's hesitating."

"Why?"

"Because of that highfalutin factor you mentioned. I'm dealing with a little of that shit."

"What's up?"

"It's his mother. I've only met her once, but that was enough to know that she can't stand me."

"Let me guess—she thinks her son's too good for you."

"That's putting it mildly. If you thought the Livingstons were stuck-up rich folk, you haven't seen nothing. When they list *snooty* in the dictionary, you'll see that Riley bitch's picture."

12

Evelyn Maureen Riley sat primly in her formal living room, carefully examining her freshly manicured nails while the maid poured a cup of perfectly brewed Earl Grey tea. After watching her add two dollops of honey and a splash of cream, she reached for the steamy brew. The maid stepped back and waited. Evelyn took one sip, closed her eyes, swallowed discreetly, and took another sip. "Perfect," she said with a brief nod. The maid smiled, heard the doorbell, and scurried to answer it. Seconds later, Evelyn's guest joined her in the room that, because of the primary color in which it was decorated, was dubbed the "White Room."

Evelyn set down her teacup, rose with the same air as would the Queen of England about to meet her subjects, and walked forward with arms outstretched. "Junior, darling." Evelyn air-kissed her son's cheeks. "This is a pleasant surprise."

"Hardly a surprise, Mother," Cooper replied, "since you practically threatened my inheritance if I didn't stop by and see you today."

"Forgive me, dear. It's just that with your new...situation... I hardly see you these days."

"Her name is Keisha, Mother, and she's more than a situation. She's the woman I love."

"Please, Cooper. I truly do not wish to fight about this. I'm only thinking of your future, darling, and how you plan to follow in your father's footsteps and become a judge. How do you think the society pages will look featuring a wife who came with a ready-made family and fathers unknown? What will that do to any future political aspirations and public opinion? I know you think lightly of these issues, but, son, these things matter!"

Cooper was well aware of how much things such as status, class, and appearances mattered to his mother. Love, compassion, and nonjudgment were foreign entities in Evelyn Riley's domain, but when it came to the right angle for one's tea-holding pinkie or charity events or dinner parties, she was the one for the job. "How's Dad?" Cooper asked in a thinly veiled hope of changing the subject.

Evelyn stifled a sigh, deciding for the moment to leave well enough alone. She knew how futile it was trying to talk sense into a man's upper head when he was thinking with his lower one. It had been that way with his father for years. That's why she'd finally given up on diverting the judge from his questionable dalliances and focused her energy on more important things: like charity work and golf and bridge. That's why she'd allowed the judge his affairs over the years. It wasn't that she hadn't known about them. She'd just learned not to care. After all, she figured things could have been worse. It could have mattered that they no longer had sex, but it didn't. And he could have been cheating with someone who'd threaten her marriage . . . like a woman. As it was, Cooper Sr.'s choices solidified the fact that she would never experience divorce unless she chose it. She knew too much.

"The judge is fine, dear," she said after a pause. "In fact, we're hosting a dinner party tonight and we'd love for you to come."

"Let me guess. You'd prefer I come alone."

"Congressman Abernathy will be here, darling, and per-haps a White House aide. I've planned a seven-course meal with intricate settings. I'd hate for your...friend...to feel out of place when navigating those pesky forks and spoons."

"Ah, yes, we can't have the ghetto girl eating the soup with the dessert spoon or stabbing her salad with the fork reserved for the steak, now, could we?"

"Please understand how difficult this is for me, son. I've al-ways tried to be supportive of your choices—"

Cooper snorted, a sound so uncharacteristic in the Riley household that the room lost air.

"I've always wanted what's best for you," Evelyn contin-ued, after an almost imperceptible regrouping.

"What about what *I* want, Mother?"

"Of course that's to be considered..."

"I'm thirty-six years old, Mother. Thirty-six! I think that by now my own wishes about my own life should be more than mere considerations."

"Just six months, son. Promise me you'll give this"—Eve-lyn swallowed lest she choke on the word—"relationship that much time before proceeding further." Evelyn knew her freckle-faced son and knew how to read the look on his face whenever he mentioned *her*. It was the same look Cooper Sr. had in the weeks before he proposed. Evelyn opened her mouth but just as quickly closed it. She wanted to address the patently nauseating issue about that woman and her bastards living in her son's home, but, again, she knew she'd reached the fairly lofty level of her son's patience. "Will you do that, Ju-nior? And in that time, I'll work very hard to give fair consid-eration to your wishes."

Cooper looked at his watch. Lunchtime was over, but since he no longer had an appetite, it was no problem getting back to the courthouse without having eaten. Besides, considering how manipulative and pushy his mother could be, this conversation had gone surprisingly well. Had he actually heard her correctly? Had she actually used words like *work very hard* and *fair consideration* in regards to how she felt about Keisha? Cooper was not a religious man, but in this moment, as he returned air kisses with his mother, he actually believed that there was a God.

Evelyn kept her pasted-on smile perfectly in place until she'd shut the door and Cooper had left the driveway. Then her eyes turned to daggers as she walked toward the solarium at the back of the house. It was filled with fountains and greenery and was where she found peace. It was also where she'd hatch up a plan to deal with Keisha Miller. Because she hadn't lied when she told Cooper that she'd work very hard concerning his floozy. Evelyn had worked hard to reinvent herself, to mold the poor, mocked girl that nobody liked into the woman that society envied. And she'd work even harder to not only get the woman who reminded Evelyn of her own past out of her son's home, but also out of his life.

13

Toussaint stood in his master suite, watching Alexis pack his suitcase. She looked perfectly decadent in a short-waisted T-shirt, booty shorts, and no bra or panties. That they'd just made love didn't matter: He was getting hard for her all over again. "You know you don't have to do that," he said, trying to distract his mind and cool his ardor.

"Do what?"

"Pack my bag. I had a life before I met you, woman, and it included taking trips and packing clothes."

"It's a labor of love, darling," Alexis cooed. She placed a last shirt into the carry-on and walked over to him. "With your schedule so busy, I have to take my time with you however I can get it." She continued in a whisper, "Besides, I like taking care of my man." Her tongue ran along his earlobe and dipped inside. Evidently Toussaint wasn't the only insatiable one in the room.

Toussaint moaned, his tongue quickly finding hers and beginning a familiar twirl. A hand slid beneath her top to tweak a nipple. Alexis laughed. He caught her joy in his mouth and deepened the kiss. "Honey, stop. You'll be late to catch the plane."

"Are you sure you can't come with me?"

"Who will watch Tiara?" Their first child, Skylar Tiara, who they mostly referred to by her middle name and often called Tee, was the couple's pride and joy.

"I told you that I talked to Victoria. Victory's nanny said it would be perfectly fine to drop off our child."

Alexis kissed him again and went back to the carry-on. "Fine with her, but not with me," she said, zipping it up. "How many times do I have to tell you that I want to be the one raising my child?"

"I hardly call forty-eight hours away from one's baby a sign of abandonment," he drawled. "Here, let me get that." He walked over and lifted his carry-on off the bed, setting it down and immediately pulling Alexis into his arms. "We need to make time for us," he whispered, grinding his body against her. "Just you and me. Will you try and arrange that?"

The telephone rang, interrupting Alexis's response. "Hold that thought," she threw over her shoulder as she walked to the home phone. "Hello?" And then, "Honey, it's your mother."

Toussaint patted Alexis's ample ass as he took the phone. "Hey, Mama, what's up?"

"That's why I'm calling," Candace replied. "We need you to find out what's up with your cousin."

"Jeff?"

"Yes. You know he wasn't at work again today."

"But I thought he called and explained that he was working from home."

"Ace and Diane are worried, Toussaint. You know how responsible Jeff is. Not going to LA, missing work . . . this behavior simply is not like him."

"What did he say when they talked to him?"

"That's just it; he hasn't returned their calls, and yesterday when Diane went over there, he didn't answer the door."

"Maybe he wasn't there."

"I thought the same thing. But Diane looked in the garage and saw his car."

"Maybe he was busy doing the nasty."

"We thought that too," Candace said with a laugh. "But there's no pussy good enough to not answer when your mama knocks."

"Dang, Mama!"

"Sorry, son. Real talk."

Watching Alexis lean over to retrieve something from the nightstand drawer, Toussaint begged to differ about what good pussy could make a man do. But there was no time to argue. He had a plane to catch. "I think we should just give Jeff some space, let him work whatever it is out. He'll be all right."

"Do you still have a key to his house?"

Toussaint stifled a sigh. His mother and aunt had obviously put their heads together and decided the next course of action. He knew she'd bug him until he gave in, so he decided to get it over with. "Okay, Mama, if he's not at work tomorrow, I'll go by his house when I get back from Vegas."

"Is that where you're headed?"

"Yes. I'm checking out a few locations on the Strip for the next Taste of Soul. Some prime real estate has just become available, so I have to move fast."

"Baby, is there any way you can push back your plane departure and check on him tonight, before you leave?"

"Where's Malcolm?"

"He's out of town, too, in New York. Remember he's unveiling the latest Soul Smoker on the *Rachael Ray* show?"

Toussaint looked at his watch. "I'll call the pilot and have him push back the flight time. But if Jeff's not there, I don't have time to go looking for him. It's not like we're teens and I'm trying to keep him away from Pauletta's fast, trying-to-get-pregnant-and-trap-a-Livingston's behind."

This elicited a chuckle from Candace, as Toussaint had hoped. "Hold on, honey."

Toussaint heard muffled voices and then Adam came on the line. "Son?"

"Yeah, Daddy, I'm on my way over there."

"Thanks, Toussaint. Ace had a meeting that he couldn't reschedule, and your aunt Diane is worried about Jeff. She feels that while he's not saying anything to his immediate family, he just might open up to you."

"I don't know about all that. Jeff hasn't totally gotten over me choosing Bianca for the West Coast job. Y'all know that."

"Yes, but now we know why he was pushing for it. All things considered, I think the situation worked out the way it was supposed to. Besides, we're family. It's been a year. Y'all need to figure out a way to resolve any differences you might have."

"It ain't me who needs to do the resolving."

"However it happens, any broken fences need to be mended. In this family, there's no room for feuds."

Twenty minutes later, Toussaint pulled up to a respectable residence in an upscale Atlanta subdivision. The neighborhood was quiet and Jefferson's house was dark. Toussaint got out of his Mercedes and looked around. Everything looked ordinary enough. He walked up the drive toward Jefferson's front door. The motion light came on. He stopped, looked in the garage window. Empty. He looked around again and noticed a late-model Infiniti parked across the street. He had a vague niggling that he'd seen the car before and went through a mental Rolodex of mutual friends they had. Drawing a blank, he shrugged his shoulders and bounded up the stairs. He knocked on the door, but even as he did so, he felt sure that Jefferson wasn't there. He headed toward his car when his mother's voice stopped him. *Do you still have a key to his house?* "The first thing she'll do is ask me if I went inside," he mumbled, turning around to go back up the drive. He made one more attempt to peek through the closed blinds, but in the darkness, nothing was visible. He pulled out the spare key Jefferson had given him when the house was first purchased, unlocked the door, and went inside.

The first thing he noticed was the smell—stale alcohol. *Not good.* His brow furrowed as he stepped farther into the living room and looked around. Shoes, magazines, and an empty pizza box littered the floor. There were two empty bottles of cognac on the table next to what Toussaint knew was Jefferson's favorite recliner, where if he wasn't checking out football on the big screen in Malcolm's man cave, he'd be sitting here watching it every Sunday afternoon.

The silence of the home bore down on him. A shiver of fear went down his spine. *Stay cool, man. Your aunt talked to Jeff earlier today. He's all right.* Still, Toussaint's breathing increased as he walked through the house—slowly, quietly, all senses alert. The open layout of the downstairs made inspection easy; there was no one in the dining room, kitchen, or downstairs bath. *Man, stop tripping. There's nobody here.* He almost laughed out loud, imagining how he must have looked, like *Law and Order*, scoping out the bad guy.

He walked up the stairs with a lighter heart, his mind already in Vegas and the next day's meeting with the commercial Realtor. He reached the top of the stairs and stopped. *Wait. Is that music I hear?* No, not music. *Creak. Groan. Huff. Puff.* The nasty . . . in full effect. Okay, now Toussaint was pissed. Not answering a door with your mother on one side and your freak on the other was understandable. But Candace was right. No pussy was good enough to not only ignore your mother's *subsequent* phone calls, but to make your cousin delay his business trip as well. *Ah, hell no.* It was about to go down.

Toussaint turned the corner, walked into the room, and stopped short. There, in the romantic hue of dimmed lighting, he saw her. Or rather, he saw it. A big, round, juicy ass high in the air. Thick brown legs on either side of another pair that stuck out in between them. Jeff. Thrashing, moaning, appreciating what the woman was obviously doing to him with her mouth. He didn't mean to stand there like he was at a two-dollar peep show, but for a full thirty seconds, he couldn't move. Just stood there, watching the woman's head bob up and down: hair swinging, butt swaying, voice asking if he liked it when she licked him like that. She turned her face to the side, her eyes closed in concentration.

That's when Toussaint recognized her. The woman who'd gone after his father, and when that hadn't worked, had placed his brother in her crosshairs. *Shit!* He stepped farther into the room. "Joyce?"

The creaking stopped.

The moaning stopped.

Jefferson pushed Joyce over and sat up straight. "Damn, man! Can't you knock?"

14

The first thing Toussaint noticed about his cousin were the bleary eyes. "I did," he drawled. "See now why you couldn't hear me, though."

Joyce, who'd gathered the sheet around her, now scooted off the bed and reached for her clothes, lying on the bench at the end of the bed. "Hello, Toussaint."

In her state of dishevel and undress, not to mention what she had to know he'd just seen, he laughed at her attempt to try and sound professional. "Joyce Witherspoon. I see you're keeping it all in the family."

She opened her mouth to speak, closed it when no words came out, and raced to the master bath.

Toussaint crossed over to where Jefferson sat rubbing his face. He reached down, picked up a crumpled pair of jeans, and threw them at his cousin. "Put those on, fool. We need to talk."

"Don't you think if I felt like talking, I would have answered the phone?"

Instead of answering, Toussaint walked over to the dimmer and put the light on full strength. Jefferson squinted before putting his hand up over his eyes. "Turn that light down, man!"

Toussaint looked at Jefferson and slowly shook his head. "Joyce! Hurry up!"

Joyce came out of the bathroom, wearing her dress but carrying her undies and shoes. Her curly short hairstyle looked a mess, as did her smudged makeup. And where was her other earring? "Listen, Toussaint—"

"Save it," Toussaint said without looking at her. "Any conversation you have needs to be with Jeff, not me."

"It's not what it—"

"Joyce." The look Toussaint gave her left no room for further argument. "Leave."

Joyce's eyes darted from Toussaint, the man she'd always wanted to chase, to the man she'd chased tonight, and caught. "Jeff, I'll call you tomorrow."

Jefferson nodded and then dismissed her. "Lock the door on your way out."

Joyce looked once more at Toussaint, her expression pleading for understanding. Toussaint continued to stare straight ahead.

A moment later, they heard a door close. "I'll be right back," Toussaint said. He went downstairs, looked around, and then peered out the window. The Infiniti was gone. Confident that he and Jefferson were indeed alone, he walked back up the stairs and into the master suite. Jefferson had put on his jeans and was now in the sitting area of the room, nursing a cognac.

"Been hitting the sauce a little heavy, haven't you, cuz? Your living room smells like a distillery."

"Yeah, well, if I'd been expecting company, I would have cleaned up."

"If I'm not mistaken, some *company* just left. Joyce Witherspoon? Really, dog?"

"What's wrong with Joyce?"

"Nothing, except that she's been on a mission for the last few years—going after Daddy and when he didn't take the bait, trying to get down with Malcolm."

"Yeah, and almost succeeded as I recall."

"But she didn't. Plus, there were extenuating circumstances that had a brothah vulnerable, as you well know. But I'm not here to talk about Malcolm. This is about you, cuz. What's going on?"

Jefferson put down the now empty tumbler. "Look, I went to a function, had too much to drink. Joyce offered to bring me home. What the hell do you care?"

"Why wouldn't I? This isn't like you, Jeff." Toussaint paused, sheer concern covering every inch of his face. He thought back to what Candace had said, how Ace and Diane had repeatedly tried to reach him over the past couple days, his no-show in LA, how they hadn't even talked about the fire. This was a Jefferson he'd never seen before, and quite frankly, it bothered him. A lot. "I can't believe you've been MIA while we've been literally putting out fires."

A humorless smile scampered across Jefferson's face. "I've been watching the happenings on TV. Ain't nothing that my little sis Bianca can't handle."

Toussaint walked over to where Jefferson sat, and plopped down on the other end of the loveseat. "Is that what this bull-shit is about? That you aren't heading up the West Coast? Are we still on that shit? Because let me tell you, if we are, we need to handle this nonsense. Daddy asked me how we were rolling before I came over. I told him that we were cool. Are we?"

Jefferson splashed a bit of cognac into the tumbler, and gri-maced slightly as the drink went down. "You've always gotten everything you ever wanted—every job, every woman, every-thing. You don't know what it's like to be me, sometimes feel-ing like the black sheep of the family."

WTH? Toussaint looked at the man sitting on the love seat and tried to find his cousin. "Are you kidding me? They're grooming you to eventually have the top position in the com-pany, man—president and chief operating officer!"

Jefferson didn't have an answer for that, and if he had, he would have had to utter it around another sip.

"Ace and Aunt Diane are beside themselves with worry. I don't know what's going on with you, cousin, but if you don't straighten up, and I mean fast, you're going to feel more heat than any fire could ever cause."

Jefferson set down the drink and put his head in his hands. "I hear you, cousin." He sighed deeply, resting his head against the seat back and staring at the ceiling.

"Do you want to talk about it? Because I have a feeling that's it not about Bianca, TOSTS, or the West Coast."

"No."

"Is it Keisha?"

Jeff slowly shook his head. Toussaint eyed his cousin for a long time.

"I'll get it together," Jeff finally said, offering his cousin a crooked smile. "And be at work tomorrow, bright and early."

"This isn't about the business, man. This is about *you*. I love you, man. We all do. Whatever it is that's bothering you, we just want to help, that's all. And if you can't tell any of us what's bothering you, you need to tell somebody." Toussaint stood. "And not Joyce Witherspoon either. Watch yourself with her, man. There's a shrewd mind behind that pretty smile and wide behind."

"You trying to say she's not just with me for my good looks?"

"I'm saying that she's been sniffing around this camp for a long time. And I wouldn't put anything past her." Toussaint's head jerked up. "Did you use protection?"

"Toussaint, I might be drunk, but I'm not a damn fool!"

"I don't know. I remember saving you once before when you were getting ready to go raw."

Jefferson laughed. "Will I ever live down you finding me in GrandMar's barn with Pauletta? I was ten years old!"

"And hard as a rock! All that dick and didn't know what to do with it!"

"Thank God for small favors! Saved girlfriend's virginity. She was, what, twelve, thirteen?"

"I don't even know, man, but she definitely thought you were older. You grew faster than the rest of us." Toussaint turned serious as he looked at his watch. "I really should be going, man. You sure you're all right?"

Jefferson stood as well and walked with Toussaint toward the bedroom door. "It's all good, Toussaint. I appreciate you, man, for real."

"I know I've said it before, but I'm sorry that I had to vote against you on the West Coast situation. It wasn't personal, dog. In the end, you'll thank me, watch."

"Yeah, but I might have to kick your ass first. Especially since you rolling up on me in the middle of some pretty good pole swabbing."

"Yeah, old girl was going at it like it wasn't her first time at the rodeo. But don't sell yourself short, Jeff. Women all over the place are digging you."

Jefferson thought about one particular woman who had been digging on him and how that attraction was partly responsible for the shape he was now in. "Tell everybody I'm good," he said, hugging Toussaint.

"I'll tell everybody you're still breathing. Them knowing you're good . . . that's on you."

Jefferson heard the door close downstairs. Toussaint was gone. He walked back over to the loveseat, reached for his glass with one hand and the bottle with the other. Then, sighing heavily, he put both back down on the table, stood, removed his jeans, and headed naked to the shower. Since the whole family was talking, there would undoubtedly be a meeting soon, and he'd be the item on the agenda. If he was going to convincingly share what they needed to hear and keep secrets better left unsaid not said, he'd need to have a clear head.

15

"Joyce Witherspoon?" Victoria Sanders Livingston's incredulity was evident in the way her voice went up three octaves. She'd disliked this would-be husband stealer ever since finding out about her interest in Malcolm and about Malcolm's battle not to act on this lust. Alexis's face showed mild confusion while Diane sat on the sofa looking resolute. Candace, who'd just shared the news with Victoria, looked ready to take off her earrings, grease her face, and kick some serious butt. One could almost hear the creaking of wood as the Livingston women came together to circle the proverbial wagons. There hadn't always been harmony among these four wives, but on this particular subject, they were all in accord.

"No, Tee," Alexis admonished as her and Toussaint's daughter, Skylar Tiara, worked to keep her balance while reaching for a magazine on the ottoman. She failed, and soon a plump, diaper-covered bottom made contact with the floor, almost sitting on her cousin, Victory, who was busy trying to eat a large, plastic ball. The babies looked at each other, laughed, and started chatting in a language only they could understand.

"Lord, if that angel doesn't look like Toussaint," Diane said, her attention temporarily diverted from the devil being discussed. "I think she's going to be tall like him too. Victory looks like you, Victoria. She's going to be a heartbreaker."

"Lord, don't remind me. I'm already going round and round with her older sister Brittany, who's trying to be the next Willow Smith, only wanting to wear skin-tight pants that show off her little booty with midriff, navel-baring tops. Oh, and she now insists on weekly pedicures because wearing the same polish more than seven days is"—Victoria mimicked her daughter—"sooo not cool."

"At what, nine years old?" Alexis asked.

Victoria nodded. "Malcolm calls her his little princess, and she believes that hype!"

"I don't know about princess, but she is her mother's daughter," Candace mumbled.

Everyone laughed.

Victoria discreetly pushed a pager button. Within seconds, the nanny came into the room. "Rosa, please take the girls."

The room waited until the toddlers had been taken. Then Alexis spoke. "Joyce isn't dallying only with Jefferson. She's been calling Toussaint too."

Three voices. Simultaneously. "What?"

"What in the hell does she want with *my* son?" Candace demanded.

Alexis shrugged.

Victoria drawled, "You have to ask?"

"Her name is familiar," Alexis said to the room. "But what is her connection to our family?"

Candace answered. "Joyce Witherspoon started Loving Spoonful a few years back and approached Adam with a business proposition—"

"Emphasis on the word *proposition*," Diane intoned.

"She offered to partner her event planning business with Taste of Soul. On paper—and in reality—it was a good idea. Our catering arm grew significantly as a result of her events

and marketing efforts. What I didn't know at the time, however, was she was also trying to cultivate another partnership as
well."

"With Adam?" Alexis questioned.

Candace nodded.

Alexis looked around the room. "She obviously doesn't
know about the legacy."

The women were quiet a moment, sipping tea and wine
while reflecting on what was part of the Livingston heritage,
begun by a great-great-grandfather just out of slavery. After
watching the love of his life get taken away on the back of a
wagon and seeing his family torn apart before his very eyes,
he'd vowed that none of his seed would ever endure such
heartache. From that moment, he instilled in the male children
that they must always remain faithful to their wives and that
there could never, ever be a Livingston divorce. As far as anyone in the circle knew, these words had been honored and the
legacy remained intact.

"Girl, please," Diane continued. "For some women, hearing that a man is married and faithful just makes him more de-
sirable. Some women like a challenge."

"Yes, and after Adam told her in no uncertain terms that
he was not interested, she moved on to my husband."

"Malcolm?" Alexis exclaimed.

"Last time I checked," Victoria dryly replied.

"Geez, when was this, and where was I when all of this was
happening?"

"You weren't in the family yet, Alexis," Victoria explained.

"In fact," Candace added, nibbling on a meat-filled puff
pastry as she recollected, "I think all this was going down at
about the same time you were dealing with Shyla and the
shenanigans she pulled at the Ritz in LA."

"Ohhh," was Alexis's understanding answer. What was it
about all of these women doing any and everything to get a
Livingston man? Then she recalled yesterday's lovemaking be-

fore the business trip, and how deeply Toussaint had buried himself in her, over and again, and she had her answer. "What happened with Malcolm?"

Victoria took a sip of tea. "Joyce went after him around the same time I got pregnant. Malcolm and I were already having problems. He was less than thrilled about the baby, and me hiding the pregnancy until I was almost four months didn't help matters. He was working on his invention, the now *world-famous* BBQ Soul Smoker, and I was so caught up in my world at the time that I didn't have a clue what was going on in his. Ms. Witherspoon swooped in and paid attention, giving Malcolm the support he needed with a project that was very near and dear to his heart. She did what I should have done," Victoria said, her voice becoming soft with reminiscent regret. "She encouraged him, cheered him on, and even set him up with one of her associates who was a producer at QVC. I almost lost him," she finished.

"But the legacy held strong," Candace said proudly. "My baby resisted!" Which is less than she'd done, but that was another story for another time. Or not.

Alexis felt like she was in the middle of a real-life soap opera. "How did you find out?"

"By watching the two of them together at a meeting about his device," Candace replied. "Even Stevie Wonder could have seen the lust that *b* had in her eyes."

"When it comes to our husbands, we don't mess around." Victoria looked at Alexis. "We'll always have each other's backs . . . always."

"So, since she wasn't successful with Adam or Malcolm, she set her sights on Jeff."

"Looks that way. But it will be a cold day in hell before she hooks up with my son. I don't know what problems Jeff is having, but whatever they are, *that* sistah isn't going to be the one to help solve them."

"What's going on with him?" Victoria asked.

Diane shrugged. "In my opinion, it's a midlife crisis at thirty-three. But don't worry. There is going to be a major change at the company, and Jeff is at the heart of it. Help is on the way."

"Okay, enough about Joyce," Candace announced. "I need to warn y'all about something in case Marietta Livingston comes calling."

Everyone looked at her. No one spoke. Diane didn't have to; she already knew where Candace was going.

"Adam told GrandMar about Q."

Gasps. Shocked looks. Concerned glances.

"Yes, he was a fool but not a complete one. He told him that Q tried to get with me. Neither one knows that he was successful. Now, Adam asked him not to, but we all know it's just a matter of time before he tells Mom Etta, if he hasn't already. So in case she calls probing, and y'all know how Marietta Livingston rolls, that's the story and we're sticking to it. Understand?"

Nods. Smiles. Relieved sighs.

"Now, back to Joyce..."

Everybody laughed, ready to get back to one of their favorite pastimes—dirt dishing.

16

Adam stood in Ace's office staring out the window, remembering what Toussaint had shared following his visit with Jefferson and wondering where his nephew's common sense had gone. As flashes of the naked images she'd once sent him came to mind, he could imagine right about the time that it fled out the window. Joyce was a brown-skinned beauty with meat on her bones, curves in all the right places, and an aim to please. But he'd always viewed his nephew as a brainy intellectual who in practical matters thought with his upper head, not his lower one.

"You think this thing with Joyce can get serious?" Adam asked, correctly guessing what was on his twin brother's mind.

"I don't know," Ace replied. "And I know that Diane will blow a gasket if that happens. But the boy is grown. When it comes to business, I have opinions, but regarding his love life, he's on his own."

The door opened and Marcus Livingston strode into the room. He looked properly respectable and distinguished in a navy suit with a baby blue shirt and pinstriped tie, his wire-rimmed glasses adding a scholarly air. His eyes were bright and his back was straight, a carriage belying the seventy-five years he'd been on the earth. "Good afternoon, Twins." He looked around. "Where is everybody?"

"On their way," Ace replied, getting up to hug his dad. "Can we get you something? Water, tea?"

"I'll have a spot of cognac if you don't mind," Marcus responded. "Since my last checkup, that mother of y'all's has put me on restriction: done replaced my beloved pig fat with some kind of vegetable oil mess, ain't fried nothing in weeks, even an egg, and seriously raided my liquor cabinet." He waited while Ace poured him two fingers of premium cognac. Marcus swirled it, sniffed it, and then had a taste. "Ah, yeah. That's good for what ails you right there."

The door opened and in walked Toussaint, looking like a younger version of Marcus and Malcolm, who was definitely Marietta's grandchild and his father's son. Pleasantries were exchanged before Malcolm asked, "Is Bianca going to be here?"

Ace shook his head. "She's knee-deep in getting that fire mess sorted out. I filled her in on what's going on and told her to handle her business. She's in full support of the decision we've made."

"What decision is that?" Jefferson asked as he sauntered into the room. He looked like a cutout of corporate America in his charcoal-gray suit, striped gray shirt, and black silk tie. His newly cut hair and freshly shaved goatee that framed his kiss-me lips made him look distinguished, and while he was the most laid back out of all of them and didn't have Malcolm's bulk or Toussaint's six-pack, his six-foot-tall, wide-shouldered frame still commanded a presence whenever he entered the room.

"Hey now, son, come on in." Ace went over and gave Jefferson a handshake, choosing not to point out the elephant—otherwise known as the MIA question—that was in the room.

Adam, on the other hand, decided to rub its trunk. "Glad you could join us," he said with a dash of sarcasm and a mere nod of acknowledgment.

"GrandMar?" Jefferson said, noticing his grandfather in the room. "You coming out of retirement?"

"Figured that every now and then I'd let you young'uns see that I still know how to get down." The room cracked up at this comment. "Plus, your grandmother is driving me crazy. That house ain't always big enough for the both of us." No one believed Marcus for a minute. Not only was Marietta the white to his rice, the butter to his jam, and the cream to his coffee, but their three-thousand-square-foot home situated on eighty acres just east of Atlanta was more room than two people would ever need.

"It's good to see you here." Jefferson hugged his grandfather and then acknowledged the other people in the room.

Adam walked over to his desk and grabbed a black leather binder. "Okay, this is a family business meeting and we're all here. So let's gather round the conference table."

Once everyone was seated, Jefferson raised his hand. "Dad, Ace, I'd like to say something before we start the meeting." Everyone looked his way. "I want to apologize for my behavior this week, not showing up in LA to support Bianca." He snuck a glance at Ace that reminded the elder Livingston how a guilty seven-year-old Jefferson had looked when, on a dare, he'd stolen a bag of cookies from the neighborhood store. "And for not returning your or Mama's calls. I've been going through some things but"—this time he looked at Toussaint—"I'm getting it back together."

"Just what have you been going through?" Marcus asked.

"Nothing for you to worry about, GrandMar."

"If it's interfering with the restaurant business, then it is *my* business."

"His work is fine, Dad," Ace said.

"Which is why we're here," Adam added. "Jeff, one of the reasons we were trying to get a hold of you this week is because of a new development involving Mark Stewart. He's retiring in thirty days."

Jefferson's head shot up. He'd had a feeling that this meeting somehow involved him directly, but that his boss was retiring never entered his mind. "You've got to be kidding," he said when his mouth started working again. "Mark Stewart is leaving the company? Why is he leaving, and why so abruptly?"

Ace told Jefferson about Mark's mother-in-law and the family's forthcoming relocation to West Palm Beach, Florida. "Adam and I have discussed it, and we feel you are ready to go to the next level. We're here to vote on your being promoted to the position of chief financial officer for the Livingston Corporation."

"Wow." The news hit Jefferson like a punch in the stomach, and he was immediately sorry for all of the cognac he'd consumed in the past several days. Even with the hot showers and strong black coffee, his mind was fuzzy. Everyone knew that Jefferson's ultimate goal was to head up the company, and as Toussaint's recent conversation had disclosed, Jefferson was being openly groomed for that role. But Jefferson had believed Mark would be with the company for another four to five years and that the President / COO position was a good eight to ten years away. Surely he'd heard incorrectly. Surely his father hadn't just put this no-show family member one rung closer to the top of the corporate ladder. "I was expecting y'all to have something to say to me. A reprimand, a cursing out, but not this."

"Yeah, well, that's coming," Ace said, emotion bringing a gruffness to his voice. "Your mama has worried herself half sick and mercilessly nagged me in the process."

"My secretary knew that I was working from home. Did you get the reports I e-mailed over?"

Ace nodded. "I got them and it's that level of excellence that gives me the confidence to cast my vote for this promotion. We know this is unexpected, Jeff, and happening faster than any of us imagined. Mark had planned to work at least another three to five years. But life happens while we're busy making plans, and with that in mind, I'd like to open the floor for discussion before we cast our vote." Ace looked around the room. "Anyone?"

Silence.

"There's nothing to talk about," Malcolm said, the first words he'd spoken since his arrival. "Pure and simple, you're the man for the job."

And just like that, in a matter of minutes, Jefferson Livingston became the number three man at the Livingston Corporation, behind Adam and Ace. The vote was unanimous.

17

Jefferson held it together until he reached his office. There—still reeling from the love of his grandfather, father, uncle, and cousins—he broke down. "You've been an A-number-one jerk, man," he hissed, angrily wiping away the tears. *Dissing your sister, ignoring your mother . . . What's wrong with you?* But deep down, Jefferson knew what was wrong, remembered the very moment, the very second that his world got turned upside down and how—no matter how hard he'd tried to get it back together—it had never been quite right again. *If you won't talk to me, Jefferson, you need to talk to somebody. We have a friend in Chicago. . . .* Diane's words came wafting into Jefferson's head, along with the pain of having caused his mother worry.

"It's time to start picking up the pieces, brothah," he said as he reached for the phone. "Bianca," he said when his sister answered. "It's your brother, the asshole."

"Boy, what the hell is wrong with you? Mama has been driving me crazy, thinking that I know why you're acting weird."

"Weird? Is that how she described me?"

"No, Jefferson, that's my word. Not returning calls, leaving Mama standing on the other side of your door . . . c'mon now."

"Trust me, it was not a good time when she came to the door."

A pause and then, "What's wrong, Jefferson?"

At the sound of concern in Bianca's voice, Jefferson's heart clenched and tears again threatened. "It's a long story, little sis. I don't want to get into it right now, but I don't want my family worrying about me anymore. I'm getting ready to step up my game."

"Well you'd better, since I hear that congratulations are in order for your noncommunicative ass."

"Okay, there you are, the feisty know-it-all with all the answers. There's my little sis. You had me worried for a minute because I didn't know who that compassionate-sounding woman was on the phone just now."

"Yeah, well, I don't either because if you get Mama trippin' and calling me nonstop again, this sister that you're talking to is going to kick your ass!"

"Ha! In your dreams, fool."

The siblings talked on the phone for another thirty minutes. And then Jefferson turned off his computer and reached for his keys. There were a few other people he needed to talk to, and this next conversation needed to take place in person.

"Mama!" The smell of a cinnamon-filled peach cobbler assailed his nostrils as soon as he opened the door.

Diane came around the corner brandishing a marble rolling pin. "Come on in here and get this whuppin'!"

"I know," Jefferson said with a laugh as he wrestled the pin away from his mother. She was laughing, too, but a part of him knew that she was just partly joking. He didn't blame her. His recent actions had sometimes made him want to kick his own ass. "I'm sorry," he said, hugging her tight. "I didn't mean to worry you."

"Well, you did," she said, stepping back to look at him and then cuffing him on the jaw.

"Dang, Mama! It was just a few days that went by without you hearing from me. You'd think I'd been MIA for months, dropped off the face of the earth."

"When you have your own, you'll understand," Diane said, heading back to the kitchen. "Come on back here with me, because if I burn up your daddy's cobbler, that rolling pin really will go upside your head!"

After an hour of conversation, during which he got Diane to do the unthinkable and cut a chunk of Ace's pie for him to take home, Jefferson headed for his car. He had a lot to do between now and Monday and knew that this would be his last weekend off in a while, at least for the next four weeks while Mark was still in town. It would take a Herculean effort, but Jefferson was determined that the transition between himself and the outgoing CFO would be as smooth as silk.

As soon as he got settled into his Beamer, he dialed the number given to him by his mom.

"Good afternoon, Dr. Morgan's office."

"Hi, is he in, please?"

"Yes, may I ask who's calling?"

"A personal friend."

There was a brief pause and then, "One moment."

After another moment, a deep, commanding voice came on the line. "This is Dr. Morgan."

"Dr. Morgan, it's Jefferson Livingston, Ace and Diane's son."

A beat and then, "The Livingstons of Atlanta? The award-winning, barbeque maestros of the nation? Those folk?"

Jefferson chuckled. "Yes, sir."

Some of the doctor's professional demeanor was replaced by a down-home friendliness. "Boy, I haven't seen your parents in years. How are they doing? How's the business?"

"The family is fine, sir, and business is booming."

"I don't doubt it. We have some of your grandfather's

sauce in our pantry right now. And that whatchamacallit that Malcolm invented is on our patio. The wife imagines herself a chef when she uses it."

"I'm sure she fair earns the title."

"And if you don't think so, that's a thought best kept to yourself." A chuckle, a pause, and then, "So what can I do for you?"

"I'm calling to schedule a visit, to see you in a . . . professional capacity."

Dr. Morgan answered without missing a beat. "Sure, son. I'd be glad to see you and offer my help. Are you living here now? In Chicago?"

"No, I'm still in Atlanta. But quite frankly I'm relieved that this visit will be away from my hometown. Black folk don't like to admit we're crazy." Jefferson's attempt to lighten the mood was only partially successful.

"There's nothing wrong with needing help now and then, son. Too many of us ignore signs that help is needed, when life's stresses and curveballs knock us down. It takes a strong person to even admit they need help, much less seek it out. Now, when would you like to come up for a visit?"

"As soon as possible."

"I'll put you back on with my secretary, but let's see, today is Thursday and the wife and I are out of town for the weekend. Will Monday morning be soon enough?"

"Sounds perfect, Dr. Morgan."

"Feel free to call me Dan, son. I'll see you next week."

18

Chardonnay sat in a downtown chicken-and-waffles joint enjoying a rare Saturday night off and away from her three children. She was there with Bobby; her best friend (whether she knew it or not), Zoe Williams; and Zoe's boyfriend and fellow Livingston Corporation marketing employee Drake Benson. Drake had taken Shyla Martin's place when she "resigned," and Zoe had moved from being Ace's assistant to being a junior marketing manager.

"How was your catfish?" Chardonnay asked, licking the juice from the spicy garlic shrimp off her fingers.

"Not bad," Zoe replied. She reached over for one of Drake's fries. He picked up his fork, as if to stab her.

Bobby guffawed. "Uh-oh. Did y'all see that? Drake, you got some brothah man in you for real, the way you're protecting that food, partner!"

"This is all Irish, fool," Drake replied. "Don't try to come between us and our potatoes!" Still, he scooted over his plate so that Zoe could have better access. Everyone knew that he'd been head over heels in love with her since they started dating two years ago. He'd give her anything she wanted, including his last name.

All jokes were put aside as the waitress brought out their main orders: fried chicken for Chardonnay and smothered chops for Drake, while Zoe opted for salmon, and grill master that he was, Bobby had to try the barbequed turkey wings. For a time, tinkling silverware and smacking lips were the only sounds heard. Zoe was the first one to come up for air. "So, Bobby," she said, placing down her fork and wiping her mouth with a napkin. "How's the cue?"

"Can't nobody get down like we do," he said, before filling his mouth with a forkful of fried corn. "These sides are banging," he added. "We might need to add a dish like this to our menu."

"What could we call it?" Zoe asked. In addition to soul music being played at every Taste of Soul restaurant, every dish was named after a soul or R & B singer.

"Freddie's fried corn," Bobby offered, taking another forkful.

"Freddie who?" Chardonnay queried.

"Jackson," Zoe answered, savoring a mouthful of yams.

"I like Parliament-Funkadelic Fried Corn." Chardonnay started to dance. "One nation under a groove . . ."

"Girl, that name's too long to put on the menu."

"I got it!" Drake said. "Frankie Beverly and Maize. You get it? Maize?"

Chardonnay's eyes widened. "Look at Mr. Blue-Eyed Soul over there. What do you know about some 'Joy and Pain,' 'Southern Girl,' and 'Golden Time of Day'?"

"My baby's got good taste, that's what," Zoe offered, kissing Drake on the cheek. "And for the record, his eyes are green."

"Thank you, baby." Drake kissed Zoe on the lips; then went back for a second smooch. "What do y'all think about the announcement?"

"What announcement?" Bobby asked.

Drake looked at Zoe. "You didn't tell her, honey?"

"You didn't give me a chance." Zoe rolled her eyes in

feigned chagrin. "Now, this news has not yet been announced, so it can't go any further than this table. Did you hear me, Chardonnay?"

"What?" Chardonnay asked with the innocence of a just-swaddled babe.

"And don't even think about selling it to the *Atlanta Inquirer* or trying to blackmail me for more information down the line."

"Damn, girl," Chardonnay sulked. "Such a low opinion of your friend."

"And which of the above did you not do?"

Chardonnay became very involved with devouring a chicken wing.

"Uh-huh . . . I thought so." Zoe took a drink and continued. "Mark Stewart is taking an early retirement. He and his wife are moving to Florida."

Chardonnay shrugged. "What the hell do I care about this Mark joker? I don't even know him."

"But you do know Jefferson. That's who's becoming the new CFO."

Chardonnay threw down her now-clean wing bone. "Shut the front door!"

"And run out the back," Zoe finished with a laugh. Zoe had once suggested to Chardonnay how great a catch Jefferson was, but Chardonnay had poopooed the idea because for her he was "too soft." "Ace's assistant typed up the memo today and let me see a copy."

"Damn, I should have listened to you. I could be married to the money man."

Bobby cleared his throat. "Uh, hello, am I mistaken or is your present husband sitting at the table?"

Chardonnay tsked. "Whatever, nucka."

"He's a hard worker, and smart," Drake said. "I think he deserves it."

"I do too," Zoe replied. "But I was still surprised to hear

that Mark was leaving the company. He's always struck me as a very dedicated employee—been there for at least twenty years."

"Then why's he leaving?" Chardonnay asked.

"His mother-in-law is ill, and they're moving to take care of her."

"At least that's their story and they're sticking to it," Chardonnay skeptically replied.

"Don't start, Char," Zoe warned. "You're always quick to add more fuel to the fire, even if there isn't one burning. And speaking of which, I've got a pretty flaming topic hot off the press."

"What?" Chardonnay asked, eyes beaming as she leaned forward. A hint of juicy gossip is the only thing that had stopped her from eating since they sat down.

"This." Zoe held out her left hand where a diamond ring sparkled. "I've been waving it around all night, but my wrist would break before you fools noticed!"

"Y'all are getting married?" Chardonnay asked incredulously.

"Congratulations, man," Bobby said.

The subdued nature of his comment caused Zoe to look twice. She had no doubt that he sincerely meant what he said. She just wanted to know, as Paul Harvey would say, the rest of the story.

Drake, who'd been walking on sunshine since Zoe said yes, was oblivious to anything but his happiness. "Thanks, man! I appreciate it!"

Chardonnay, who'd begun eating again, asked a question around a mouthful of chicken. "When's the big day?"

The plot thickens. Like Bobby, her over-the-top friend seemed underwhelmed. "Neither of us wants to wait and neither of us wants a big wedding, so we're thinking in three months, on the Fourth of July. You know, with fireworks and all?"

"Why don't you cut out all the nonsense and marry in

Vegas, like me and Bobby? Or save even more money by going to the courthouse and calling it a day."

"Girl, don't go getting all romantic and syrupy on me," Zoe cooed, cracking up so hard that she couldn't be mad. She'd learned a long time ago that Chardonnay Wilson's bark was much worse than her bite, and that a tough hood life in which she was sexually assaulted by her stepfather at fifteen had hardened a lot about her. But underneath all of that was a person who wanted to be loved like everyone else. And who lashed out when she was hurting. Now, it seemed, was one of those times. "Come to the bathroom with me, girl," Zoe said, rising. "I want to show off these sparkles in good fluorescent light."

They'd barely gotten the door closed before Zoe rounded on her friend. "All right, out with it. What's going on?"

"What?"

"You know what," Zoe shot right back. "You and Bobby have been talking all night, but not to each other, and I've seen more enthusiasm at someone's funeral than what was just showed at my marriage announcement. Now out with it. What gives?"

"Two things," Chardonnay said, her normally boisterous voice now barely above a whisper. "But you can't tell anybody."

This answer definitely called for a hands-on-hip moment, and Zoe did it with aplomb. "Like I've ever told anybody what you've shared with me."

"Okay, damn. Don't get an attitude." Zoe raised her eyebrows. "That's my territory."

So Chardonnay told Zoe what was troubling her, to which Zoe could only utter three words: *Oh. My. God.*

19

Cooper put his arm around Keisha and pulled her into his embrace. After the tears she'd shed at being left out of the Rileys' gatherings and life in general, and the midweek dinner party in particular, he knew it was time to put his argyle-sock-wearing, loafer-clad foot down. "Mother, I told you," he continued, fortified by the presence beside him, "I do not wish to join the family for Sunday dinner unless Keisha and her sons are included in the invitation. We've had an in-depth discussion about this already, at which time I thought to have made myself perfectly clear."

On the other end of the phone, Evelyn fought to maintain her composure. *What in-depth discussion is he talking about?* She distinctly remembered having his agreement that for the next six months she'd not have to deal with Keisha, that she could act as if the...woman...didn't exist until that fervent hope became a reality. And the dinner party had gone so well; the young doctor she'd invited as Cooper's escort was a perfect match! Since then, however, someone else had obviously done some talking to him, and Evelyn knew just what set of lips had been used.

"Junior, this isn't a personal slight toward the...young

lady"—*shameless hussy*—"with whom you're illegally cohabitating. But as you know, these dinners are family affairs."

"The party was not a family affair, but she wasn't invited to *that* either."

"We have a reputation to uphold, son, not to mention an example to set. How would it appear to bring a . . . disjointed . . . family around your niece and nephew? Those boys"—*heathens*—"in your home are quite unruly, and Charles Jr. is at such an impressionable age. I'm afraid Kathy shares my feelings—"

"You've discussed this with my sister?"

"Dear, this involves *family*. I value both her and Charles's opinion, and yes, your sister and I and your father and I have discussed this at length. Now, darling, everyone will be expecting you. Let's say aperitifs at three?"

Cooper slowly placed the receiver back in its cordless cradle. He had a mind to totally disregard his mother's edict and bring *his* family to the Riley's Sunday brunch. In fact, he decided he'd do just that. "Honey, I—"

"Give it back, asshole!"

Dorian ran from the den where the TV, Xbox, and Wii games were housed, through the living room, and into the dining room. He held a set of game controls high above his four-foot frame.

"Fuck you! I had it first."

Cooper's face could have appeared next to *aghast* in the dictionary.

"Y'all, quit that damn fighting!" Keisha spoke this in a tone that suggested this was not her first time at this particular rodeo.

The sound of two small bodies falling and tousling on hardwood, along with expletives that should never be uttered from mouths under the age of say, eighty, followed.

"Dorian! Antwan! I'm going to beat your asses!"

Crash!

"Shit!" Keisha jumped up from the couch and ran into the dining room. The boys continued fighting, totally oblivious to the fact that they'd broken glass.

Cooper imagined this scene taking place at his parents' home, amid their priceless paintings, crystal, and antiques. His blood pressure soared. "Boys! Stop it this instant!" Standing in the dining room entryway, his stance was the same as if he had said, "Objection, Your Honor!"

Keisha entered the fray, pulling Antwan by his leg while smacking Dorian across the face. "Un-huh, I'ma kick both your asses! Give it here!" she screamed, holding out her hand and demanding the controls from Dorian. When he didn't give it to her quick enough, she snatched it from him and whacked him upside the head with it.

"Ow, Mama, that hurt!"

"I intended for it to hurt."

"Keisha, please! Let's not resort to violence."

She whacked him again.

Dorian ran up on Cooper. "Stop hollering at my mama, fool!"

Antwan began jumping for the remote. "Mama, give it to me! Mama, give it to me! Mama! Mama! Mama!"

"Here, boy!"

And just like that, it was over. Antwan took the control and ran from the room. Dorian trudged into the kitchen and seconds later came out eating from a large bag of chips as if what had just occurred had not even happened. Cooper stood with eyes wide, his breathing heavy and tie askew. It felt like the calm after a tornado, when after wreaking abject destruction in mere seconds, the twister moseys on its way as quickly as it came.

"Sorry about that, baby," Keisha said, calmly picking up wineglass fragments from the floor and placing them on the table, along with what remained of two bone china plates. "I'll speak with the housekeeper. These dishes should not have been on the table in the first damn place. We ate hours ago!" Satisfied that she'd gotten the biggest pieces, she continued. "What were we talking about? Oh, yes, dinner with your family. That sounds cool with me. When are we leaving?"

"Uh, sweetie, about dinner. Mother is still putting up a bit of a fuss in regards to having you join us."

"And? You're going to let her dictate your life and tell you what to do?" She sidled up to him and grabbed his crotch. "That's not what you said last night."

"In general, no," Cooper replied, disengaging her hand. Although, seriously, there was no need. In his present discombobulated state, he doubted an erection would occur even with a penile pump. "But in this case, yes." Cooper took a deep breath. He wasn't used to such outbursts of verbal anger, let along actual fisticuffs taking place in someone's home. Quite frankly, he was appalled. He looked at his watch and was relieved to see that he actually needed to leave. Right now. Arriving late at Evelyn Riley's dinner table was not an option. He began retying his tie. "Look, sweetheart, I'll talk to my parents today, get them to see reason—"

"Yeah, whatever, Cooper. You're ashamed of me and my boys."

"No, darling—" He reached out to Keisha.

She jerked away. "No! Just go over to your stupid mother's house, with her stuck-up ass. The food is probably nasty anyway!"

There was absolutely, positively no appropriate response for Cooper other than to nod curtly, turn on his heels, grab his keys, and walk out the door.

Twenty minutes later, Cooper entered the Riley household. It was as if he'd been wandering through the darkness and now entered the marvelous light. The smell of something delicious wafted from the dining room, mixing with the scent from the large bouquet of cut flowers showcased in the foyer.

Strands of Wolfgang Amadeus Mozart's *Symphony No. 29 in A Major* tickled his ears. Cooper took a deep breath and inhaled peace and quiet. How could he ever have turned his nose up at this banal way of life? It hadn't dawned on him until the drive over that he had taken for granted the art of civilization.

In all the years he'd lived at home, which was until he was thirty-five, he'd never once heard a raised voice. He never heard his parents argue, and even their debates—say, regarding politics or wallpaper swatches—were conducted in hushed, quiet tones. He and his older sister, Kathy, had modeled their cookie-cutter parents and had been perfect children. He'd practiced good manners, done what he was told, and for the most part, lived a contented life. Boring as watching television static, but content.

Cooper removed his shoes and moved toward the low murmuring of conversation he heard in the distance. He passed the dining room and nodded at the maid who delivered a covered platter to the buffet on noiseless feet. Continuing on to the den at the back of the house, he turned the corner and witnessed a perfect tableau. His father, Judge Riley, sat looking properly respectable in a pair of black trousers, a button-down white shirt, and black-patterned tie. Charles's attire was similar, except his shirt was pinstriped, and a suit coat was carefully positioned over the back of his chair. Kathy and his mother sat on a settee with backs straight and legs properly crossed at the ankles. Kathy wore a knee-length dress, with hose and modest heels. Evelyn opted for a black pencil skirt paired with a silk, paisley-patterned blouse. Both women wore pearls. The children sat quietly at a nearby table. Six-year-old Rebecca played with a doll. Eight-year-old Charles Jr. was tackling the last Harry Potter tome. He was the first one to see Cooper.

"Uncle Junior," he announced, closing his book and standing. He walked over and held out his hand. Cooper smiled and shook it. Banal. Civilized.

"Hello, everyone." Cooper walked into the room. "Sister," he said, bending down to kiss Kathy's cheek. "Charles." The men shook hands. "Father, Mother." He kissed Evelyn's cheek and shook the judge's hand.

Evelyn stood, surreptitiously looking over Cooper's shoulder. "Son, you came," she said, the tiniest of chinks in her unflappable armor. "And your guests?"

"At home, Mother," Cooper replied.

"Ah," Evelyn said cheerfully, hands clasped together in restrained glee. "May I get you a Campari and soda, darling?"

"I'll help myself, Mother, if you don't mind." Cooper walked over to the bar, poured two fingers of Scotch, downed it, and poured two fingers more. Four pairs of eyes observed. Four mouths said nothing. Evelyn, meanwhile, excused herself and left the room. When she returned, her eyes were shining.

The meal was properly delightful. Banal. Civilized. As dessert was being served, the doorbell rang. Moments later, in walked Michelle Hopkins, the attractive OB-GYN from Wednesday night's dinner party, wearing a form-flattering pair of rust-colored Donna Karan slacks, a simple knit shell, and a triple strand of Tahitian peacock pearls. Her shoulder-length hair was pulled back in a soft ponytail. Her makeup was light and flawless.

"I'm sorry to have missed dinner," she said after greetings. "There was a slight complication with a delivery, so it took a bit longer than I thought."

"But everything came out okay?" Judge Cooper intoned with his dry brand of humor. "Or should I say *everyone*?"

"Yes," Michelle answered after laughing lightly at the judge's remark, as was required. "The eight-pound baby and mother are both doing wonderfully."

"You're just in time for dessert," Evelyn said as she motioned for Michelle to sit. "Please join us."

Cooper watched with rapt interest as Michelle picked up

the proper fork, in the proper manner, and took dainty bites of cheesecake while not leaving crumbs on her lips. Her being in his home felt almost surreal, as though he'd not met her just days ago. He listened to her intelligent and lively conversation with new ears. *Quit that damn fighting. I'ma kick both your asses.* And appreciated her stunning beauty—not to mention civility—with new eyes. Not even Keisha's river of tears and expert sex could erase the fact clearly evident before Cooper in this moment: Michelle Hopkins fit in perfectly with the Riley tableau, and Keisha never would.

Back at Cooper's luxury townhome, Keisha sat in the middle of their master bedroom, high and drained. After cursing her kids out (and crying her eyes out), she'd taken them out to eat, went down into the hood, and copped a dime bag, and now sat trying to figure out what to do with her life. For the past two years, she'd tried various ways to make things better for her and the boys—both illegally and legally—but things weren't working out. Maybe her brother was right. Maybe one couldn't change who they really were, or move out of the hood and into the well heeled. *When it comes to people like the Livingstons, people like you and me are good enough to fuck but not good enough to marry.* That's what Q had said when she'd fallen in love with Jefferson, when she'd actually believed there was a chance that she could become his wife. And that's what he'd said about Cooper too. *He loves what's between your legs, little sis.* Well, there was no doubt that this was true where Cooper was concerned. That, and what she did to his little soldier with her mouth. "Fuck it! I'm tired of trying to fit in with these phony clowns!" *I'll go back to LA, maybe hook up with Rico and try to make hella paper on the other side of the law.* Decision made to get out of the golden carriage and step back into a pumpkin, Keisha slid off the bed, walked into the master suite, and promptly threw up all over the floor.

20

The Midwest was experiencing April showers, and Jefferson felt a chill in the air as he walked down Chicago's Magnificent Mile. But upon entering Dr. Dan Morgan's warmly decorated office, he immediately relaxed. The walls were a soothing shade of blue, the carpet chocolate brown, the lighting subdued. Huge leafy plants filled the corners and pictures of the doctor's family littered his desk. A cushy love seat anchored the far wall. After shaking hands, this is the area to which Dr. Morgan directed them to sit.

"Can I get you anything? Coffee? Tea?"

"No, Doctor, I'm fine."

"You may call me Doctor if you'd like, but really, Dan is fine."

"Okay, Dan."

"Okay, Jeff. What would you like to talk about?"

And with that simple, straightforward question, Jefferson began to regurgitate the past two years of his life: meeting Keisha, falling in love, being betrayed by her thievery, his duplicitous actions in her brother's imprisonment, and his abject loneliness since she and the boys had left his life. The emptiness that alcohol had increasingly filled. He then shared his hurt at being overlooked for the West Coast position, even as he acknowledged the healing effects of his recent promotion—the primary act that had driven him here.

Aside from a clarifying question here and an affirming grunt there, Dr. Morgan listened quietly. "That's quite an emotional roller-coaster ride," he said when Jefferson finished. "Any one of those incidents could have sent the average person reeling. But all of this, combined with the family and business dynamics, is a lot to hold inside you. And that's what you've been doing, haven't you? Holding it in."

Jefferson nodded.

"And trying to drown it in alcohol," the doctor added.

Another nod.

"We can get you into treatment for the drinking, if you feel you need it, and discuss some fairly simple and clear-cut methods to bring you back to being firmly and fully in control of your life. Many of us, and I'm talking people of color here, and especially men, don't like to discuss our problems. We tend to hold it in and by doing so end up carrying the weight of the world on our shoulders and in our hearts. This, and lack of diet and exercise, affects us not only mentally, but also physically. Chitterlings and fried chicken aren't why we lead the nation in hypertension and heart disease. No, son. Stress is the leading cause of sickness in our community. I firmly believe that when we relieve the stress that the events of the past two years have caused from your life, we'll relieve your need for alcohol"—the doctor smiled warmly—"and your need to see me." The doctor jotted down a couple of notes, then looked at Jefferson. "So the two issues we're going to deal with and get through are the failed relationship and the failed career move."

"Yes."

"Anything else?"

Silence.

Dan leaned back, mirroring the casualness of his body language in the sound of his voice. "Jeff, problems have to be acknowledged before they can be dealt with. In order for us to effectively work together, I need to know if there's anything else that's bothering you."

"There is one more thing." Jefferson said after a lengthy pause. Deep down, he knew that what he was about to share was the catalyst for his downward spiral, the proverbial straw that had broken the camel's back, even more than Keisha's betrayal. He'd never wanted anyone to know what happened. But to successfully head up the Livingston Corporation and be free of his past, he had to keep it one hundred. "About a year ago," he started, forcing himself to look the doctor dead in the eye. "I made out with a beautiful woman . . . then found out she was a man."

Twenty years of counseling allowed Dr. Morgan to absorb this information without flinching. He simply nodded, crossed his right foot over his left knee, and said, "Let's talk about that."

Jefferson may have had problems with male-on-male encounters, but for Taste of Soul sous-chef Bobby Wilson, it was another story altogether. As requested, he'd come down to the courtroom on the pretense of delivering a meal. Well, he'd indeed brought the judge his favorite TOS menu item: James Brown's Baby Back Big Rib Snack with BBQ beans and potato salad. He enjoyed the ribs while Bobby devoured a Blue Notes Burger with Five Stairstep Fries—seasoned with a top-secret five spices. But the bone Cooper Riley Sr. had really wanted was the one that was nut-deep in his booty right now.

"Ohhhhh," the judge moaned, holding on to his desk.

Bobby threw his head back and did a Jermaine Jackson. He got serious. Grabbing the judge around his flabby middle, he shifted his body, rose up on his toes, and pounded anew. Sweat poured off of both men as they raced toward a climax. The judge's member waved back and forth in semi-hard splendor while Bobby's ironlike pipe continued being laid. "Here I go," he began to pant, moving faster and faster until his hip movements almost became a blur. "Here I go, here I go, here I go!" He thrust forward so hard that the judge lost his balance. The chair flew out from under him and he hit the floor with a thud. He was too tired and too satiated to care. After taking a moment to gather his breath, he simply turned over, sat up, and said, "Bobby, please help me up."

First the judge and then Bobby performed separate ablutions in the judge's private bathroom. When Bobby returned, he noted the pine smell of some type of disinfectant the judge had sprayed. He started to get pissed, but then, on second thought, felt that a whiff of sex or some errant cum on a lawyer's slacks wouldn't be a good look. He walked over to where he'd left his keys and frowned when he saw a huge stack of bills lying beside them.

"What the fuck is this?"

"Some fun money," the judge replied. "I thought that perhaps you could take a couple days off soon and that we could go somewhere like Vegas, Atlantic City . . . or even Mexico."

"Ah, hell, man. Don't go getting all hung up and possessive and shit. That's what slowed me and Abernathy's roll."

"Which he is still none too pleased about. He doesn't know that I know who he's talking about, but when reading between the lines of his comments, it is clear that he wants to make you a permanent fixture in his life. It's the main motivation behind him funding your restaurant."

"Yeah? And what's yours?" Bobby had been shocked but not surprised to find out that the upper crust of the black gay community not only knew of each other, but had each other's backs as well.

"I want to help a man with potential realize his dreams." Judge Riley met Bobby's skeptical stare and continued. "I've been married forty years with a sizeable bank account and a comfortable life. I love Evelyn and have absolutely no plans or desire to ever leave her."

"That's your position, but what about hers? Do you think she'd ever leave you?"

The judge seemed genuinely perplexed. "Why would she ever want to do that? She knows about my...proclivities... but she also knows that there is nothing that would ever threaten our marriage. That's what you need to have to be successful in life, son. An understanding wife."

Bobby thought about Chardonnay and almost burst out laughing. There was no doubt that Mrs. Riley was nothing like his boo. Mrs. Riley might turn the other butt cheek while her husband spread his, but Chardonnay Johnson Wilson wasn't going to go out like that. She'd told him in no uncertain terms that if she was going to give up her dial-a-dick options, then he'd have to turn in his pick-a-pussy card. Which is why he had to make a decision, and soon. The family he had or the restaurant he wanted? Because knowing the strings that the restaurant came with...Bobby knew that he couldn't have both.

21

Toussaint's secretary buzzed him on the intercom. "Joyce Witherspoon is here to see you, Toussaint."

"Thank you, Monique," Toussaint answered. "Send her in."

Seconds later, Joyce entered Toussaint's office. She had dressed to impress—and she did. Her tailored, cream-colored suit complemented a complexion the color of pecans and accented curves that were envied by those lesser endowed. Her understated elegant look continued in the light yellow shell she wore, with simple gold jewelry. Her flowery perfume was subtle, yet evident, as was her smile as she approached him with hand outstretched. "Toussaint, thank you so much for agreeing to see me."

Toussaint shook her hand. "The proposal you sent was impressive," he responded while shaking her hand. He took her elbow and gently led her over to the office's sitting area. "I'd never let personal opinion get in the way of potential profit."

"Spoken like a true businessman."

"You know the deal. Coffee?"

"No, thanks."

"Water?"

"I'm fine, thank you."

Toussaint poured himself a glass of lemon water and joined Joyce at the table. "So . . . have you talked to Jeff?"

Joyce resisted the urge to look embarrassed. Both she and Jeff were two grown-ass people who'd been interrupted while doing grown-ass things. She had nothing for which to apologize. "No, I have not. I left a couple messages, but they weren't returned."

"Don't take it personally. Jeff's been busy."

"I totally understand. And while you probably think I'm just trying to get with yet another Livingston, *and you'd be right,* I want you to know that I truly respect your cousin. He's a good man."

"You're right—he is." He reached for the proposal his assistant had printed out before Joyce's arrival. "Considering our last encounter, I was surprised to receive this from you."

"I'd prepared it before running into Jeff last Wednesday."

"Where did you guys hook up anyway? FGO?"

"Would you believe Starbucks?"

"Ha! Only because that answer is too crazy to be a lie."

"He was coming from some type of benefit and had stopped by Starbucks for a cup of sober-up. I thought he was too tipsy to drive and offered to give him a ride home."

"I guess I should say thank you."

"It's what any concerned citizen would do."

"Ha! What about what happened after that?"

"That's between me and Jeff." She met Toussaint's stare without flinching.

Toussaint had to give it to old Joyce girl. She knew how to roll with the big boys and didn't back down. He liked that. He scanned the paper in front of him. "As I've stated, Joyce, this proposal is superb. But I must ask the obvious. With all the bad blood between us, more specifically between you and the Livingston women, why would you even come our way to do business again?"

Joyce answered without hesitation. "When it comes to soul food, you're the best. And because of our liaison when my company began, Southern cooking became synonymous with Loving Spoonful events, a part of the brand, if you will. This is the South, and when I host events, especially for out-of-towners, the Southern-inspired menu is always a hit. Similarly, when I host events out of town, it's like bringing a little bit of my Southern heritage with me. I can serve any number of cuisines and have: Italian, Mexican, Indian, Greek. But by far and away the most popular and the most often recommended is soul food.

"About six months ago, I received an excellent contract, a game-changer really." Toussaint's brow rose. Joyce continued. "A partnership with the Democratic National Convention to not only plan events surrounding their convention in August, but also to work individually with a number of congressmen and senators in their individual races—fund-raisers and the like. These events range from small and intimate, say a dinner party of a dozen or so, to a ballroom filled with five thousand folks. The week before the fire, I'd spent a considerable amount of time on the TOSTS Web site and found Bianca's ideas of tapas-style soul-food appetizers to be genius. I immediately envisioned these tasty treats being passed around at all of these functions. After seeing the fire, I thought this could be great positive publicity in the face of negative circumstances. During the dormancy of their rebuilding, TOSTS could expand their name recognition, and I could offer exclusive menu items. From this perspective, the idea to contact you was a no-brainer. Like you, I'd never let personal opinion get in the way of potential profit."

Toussaint nodded his understanding. "Touché."

Over the next hour, Toussaint and Joyce discussed her proposal. He'd even tried to reach Bianca, but his cousin was busy meeting with the company who would rebuild TOSTS. By meeting's end, he was convinced that her plan was solid enough for serious consideration. But he knew that the decision was not his alone to make. "I'll run this by the appropriate personnel," he said, closing the folder—an indication that their meeting was over, "and get back with you sometime in the next few weeks. In the meantime, I'd suggest you do a little fence mending."

"Don't worry, Toussaint. I won't stop trying until I talk to Jeff."

"You definitely should talk to my cousin, but I'm not talking about him. I'm talking about my sister-in-law, Victoria, and my mother. I know that women can be scandalous, but what you tried to pull with my uncle and brother was some foul shit. You owe both women an apology. I strongly suggest you make that happen . . . and soon."

22

The next morning, Jefferson arrived at the Livingston Corporation bright and early. He wanted to speak with his father and knew that Ace, an early riser, was often one of the first employees in the building. He turned the corner and sure enough saw a shard of light peeking from under Ace's double office doors. What surprised him, however, was the tinkling laughter he heard as he neared. He tapped the door lightly.

The laughter stopped.

He tapped again. "Ace, it's me."

Pause. "Hold on just a second, son."

Jefferson frowned. One second passed. Two. Five. The frown deepened, followed by the crossing of arms. He was just about to knock again when the door swung open. "Mom?"

"Hello, son," Diane said a bit breathlessly as she walked back into the office. "Your father left extra early this morning, so I decided to surprise him with . . . breakfast. Come on over to the conference table. There's a couple biscuits left. I'll warm one up—got some jam, too, that Mama made. The strawberry kind that you like." She had to finally stop her nervous chatter and catch her breath. "You want some?"

The slyest of smiles scampered across Jefferson's face as he followed his mother to the table where, indeed, remnants of what looked like a hearty breakfast remained. There were a few other noticeable remnants in the room, a certain odor that probably explained why his mother's hair was askew, but Jefferson shut his mind down before it could go further. When it came to parents, some things were best not thought about.

The toilet flushed and soon Ace came out of the office, wiping his hands on a monogrammed towel and smelling like too much Hugo Boss. "Good morning, Jeff. You're here early."

"Taking a page out of your book, I guess." He accepted the warmed up biscuit from his mother that was oozing with butter and jam. "Thanks, Mom. Lots of work to do, so I wanted to get a jump on the day."

"Good practice, son."

"Speaking of work, I should be going. Wouldn't want to interrupt the flow!" Diane kissed the top of Ace's bald head, then walked around and hugged her son. "Why don't you stop by later, baby. Tell me how your visit with Dan Morgan went."

"I will, Mom. It went good."

"Excuse me, son. Let me walk your mama to the door."

Jeff waited and, unless they'd moved the door he'd just entered to the other end of the hall, knew that his parents' goodbye included tongue-thrashing and lip-locking. He guessed he should be grateful to have been raised by two people who were still in love. *Maybe I'll have that someday.* He instantly thought of another woman and remembered that he owed Joyce Witherspoon a call.

"All right, then, Jeff. What's on your mind?"

Besides you in here throwing down with my mama? Mack Daddy? Player, player, play on? "Ha!"

Ace looked up from his coffee. "What's funny?"

"Ahem." Jefferson cleared his throat. "Just thought of something, that's all."

"How was your trip?"

"It went well."

"How's the good doctor?"

"Dr. Morgan looks well, Ace. He asked about y'all."

"Me and Diane need to get up to Chicago. It's been a while."

"He said as much. He also said you have a standing invitation."

"We just might take him up on that in the not-too-distant future." Ace nodded toward Jefferson's hand. "What's that?"

Jefferson had almost forgotten the paper in his hand—a rough outline of the items he wanted to tackle during the thirty-day transition period where Mark Stewart would hand over the reins, followed by his first ninety days as the official CFO. "Just a few things I came up with on the flight back."

Ace scanned the paper, nodding as he read. "I like the strategic direction you're heading in relation to portfolio management and franchise expansion. By the time the board meets in October, you'll have a few months under your belt and a more in-depth report.

"Come on over to my desk, Jeff. I want you to take a look at the operating expenses for this next quarter. I'm thinking that—" Ace's office phone rang. "Excuse me." He answered it. "Ace Livingston."

"Good morning, Ace. Sterling. Figured I'd catch you at work already."

Ace looked at his watch. It was not quite eight-thirty. "You're rolling pretty early as well. What can I do for you?"

"I was hoping to either come by your office around nine, or have you and Adam meet me here, at my office."

Ace was immediately on alert. "Why? Is there a new development?" He asked this already knowing that Sterling wouldn't provide a direct answer. He never discussed details of any kind over the phone.

"I'd like to meet. Which location works best?"

Ace looked at his watch again. "Let me try and catch Adam before he leaves the house. We'll meet at your office." Ace ended the call. "Sterling wants to meet with Adam and me. I imagine it's something to do with the fire."

"It wasn't an accident?"

Ace gave Jeff a look. "That's what we're getting ready to find out."

23

Ten minutes later, Ace and Adam entered the Bank of America building in downtown Atlanta. They joined a slew of office workers headed to their nine-to-fives, but once they'd reached the fiftieth story, they stepped off, walked down the hall to a nondescript door, and pressed the buzzer on the silver plaque that bore one word: STERLING. They were immediately buzzed in.

Sterling greeted them, shaking hands. "Ace, Adam, my secretary is out sick today. Come on back."

They walked back to his large corner office, tastefully decorated in black, ivory, and silver understated elegance. Adam accepted a cup of coffee. Ace declined but accepted a bottle of ice-cold water.

"Well, gentlemen," Sterling began after unscrewing his bottle of water and taking a swig. "Looks like we may have a situation."

Ace and Adam looked at each other. "Meaning?" Ace asked.

Sterling leaned back, speaking in his usual low, calm, authoritative voice. "My investigation has yielded an eye witness who was evidently missed during the fire department's search, the second one you requested after the first yielded no clues. Evidently he went on vacation the day of the incident and by the time he returned, their exploration of the incident had ended."

Adam worked to hide his impatience. "What exactly did this person witness?"

"Someone loitering in the alley, near your establishment's back door shortly before the explosion."

"Did he get a good description of what this person looked like?" Ace asked.

Sterling shook his head. "At the time, the worker didn't pay much attention to the guy. He only noticed him because it was early, and this cook knew just about everyone who was up and stirring in the neighborhood that time of morning. Plus, he said the man wore dark clothing: baggy shorts, a baseball cap, and a black T-shirt."

Ace sat back in his seat. "Damn."

"There is one tidbit of information that may be useful—a tattoo. The worker said it stuck out because it had welted the man's skin and was therefore slightly raised from the arm."

Adam rubbed a frustrated hand over his close-cropped hair. "Did this potential witness see what the tattoo was?"

"He thinks it was a cross but wasn't one hundred percent sure."

Ace took another swallow of water. "So was this guy white, black, Hispanic?"

Sterling's pause was ever so slight. "He was African American."

The room was quiet for a moment while this news sank in. "Well we know one person who it isn't," Ace finally said. "It's not Quintin Bright. Not unless he's escaped from prison." There was no joy in the laugh that followed.

"Well, that's the second piece of news that I have."

An almost imperceptible glance passed between the twins.

"Quintin Bright was behind bars when this happened, but

I have it on good authority that Cooper Riley is working tire-lessly to get him released."

Adam and Ace exchanged a look. Both had no doubt as to what the other was thinking in that moment: *One, hell hath no fury like an attorney scorned, and two, Keisha Miller's snatch must be made out of gold!*

"How can that son of a bitch be getting out already?" Adam asked. "It wasn't more than a month or so ago that you were telling us that he'd been involved in a fight and gotten more time."

"And that's all true. But you shouldn't underestimate the Rileys. At times, their judicial pull can be impressive."

"So he's gonna walk," Ace said. "Just like that."

"Believe it or not, this may work in our favor. His actions will be easier to track once he comes out from behind bars."

Ace leaned forward. "So you're tracking him because you think he's somehow connected to the fire."

"I'm tracking everyone who's ever had a beef with your family in the last few years, including ex-employees. Now, tell me, do either of you gentlemen recall Quintin having a tat-too?"

Both men shook their heads.

"These days, lots of men have tattoos," Ace said. "And I'm sure that here in the Bible Belt there are more than a few crosses among them."

"Somebody must not be too holy if they blew up our business."

"Let's not jump to conclusions, gentlemen. This informa-tion may mean something, but then again it may mean noth-ing at all. It's not a crime to walk down an alley or even loiter at the back of the building. I've called in a fire expert who is going over the evidence collected by the fire department and who will also comb the premises with his team. I'd rather not speculate but wait for the facts."

Adam nodded. "So when will we know more?"

"Probably no more than a week or so. These specialists I hired are top-notch. One of them worked on Ground Zero after nine-eleven; the other one is a retired military reconnaissance expert. Both are also good friends of mine. If there is a clue anywhere in that debris, they'll find it."

"That tattoo-wearing asshole," Ace said, rising. "That sounds like the debris that they need to find."

Sterling smirked slightly as he, too, rose and shook the hands of both men. "Barbequing is your business, brothers, investigating is mine."

"Well, get to handling your business, then!" Ace said.

"Haven't you been listening? I'm handling it now." With that, Sterling walked the gentlemen to the door and wished them a pleasant rest of the day.

As Adam was leaving Sterling's office, someone was arriving at his front door. Candace was only mildly surprised when she looked out and saw who it was. Toussaint had told her that Joyce was trying to reestablish a connection with the restaurant. She took a deep breath and opened the door.

"Good morning, Candace."

Candace looked her up and down. "Joyce."

"May I come in?"

Candace thought about having this conversation take place on the porch, but having been given a healthy dose of brought-upsy by her mother, she opened the door and motioned Joyce in. The porch would have showed absolutely no genteel manners. But Candace figured that when it came to the woman who tried to steal her husband and eff her married son, the foyer was about as polite as she could get.

Joyce stepped in and looked around, immediately noting the high ceilings, marbled entryway, and sparkling chandelier. "Your house is lovely, Candace."

Candace crossed her arms. "I imagine you're not here to discuss interior design."

Joyce's smile was small but sincere. "Of course not. Toussaint may have told you I'd be coming over. I'm here to apologize."

"For..."

"For my inappropriate actions with your husband. We were never intimate," she hurriedly added. "But that was more because of your husband's faithfulness than any conscience on my part." At the three-syllable F-word, Candace uncrossed her arms and lessened her judgment, less someone throw a rock at her glass house. "There is absolutely no excuse for going after a married man. I always knew that and always said I'd never be that kind of woman. But when I met Adam, and saw how kind and wonderful and powerful he was I...Candace, I just lost my mind. Plain and simple."

"You did that, all right."

"I'm very sorry, Candace. Not only for trying to mess with your husband, but also for crossing the line with your son. I've placed a call to Victoria, but when you talk to her, can you let her know why I'm calling? I'm wanting her forgiveness. Do I have yours?"

Candace gave Joyce a long look. She was a fairly good reader of people, and all in all, she felt Joyce wasn't a bad person, but like so many other sistahs out there, just desperate and lonely. "I'll forgive you," she finally said, walking toward the door to signal the end of the discussion, "because none of us are perfect. But I won't forget. So I hope you've learned your lesson about coming after a married man."

"I have, Candace. Again, I'm very sorry for what happened and am hoping we can somehow put it behind us. I've secured a major contract with the Democrats and want to partner with your company to cater these events. I'm hoping my...deplorable actions of the past won't jeopardize what could be a very profitable venture."

Candace's eyes narrowed. "I hear you're after more than our catering services."

Joyce wasn't surprised at what Candace knew. The Livingstons were a close-knit clan. "You have a problem with me seeing Jefferson?"

"What do you think?"

"I think that if you do, then I am not truly forgiven."

24

It had been months since Joyce had visited a TOS site, and probably years since she'd visited the Auburn location. But as soon as she stepped inside the small yet tastefully decorated restaurant, she felt right at home. Like the Buckhead Taste of Soul location, this one boasted a red and black color scheme, with a dark wooden floor and tables and stark-white walls. Most of the framed black-and-white pictures on the wall had been signed, a combination of politicians, actors, and singers whose names had been immortalized in dishes such as Luther's Limas, the Pendergrass Pork Chop Plate, Marvin's Mellow Meatloaf, and most recently, Michael's Mixed Plate. This slight nod to vegetarianism (slight because some of the vegetable dishes were seasoned with meat) offered four vegetable sides and a soda pop. Because Joyce had begun watching what she ate, she ordered the latter but couldn't resist adding an appetizer of Ruffin's Rib Tips to assuage the need for cue that walking into a Taste of Soul joint always evoked. She'd just received her rib tips, placed a heaping forkful inside a buttery roll, and taken a bite when a shadow crossed her table.

"Joyce?"

Joyce's first thought was, *If this is someone important, please don't let me have sauce on my chin.* She surreptitiously ran a hand over her mouth as she looked up. *Shyla Martin? On Auburn Avenue?* Not important, per se, but definitely interesting. You normally wouldn't catch someone like Shyla Martin around these parts. "Hi, Shyla."

"Mind if I sit down?" Shyla asked.

Joyce picked up her fork and resumed eating. "Not at all."

The waiter brought over a menu and water. Shyla waved away the plastic-coated paper. After more than two intense years as the Livingston Corporation's marketing director and having eaten at the restaurant regularly during that time, she was well aware of everything on the menu. "I'll have the Bloodstone's Baked Chicken Plate."

"With two or three sides?"

"Two: Commodores Coleslaw and the Dramatics Dirty Rice." After the waiter left, Shyla turned to Joyce. "I'm surprised to see you here, Joyce," she said, confirming that she and Joyce had been thinking the same thing about each other. "You're more of a Buckhead kind of sistah, if you know what I mean."

Joyce smiled. "I am and I do. Next month, I'm doing a fund-raiser in this area for one of my clients and was inspecting the space."

"Anyone I know?"

"Everybody knows him. Jon Abernathy."

"Ha! The people's politician," Shyla said, quoting one of his campaign ad taglines. "That is one gorgeous man."

"I concur."

"He's not that tall, what five eight, nine—"

"Ten, according to his publicist."

"Well, he may have that extra inch somewhere but it's not on his stature."

"Ha!"

"But he blesses a suit with that compact tight body. He reminds me a little of the Buckhead sous-chef, Bobby Wilson."

"Yup, a darker, more handsome version." Joyce moved her plate of rib tips aside as the waiter placed down her entrée. "Can I have some hot sauce?" And then, "You know what, Shyla? Although we've often traveled in the same circles and even worked with the same company, I believe that this is the longest conversation I've ever had with you."

"I think you're right. But then again, many of the occasions were at affairs your company organized. You make it look easy, but event planning is no joke. It seems as though you're needed everywhere, yet you carry a smile all over the room."

"Yes, it's usually hiding the fact that I'm about to kill somebody."

"Ha! Seriously, everyone clamors to attend a Loving Spoonful event. You must be proud of what you've been able to do in a few short years."

"I'm very pleased with my company's current position." Joyce enjoyed a forkful of perfectly seasoned cabbage. "What about you? How's life after the Livingstons?" She really wanted to ask how life was after Toussaint, but they were having a pleasant conversation and Joyce planned to keep it that way.

"Honestly, they are a hard act to follow. But I'm doing okay." Shyla told Joyce about working at the advertising company. "I also consult on the side," she concluded, reaching for her purse and digging out a business card. "So if one of your clients ever has need of marketing or public relations assistance, please feel free to pass on my information. In fact"—she reached into her purse again—"here's a few cards." Joyce took the cards and pocketed them in her briefcase. "What about you? Is Taste of Soul still your main caterer?"

Joyce looked at Shyla, expecting to see the sarcasm in her eyes that hadn't been in her voice. But then she realized that being out of the loop, there was no way for Shyla to know what had gone down between her and the Livingstons in general and between her, Malcolm, and Victoria in particular. And

there was absolutely no way for her to know what had happened with her and Jefferson. She'd finally heard from him,
and it came as no surprise when he informed her that what
had happened that Wednesday night was a situation that he
blamed on the alcohol. He might have been drunk, but Joyce
wasn't. She'd been stone cold sober during their encounter and
knew that what she now felt for him was only partially inspired by his last name. The other part was the desire of a basically good woman wanting a basically good man. Realizing
that Shyla was still waiting for an answer, Joyce spoke. "As my
clientele has diversified, so has my menu," she said. "But we
still partner on occasion. In fact, I met with Toussaint a couple
weeks ago and am very excited about a new venture that he
and I discussed."

Hearing Toussaint's name almost took Shyla's appetite.
Then the waiter set down an aromatic plate of baked chicken
seasoned with fresh herbs and spices, and the need to feed
came right back. "How is he?" she asked, knowing she could
have won an Oscar for the casualness of her tone.

"Finer than ever," Joyce readily replied. "Married life
agrees with him. He looks good and he's the consummate
family man. Alexis is almost always with him when I see him
socially, and pictures of their daughter are all over his office."
And then, because she simply couldn't resist, "I always thought
you and Toussaint made an attractive couple."

Shyla pushed around the Commodores Coleslaw with her
fork. "At one time, so did I."

"I won't ask what happened because it's none of my business."

"Life happens. We move on."

The ladies chatted amicably as they shared lunch, discussing
mutual acquaintances, President Obama's reelection campaign,
and, of course, the Livingstons. Later, as they parted, they agreed
to keep in touch. Each woman had her own self-serving rea-

son. Shyla was good at what she did. In Joyce's opinion, there could quite possibly be some joint business ventures down the line. Shyla's intent was more focused. She had every intention of working with one of Joyce's clients, a man who like all others had once been hidden behind Toussaint's shadow but whose star was on the rise. Joyce was hosting an event for Congressman Jon Abernathy who was now running for the U.S. Senate. Shyla figured if she could get connected to the political game, she could have enough business to start her own firm. And perhaps she could start something else with the would-be senator, something personal.

25

"You know you're being a rascal, don'tcha?" Marietta giggled as Marcus scooted closer to her in the bed and poked something familiar into the small of her back. "I ain't stuttin' you, Marcus Livingston. You might as well turn over and go to sleep."

"Just let me put it in a little bit." He paused. "Just the head."

Marietta laughed out loud now and Marcus joined her. This was the line he'd used around fifty-five years ago, a move that, combined with his smoldering good looks, had talked a perky and cute Marietta right out of her panties. She'd been only sixteen but was already in college, having been academically light-years ahead of her one-room country school class.

"If I remember correctly, somebody forgot all about 'just the head' once he got inside me."

"And if I remember correctly, somebody was pretty glad I forgot it."

"You just keep on thinking that, you hear?"

"I don't have to think it, woman! All I got to do is look at the twins to know for sure what I'm talking about!" The room was quiet for a moment, and then the poking began again.

"C'mon, Etta. Why you have your man begging? Give me some of that poontang. You know at my age that every stiff is a gift."

"Because old man Arthur is talking too loud for me to hear what you're saying. If I spread these old legs for you this evening, I might not get 'em closed again!"

"Ha!" He nuzzled her neck and put his arms around her stomach. "Well get on down there, woman, and suck on it or something!"

"Boy, you really feeling frisky tonight. Did you go and finally order some of them little blue pills?"

Talk about arthritis and Viagra aside, few would believe this was a conversation happening between two seventysome-things who'd "done the do" together for almost sixty years. But it had always been this way with Marcus and Marietta. He'd had no problem upholding the legacy because Marietta had been his one and only true love and almost his singular attraction. Her five-four frame against his six-two was, surprisingly, a perfect fit and her feistiness matched his fervor from the moment they met. Even after the babies, it was never long before this couple would be back in the sexual saddle, making sure that both were totally satisfied. For the most part, this fire had passed down to the children and grands. Ace was a workhorse, ready anytime and anywhere. Adam was less ardent but even after an affair and a videotaped exposure of his wife, he was once again starting to hold his own. But for Marcus and Marietta, the love had been constant, and even now, in these winter years of their life, it was a rare month that went by without at least one round of intercourse.

"I know what this is really about," Marcus said after Marietta had swatted his hand away from her poontang once again. "You're still smarting because I won't tell you what Adam and I discussed." Silence. "How would that look for me to tell you something that he told me to keep to myself?"

Finally, Marietta turned over. "It would look like you've got some sense, that's what! In marriage, the two become one, so him telling you is like him telling me. Man, we've been together more than half a century. And you're evidently starting to forget some of my home training." Her words were gruff, but she reached out her small hand and encircled his dick. "Am I right?" she asked, slowly pulling on his member, feeling it grow beneath her fingers.

"Aw, shit, woman, you know you're right about it!"

"So what did he tell you?" A few more pulls, a few more moans. A fingernail lightly skimming across a big, juicy head followed by a hissing sound. "If it was something about the business, just say that's what it's about." She fondled his nuts, then went back to stroking. Then she stopped. "Never mind, I'm going to sleep."

"It was about business, but that ain't all," Marcus said quickly. Etta turned back over, started stroking again. It was a good thing it was dark because the smile on her face would be a dead giveaway to her blatant manipulation. "It was about Candace."

"What about Candace?" Squeeze. Pull. Rub the tip.

"A brothah pushed up on her, and if it hadn't been for Adam, she would have had an affair."

Screech!

"An affair?!"

"C'mon, now, Etta. This is why I didn't want to say nothing. And I'm telling you now that Candace feels bad enough already without your bringing it up all over again. According to Adam, this happened years ago. And when he confronted the young blood, the boy copped an attitude and that's why Adam got shot."

Etta rolled onto her back. "I knew there was more to that story. I always had a feeling about that thing."

"Well, you were right. Now, you happy?"

"How am I going to be happy about that?"

"Happy that I told you, woman."

"It's no more than what you should have done, and you should have done it weeks ago." Marcus sighed and again, Marietta smiled into the darkness. "But I appreciate you telling me now."

"How much?" Marcus asked, reaching for Marietta's hand and rubbing it over his crotch.

"Enough to try and spread these creaky old legs. But hurry up and do your business. I'm ready to go to sleep."

26

What did some of his clients say? That money talked and bullshit walked? Well, Attorney Cooper Riley Jr. didn't know about that, but he did know that on this bright Tuesday morning in May, one of his clients was walking out of prison, and with a conditional, five-year probation, he would technically be a free man. Quintin had actually balked at the lengthy time under scrutiny of the state (the nerve of him!), but it was the exchange for getting the would-be Mike Tyson's sentence reduced. Again. And as it was, Quintin would still be allowed to travel outside of Georgia as long as his whereabouts were known. Sure, it had cost Cooper Jr. a few favors and hands being greased, but for the happiness it would bring Keisha, it was money well spent. And he did want to bring her happiness. Especially now, when he was getting ready to break her heart. But there was no getting around it. After a month of spending quality time with Dr. Michelle Hopkins, one thing was very clear: Opposites may indeed attract, but they weren't supposed to marry. He would always love Keisha and see that she was taken care of. But his mother asking him to wait six months before proceeding further in the relationship was the best thing she could have done. Michelle didn't have Keisha's fire, but fires burned out. Michelle had what kept couples laughing after thirty years of marriage, and talking after forty. It was too early to entertain thoughts of marriage, but Cooper looked forward to dating Michelle. His family was planning a trip to Florida for the Fourth of July and yachting around the Keys. By then, Keisha would be in his rearview mirror, and, if her delivery schedule allowed it, Michelle would be by his side.

But first things first: giving Keisha a healthy dose of good news to help the disappointing news go down easier. He'd planned a surprise for her this evening, had made Quintin promise to let him break the news to her about her brother's freedom. In the throes of that happiness, he'd use his mother as the fall person and admit that there is simply no way she'd ever accept Keisha and that she'd make their lives together a living hell. No, he didn't want to leave her, but what choice did he have? He would never put her in a position to be ridiculed the rest of her life. But he wouldn't leave her high and dry. He was prepared to give her some "go away" money, help ease the transition for her and the boys. Contrary to his mother's belief, Cooper did not think them hoodlums, just grossly untrained. Unfortunately, Cooper realized this job would have to fall to someone with bigger balls than him. Someone with a military background perhaps. And a Taser.

Cooper's phone rang. He looked at the caller ID and smiled. "Hey, Beautiful."

A melodious yet professional voice oozed through his car speakers. "Hello, Mr. Attorney-At-Law."

"How's the good doctor today?"

"Very good, thanks. And you?"

"Excellent. Things went well at the prison and my client should be walking out"—Cooper glanced at his watch—"in about two hours. I've arranged for someone to meet him at the prison, give him some funds, and put him up at a hotel for a couple days. Get him reacclimated to society."

"That's very thoughtful of you, Cooper."

"It's the least I could do." That's one of the things he truly appreciated about Michelle: her level of compassion and understanding. He'd told her everything about Keisha, and even after giving her a myriad of legitimate reasons why he could not continue on with the woman living in his home, Michelle had suggested caution and patience in his moving forward to the dissolution of the relationship.

"She's young and probably vulnerable," she'd explained with concern.

"She's twenty-seven and has probably experienced more in those short years than some have in a lifetime. I'll take care of her," Cooper had assured her. "She'll be better off upon leaving than when she arrived."

Two hours later, a properly suited Cooper and radiant Keisha sat at the back of a quaint restaurant. Cooper had purposely chosen one on the outskirts of town. He'd given the pretense that it was one of his favorites, but actually it was one in which he risked the least chance of running into someone he knew. But it was a beautiful Italian establishment and Keisha was duly impressed.

He had to admit, she looked positively stunning. Because he'd told her that this was a celebration of sorts, she'd taken extra pains with her appearance. Her long, naturally curly hair was piled on top of her head, with flirty tendrils framing her face and teasing her neck. Her dress was different from what she normally wore, but Cooper loved it. Keisha typically went for the short, formfitting numbers, but this dress, while short, had an A-line cut that gathered at the bodice before flaring out in playful pleats. Her four-inch heels complemented shapely, blemish-free legs, and she wore very little makeup. She truly didn't need any.

After placing their entire dinner order, Cooper nodded for the waiter to pop the bottle of bubbly chilling in a pail. Once done, he raised his glass and offered Keisha a sincere smile. "To one of the most beautiful women in all the world," he said.

"One of?" Keisha asked, her voice soft, her look teasing.

"Okay, okay. The most beautiful," Cooper restated. He took a long sip of the semidry brut, and then another, noting Keisha's dainty sip before she placed down her glass. For a moment he faltered in his decision, imagining that perhaps somehow, some way, this vixen of a woman could truly fit into his world. Out of respect, he hadn't broached intimacy with Michelle Hopkins—he had experienced no more than hugs, caresses, and chaste kisses. But he doubted what they'd share would come close to what he'd experienced with Keisha. Goodness, the things she'd done to and with him. His mother would be beyond appalled! But then he thought about the long, stimulating conversations he'd had with Michelle, how easily they bantered about the most complex of topics and shared commonalities like a love for classical music and traveling to Italy and France. No, he was doing the right thing. Best to get on with it.

"So, then, it's time to disclose the reason for our celebration." His heart softened as Keisha's eyes lit up. "Better yet, there's someone I want you to talk to." He noted the slight confusion that crossed her gorgeous face and felt like a boy with a brand-new marble at the joy he'd shortly bring her. The person on the other end of the phone picked up on the first ring. "Hello." A pause and then, "Yes, if you have a minute, I'd like for you to say hello to a very special lady."

He handed the phone to Keisha. "Hello?" she said cautiously.

"Hey, baby sis," was the rumbling answer.

A look of deeper confusion. "Q?"

"Who else, fool?"

"But this isn't a collect call." She looked at Cooper. "How were you able to call him? Is this some kind of lawyer-privilege thing?"

"No, baby girl," Q answered, having heard the question. "It's a brothah-man-been-freed kind of thing."

"What?" Keisha's exclamation turned a few heads and she covered her hand with her mouth. "What? Are you out?" she frantically whispered, barely caring about the other patrons. If her brother was out of jail, it was getting ready to be a straight up party in here!

"Yeah, girl. Hanging-With-Mr.-Cooper did his thang and got a brother sprung."

Tears glistened in Keisha's eyes as she looked at Cooper. "Where are you?" she asked Q.

"They got me on some kind of debriefing shit. I'm at a hotel about an hour away from the pen. Soft bed, clean sheets. I think I stayed in that marbled shower for over an hour. This is taking me back to how I'm used to rolling."

"When will I see you?"

"In a couple days. Have old boy give you my number, and call me tomorrow."

"Okay, I will. I love you, Q!"

"Love you, too, sis."

The moment was so wonderful and she was so high that Cooper felt even worse for the second part of the surprise. But this was undoubtedly the best time to do it—now that her brother would be here to offer his support. "Darling, there's something else I need to tell you."

"No, wait," Keisha said, shaking her head and laughing. "There's something I want to tell you first."

"Oh, really?" Cooper asked, his tone amused as he poured more champagne. "What's that?"

"It's good news, but I don't if it tops your surprise." A pause and then: "I'm going to have your baby."

"She what?" All pretense of decorum left as Evelyn Maureen Riley jumped off the couch. The refined woman was replaced by remnants of the braid-wearing country girl who used to chase lightning bugs and go barefoot before her parents went north, went to college, got an edge-a-ma-kay-tion, and changed their lifestyles. "Uh-uh. There's no way that woman is pregnant with your child." This sentence came out in a growl, her eyes bugged out bigger than Cooper had ever seen them. In fact, he'd never met this spittle-spouting woman who stood before him. And he was quite concerned.

"Mother, please, I'm as upset as you are."

"You can't possibly be as upset as I am." Evelyn turned on her heels and collapsed on the couch. "This will surely bring on the heart attack I've feared and force me to die young."

"Mother—"

"No!" The crazy woman abruptly sat up, closed her eyes, and took deep, steady breaths until the banshee receded and the cool, calm, collected woman most often referred to as *Mrs. Riley* or *the Judge's wife* returned. After a few minutes, she opened her eyes. Her manner was so calm that Cooper now wondered if he'd imagined the banshee. "She is lying, Cooper."

"I went with her to her doctor's appointment today," Cooper replied. "She is three months along."

"And you believe it's yours?"

Cooper sighed. "Yes, Mother."

An eyebrow arched in aristocratic fashion. "But can you be sure?"

"In time, yes."

"Cooper, your father gave you the talk when you were sixteen years old! Using protection should be second nature. That woman has . . . been around. Who knows what she's"—*contracted*—"been through."

Cooper and Keisha had both been tested for AIDS and STDs before they decided to abandon the condoms. They'd agreed to be exclusive and Keisha was on the pill. He knew she took them. He often watched her. But obviously she'd either missed a few, or they'd fallen into the unlucky 2 percent, one or the other. At first he'd been as shocked as his mother, and disappointed to watch his dreams of life with the doctor fade. But secretly, loss of Michelle and perfect Riley tableau aside, Cooper was delighted that Keisha was having his baby and that he was becoming a father. As unsophisticated and uncouth as she sometimes was, other parts of her were truly endearing. Plus, he thought he'd make a great dad. He also thought it best not to share these thoughts with his mother.

"Did you tell her about Michelle? Did she know that you were planning to leave her?"

"She hadn't a clue. And I won't tell her now. In fact, I'm planning to fly us to Mexico this weekend so that we can be married."

"Son. Please. Don't."

"You would have the child born out of wedlock, Mother? You'd prefer a bastard seed?"

I'd prefer my plans be realized and you marry the woman of my choosing! "I'd prefer you wait until you know for sure that she's carrying your baby. And even then, if this is so, there are options that can prevent your being obligated to her."

"Mother, if Keisha is carrying my child, then she will become my wife. That is how you and Father raised me—to be an upright man, a law-abiding citizen, and responsible. I have tried to do that in the past, and I fully intend to make you proud."

That night, Evelyn Maureen Riley did something she'd never, ever done before in life: She drank several shots of bourbon and half a bottle of wine, and passed out. In short, she got drunker than a skunk. Unfortunately, when she awoke the next morning, dazed and hungover, she realized that alcohol hadn't taken away the pain, and she hadn't been dreaming. Keisha Miller possibly being pregnant with her grandchild was a living nightmare.

27

Chardonnay would not have labeled her situation a night-mare but she wouldn't have argued with the definition "very bad dream." "Where in the hell are you going, Bobby?" she demanded, following closer than his shadow as he traipsed from the bathroom to the bedroom and back to the mirror. He'd just gotten out of the shower and with only a towel wrapped around him, stood shaving. "You've got the night off. We've both been working all week. Your sister's got the kids. Hell, we should be doing something together. Instead you're talking about going to some punk-ass business meeting? What, you think I'm stuck on stupid? You think I don't think you're going out there after some pussy? Or is it some dick?"

Bobby's razor stopped midway between the bowl and his face. But he recovered quickly. Chardonnay was no fool and with the hints she'd been dropping lately, he knew that his cover was very close to being blown. A part of him was scared to death of what she'd think of him if he ever told her, but the other part of him really wanted her to know. Chardonnay was the woman he loved, and he hated having this secret between them. "Oh, it's like that, huh?" he said, delivering smooth strokes that resulted in a hairless jaw.

"You tell me what it's like. It's obviously something out there you want since you're so set on going out no matter what I say."

Bobby stopped, turned around. "Char, why you trippin'? I told you this was business."

"Yeah, right. Somebody wanting to talk to you about having your own restaurant. What's with that? I thought you were all in tight with Chef, that you wanted to become the executive chef at Taste of Soul?"

He took a step toward her. "You're so busy yapping your jaws that you don't have a clue what the hell I want. Have you ever asked me?"

Instead of backing off, Chardonnay took a step closer as well. "I'm your wife. I shouldn't have to ask you. You should offer up the information, let me know what the hell is going on!"

"I'm telling you what's going on!" he exclaimed, their faces so close that Newport cigarette and white-wine breath mingled with mint mouthwash air.

"What?" Chardonnay challenged, standing breast to chest.

"This!" Bobby snatched off the towel, swung it around Chardonnay's neck, and pulled her close—swallowing her sharp retort in a bruising kiss. Chardonnay struggled, but her five-foot-four slender frame was no match for Bobby's wiry yet powerful five-foot-nine and a buck seventy-five physique. She pulled back again and they tumbled from the master bath into the bedroom of their two-bed, two-bath condo, tripping over the shoes that Chardonnay had hastily discarded after work and Bobby's twenty-five-pound barbells. Landing on the bed with a *thunk*, Bobby quickly reached for the waistband of the drawstring warm-ups Chardonnay was wearing.

"Get off of me, nucka!" She twisted and—fortunately or unfortunately for her—this freed the material that was under her round, high booty. Bobby's sizeable asset nodded its pleasure at this turn of events, and he made quick work of pulling pants off of thrashing legs, getting more and more turned on by the moment as Chardonnay continued to act as though the very thing she wanted, what she always wanted when Bobby was around, wasn't going to happen. She scooted away from him. He pulled her back. She planted her feet against his chest and pushed. He fell back and off the bed. She scrambled off the bed and tried to run past him.

"Uh-huh," he said with a chuckle, grabbing her leg as she passed. She stumbled. He took advantage of their mutual acquaintance with the floor. "Come here." He pulled her underneath him, came up on his knees, and plopped his face smack dab in the middle of what he wanted. Chardonnay put up a last veiled attempt at a struggle, but there was no use. If there was a category for best at oral sex, Bobby's tongue could have gone in *Guinness*, the Smithsonian, Madame Tussauds Wax Museum...somewhere. He spread her legs, dipped his long, stiff tongue between her folds, and lapped like a kitten at a bowl of sweet milk. He nipped her nub and then lengthened the licks, slowed them down, and then sped back up.

"Damn, Bobby," Chardonnay panted. "Stop that right... ooh..."

He chuckled, even as he rolled her over and continued in the back what he'd done in the front. "Get up on your knees. I'm getting ready to own this piece."

"You're not owning shit," Chardonnay said, scrambling to her knees so fast she almost got carpet burn.

Bobby grabbed her hips, placed his tip against her lips, and took the plunge with a satisfied growl. He was both long and thick, and he punctuated each thrust with a grunt or a word: *This. Pussy. Is. Mine.*

Chardonnay threw away all pretense of anger, grinding her butt back against his heat, head down, weave swinging to the Bobby beat. "Harder, Bobby, harder!"

Bobby pulled out, pulled her up, then pushed her onto the bed. "What do you want, huh?"

Chardonnay reached for him. "You know what I want, come on!"

"No, I don't," Bobby countered, swinging his hard, massive no-I-don't from side to side.

Chardonnay crossed the bed on her knees and tried to grab it. "You pimply-faced walnut head—"

Bobby dodged her, laughing.

"Dish washing, chipped-tooth-looking—"

Bobby jumped onto the bed and onto her, plunging into her wetness with all of the precision of a seeker missile.

"Ahhh! Yes, give me this dick. Give. Me. This. Dick!"

And it was on. Skin slapping, moaning, groaning, sheets getting twisted, pillows on the floor. The bedsprings creaked in protest, punctuated by Chardonnay's head hitting the headboard. For a slight guy, Bobby packed a punch, and he packed it all inside of Chardonnay, turning her out for the umpteenth time.

"Bobby!" she screamed as an orgasm overtook her. "Yes!" she hollered, as if it were the Olympics and he'd scored a perfect ten.

Soon, Bobby shivered with the intensity of his own release. Then he got up, walked into the bathroom, and took another quick shower. Afterward, he finished shaving, dressed, and left the house. Chardonnay was too tired to talk; Bobby was too preoccupied. Screwing his wife had taken fifteen minutes, the added toiletries another ten.

Damn! He quickly walked to his brand-new Camry, popped the lock, and within seconds was zooming out of the parking lot. Not only was he now late for his appointment, but also he was drained and needed to quickly regain his energy. He'd been fending off Jon for months now but knew that if the congressman had his way, it was going to be a long night.

A short time later, Bobby pulled up to Jon's house. That's when he dealt with the second person having trouble with the N-word.

"What do you mean, no?" Jon asked, a professionally arched eyebrow raising a notch.

"I didn't say no outright," Bobby corrected, taking a sip of his Hennessy and Coke from Jon's well-stocked bar. "I just said I'm having second thoughts about this whole thing." The second thoughts had started before Chardonnay's outburst tonight but had increased with her comments and the amazing-as-always sex. He was still dog tired, and for this normally Energizer-Bunny-like dog, that was saying a lot.

"Well, the fellas are waiting for an answer," Jon said. "And so am I. There are a lot of would-be business owners who would give their eyetooth for the kind of chance that we're offering. So don't make us wait too long."

Bobby finished his drink and slid off the barstool. It was early and he'd told Chardonnay that he'd be home late. He said this because he'd fully planned on sticking the congressman. But he'd changed his mind.

"Where are you going?" Jon asked, his expression one of confusion as he followed Bobby to the door.

"Home to my family," Bobby responded. "I'm in the mood to be a good husband and father."

"But, Bobby. I thought—"

"I did too. But it ain't happening. Goodnight."

During the drive from Jon's upscale neighborhood to Bobby's middle-class townhome, he had fifteen good minutes to go over what had recently transpired. It had been a few weeks since Bobby had gone to Jon's home and met the three silent investors who, along with the congressman, wanted to finance his restaurant. The first surprise had been that Cooper Riley Sr. was among them. It wasn't like Jon didn't know about Bobby's dalliances with the judge. During one of Jon's jealous rages, Bobby had chosen to drop this dime. And even though the judge knew Jon, neither one of them were aware that Bobby knew more about the third investor—a famous football player—than any of his coaches, or wife, ever suspected.

The truth of the matter was, this whole bi-slash-down-low-slash-cheating situation was starting to wear on his nerves. Tonight, Chardonnay's suspicion had turned into an out and out allegation but even before the argument they'd just had, Bobby had been thinking of how to get out of a situation that he could hardly believe he'd gotten himself into in the first place.

At first, it seemed an act of necessity. He had been twenty years old and doing a twelve-month bid for marijuana possession with intent to distribute. He'd always been a very virile brother with a high sex drive, and when he got locked up, he quickly discovered that that didn't stop just because no females were available. And he also discovered that after being used to penetration since he lost his virginity at a young twelve years old, jacking off could satisfy for just so long. And finally, he discovered that there were men willing to be penetrated. Almost none of these men called themselves gay. And neither did he.

Moving to Atlanta made this double-sided lifestyle easy to continue. At first it was just a dude here or there for variety, but then he'd met Jon Abernathy and that had changed. The congressman had wanted him to become his man and shit, and Bobby wasn't down with that. However, he was content to accept pricey gifts, high-end trips, and other perks. He knew of other dudes who were supported by high-profile men and realized that falling into that trap could be hella easy. It had almost happened to him.

Especially when Judge Cooper Riley came along. Now, for all the buzz he'd heard about married, gay men, that one he hadn't seen coming. It was during one of Jon's lavish dinner parties. Bobby had prepared the meal: rib-eye steak, gourmet scallops, fingerling potatoes, and asparagus. A high-end, bougie dinner that ended with crème brûlée, cigars, pipes, and lots of alcohol. He'd been cleaning up in the kitchen and thought that, as often happened, the judge had come in there to thank him for a good meal. The man had come in there looking for more meat. And Bobby had given it to him. Hard.

The football player had come into the restaurant one evening around closing time and after a brief conversation, had given Bobby tickets to the next home game. Afterwards, he'd invited Bobby to hang out with him "and the fellas." Bobby arrived at the house to a party of two. Of these three men, he felt Mr. NFL was the only one truly in it for the investment. The judge and the congressman were in it because they were trying to hang on, get Bobby caught up. And he wasn't going out like that. For all the male-on-male effing he did, he actually loved his wife, loved his kids. And this is why his dream of owning a restaurant just might have to wait a little longer. Because Bobby Wilson could be rented, but he could not be bought.

28

The Livingston men sat in Adam's study, having decided to move their meeting from the office to the home. Too many sensitive things to discuss, and with all of them burning the candle at both ends these days, they'd temporarily tired of the workplace. Later, all of these matters would be discussed in a more formal setting, attended by additional Livingston execs, but if anyone ever doubted who owned the company, they need look no further than the fact that everything that happened both began and ended in a room full of Livingstons.

"So Quintin is out of jail?" Malcolm asked, a calmness belying the anger he felt. "How in the hell did that happen?"

"Cooper Riley's camp," Ace responded. "At least that's what Sterling thinks. And I'm inclined to agree."

"I'm glad he's out," Toussaint said. "Gives me a chance to catch his ass in a dark alley somewhere."

"Now, son," Adam cautioned, "calm yourself. In fact, I want all of y'all to just take it down a notch or two regarding that muthafucka." Adam's face contorted as he spat these words, causing everyone to crack up. Clearly, he'd have the hardest time following his own suggestion, but the futility of a Livingston being anything but highly pissed where Quintin

Bright was concerned helped some of the tension leave the room.

"Where's Bianca?" Jefferson asked, looking at his watch. "I have a meeting with the finance department at three."

"And you'll make it, big brother," Bianca said, coming around the corner looking like Ms. LA. She'd cut her hair again, Halle Berry short, and her flawlessly made up face was covered by large designer glasses. The stress from the fire combined with long work hours and little food had caused her to lose weight, but her curves still did justice to the formfitting floral dress she wore with large hoop earrings and Louboutin pumps. "Hey, everybody," she said, addressing the room and giving hugs all around. "Sorry I'm late, but that's what happens when a sistah has to fly commercial. There was some kind of mechanical issue that caused the hour-long delay."

"It's all good, cousin," Toussaint said, offering his seat while he rose to fix himself a glass of sparkling water. "Life seems to still be treating you good on the West Coast."

"Where's Xavier?" Malcolm asked.

"Meetings. Family business," Bianca replied. "Daddy, you need to be careful when dealing with people for whom English is their second language. You told him to protect me and he's taken that literally. He barely leaves my side and I had to go sistah-girl black on him not to hire a security detail."

"And your problem is . . . ?" Ace drawled.

"The problem is that I'm being suffocated. I can barely go anywhere by myself. If we spend the rest of our lives looking over our shoulders, then whoever was responsible for the fire has won. I refuse to live that way. I simply won't stand for it!"

Ace's eyes twinkled as he watched his fiery daughter, so much like him and his mother. "You just remember to let that man be the head of the household," Ace admonished. "If he wants to hire the National Guard and surround your house with them, let him. We need to feel in power and control like we need air to breathe."

Bianca wisely remained silent. Her mother and aunt were not in on this meeting, and she knew she'd get no backing in this testosterone-filled room.

"How are the building plans coming, baby?" Ace asked.

Bianca gave him an update and then added, "Unfortunately, everything seems to take longer than planned. The last estimate they gave me is ninety to one hundred and twenty days before TOSTS is back up and operational."

"I might have a solution for that," Toussaint offered.

Bianca was immediately all ears. "What?"

"All right, now, let's not get ahead of the agenda. The first item on it was the fire, so my question wasn't asked out of turn." Various moans and facial expressions commenced. Ace laughed. "Next is an update about finance. Jeff."

Jeff opened the leather portfolio that contained the concise financial summary contained on a single sheet of paper. Every day he awoke thankful that the promotion had come when it did. Focusing on work and not his issues had been almost as therapeutic as his visits with Dr. Morgan. After two in-person sessions, the rest were being conducted by phone. In short, Jefferson was close to being back to his old self. "I'm pleased to announce that our profits are stronger than ever," he began, before giving a rundown of the eleven restaurants in the Taste of Soul chain. "Our catering arm is actively seeking out venues to further promote the brand, and while the Food Network and Soul Smoker profits are not a part of the Livingston Corporation monies"—Ace and Adam coughed simultaneously and the room laughed—"their national presence continues to provide valuable exposure. You'll see from the statement that sales of barbeque sauce are through the roof." He continued for another ten minutes, making everyone in the room proud of their decision to elect him CFO, and even happier to have the old Jefferson back.

"Thanks, son," Ace said once Jefferson concluded. "Toussaint?"

"Finally," Toussaint said in an exaggerated tone. That's one thing that helped this family that worked and played together stay together. Even though they were often discussing multi-million- and billion-dollar situations, they never forgot to have fun. "Two things," Toussaint said, standing so he could see everyone's reactions to what he was about to say and therefore to judge them more accurately. "One, the trip to Las Vegas. I already shared my initial thoughts with Daddy and Ace, but for everyone else, the timing couldn't be better for this move. I looked at several properties, and two stood out the most: one on the north end of Las Vegas Boulevard, closer to the Fashion Show Mall—which gets a lot of middle-class tourist foot traffic—and the Riviera and the Stratosphere. The other spot is on the south end. Now we're talking Bally's; Bellagio; Paris Las Vegas; New York-New York; MGM. This is the higher end side of the hotels on the Strip and that, my dear cousin Bianca, is where my next item point comes in."

"No, Toussaint," Bianca answered, already well ahead of her cousin. "TOSTS is to be an LA exclusive until that brand is solid."

"Right now, TOSTS is exclusively *closed*," Toussaint calmly retorted. "So shut your mouth and open your ears, baby girl. I'm getting ready to help you save your dream." He then launched into an expertly prepared presentation of opening two locations in Vegas: a full-sized Taste of Soul restaurant on the north end of the Strip and a smaller, upscale TOSTS on the south end, possibly in one of the four- or five-star hotels. Discussion ensued, and the longer it went, the more everyone in the room warmed to the idea.

"I guess you're right, cuz. Vegas does sounds like a good bet for a second TOSTS location," Bianca said. "Especially since it's close enough for me to still be hands-on, which is a must for growing this brand the way I'd like." She looked down at the outline Toussaint had prepared. "Eighteen to twenty-four months out?" That's a good time for establishing this as a Taste of Soul concept . . . and for me to decide whether or not I'm going to give it my blessing." A playful smile belied her words.

"That's good to hear, Bianca," Toussaint seamlessly continued, "because the next agenda item would create such a tremendous buzz for TOSTS that when it's over, this establishment, and not oceans and casinos, will be why people travel to LA and Vegas." This comment was enough to quiet the room. Toussaint had everyone's undivided attention, which was just the way he liked it. "I've been approached with a partnership idea, one in which at this strategic time of our nation I think is an excellent opportunity. It is a connection with the Democratic Party in general and the DNC in particular."

"As in the Democratic National Convention?" Jefferson asked.

"Yes."

"I'm intrigued, nephew," Adam said. "Tell us more."

"Well, this person has developed an extensive liaison with members of this party, and since this is an election year, it has a slew of events: fund-raisers, parties, campaign events, private hosting, and so on, with congressmen, senators, a couple high-profile mayors, and yes, even the White House. She wants to make us the exclusive restaurant used to cater these events and highlight Bianca's creations."

Bianca's female antennae began to ping. "She?" she asked. "What *she* are we talking about?"

Here's where it gets tricky. But Toussaint was so cool he could have chilled Asti. "Joyce Witherspoon."

You could have heard a mosquito pee on cotton.

Toussaint looked around the room.

"Joyce Witherspoon back in Livingston territory?" Malcolm asked, somewhat incredulously. "Uh, that would be a negative."

"So that's what her visit to Candace was about," Adam drawled.

"I think that visit was about sincerely apologizing," Malcolm said. "She talked to Vickie, too, and she believes Joyce was serious. But wives forgiving her is one thing. Doing business again is another."

"I think we should consider it," Jefferson said. "No matter what we think about her personal choices, she's one hell of a businesswoman."

"A few select TOSTS locations is a good idea, Toussaint," Bianca said. "Mass-producing soul-food tapas is not. This concept is meant to be high-end, exclusive, something that can't be eaten every day and definitely not everywhere. Now, maybe five, ten years down the line, we could revisit this idea, after we've made this brand solid through proper marketing and PR. They think I don't know this, but chefs from similar establishments have already come to the restaurant to check out my idea and how we execute it. Imitators will come out of the woodwork soon enough. But it's too early to spread this idea right now. And since it is *my* baby," she concluded, making eye contact with everyone in the room, "I'd like my words to be seriously considered."

Toussaint eyed Bianca a moment. "Fair enough. Let's table the idea of incorporating the small-plate appetizers into the catering concept and focus strictly on reestablishing a partnership with Loving Spoonful." Toussaint handed out a one-page outline, with bullet points of advantages to such a liaison. "Joyce has parlayed the work she's done for Jon Abernathy and other local politicians into a national presence on the Democratic landscape. I've seen her calendar and, again, because this is an election year, her event list is through the roof. She wants to bring us in on this action and hone her menu down to where when one thinks of her Southern-based event business, they think of Southern cuisine."

"We're not the only soul-food chain out here," Malcolm interjected. "Why can't she partner with someone else?"

Toussaint gave Malcolm the look that a patient father might give a child. "We may not be the only soul-food restaurant, but we're the best." He looked around the room and continued. "We're talking millions of dollars here, and exposure that money simply cannot buy. You know Barack will be making at least one stop in Atlanta. Can you imagine the popularity of a Barack Baked Potato or Obama's Okra?"

"Uh, excuse me," Bianca countered. "With all due respect, President Obama is politics, not R and B. Our dishes reflect good music."

"If that brother gets in for four more years, that will be music to my ears," Malcolm murmured, walking over to the bar for a glass of juice.

"I think that we can make an exception, Bianca. Especially considering it's the president of the United States, not to mention an election year."

"Some things are about more than money," Malcolm argued. "I say that Joyce Witherspoon has showed us her colors more than once. It would be the epitome of insanity to invite her back into our company, and our lives. Let me put it this way, and I don't need to review the proposal to say this. I don't want her in this company. She doesn't need to be here."

"I say we take it to a vote," Jefferson said.

Discussion ensued and unlike during the West Coast expansion debates, this time Toussaint and Jefferson were on the same side. And after the vote had been taken, Joyce Witherspoon was in partnership with the Livingstons once again.

29

Jefferson walked back to his office and noticed that he'd missed a call from Dan Morgan. *Oh, man!* Since getting the promotion, Jeff had had a one-track mind and had totally forgotten about the weekly therapy both had agreed could continue by phone.

"Dr. Morgan's office."

"Jeff Livingston. Is the doctor in?"

"He's been waiting to hear from you, Jeff. One moment."

Jeff began speaking as soon as the doctor answered the phone. "Sorry about missing the session, Doc. With the promotion and all, I've been swamped."

"I'm sure you have, Jeff. But I don't want you to lose focus of what I asked you during the last session, about dealing with the situation that landed you in my office. When you are ready to face that fear and confront the person who betrayed you, then you will totally get your life back. And keep in mind what I told you: the actual consequence of that betrayal happened in a matter of minutes, but you shared a very real friendship with this person for years. That means that for you a bad thing happened, but this isn't necessarily a bad person. You're sensitive but you're also strong. You can do this, Jefferson. Believe it or not, this Divine person may provide insight that causes you to look at her in a different light, and therefore the situation in a different manner. I strongly suggest you examine why you're not contacting her—"

"Him—"

"This transgendered individual, and upon completion of that examination, come full circle with this incident so that you can put it behind you. Then, I guarantee you, you'll be able to move on with your life."

It took two more weeks for Jefferson to conduct this examination, but when it was over, he found himself where he never thought he'd ever be again—parked outside Divine Art, the gallery where the incident that tipped the scales and initiated his downward spiral took place. He looked at the colorful storefront, heard the world-beat music wafting out of the open door. *Nothing is ever going to feel right about this,* Jefferson concluded as he reached for the door handle. *Might as well do it in this uncomfortable state.*

He walked into the studio. As Jefferson had expected, there were no other patrons. It was why Jefferson had chosen a weekday, and the middle of the afternoon to come here. Most of Divine's activities took place in the evenings and on weekends. During the day, Divine painted and as Jefferson walked past the gallery and into the studio, he saw that it was what was happening now.

At the sound of footsteps, Divine turned around. The smile she wore ran away from her face. Her eyes widened and she quickly stood, backing away from Jefferson until she reached the wall. "Jefferson," she said, her visibly frightened countenance enhancing the beauty that even with his hatred of her was hard to ignore. She held up her hands in defense. "Please don't hurt me."

Jefferson took a deep breath. He totally understood Divine's fear. In the days following The Incident, she'd tried to contact him several times. Finally, he picked up the phone, only to tell her that if she called again, he was going to come down to the gallery and finish the ass kicking he started. And then, after further threats on her life if she ever shared what happened, he said he'd expose her secret, a move that—considering the number of high-profile men on who's arm she'd been squired—would amount to a death sentence. But in this moment, with her deer-in-the-headlights look and pleading voice, it was hard to imagine that this was not a true female standing in front of him. The doctor's words began replaying in his head. *You had no way of knowing, no reason to suspect. Jefferson, this wasn't your fault.* "Chill out, Divine" he said finally, leaning against the doorjamb. "I'm not going to hurt you. I still hate you, but I'm not going to hurt you."

Divine visibly relaxed. "Why are you here?"

"It's part of my therapy."

Divine's eyes widened a bit, before filling with tears. "I'm so sorry, Jefferson. I should have told you before anything physical happened. I realize that now. If I could, I'd take back every single moment of that night. In fact, I would never have befriended you. It would have been better to never know such a good person than to know them and then lose them. You are the best friend I ever had, Jefferson, and I'm so very sorry." The tears raced down her cheeks. "I'm in therapy as well."

"Why? You know what you are! It's everybody else who's in the dark about it."

"There's a lot you don't know about me, Jefferson."

"That's an understatement," Jefferson mumbled.

The briefest of smiles appeared on Divine's face. "Besides that."

This Divine person may provide insight that causes you to look at her in a different light, and therefore the situation in a different manner. Remembering the doctor's words, Jefferson walked into the room and sat on an ebony chair that was shaped like a woman's head, her big, wide Afro being the chair's back. "Why don't you enlighten me?"

Thus began an hour-long conversation in which Divine shared things that she'd kept bottled up for most of her twenty-nine years. It was a tragic tale that involved isolation, drugs, alcohol, sexual abuse from the age of four, domestic abuse . . . and more. "I was seventeen years old and had just broken up with my latest sponsor. It was like, four o'clock in the morning and I didn't have anywhere else to go that time of day. So I went home." Divine's voice got soft and her eyes far, far away. "I hadn't been there in months, and when I walked in and saw her . . . my mom . . . sitting on the couch, I almost didn't recognize her. She wasn't wearing a stitch of clothing and was thinner than I'd ever seen her. But that wasn't the main reason why she looked so different. It was what my stepfather had done not only to her face, but also to her whole body. I'd seen her with black eyes and busted lips—hell, he'd given me my share of those. But this time he'd used a belt and beaten her off and on all night. Besides the eye that was swollen shut and the dislocated jaw puffed out to twice its size, there wasn't a spot on her that wasn't bruised. There were these large welts every-where—across her neck, chest, stomach, back, legs—every-where, and huge gashes where the buckle had landed. The only reason the beating stopped is because he'd run out of al-cohol. He'd told her to sit on the couch and dared her to move. He said that when he came back, he was going to kill her."

Jefferson slowly shook his head, his stomach roiling from the events Divine recounted. "I can't even imagine," he finally said.

"Well, I don't have to imagine it. I lived it. It wasn't enough for him to fuck me, but sometimes he . . . used other things on me. Do you know what I'm saying? He used other things to penetrate me. That's why as much as I loved and feared for my mother, I finally ran away.

"When she told me that she was too afraid to put on the robe I brought out to her because that son-of-a-bitch had dared her to *move*, something in me snapped. I didn't know it at the time. No, I thought I was handling the fucked up situation rather well. And when I went into the kitchen and got the biggest knife I could find, I told myself that I was just going to scare him, get him to leave us alone long enough for me to talk some sense into my mother, talk her into getting away from him once and for all. But that isn't what happened. He came back, drunker than I'd ever seen him. Obviously he hadn't waited until he got home to bust that bottle's label. When he saw me standing there with the knife in my hand, he started laughing, mocking me, and threatening me to do anything to him. He said he was glad I was back, that he'd missed my nice lips and tight ass. My mom pleaded with him to leave me alone, to let me leave so that he could finish with her."

Fresh tears fell as Divine continued, her voice barely above a whisper. "He told her to shut up, that he now was going to beat her for trying to tell him what to do, that I was going to watch him beat her, and then she was going to watch him fuck me." Divine swallowed hard. "It wouldn't be the first time for that. Anyway, when he took off his belt, his pants fell and he was already hard. He took one step toward my mom and my mind must have blacked out at this point because I swear the next thing I knew I was standing over his dead body with blood dripping from the knife and all over me, and my mother was huddled in a corner." Now Divine's voice was mechanical, as if she were outside herself telling the experience and listening as well. "We kept the body in the house all day. Then, around midnight, me and my mom rolled that asshole into a blanket, carried him downstairs, and threw him in a Dumpster. I helped my mom clean up the place and get all her things. The apartment was in his name and it was mostly his stuff, so she didn't have much. She moved into a shelter and I went on the run. Because of my age, I knew I'd get tried as an adult, and if I ever went to prison, my life would be over. The sponsor I'd just broken up with is a very rich man. I went to his house and begged him to help me. He had mercy and said he would, told me if there was ever any chance of my not getting caught, that I would have to disappear.

"Now, this is going to sound like some movie shit, but I swear it's true. He paid one of his police officer friends to let him know the next time they found a derelict's body. In the meantime, my transformation began. I went to a dentist and had them pull four back teeth, which helped make my face less rounded, my cheekbones more prominent. I had five plastic surgeries, a breast augmentation, ass implants, and lip injections. During this time, my ex-sponsor received the call that an unknown had been found. He paid to have this body burned to beyond recognition and to have my teeth planted at the scene. When they identified the bum through dental records, my name came up."

"Divine?" Jefferson had barely spoken in almost an hour and even now, his voice was just above a whisper.

"No," Divine said with a smile. "Dale. That was my name, Dale Oberson. But he died twelve years ago. And Divine was born. Three weeks after my last surgery, I cut all ties to Oakland, bought a one-way ticket to Atlanta, and immersed myself in this city's art culture and life in Five Points. For the first time, I felt like I was home."

Jefferson was not ashamed of the tears that he wiped from his face. And for the first time, he was not ashamed of what had happened either. The only embarrassment he felt at the moment was for his behavior, his reaction in the past year. Here he'd gone and lost his mind for accidentally feeling a dick, when Divine should have lost her mind a long time ago—for very legitimate reasons. Suddenly, he remembered their conversations in a new light, how discussion of family were always one-sided and how he'd never met any of the people Divine had said she was dating.

"Where is your mom now?"

Divine truly smiled for the first time since Jefferson arrived. "Here."

"In Atlanta?"

"No, Augusta. When my art started selling and the money started rolling in, the first thing I did was get her relocated. She lives in a little house on a nondescript street. She's married to one of the nicest men you'd ever want to meet."

"You've met him?"

"Yes. She introduced me as her adopted daughter. I visit her almost every week and she's been here a couple times but only at night, when the gallery is closed. The more time passes, the less likely I feel that my secret will ever be discovered. But there's a part of me that will probably always look over my shoulder and be extra cautious. That's why no one here in Atlanta has ever heard this story, and why no one else ever will. That's why even though I know it's an awful lot to ask but—"

"Your secret's safe with me, Divine. Aside from my therapist, no one knows the details of what happened that night. And now no one ever will. But what about all those guys you told me you were dating whenever I was in between relationships?"

Divine smiled again, but this time it was bittersweet. "A figment of my overactive imagination, nothing more. Divine has never seriously dated anyone. Oh, she's squired around town and makes sure that she makes the society pages. But all of those men understood that there would be no sex, that my man lived in another state and that I was faithful." She stopped, obviously carefully considering her next words. "Divine only dared to love one time"—she looked at Jefferson—"and it cost me dearly."

"I'm sorry for hitting you."

"Don't you dare apologize. I deserved it."

"So answer me this. Did you know you were gay when you were little, or did your stepfather turn you out?"

"Oh, no, Jefferson. This sistah has always been strictly dickly."

For the first time since beginning to see Dr. Morgan and becoming CFO, Jefferson spent the afternoon away from the office. He and Divine talked the rest of the afternoon and into the evening, ordered in dinner and talked some more. As he drove home, he couldn't believe how light he felt now that his burden had been lifted, how once again he loved life. And while he loved pussy too much to ever doubt that he was anything but heterosexual, he could now unabashedly say that he loved Divine as well.

She deserves to be happy. This is what Jefferson was thinking as he pulled into the garage of his upscale home. And then another thought hit him, one based on another secretive conversation he'd had some months ago with his cousin Malcolm. *I wonder if that would work?* The more he thought about it, the more excited he became at the possibility. And by the time he'd gone to sleep that night, Jefferson the organizer, the strategist, the brain, had a whole plan laid out, just waiting to be put into motion.

30

Quintin Bright sat in a four-star hotel just outside of Atlanta, enjoying a room service meal of steak, potatoes, and apple pie. It had been a week since being released from prison, and he had to admit that life looked a whole lot better on this side of the bars. He's spent the day before with Keisha and his nephews. He hadn't realized how much he'd missed those boys until he held their bad asses in his arms. Dorian held on so tight that Quintin thought he'd never let go. And Antwan had gotten so big! And then a thought came from out of nowhere that hit Quintin square in the face. The thought was that if Quintin died that night, there was nobody on earth to carry on his blood or his name.

"What the hell do I care about that? I've been dodging bullets by not having a bunch of kids all over the place. Damn, man, that time behind has made you soft," he whispered, spearing another chunk of medium-well beef and shoveling it into his mouth. That was followed by a healthy bite of broccoli-and-cheese-filled baked potato and a huge bite of Texas toast. He washed all of this down with a large swig of Cristal, straight from the bottle. Yeah, he'd been out of prison for a week, but he was still celebrating the miracle of his release. *Shoot a nucka, steals hella paper, and walks in less than twenty-four. Not too bad, son.* Quintin laughed and took another long drink of the effervescent champagne. He thought of the phone call he was about to make and laughed harder. Life was good—better than good. *Hell to the muthafuckin' yeah!*

He unwrapped the temporary phone he'd purchased, punched in a series of numbers, and soon a melodic voice with a clipped, Jamaican accent came on the line. "Hello?"

"Is this my Jamaican joy?" Quintin drawled.

A scream on the other end was his answer. Constance Ward was the woman who'd befriended Quintin more than a year ago when he ended up in Jamaica rich in money but after Shyla returned to the states, poor in friends. "Quintin, this is you? I can't believe it, mon. You're really calling?"

"Yes, it's me, baby girl. I told you to hang tight and that you'd hear from me."

"But it's been over a year. I didn't know what had happened."

Quintin immediately became quiet. And suspicious. "What's that supposed to mean? I said I'd call you. What, you gone and found a new man or something? You couldn't wait on a brothah until I got out?"

"Don't you get snippy with me, black man," Constance said in a voice that suggested she was far from being afraid of one Mr. Quintin Bright. "I don't hear from you for a long time. You're not writin', you're not callin' ..."

"I started writing ... eventually."

"Yes, after six months or more. Thanks a lot." One could barely hear the sarcasm for all of the joy in her voice.

"No, baby," Quintin said, his voice once again soft and flirty. He never imagined Constance wouldn't wait on him and was more than a little surprised at how the thought that she might have moved on affected him. "Thank you. Those letters you sent me every week is what kept a brothah alive in there."

"I'm glad to hear from you, Quintin."

A pause, and Quintin could have sworn he heard a sniffle. *Wait, that* was *a sniffle.*

"I missed you." Another pause and then, "So, when are you coming to see me?"

"That's why I'm calling," Quintin responded. "I just got out last week. My attorney has to take care of some things, make it all right for me to leave the country. And then it's on, baby girl. I'm coming straight to see you. Is everything all right down there? Everything still where it's supposed to be?"

"I kept all of your belongings," Constance responded. "Everything is still here. Waiting for you."

They talked for almost an hour, and when they hung up, Quintin let out a whoop. How he'd managed to find a woman like Constance was beyond him—someone loyal, faithful, and loved him so intensely that he could feel it through the mail. He thought of other women he'd dated or slept with, including Candace, Shyla, and Chardonnay. All of them had their attributes, but at the end of the day, Quintin concluded, none were worthy of his love. *Candace's bitch-ass was willing to pay for the dick but not defend. Shyla was willing to play with the dick but not stay with it, and Chardonnay* . . . Quintin smiled. Of those three, Chardonnay was the one he most respected. She might not have the money or the class of the others, but she had something he felt even more valuable—honesty. With Chardonnay Johnson—*oh, it's Wilson now, my bad*—what you saw was what you got. But the woman waiting for him in Jamaica was one of a kind. Hadn't she just told him that *all* of his belongings—translated, undiscovered Benjamins—were still in Jamaica? The last chunk of money he'd stolen from the Livingstons, courtesy of their punk-ass son Jefferson, was still in place. With proper investment through a connection he met on the inside, Quintin knew that his life of crime could truly be over. He could hang up his gangsta badge and go legit.

Quintin finished his meal and reached for the phone. He'd had a lot of ups and downs in his life, but right now, it was almost perfect. He just needed to make one more call. . . .

31

Barely two weeks after the meeting in Adam's study, a paired down Taste of Soul menu appeared at a Loving Spoonful event. It was the fund-raiser for Jon Abernathy on Auburn Avenue, with some of the supporters who'd been with him since his attorney days. There was a crush, and some of everybody was there. Along with the city's political elite were a few R & B singers, a number of athletes, and a couple megachurch ministers and their wives mingled around the room, balancing plates piled high with soul food along with a signature drink—the Congressman—that Bobby had created. With a nod to Jon's penchant for Seven and Seven, this drink included those ingredients along with Grand Marnier and a touch of absinthe. The drink was set on fire before being served. "Just like I want you to set me on fire," Jon had whispered. He had tried to talk Bobby into seeing him later only to be told yet again that Bobby was going home to his wife. Still, Jon took Bobby's design of this concoction as a message that what they had wasn't over. But considering how Bobby dodged him all evening, he'd eventually come to believe that their little dalliance—like the drink—had gone up in flames.

One of the couples enjoying the drink that Bobby had

created was Judge and Mrs. Cooper Riley Sr. The judge made a big deal of introducing his wife to the chef, and they toasted their love with the Congressman. Evelyn took a couple polite sips of the concoction, but knowing her low tolerance for alcohol, she mostly held the glass. This was an important night filled with important people, and she would not take the chance of becoming inebriated. And it was a good thing because had she been drunk, she may have gone over and thrown her drink in the face of someone just entering the room. As it were, she reached over and squeezed her husband's arm. *Squeezed* is an understatement. Her nails nearly dug through the wool and cotton of his suit coat and shirt.

Cooper Sr. used to his wife's subtle histrionics, calmly turned toward her. "What is it, dear?"

"Your son is here." She said this while maintaining the fakest of smiles. Had her mouth moved any less, she would have been a ventriloquist.

The judge drily retorted, "And that is causing you to almost squeeze blood from my arm because...?"

There was no use. Evelyn knew she'd need major fortification to get through these next moments. So after taking a healthy swallow of the Congressman, she hissed in a whisper meant for Cooper Sr. alone, "Because he's with *her*."

Uh-oh. At once the judge knew who his wife was talking about and it wasn't Dr. Hopkins. He turned just as his son approached with a woman as stunning as any in the room. Keisha wore a light turquoise dress that gathered at the bodice and flared out in miniscule pleats, effectively hiding her baby bump. The color complemented her café au lait skin, and each step in her four-inch heels revealed the toned calves of nicely shaped legs. Her hair was loosely piled atop her head with errant tendrils creating just the right amount of mischief so as to not make the style severe, and the diamond studs she wore spoke of wealth and good taste. In short, she looked stunning, and every male eye, and almost every female one, followed her progression as she crossed the room on Cooper's arm.

"Mother, Dad," Cooper addressed his parents as he placed a protective arm around Keisha's shoulders. "You both remember Keisha."

"Hello, Mrs. Riley," Keisha said. She held out her hand, her smile bright, eyes challenging. She spoke in a soft, cultivated voice with no traces of hood.

Of course, Evelyn had to shake Keisha's hand. What else could she do with the room watching? "Hello, dear," Evelyn responded with a smile that came nowhere close to reaching her eyes. "Cooper, may I have a moment?"

"Not now, Mother. There are a few people I want Keisha to meet, and then we have dinner reservations."

Rapid eye batting was the only outward sign that Evelyn Maureen Riley was about to blow a gasket. Had she gripped the glass in her hand any harder, it would have shattered.

Keisha turned to Cooper Sr. "Judge Riley, it is a pleasure to see you again. That's a beautiful tie. I believe Cooper has one just like it."

Almost as much a sucker for a beautiful woman as he was for a big dick, the judge beamed at her praise. "Hello, Keisha," he said, taking the woman's hand and—gasp and sputter—bringing it to his lips for a kiss. "You look positively radiant."

"Thank you," Keisha responded, and then leaning forward, she whispered in his ear, "It's the pregnancy glow."

"A few seconds, Junior, if I may?" Evelyn repeated, appearing to gently grab Cooper's arm when in reality the hold felt like the Jaws of Life.

But before she could pull him away, they were joined by the event organizer. "Hello, Cooper," Joyce said, giving him a light hug. "So glad you could make it." She turned curious yet kind eyes at Keisha. "Hello, I'm Joyce Witherspoon."

"Hello, Keisha Miller. Nice to meet you."

"Honey, Joyce is an event planner. She is the one responsible for this classy setup."

Keisha looked around the room and back at Joyce. "It's very nice."

Noticing their empty hands, Joyce continued. "Please visit the buffet, and you must try the night's signature drink, the Congressman."

"Oh, I couldn't," Keisha began. "I'm—"

"Joyce!" Evelyn interrupted, in a tone more loud and forceful than she intended. "I simply love that suit you're wearing. It looks to be classic Chanel. Am I right?" She cut a warning look at Cooper, who led Keisha over toward the buffet.

"Yes, Mrs. Riley, it's Chanel." Joyce watched Cooper take Keisha's hand as they walked away. "What a lovely young woman with Cooper. I don't remember seeing her around."

And if I have my way, you never will again! "Yes, well, she's ... uh ..."

Joyce's brow creased slightly. There was a first time for everything because she'd never, ever heard the ever-so-well-spoken Evelyn Riley stumble over her words.

"She's rather new in town."

Rather new? Interesting choice of words. Joyce felt there was a story there, but before she could examine it further, one of her assistants came over with yet another fire to put out. "Judge, Mrs. Riley, if you'll excuse me."

As soon as Joyce was out of earshot, Evelyn rounded on the judge. "I. Am. Furious!"

"Careful, darling," the judge responded, as cool as you please. "Your veneer is slipping."

"Positively radiant? Really, Cooper? When you've barely looked at me all evening, much less offered a compliment?"

"Now, Evelyn."

"Don't you *now* me. I put up with a lot from you, but I won't put up with—"

"Evelyn! Judge Riley I thought I might see the two of you here."

At this moment, Evelyn wished she could turn into the Wicked Witch and melt into the floor. Instead, she practiced the restraint that had been honed ever since she left the south side of Chicago. She turned and smiled. "Hello, Michelle, what a pleasant surprise. I'm amazed that you could get away from the hospital."

"I can't stay long. Is Cooper here also? I've been trying to reach him without success. But then, I'm sure the life of an attorney can be as hectic as that of a doctor."

"Honey," Evelyn said, turning to the judge, "could you please bring me another Congressman?" Evelyn knew she was going to need it because it was going to be a long night.

32

If Alexis had her way, the night would be short. Given her husband's busy schedule and frequent trips to the West Coast, she was more than happy to accompany him. But having already been there almost an hour, she was equally ready to leave the affair now. Since becoming a mother, she'd also become a homebody, having handled only a couple interior decorating clients all year. These days she could mostly be found wearing comfortable miniskirts or jeans and a tank top or casual sundresses. She couldn't remember the last time she'd worn heels, and the way her feet were talking to her, she imagined it would be a minute before she did so again.

"Baby, I'm going to the ladies' room."

Toussaint nodded, even as he eyed the scene across the room. "Okay, baby." Without Alexis there to distract him, Toussaint couldn't help but saunter over to where Cooper and Keisha stood in quiet conversation.

"Coop De Ville," he said, addressing Cooper as he had for almost thirty years, back when they were friends. But his tone was about as warm as the ground in Antarctica.

Neither man offered their hand for a shake. Toussaint pointedly ignored Keisha.

"Good evening, Toussaint," Cooper replied, his heart beating faster at being in the proximity of the son of the man who his client had shot and who'd recently been released. "How are you?"

"Fantastic," Toussaint replied. "What about you? You must be feeling pretty good since you were able to get one of your criminals released early."

Exit culture, enter hood. Keisha stepped to Toussaint. "Nucka, who are you calling a—"

"Darling, please," Cooper said, his grip almost as firm on Keisha's arm as his mother's had been on the judge's. He placed her slightly behind him before continuing. "About what's happened, Toussaint—"

"Yes," Toussaint asked, his face a study in politeness but his voice razor sharp, "what about it?"

"I believe that every soul is worthy of redemption, and as a defender of the less fortunate, I guess you could say that I'm just doing my job."

And I'd just be doing my job if I kicked your ass, huh. "As long as you can sleep at night, Cooper."

"Thanks for your concern, Toussaint. I sleep just fine."

"Toussaint!" Jon Abernathy smiled big as he made his way over. "Glad you could make it, man." They did a soul brother's handshake. "With the way you're all over the television, I'm surprised you had any time left for us little folk."

"Just here representing the family, brothah," Toussaint replied, giving Cooper one last cutting look before he walked away. "Putting in an appearance, you understand."

Jon nodded. "So Malcolm couldn't make it? Or Jeff?"

"Malcolm had a prior commitment but Jeff said he'd try and swing by."

"That's right. I heard about Jefferson's promotion to CFO. That brothah is probably chained to his desk."

"Pretty much."

As always, Jon's eyes continued to scan the room. "Damn."

"What?" Toussaint said, taking a sip of his drink.

"That's a face I haven't seen for a while."

"Who?" Toussaint said, turning to see the person who had caught Jon's eye.

"Shyla Martin. She just went around the corner, though, probably to the restroom."

Ah, hell. "Uh, excuse me, man." Toussaint walked in the direction Alexis had taken earlier, but before he could take two good steps, Joyce approached him.

"Toussaint! So glad I caught you. I'd like to introduce you to one of President Obama's aides. Parker, this is Toussaint Livingston, the owner of the restaurant that needs to cater your next White House event."

And just around the corner...

"Excuse me!"

"Oh, I'm sorry."

And then... recognition.

In a defensive gesture, Shyla rose to her full five foot eight and wished she'd been wearing her usual three-inch heels. As it were, being aware of Jon's less-than-massive stature, she'd worn only one-inch heels. Still, she towered a good three inches over Toussaint's four-inch-heel-wearing wife.

Alexis, whose mind had been on how much her feet hurt and how much she was ready to go home and hug her daughter, immediately recognized the woman who'd almost mowed her down. She felt a plethora of emotions at once: shock, anger, confusion, hurt. But then she remembered the conversation she'd had with her sisters a few weeks ago, and the one she'd had with her husband just last night. She was the one married to the man this woman wished she could have. There was no need to be anything but cordial.

"Hello, Shyla."

"Hi, Alecia."

A chuckle and then, "It's Alexis."

"I'm sorry. Unless a person matters to me, it's hard to remember their name."

Okay, b, I was trying to be nice. "I'm sure you have that problem with your male friends as well, being as there are so many."

"Yes, including your husband."

"I understand your anger toward me, Shyla." Alexis lowered her voice. "I took away from you some very good dick."

Shyla stood even straighter and held her chin even higher. "Glad you're enjoying my seconds."

"Immensely, sweetheart, and every night. In fact"—she looked at her watch—"it's about time for me to enjoy some now." Alexis passed Shyla, then stopped and turned. "Oh, and, Shyla"—she waited until Shyla turned around—"the color green does not look good on you."

Shyla looked down at her chocolate-brown suit, then up at Alexis's back. By the time it dawned on her what was meant by that statement, Alexis had rejoined her husband and asked to go home. Moments later, Shyla stepped back into the room, spotted Joyce, and immediately walked over. "Have you seen Toussaint?"

"Uh-oh, what happened?"

"Nothing. I just heard he was here and wanted to say hello."

"Yes, he was here, with his wife. They left a few minutes ago."

Shyla nodded toward Jon, who was now talking to the presidential aide. "Don't you think it's about time I met the congressman?"

Joyce smiled. "Absolutely. Come with me."

Because she'd taken Shyla into the other room, where the congressman was now happily holding court, Joyce didn't see the various reactions—envy, appreciation, curiosity—when her next guests arrived. It was Jefferson Livingston, looking quite dapper and handsome in a vested suit with chain watch. On his arm was one of the most beautiful women in the room, even more striking and causing more whispers than when Keisha had entered.

Meanwhile, Shyla met Jon and she could immediately see that he was smitten with her. And why shouldn't he be? She'd worked hard to keep her body fit and firm, and her mind sharp. And while not daring to think of anything long-term so early in the game, she did feel that she'd make an excellent senator's wife. They'd just made plans for dinner the following evening to discuss her participation on an upcoming marketing campaign. The night was going exactly as she'd planned it. And then they were interrupted.

"Jefferson!" Jon exclaimed as he noticed him behind Shyla's shoulder. "Good to see you, man. Toussaint didn't know if you'd make it."

"I almost didn't. But I finished earlier than anticipated and thought I'd come out and show my support. Hello, Shyla."

"Hello, Jefferson." She spoke to him, but her eyes stayed trained on the woman on his arm. She'd seen her before, at a Livingston function, and was trying to place her.

"Shyla, you remember Divine. She came to a couple company dinners."

Right! She was Jefferson's date. "I knew I'd seen you before," Shyla said, obviously relieved that this stunning woman was with Jefferson and therefore not a threat. She held out her hand and said warmly, "Shyla Martin." It was the warmest words she'd ever have with or for Divine.

"Divine, this is the friend I told you about, Jon Abernathy. Jon, this is a very good friend of mine, Divine."

"You absolutely are," Jon said, kissing her hand.

"Divine has the gallery over in Five Points. I told her that you were an art connoisseur and that maybe y'all should set up a private appointment."

"I'd love to."

"I also warned her about you, Jon. She's newly single and I told her that you had a thing for attractive, unattached women. So she's already on to your game."

"Well, since that's the case, let the playing begin. Have you been to the buffet or gotten a drink?"

Divine coyly shook her head.

Jon turned to Shyla. "Let's finish our talk about the marketing campaign tomorrow, all right?"

"Sure, Jon," Shyla said, just a tad too brightly.

He shook Jefferson's hand. "Now, if I can steal Divine away from you for...the rest of my life..." He guided Divine a short distance away before turning back and giving Jefferson a surreptitious thumbs-up. Divine didn't see it. Shyla did.

It was an interesting evening to say the least, and by the end of it, a few lines had been drawn. Against his mother's wishes and much to Dr. Hopkins's surprise, Cooper was standing with Keisha. Shyla's plans to get over the man she thought she'd already gotten over, Toussaint, with another one, Jon Abernathy, had met a hitch in the giddyup named Divine, one she planned to eliminate in rapid fashion. Divine decided to trust her friend's instincts and give a chance to one of the Atlanta men who Jefferson believed might be able to accept her just as she was *and* keep it a secret. Jon, smitten with this new woman who seemed to know his soul, decided to see if he could "go straight," and if so, for how long. And Quintin Bright, who'd watched the comings and goings from a hidden position across the street, figured that now was as good a time as any to settle one more debt before leaving town. Toussaint Livingston had visited him at the jail once and basically dared him to ever come near his family. Quintin was getting ready to leave that cocky trust fund dude a Bernie Mac–style message: *I ain't scared of you, mutha. . . .*

33

"She looks more like you every day," Alexis said as she and Toussaint observed their sleeping daughter.

"That's a good thing, right?"

"Absolutely, baby." They each kissed their daughter before leaving the nursery and heading to the master suite.

"What can I say," he said as they entered their room. "I've got the touch."

Alexis turned around and stepped into his arms. "That you do." She moaned as Toussaint's soft, full lips descended on hers, and his skillful tongue flicked against her own soft lips until they parted. He was instantly hard. She felt his excitement pushing into her stomach, even as she felt his hand sliding under her top, relished the feel of his strong, long fingers as they pinched her nipple. She wrapped her arms around him, leisurely rubbing his broad back as they slanted their mouths and deepened a kiss that went from searching to scorching in nothing flat. One would think that making love almost every night for twelve months straight would lessen this couple's ardor, but it seemed to intensify it. Toussaint began grinding his pelvis against Alexis, his tongue mimicking the movement.

"I think we should take a cue from Tiara and go to bed too," he murmured after licking her ear.

"Why do I get the feeling that sleep isn't what you have in mind?"

The two continued chatting as they undressed. Having already discussed Shyla being a nonissue on the way home, they were now content to keep the conversation mainly focused on them and the vacation for which they were long overdue.

Once they'd settled into bed, the kissing resumed.

"Have I told you that I love you today?" Toussaint asked when they'd come up for air.

"You've told me," Alexis responded, reaching for his rock-hard shaft. "But I'd rather that you show me."

Toussaint's eyes darkened with desire as he kissed her lips once again before dipping his head down to a dark, hard nipple. He circled it with his tongue before sucking it into his mouth. Alexis hissed her pleasure, rubbing the soft, curly hair on his head while rubbing his other head with the ball of her foot. He continued the journey, placing a trail of kisses down her stomach, stopping briefly at her navel before continuing the journey into the deep. He spread her legs, slowly, lovingly, placing wet kisses on each inner thigh. Alexis trembled with anticipation, her stomach clenching when he lightly, ever... so... lightly... ran his tongue along the folds of her heat. Back and forth, as if he had all the time in the world, he lapped her nectar while spreading her even wider, exposing her nub. Alexis felt vulnerable and wanton, her thighs in the grips of Toussaint's sure, steady hands, her legs now high in the air, her body humming with need.

He flicked her nub. Once, again, and then he covered her pussy with his mouth and acted as if he were dining on a gourmet meal. He smacked, she purred, as they poured all the love they had for each other into the moment. Just as she was about to reach her peak, Toussaint released her legs, covered her body with his, and joined them together with one sure thrust. For a moment, they simply lay there, totally connected. But before long, their hips began dancing without anyone's permission, making lazy circles, the same way their tongues swirled. Toussaint rose up as he thrust into her, looked deep into the eyes of the woman who'd made him whole when he'd never even known there was a part that was missing. Harder he plunged, more deeply. He wanted to touch the very core of her existence, wanted to brand her forever with his love. He got on his knees, took her legs, placed them over his shoulders, and drove himself even more deeply inside her. Alexis moaned loudly as her muscles clenched around his massive shaft, and she tried to pull him deeply inside of her and hold him forever. "I love this," Toussaint growled, pumping harder, deeper, faster. "I love you," he said again between clenched teeth.

"I love you, too, baby," Alexis panted, the familiar tightening at her core signaling the eminent shattering of her control. "Oh, yes, right there, right there! I love you!" Alexis went over the edge.

"I love you!" Toussaint followed her into bliss.

Seconds later, they lay cuddled in each other's arms. Alexis drew lazy circles on Toussaint's arm while he ran a finger up and down her body and over her now-soft nipple. "What did I do to deserve you?" he asked, his voice one of wonder as if he really had no idea how fine, intelligent, and good-hearted he was.

"I don't know, but if you keep putting it down like you just did, you don't have to worry about me going anywhere!"

"Ha! Thank you, baby."

"No, thank *you*." Alexis placed Toussaint's arm over her stomach. "You think it will always be like this between us, even ten, twenty, thirty years from now?"

Toussaint kissed the top of Alexis's head. "Sure, why not? Look at GrandMar and Mom Etta? They've been married for fifty years, and believe me, when Marcus looks at Marietta, I still see a sparkle in his eye."

Alexis turned her body and spooned back against him. She went to sleep thanking God for Shyla's seconds.

The next morning she was up early, a full list of to-dos ready to fill up her Saturday. First on her list was grocery shopping. She finished in just over an hour, wheeling a full cart out to the parking lot. She popped the trunk, positioned the cart against the car to prevent it rolling, and then placed Tiara into her car seat. When she rose up from buckling her, she was startled to see a tall, dark, attractive man placing her groceries into the trunk. Something about the bold act was unsettling, but she chose to take the high road, keep the exchange light—and fast.

"Thanks, but you didn't have to do that," she said, reaching in to take one of the bags herself.

"I never pass up the opportunity to help someone as fine as you," the stranger drawled, his muscles rippling as he picked up the heaviest of the bags and placed it into the trunk.

Alexis was pissed at the guy's forwardness but again chose to let it slide. All she wanted to do was get away from his lusting eyes. She closed the trunk and headed for her car door.

"And that little girl is as pretty as her mama," the stranger said as Alexis sat down in the driver's seat.

Alexis's head whipped around for a smart retort, but the man was ambling away from her, his long legs carrying him far, fast. She started the car, taking a breath when she realized her hands were gripping the steering wheel. *Where did he come from?* Normally, Alexis made a point of being aware of her surroundings, especially when Tiara was with her, which was practically all the time. "Shake it off," Alexis whispered. "It's a shame we have to get paranoid at kindness these days."

However, when Toussaint returned home from putting in a few weekend hours at the office, the niggling feeling about the encounter hadn't left her. After Toussaint had shared the events of his day, he asked about hers.

"Busy," she answered as she removed dishes from the cabinet to set the table. "But interesting."

Toussaint took a bite out of an apple. "Yeah? How so?"

Alexis held a plate against her chest as she turned and leaned against the counter. Her expression was one of thoughtfulness as she answered. "I ran into this guy in the Whole Foods parking lot. He helped me with my groceries."

"Wow, baby, if you think that's interesting, it's time for you to get back into the workplace."

"Ha!" Alexis swatted Toussaint playfully as she took the dishes and walked into the dining room. Toussaint followed her. "I don't know how to explain it except that it felt weird."

"What do you mean, baby?" Toussaint took the silverware and helped set the table.

"First of all, I was buckling Tee into her seat and didn't see him approach the car. When I turned, he was already placing bags into my trunk."

This gave Toussaint pause. "He didn't ask you?"

Alexis shook her head. "I told him thanks but that he didn't have to help me. Then he started flirting."

Toussaint relaxed. As fine as she was, he wasn't surprised that somebody made a move on her. Quite frankly, he'd be shocked if a brothah didn't try and hit on her. He walked around the table and grabbed her around the waist. "That's what you get for being so fine, with all of this"—he squeezed her titties—"and this." He squeezed her butt.

Alexis wiggled out of his embrace. "You're right. I'm probably just tripping. But he gave me an eerie feeling. Oh, and then there's the comment he made about Tee, that she was as pretty as her mama."

"Wait, I thought you said Tiara was already in the car."

"She was."

"Then how did he know what she looks like?"

"Maybe he saw me put her in the car."

"But you said he didn't walk up until after you put her there."

Alexis just looked at Toussaint. She didn't have an answer for that.

Now it was Toussaint's turn to feel an uncomfortable niggle. "What did this guy look like?" he finally asked, crossing his arms.

"Tall, dark, bald head..."

Toussaint's heartbeat quickened. "Real muscular dude?"

Alexis nodded.

"Come with me." Toussaint turned and walked to his office.

"What is it, Toussaint?"

He reached his desk and toggled the mouse, taking his computer out of sleep mode. He went to a search engine and typed in *Quintin Bright*. Several images appeared on the screen. He found the one he wanted and enlarged the picture. "Is this him?" Toussaint asked.

Alexis eyed her husband's stormy countenance as she walked around to his side of the desk.

"Yes," she said, a bit surprised that her husband had found him. Then she looked at the name. And gasped.

Without another word, Toussaint strode past her on the way to the front door.

"Toussaint!"

He didn't break stride as he reached for his keys on the table in the foyer.

"Toussaint, wait!"

He was out the door.

She hurried behind him. "Toussaint, wait, let's talk about this."

"Get back in the house and don't open the door. I'll be back."

"Toussaint, please don't do anything..." The rest of her statement died on her lips as Toussaint backed out of the driveway and burned rubber as he raced down the street.

34

Toussaint ignored Alexis on the caller ID and dialed his brother.

"What's up, bro?"

"Malcolm, I need you to meet me at the office."

The stress in Toussaint's voice carried over the wire. "Toussaint, what's wrong?"

"Quintin threatened my family."

"What?"

Toussaint told him what happened.

"I'm on my way."

Toussaint hung up, having heard the exact response from Malcolm that he expected. Anyone outside the clan may have accused him of overreacting, but given Quintin's history of Livingstons and parking lots, he'd obviously felt his brother's concern well warranted. Toussaint punched in Jefferson's number. "Cuz, I need you to meet me."

While Toussaint talked with the men, Alexis reached Victoria. "Hey, Victoria, it's Lexy. Is Malcolm there?"

"No," Victoria said, switching the phone from one ear to the other so that she could mute the TV. "He just tore out of here like a bat out of you-know-where. Do you know what's going on?"

Alexis slumped into the living room couch. "I'm afraid I do." She told Victoria what happened. "I'm so frightened for him, Vickie. What should I do?"

After a brief hesitation, Victoria answered. "Let's pray."

A short time later, Toussaint, Malcolm, and Jefferson sat inside Toussaint's office, discussing what had transpired. "I can't believe the nerve of that asshole," Jefferson said, showing anger uncommon for this usually placid soul.

"I can," Toussaint replied. "I've been waiting for this."

"I know you're angry, brother," Malcolm said, trying to coax a semblance of calm into his voice. "And I totally understand it. I'd feel the same way. But we've got to keep our head here—"

Toussaint snorted.

"It's why he's doing it, Toussaint. He wants you to lose your cool, do something that can make the evening news. Let's not give him the benefit of exploding, man. Let's calm down and think of a way to handle this."

As if Malcolm hadn't said a word, Toussaint punched a series of numbers into his phone. "Chardonnay, it's Toussaint."

Pause. No response.

"Look, I've got a situation and I know you think we jacked you around, but I don't have any time for bullshit."

"What's going on, Toussaint?"

"Have you seen Quintin since he got out of jail?"

"I didn't even know that he was out."

"So you haven't seen him?"

"No."

"Have you talked to him?"

"No!"

Toussaint took a breath, and tried to calm down. "I need to see him. Do you have any idea where he hangs out in Atlanta?"

Chardonnay gave him the name of a club and a game space where guys played pool.

"Let me know if you hear from him." Toussaint disconnected the call.

Because it was early, not yet 8:00 p.m., the brothers and cousin decided to check out the game space. After casing the entire perimeter, including the bathroom and parking lot, they deduced that Quintin wasn't there.

"What do we do now?" Jefferson asked, his adrenaline pumping with what was for him highly unusual activity.

Toussaint's phone rang again. "Baby, I'm all right."

"Goodness, Toussaint!" Alexis exclaimed. "I've been so worried."

"Well don't be. I just needed to chill out. I'm hanging with Malcolm and Jefferson for a minute. Don't wait up for me. We'll probably have a drink at the club."

"Okay, baby," Alexis said, assuming that Toussaint referred to FGO. "I'll see you when you get home."

Ninety minutes later, Toussaint, Malcolm, and Jefferson walked toward the entrance to the club that Chardonnay had mentioned. They'd sat outside with a clear view of the club's entrance for almost an hour before their casing paid off. Quintin had walked in fifteen minutes ago. They'd waited because they wanted him good and comfortable when they entered, caught totally off guard and hopefully surrounded by witnesses. Quintin's aim may have been to provoke the Livingstons to anger, but if they had their way, he'd be the one going back to jail.

Any suited group of guys walking into a club specializing in hip-hop would have stood out, but these three men strolling in shoulder to shoulder, eyes hidden behind dark glasses, made a particularly striking scene. The crowd immediately parted, like when Moses held up his staff at the Red Sea. Whispered comments followed the men as they walked toward the bar where Quintin sat quietly sipping a drink. Someone tapped him on the shoulder and he slowly turned around. When he did, a smile spread across his face. He leaned back into the bar and spread his arms out along the mahogany.

"Well, well, well, if it isn't the Livingstons gone slumming."

Toussaint waited until he was directly in front of Quintin. "You are one punk-ass bitch," he spat, and watched with veiled relish as Quintin's smile disappeared and an anger-induced vein popped out on the side of his neck.

Quintin slid off the bar stool. "You'd better back the fuck up off me."

Malcolm stepped forward. "Or what?" Quintin glared at him, his hands flexing into fists, but said nothing. "Just like I thought," Malcolm continued, increasing his volume for the gathering crowd. "When it comes to stepping to women and children, you're as bold as they come. But when a man gets up in your face," Malcolm spat precariously close to Quintin's brand new Jordans, "you ain't shit."

Quintin's reaction was to push Malcolm with a force that would have felled a lighter man.

It wasn't the same as throwing the first punch, but it was close enough for jazz. Toussaint stepped in and threw a cross punch so hard that Quintin's neck snapped back. Before Quintin could recover, Toussaint added a punch to the gut and an upper cut to Quintin's chin. Quintin's blow grazed Toussaint's temple but the fist meant for Toussaint's mouth was blocked by Toussaint's forearm. That Quintin had downed several shots of Patrón before he came to the club and had had two since arriving worked to Toussaint's advantage. Still, Quintin lunged at Toussaint and the crowd parted as the two men went down. At first, Quintin was on top and got in a good lick to Toussaint's chin. Now, Toussaint was really pissed off. He rolled them over until he was on top and, thinking about his mother, father and wife, began to pummel Quintin with both fists. Blood now poured from Quintin's mouth and nose.

"Come on, man," Jefferson said, stepping forward to pull Toussaint off of Quintin.

But Toussaint jerked away, even as he bent down and whispered in Quintin's ear. "Come near my family one more time . . . and I'm going to fuck you up for real."

This time, Toussaint allowed himself to be pulled off Quintin, but couldn't leave before kicking his booted size thirteen foot into Quintin's side.

"Any of y'all see anything?" Malcolm asked the crowd. No one answered. He pulled out a few Benjamins, and gave them to the bartender. "Sorry for the disturbance, man. Drinks are on me."

During this time, Jefferson had escorted Toussaint to the door. They now turned and watched as Malcolm came toward them, making sure that Quintin didn't get up and jump him from behind. After tipping the bouncer another few hundred for not interrupting the Livingston / Bright "conversation," the men headed toward Malcolm's car.

"Damn, man," Jefferson said, once they were safely headed away from the club. "You were supposed to provoke him, not punch him out."

"Muthafucka got off easy," Toussaint replied, his face still in full scowl as he rubbed sore knuckles. "Because if he comes near my family again, he's going to lose more than a little blood . . . he's going to lose his life."

35

Shyla walked up to FGO feeling like a million bucks and looking the same. She'd dressed to impress in a tight white Prada mini, with chunky silver buttons and iridescent-jeweled pumps. Her weave was fresh and flowing, and heads turned as soon as she appeared at the host stand.

Harold, the friendly gray-haired gent who'd been the club's host for thirty years, greeted Shyla with an appreciative smile. "Hello, pretty lady."

"Hello, Harold. You're looking as handsome as always."

"Ah, I guess I'm doing all right for an old man."

"Don't let anybody fool you, Harold. You can give these young bloods a run for their money."

Harold's eyes twinkled. "I might give them a walk for their money, but I'm not running too many places these days. Come right this way, Shyla. Jon is already here."

Shyla's heart thrilled at this news. The congressman had obviously told Harold that she was his date and to be expecting her. She already liked how he rolled. She rounded the corner to the semiprivate booths and immediately heard Jon's sexy, deep voice. "Hello, Jon," she said, leaning over to place a kiss on his mouth.

"Uh, hi, Shyla." A look of discomfort was on Jon's face as his eyes darted from her face to that of the person who was obviously behind her, sitting on the other side of the booth. Before even turning, she knew who it was. But she turned anyway.

"I hope that you don't mind my having asked Divine to join us," he said quickly, having sufficiently recovered enough to rise from his side of the booth, motion for Shyla to sit there, and then joining Divine on the other side. "I was given a quick tour of her gallery last night and think it would be the perfect place for the event that you're marketing."

Shyla, girl, you should have known that this was strictly business. There's no way Jon is feeling anyone else the way he is feeling you. Shyla figured that if she told this to herself often enough and long enough, then maybe she'd believe it.

"You do remember her from last night, right?"

"Of course," Shyla said, trying to force a smile onto stiff lips. "Hello, Divine."

"Hello, Shyla."

"What are you drinking, Shyla?" Jon asked.

Shyla, she noted. *Not baby, or beautiful, or any of the other terms of endearment you used before taking this woman's arm and basically disappearing for the night.* When she'd asked Joyce about Jon's whereabouts, she'd been told that he had other "pressing engagements." She could just about imagine how he'd been engaged and what had been pressed. "I'll have a Moscato."

"Beautiful! Divine likes that wine as well, so I'll order a bottle." He motioned for the waiter. "Are you hungry? We're planning to order dinner but wanted to wait for you."

At the moment, Shyla felt that if she tried to swallow anything other than saliva, she'd regurgitate. But they were ordering dinner. What would she do while they ate? "I had a big, late lunch, so I think a salad will suffice for me."

Jon smiled politely. "Divine?"

"Darlings, I am starving! I'll have a salad for an appetizer, and then...let me see...I'll have the rib-eye steak, a baked potato, corn on the cob, creamed spinach, and, Jon, would you like to split an order of Hawaiian rolls?"

Jon's smile was wide and appreciative. "You've got to be kidding, right?"

"Oh," Divine said, looking honestly confused. "You want a whole order of rolls yourself?"

Jon cracked up. "What a breath of fresh air you are, Divine. Most women eat like rabbits when they're out, but you ordered like a man!" Divine's smile faltered. "No, please, don't feel uncomfortable about my saying that. I love a woman with a hearty appetite, someone comfortable enough in their own skin to come into a restaurant and throw down!"

"Well," Shyla said, taking a dainty sip of lemon water. "Had I known how impressed it would have made you, I would have ordered the entire cow, with snout and tail included."

"I don't know about cow snout," Divine said, "but my auntie could make a pig snout so delicious that a vegetarian would eat it."

Jon cracked up again.

Shyla smiled politely. *Is this the distinguished FGO, or* Def Comedy Jam? "So your aunt is a good cook, Divine?"

"Yes, girl, the best."

"Does she live here? Is your family from Atlanta?"

"My roots spread out all over America," was Divine's noncommittal answer. "I'm from some of everywhere."

The waiter came to take their orders and bring their wine. After making a great show of the opening, swirling, and sipping of the drink, Jon nodded his approval and the waiter filled their glasses.

"You say you visited the gallery last night, Jon?"

Jon nodded.

"Is this a twenty-four-hour gallery, Divine?"

Divine laughed. "Not at all. But as the owner, artist, and curator, it is open whenever I say it is. When I described my gallery, Congressman Abernathy—"

"Jon," Jon corrected.

"Jon," Divine replied, "was kind enough to consider it as a potential event site and because the event is happening soon, we needed to move quickly." A quick looked passed between the congressman and the curator.

Shyla nodded, figuring that later would be time enough to make her move on Jon Abernathy. The woman across from her was attractive but not intelligent, the kind of woman who men like Jon tired of in no time flat. Even if he hit it, Shyla gave him a month, two months max and this little fixation would be over. She planned to work with Jon for the foreseeable future and figured she'd be around long after this little gallery affair. "So," she said, taking out a mini-computer and placing it on the table. "Shall we talk marketing and campaign wins?"

Jon raised his glass. Divine did too. Shyla winked as she toasted Jon: "To your success!"

Later that night, Jon once again accompanied Divine to her gallery, but this time a viewing of her personal domain was added to the tour. At one point, she turned and with a very serious look said, "There's something that you need to know about me."

And much later than that, Jon was still there, proving that he was okay with what he found out.

36

Someone else was finding something out, but the jury was still out on how they felt about it.

"I knew it," Chardonnay hissed after Bobby had revealed to her what he described as *bi tendencies*. "I knew there was a reason that I didn't like Jon Abernathy and I knew that you liked dick. You've been cheating on me, Bobby! And with a damn dude! How do you think that makes me feel, huh?"

"But that's why it's not really cheating, baby, because it's a dude. Do you think he could ever compete with you? It was just fucking, Chardonnay!"

Chardonnay looked at him as if he'd grown a dick between his eyeballs. "So let me get this straight. If I make love, it's cheating. But if I fuck, it's all fair game?"

"No, baby, but let's say I walked in on you with another woman. I wouldn't call that cheating; I'd say you were just . . . you know . . . getting your freak on."

"You are a disgusting, lowdown, cheating muthafucka, you know that?"

Bobby hung his head. "I know, baby, and I'm sorry." When he looked up, there were genuine tears in his eyes. "But that's why I'm telling you all of this, baby. I'm done with all of that.

Life was hard where I come from, baby. New Orleans is not a game and Hollygrove is no joke, believe that. I never thought I'd have what I have with you—a good woman by my side, a family. I got caught up in some bullshit, Char, but it didn't feel good to lie to you."

"How long has this been happening?"

"What?"

"Don't what me, like my kids Yak or Ray-Ray would do. How long have you been cheating on me?"

"Does it matter?"

Chardonnay jumped up off the couch. "If I'm asking, then it must matter. How long have we been rolling raw while you've been putting that shit where it don't belong?"

"Oh," Bobby replied, having the nerve to look relieved and cracking a smile. "Don't worry about that, baby. I always use protection when I roll like that. You the only one I'm raw with."

"You say that shit like I'm supposed to be proud about it. Yeah, y'all," she said, mimicking a Southern drawl, "he cheat on me, but he use a rubber while he does it so, you know, I'm good and shit. Boy, you out your goddamn mind."

Bobby stood and reached out to her. "Please, Chardonnay."

"Don't touch me!"

"But I love you!"

"Yeah, me and Jon Abernathy!"

"Keep that shit down, Char. I told you nobody knows this shit, and I'm telling you, now, things will get real serious if you even think about talking out of school on homeboy. This isn't the Livingstons and a secret marriage. This is people's reputations, their lives, their money. I've seen the kind of people who roll with Jon, and I'ma tell you now, messing with him can get you six feet deep."

"If you're trying to scare me, it ain't working." Chardonnay stopped and spun around. "Is he the only one?"

"What?"

"Damn you're slow. Is he the only bitch you've been with besides me?"

"Yes," Bobby answered without hesitation. He'd decided before this conversation began that a single confession could cover a multitude of faults. "Look, I just know how you think, Char. You're always trying to get over. But you don't want to go down this road. Look how long you've been trying to screw over the Livingstons, even though they sign your checks and feed your kids."

"Yeah, I'm still trying to think of a way to get payback on their lying asses."

"Girl, you sold Bianca's story to the *Inquirer*!"

"The choice was hers, pay or play. She wouldn't give me the paper, so Mama had to play."

"Yeah, well, how's that working out for you?"

"How's slaving over that stove working out for you? And what about that business venture? Is Mr. Money Bags going to still be interested when you cut off the pipe?"

"I'm not going into business with Jon. Toussaint and Ace want to talk to me about moving up in the Livingston Corp., taking over for Chef on the catering arm or maybe even managing one of the new chains."

"Look at you," Chardonnay snarled, her lip curled up as if she were smelling Bobby Jr.'s dookey diaper. "All up in they asses."

"Whatever, Char."

"I'm still looking for big money, like they promised. And in the meantime, I just might see what I can do with this Abernathy news—"

Bobby grabbed her arm so fast and squeezed so tight that for a minute, Chardonnay felt fear. "Let go of me, Bobby."

"Don't play with me, girl," Bobby said, his voice deceptively low. "I let you get away with a lot of bullshit, but don't mess with me on this right here."

"Oh, so it's not just Jon you're worried about getting exposed—it's your sous-chef up-and-coming ass."

"Damn right." He let her go. "I mean it, Char. Don't play." There was a moment of tense silence before Bobby said, "So, that's it. I have no more secrets. We still together, right?"

"You expect an answer now? Tonight? Let me think about it, and in the meantime, the couch is your new castle."

"That's fair enough. At least you didn't straight out kick me to the curb."

"That would take too much energy and right now, I have to get ready for work."

Bobby headed for the bedroom, and when he reached the doorway, he turned around. "Chardonnay."

"What?"

"Do you have any secrets that you want to tell me?"

"What the hell do you think?"

"I'm just asking."

"And I'm just telling."

"Do you?"

"Boy, please. I'm done with this conversation."

And she was. Moments later she was dressed, out of the house, and on her way to Taste of Soul. Her and her secrets . . .

37

Her doorbell rang, and Keisha didn't have to look out of the peephole to ID the visitor. She'd seen the shiny white Lincoln when it pulled into the driveway. With her woozy head and queasy stomach, she'd rather have faced down a rabid pit bull than spend two seconds with the person on the other side of the door. But since she doubted Evelyn Riley would go away quietly, she opened it.

"Yes?" No greeting, no smile.

Evelyn's chin rose ever so slightly. Her least favorite person in the world was ill-bred, not to mention someone who was still wearing loungewear in the middle of the afternoon, pregnant or no. Determined to show how one behaved when not raised by a pack of wolves, she forced a smile. "Hello, Keisha. May I come in?"

"Cooper isn't here, which you well know since it's Monday, and the middle of the day."

"Yes, Keisha. I am well aware of my son's schedule. I'd like to have a chat with you, which is why I'm here. May I enter?"

Keisha leaned against the doorjamb and folded her arms. She knew that she gave off an air of insolence, but in fact, she was trying to keep down the crackers she'd eaten. "Look, Evelyn—"

"It is Mrs. Riley, young lady . . ."

"Whatever, *Evelyn*. We might as well not even play these games. I know that you don't like me and the feeling is mutual. I also know that you're not happy about becoming a granny again."

A slight flaring of nostrils was the only sign of Evelyn's utter disdain. "I'm reserving my joy for children I am sure my son has fathered. Given your history, even you should be able to understand my"—*disbelief*—"uncertainty."

"Cooper is certain that it's his and so am I. Which means I'm not going anywhere."

"And neither am I, not until I've had my say." Evelyn brushed past Keisha and entered the home. Her eyes widened briefly as she took in an array of magazines spread across the sofa and a can of soda on the coffee table. *My goodness, she ingests all of that sugar and wasted calories? And directly out of the can?* To say she was tasteless, Evelyn decided, would be to move her up the scale a notch or two. "Where is the housekeeper?"

"Why, do you plan to do any cleaning?"

As she turned, Evelyn's back was so straight and rigid that it could have substituted for a really good ironing board. "Really, Keisha, this insolence is very unattractive and speaks to the insecurity you're trying hard to hide. Given your history, this vulnerability is totally understandable."

Keisha rolled her eyes, plopped down on the couch, and began flipping through the *Atlanta Inquirer*. This move in no way detracted Evelyn from her goal. In fact, she one-upped her by joining her on the couch, picking up a magazine as well and continuing to chat as she flipped through it. She, like Keisha, didn't see a word on a page.

"I'll admit that you are not my first choice for Junior, nor are you someone with whom I see sharing tea and crumpets on a regular basis."

"Naw, I'm more of a Patrón and pig skins kind of chick."

"But my son has invited you into his home, which makes

you my business. And that's what I'd like to discuss—business."
Evelyn put down the magazine and reached for her purse. "I
believe your feelings for Junior involve gratitude but not love.
He did represent your"—*thug, criminal*—"brother and helped
secure an early release. But do you really feel you're compati-
ble with someone as"—*sane, intelligent, human*—"conservative
as my son? Can you truly envision a life with him?"

"You don't give Junior very much credit, do you? Hell,
yeah, I'm grateful. But I love your son. And he loves me *and*
my kids."

Kids are goats—an appropriate description. Evelyn knew there
was no sense continuing a conversation with someone possess-
ing this level of intelligence. She decided to end by speaking
the language she was sure that Keisha understood. She reached
into her purse and pulled out a check. "I'm sure that you have
some feelings for my son, but I do not believe that you truly
love him. I believe you love the lifestyle he affords you: this
home, your car, a role model for your"—*brats*—"sons. I'm here
to offer you those things and the chance to enjoy them with
someone more to your"—*low level*—"liking. Say, a hundred
thousand dollars to bow out of my son's life. You could return
to"—*the hole that you crawled out of*—"Los Angeles and live in
style. How does that sound,"—*wretched wench*—"dear?"

Keisha's laugh was harsh and immediate. "Sounds like you
don't know the cost of living on the west side!"

You greedy little tramp. "I know that the sum of money I'm
offering is much more than you've ever had on your own. I
also know that it will afford you to live better than you did before you met my son."

"I lived *very* well before I met Cooper."

"Oh, yes, forgive me." Evelyn's stoic veneer that she'd worked
a lifetime to build began to wear thin, and the South Side
Chicago, before-her-parents-got-edge-a-ma-kay-ted, threatened
to come through. "You sponged off one of the Livingston men

before setting your sights higher. I must say, Keisha, you're nothing if not ambitious."

"Ha! You don't know the half."

"And I'd prefer not to, dear."

"Then what the hell are you doing in my house?"

"Your house?"

"Look, I got things to do. You need to raise up off my couch and get the hell on!"

Evelyn settled her back against the sofa. "Two hundred thousand."

"Is that all you think your son's freedom is worth?"

Evelyn's eyes narrowed. *Greedy bitch.* "Two-hundred and fifty thousand dollars, Keisha. That is my final offer."

"Good, then I'll walk you to the door." Keisha got up, walked to the door and jerked it open. "Cooper!"

"Hello, Keisha. Is that Mother's car out front?"

"Yes, and you're just in time to tell her to exit stage gone."

"Please, Keisha, she's my mother. Show respect."

"You tell her to show *me* some! Instead of coming in here and trying to bribe me into leaving you and taking your baby with me!"

Cooper's brow creased as he turned toward Evelyn. "Mother . . ."

"Son, it isn't how she's describing."

"It was exactly that way, bitch!"

Cooper and Evelyn matched gasps. "Keisha!" Cooper cried in an uncharacteristically loud voice. This was followed by the solid stomping of one foot. "I will not tolerate this type of behavior!"

"Me neither. Either she goes, or I will. And if I leave, Cooper, I'm not coming back."

Cooper looked from his mother down to the hand Keisha had unconsciously placed on her stomach. It was the same spot where he'd placed his hand just this week, and for the first time felt the baby kick. "Mother, I'm sorry, but I must ask you to leave."

"Junior, you cannot possibly—"

"Yes, Mother, I can." He placed a firm grasp on Evelyn's elbow and steered her to the door. "Tempers are obviously frayed here, causing further conversation at this juncture to be counterproductive. Return home, Mother, and try and calm down. I'll call you later."

Three hours after the Confrontation, Evelyn still reeled in shock. Memories of the one and only hangover she'd ever had in her life caused her to resist pouring some of the nearby amber liquid into a tumbler and drinking it straight. But just barely. *That piece of ghetto filth has a Riley growing inside her gold-digging belly?* Gasp and sputter and gasp again! She'd been on autopilot since leaving Cooper's townhome, with barely a word shared through a dinner that mostly remained on her plate. Now she sat across from a stoic-looking Cooper Sr., who was nursing his nightly glass of Scotch with furrowed brow.

Memories that Evelyn mostly kept under wraps invaded her thoughts. How when they'd moved from the south to Chicago, she'd been the black, ugly, unrefined outcast among her lighter-skinned, cultured, citified friends. How it had taken her years of study, schmoozing, and her father's ascension to dean at a prominent college—not to mention lots of money— to reinvent herself and become accepted. The day she'd gotten accepted into a sorority, Evelyn had made herself a promise: that she would never, *ever* be included among the outcasts again. "She can't keep it," Evelyn finally said into the silence.

"What?"

"The baby. I believe she's only four months along. I'll talk to Michelle and find out the feasibility of having this mistake aborted. I know that woman has a price. I just have to keep making the offer until I reach it. And believe me, when it comes to getting that girl out of my son's life, no price is too high."

"Easy, Evelyn," the judge murmured, still chagrined by his wife's earlier actions. "You're thinking of tossing my money to her in reckless abandon. We're not even sure that's our boy's child."

"I don't want to take the chance of finding out!" Evelyn stood and began to pace. "She's got to get rid of it. We have to make her get rid of it! We cannot have that woman become a part of this family."

Cooper Sr. tossed back his Scotch. "If she's telling the truth and that's Cooper's baby, then she's part of the family already."

"Oh, God!" Evelyn put her head in her hands, imagining a dinner table with a Patrón-swigging, foul-mouthed Keisha and her untrained heathens in tow. Then she straightened her back and lifted her hands toward heaven. "Lord, it's Evelyn. Please, just take me now."

38

"Boys, put your shoes on. We're going shopping." Feeling her stomach settled for the first time in months, Keisha was ready to go out and soak up some of the warm, spring sunshine. She was still reveling in the small victory she'd experienced yesterday when she'd made the great and powerful Evelyn Riley back the bump up. She wasn't at all surprised that Cooper had left the house shortly after his mother, undoubtedly running behind her like a puppy dog to make amends. Fine with her; his absence had given her the time she needed to move her things out of their master suite and into the guest room. He came home to a quiet house and a locked bedroom door. The only two words she'd blessed him with were "go away." The separation wouldn't be long, no more than a week or so. But getting back in her good graces would cost him. It was time to add to her "rainy day" fund.

She turned to Dorian and Antwan. "Okay, I'm telling y'all now, you're getting one game each. Now act a fool and you get nothing. Understand?" The boys nodded and the trio turned into the video game aisle, occupied with another family: a mother and her three kids.

"Well, well, well."

At the sound of the familiar voice, Chardonnay quickly looked up. Her eyes narrowed as she recognized the woman who'd spoken. "Well, well, well," she said, crossing her arms and adopting an I-don't-give-a-damn pose. "If it isn't Miss Bad-Ass from LA."

"If it isn't the bitch who helped put my brother behind bars."

It was the first time these women had seen each other since Quintin was arrested more than a year ago. Obviously, there was still no love lost between them.

"Ho, don't come to me with some bullshit," Chardonnay quipped. "You're talking out the side of your neck, the way ignorant people do when they don't know shit."

"Takes a ho to know a ho, don't it."

"No, it takes a ho to play silly-ass games and I don't have time for it. Yak, Ray-Ray, come on. Ray-Ray, I thought I told you to watch your little brother?"

"He's right over there. I'll get him." She then yelled like he was four miles instead of four feet away. "Bobby! Get over here!"

Meanwhile, the air crackled as these two streetwise sistahs squared off in between the Mario Brothers and Just Dance. Feeling the intensity of the moment, and becoming immediately defensive, Dorian looked over at Cognac, whose little hands were already balled up into fists. "What you looking at?"

Nine-year-old Cognac puffed out his chest and took a step. "You, fool!"

"Shut the hell up, Yak," Chardonnay admonished, reaching out and grabbing little Mike Tyson before even more hell broke loose.

Keisha cut her eye at Dorian, then looked back at Chardonnay. She'd often wondered what she'd say to the woman who'd befriended her when she first arrived in Atlanta then, as far as she could tell, stabbed her in the back for some reward money. "Are you trying to stand there and say that you didn't snitch on Q, turn him over to the cops?"

"That's exactly what I'm saying. How was I supposed to have done that, Keisha, when I hadn't heard from him in months and had no idea where he was?" She narrowed her eyes and crossed her arms, taking her time to look over the enemy. "Hell, you're dressed pretty good, got your nails done and your hair laid. Maybe *your* ass turned him in and took the money."

Keisha took a step toward Chardonnay.

Chardonnay took one herself.

Dorian and Cognac glared at each other. "Stop looking at me," Cognac warned.

"Why don't you make me?" Dorian suggested.

To little Cognac, that sounded like a plan. He leaned into it and did an uppercut proud, clocking the slightly taller Dorian on the chin. Dorian pushed Cognac into the bin of games. The two boys started scuffling, with Chardonnay and Keisha grabbing arms and legs and bits of clothes to pull them apart.

Suddenly, a miniature scream stopped all the action. Bobby Bicardi stood wide-eyed, while tears threatened to fall from his big, brown eyes and run straight down his chubby, brown face. It was the first time Keisha had paid attention to the little boy who looked to be around a year old. Chardonnay had had a baby? *WTH?*

Keisha narrowed *her* eyes and crossed *her* arms.

"What?" Chardonnay asked, pulling Bobby toward her with one hand, keeping her other one firmly on Cognac's neck.

"That your little boy?"

"What's it to you?"

"I didn't know you had another baby."

"There's a lot about me that you don't know." The toddler headed back out of the aisle. "Get back here, Bobby!"

Keisha immediately recognized the name of the man who

worked at Taste of Soul and who'd babysat when she and Chardonnay had gone partying. He was nice as she recalled, even buying her sons a pizza the evening they spent there. She looked at Chardonnay's left hand. *Yes, Virginia, there is a ring.* "Oh, and married too. Look at you trying to go all legitimate and shit."

"What I am or am not trying to do is none of your business."

Keisha took a breath and decided to try a different tactic. An old LA neighbor used to always tell her that she could catch flies faster with honey than with vinegar, and quite honestly, she could use a friend in this town. Someone more on her level, someone with whom she could interact with and simply be herself, without judgment. "Look, Chardonnay, at one time we hung out, so I know you can be cool when you want to be. And I have no reason not to believe you when you said you weren't involved in my brother going to prison. *And if you believe that, I've got some ocean property in Mississippi to sell you.* Besides, he's out now."

Because of the call from Toussaint, the reason behind which Chardonnay was still trying to figure out, she knew this. But she played the ignorant card. "Oh, Q got out?"

Keisha nodded. "Just a few days ago. And since I'm living here—"

"I thought you and Jefferson broke up."

"We did." Keisha paused before adding, "I'm with Cooper Riley."

"Riley as in Judge Riley's son?"

Keisha nodded again.

"Humph, and you're talking about me going legit? I see your ass is still trying to come up."

"We got close when he represented my brother." Again, Keisha looked at the little toddler playing on the floor. "That Bobby's baby?"

"Who else?"

"Sorry, girl, my bad." Silence, as Keisha continued to ob-serve the child. "He's cute. When did y'all get married?"

"A while back." Chardonnay picked up Bobby. "Come on, y'all."

"Mama! I want to get this one!" The fight totally forgot-ten, Dorian now ran up to his mother with the excitement of the child that he was instead of the man he oftentimes pre-tended to be.

Keisha looked up to see Chardonnay at the end of the aisle. "Chardonnay, wait!" She turned to her son. "Okay. Antwan, which one are you getting?" Antwan held up a box. "Okay, come on, y'all." Then she turned to Chardonnay, who'd now put Bobby in the top of the basket and was tying his shoe. "I have a lot of running to do today but, hey, do you still have my cell number? Maybe we can meet up for a drink. Clear the air between us."

Chardonnay studied Keisha for a minute, weighing the pros and cons of keeping in contact. The cons won. Because anyone who'd threatened her once could do so again. And that's exactly what had happened when the situation with Q went down. Plus, Chardonnay wasn't convinced that Keisha believed she had nothing to do with Q's arrest. Best to stay clear of this all the way round. "Look, Keisha, nothing personal but I'm not interested in meeting you for drinks or anything else. We might have hung out at one time or another, but you and me ain't down like that no more."

"You sure you want to play it like that?" Keisha asked, feel-ing the ice that had rolled off that statement. "Because I was going to tell Q I saw you, thought you'd want to say hey to an old friend."

"You can tell Q I said hey, but me and him ain't down no more neither."

"Oh, it's like that, huh?"

"Yeah, it's like that."

"That's cool, then. See you later." She headed straight to the checkout counter, and once she'd purchased the games for the boys, she made a beeline to her car. Once there, she dialed her mother's number. "Mama, it's Key."

"Keisha?"

"Yes, Mama, Keisha, your daughter." Keisha smiled at the surprise in her mother's voice. Their relationship had been strained at best, but in the last six months, since Q had insisted their mother was trying to stay clean and sober, Keisha had tried to bury the hatchet and salvage some sort of relationship with the woman who gave her life. "Look, I'm calling to ask a favor." She told her mother what she wanted, but since Marilyn didn't know a thing about computers, Keisha got her younger cousin on the phone and explained again. "I need you to do it ASAP. Don't forget, okay?" She finished the call, and seconds later got off the phone with a satisfied smile on her face. "What goes around comes around," she muttered as she started the car and headed for the parking lot.

"What goes around, Mama?" Antwan asked.

"Payback, baby," Keisha said with a bob of the head. "Payback."

39

Sterling sat in Toussaint's living room, listening along with Jefferson, Malcolm, Adam, and Ace. He paid close attention as the men relayed the past weekend's events. Every now and then, he made a note on his ever-present pad. When he was sure that Toussaint, Malcolm, and Jefferson had finished speaking, he sat back in his chair, thinking.

"First of all, I'm sorry this happened. You'd think that someone who spent just a little over a year in prison after everything he did would leave well enough alone. That said, I wish you men had called me on Saturday instead of today, before you paid Quintin a visit. That situation could have turned out much worse than it did."

"What was I supposed to do?" Toussaint queried. "Let that dude's actions go unchecked? After he had the nerve to come near my family? I don't think so."

"I'm sure the knowledge that he'd been that close to your wife and child was quite unsettling—"

"Damn straight it was."

Sterling took a deep, calming breath. Tempers as explosive as TNT simmered just beneath the cool Livingston exterior, and Toussaint was probably the most volatile of all. His voice was low and steady as he continued. "Unfortunately, and as much of an a-hole as he is, Quintin is still protected under the law."

"I don't give a damn," Toussaint insisted. "He started the fight. I finished it."

Malcolm's voice rose along with his anger. "He knew exactly what he was doing when he approached Alexis in the parking lot. Toussaint told him to stay away from our family and his action was a blatant 'kiss my ass'."

Toussaint nodded. "Quintin threatening my wife is not going to go unchecked. Not on my watch. Not at all."

Adam and Ace exchanged a look. There was nothing they could add to the conversation that hadn't already been said by their sons.

Sterling was the lone voice of reason. "That's assumption, Toussaint, not fact. According to Alexis, all he did was approach her, flirt a little bit, and help put groceries in the trunk of her car. Hardly a crime."

"Look, man—"

Sterling held up his hands to stop Toussaint's rant. "Listen, Toussaint. Believe it or not, I'm on your side. I'm just explaining how this would bear out in a court of law, not that I think Quintin will do anything foolish like try and file charges. It would basically be you and your brother's word against him and whatever witnesses he presented. Probably the best thing that came out of this is that he showed his hand, proved that he hasn't put his hatred of this family behind him. I'll put a tail on him for the next few weeks, see where he leads me. Meanwhile, I want your wife to file a restraining order against him. In fact, let's talk with Percillius about filing a restraining order for your entire family. I think that considering the circumstances, the judge will allow it."

Various murmurs of approval were heard around the room. Everyone there respected Percillius Phelps, the Livingstons' attorney who'd prosecuted Quintin. He might even have other legal options for them. Adam texted him to set up a meeting as soon as possible.

"What about the investigation?" Ace asked. "Any news?"

Sterling shook his head. "Quite frankly, that's going much slower than I'd like. Aside from the lone witness and the mystery man with the tattoo, there have been no leads." Sterling had even considered the fact that there was no man with a tattoo, that the witness had been mistaken. But he'd questioned him again just last week, trying to uncover anything new, and the worker had stuck to his story. "It's been only a month, so technically we're still early in this type of process."

"I thought the longer it took to solve something like this, the lesser the chances," Adam said.

Sterling smiled. "In some instances, yes. But other cases take years. I'm not saying that is going to be the situation here, nor am I saying we'll ever be able to fully know what happened on the west side that morning. Unlike on TV, in real life not every case gets solved." Sterling stood. "But I'll stay on it. In the meantime, no more gangster moves, got it?" He held Toussaint's stare until he received a curt nod. "I know you're antsy to do otherwise, but I'm asking you to please trust me. I've got this."

Back at his office, Sterling sifted through the information he'd obtained on Quintin Bright during his last investigation. A frown marred his smooth, brown skin. As assuring as he'd been to the Livingstons, it bothered him that he hadn't put the tiniest crack in this case, had come up against stone walls at all turns. "What is it, man?" he murmured to himself. "What is it that you're missing?" He rocked back in his chair, his mind methodically going through every possibility and every angle. Suddenly he sat up. "Interesting . . . but it's worth a try."

Soon he was rapidly typing on his keyboard, sending messages to his contacts in Kansas City and North Carolina. These were two of the places found while researching Quintin's money trail. Quintin may have been in prison, but Sterling grew increasingly convinced that this man was somehow connected to what happened in LA. And if he found out that this was the case, and if there was any way that Sterling could prove it, then Quintin Bright was going down—for good.

40

Adam, Candace, Ace, and Diane were in Lithonia, Georgia, enjoying Sunday dinner—a formerly common ritual that was now all too rare.

"When is the last time we did Sunday dinner with the folks?" Adam asked, piling a heaping helping of fresh-cut green beans and new potatoes on his plate.

"I don't know, but it's been too long," Ace answered, licking the fingers that had just maneuvered the fall-off-the-bone baked barbeque ribs onto his plate. "Daddy, I don't know how you do it but man! These ribs are finger-lickin' good!"

"Ain't no secret," Marcus said, putting a meaty short rib into his mouth and pulling it out clean. "Just low and slow like I taught you, son. Low and slow."

"That's how he does it," Diane said to Marcus. "And don't get me wrong. Ace's ribs are the bomb. But they're not quite like this . . ."

A twinkly look passed between Marcus and Marietta. The twins caught it.

"What?" Adam demanded. "Y'all keeping secrets from your children? Tips that should be passed down by right?"

"And they will," Marietta calmly replied, "in due time."

"What's due time?" Candace asked.

"After we're gone. Otherwise, how are we going to get y'all to continue to come over here?"

"We're your children," Ace intoned. "That's why we come over."

Marietta chuckled. "Baby, I know you're lying, but it sure sounds good."

"He sure is," Adam said, finishing off his fifth bone, along with a bite of freshly baked corn bread, the kind with actual corn kernels present throughout. " 'Cause this brothah is coming over for the food!"

Everyone laughed.

"I know it," Marietta continued. "That's why every iota of what we know about food, all the secrets we haven't shared, are locked up, to be released only upon our death."

"Quit playing, Mama," Diane said, her tone serious. "I don't like this talk about dying and wills. You're going to live a very long time."

Marietta fixed Diane with a compassionate gaze. "In case you've forgotten, I'm seventy-three. Some would figure that's pretty long already."

"No," Ace said, shaking his head. "Long is a hundred and five, like Miss Jane Pittman."

"Or Methuselah," Marcus said.

"He's from the Bible, right?" Adam asked. Marcus nodded. "How old was he?"

Marcus shook his head. "Don't start me to lying."

"With a name like that, does it matter?" Ace countered. "His mama must have been drinking Jesus juice!"

Everyone laughed, Marietta the hardest. "You got that right."

The banter continued as they ate their meal, and afterward, as was common in the Livingston households after dining, the men went one way for cigars and a spot of cognac and the women went the other for tea and a spot of gossip.

On the way, Candace managed to quickly pull Diane to

the side and nodded toward Marietta. "She ask you anything yet?"

Diane shook her head.

"She hasn't called?"

"Oh, she's called. But your name hasn't come up, not about that."

Candace frowned.

"What's the matter? I told you that she hasn't asked me a thing."

"Yeah, but with Mom Etta, her not saying anything is sometimes worse than saying something."

At first, Candace had been upset that Adam had mentioned her and the Quintin connection to his father. Two years had passed and they'd been working very hard to put her affair behind them. How could he have possibly justified this need to know? Thankfully, Diane had been the voice of reason in the situation. "She doesn't know everything, Can," Diane had patiently told her. "And you know this family. There are very few secrets among us." At the time Candace had hotly retorted, "Yes, and it looks like things are going to stay that way." Candace watched her mother-in-law, still spry at seventy-three, and tears welled in her eyes. She fairly worshipped the ground that woman walked on and ashamed was the last thing she wanted to make Marietta Livingston. For the umpteenth time, she cursed the fact that she'd ever stepped foot into Q's gym.

"What y'all girls back there putting your heads together about? I hope it's not the Memorial Day picnic menu because I've already decided. We're going to let the men handle cooking duties that day."

Diane and Candace followed Marietta into her large, airy, country-style kitchen, placing the dishes they'd brought from the table into the sink.

"Fine with me," Candace said, rinsing the dishes and placing them in the dishwasher. "I'll eat some of GrandMar's cooking any day."

"Ha! That boy Malcolm sure changed that man's name, didn't he?"

"Sure did."

Marietta wiped her hands on a dish towel. "How are Malcolm and Victoria doing? I don't see much of them these days, especially her."

"They're busy but fine," Candace replied. "I never thought I'd see the day, but Victoria is actually coming down to earth a little bit."

Marietta put her hand on her hip. "Honey, five kids will snap your head out of the clouds real fast."

"Ha! Thankfully, I wouldn't know. But my son is happier than I've ever seen him and anyone who can do that for him is fine by me."

"Yes," Marietta said as she sat at the island and stared into the distance. "Amazing what children can do. Even when you don't want them, they turn out to be a blessing."

Diane and Candace exchanged looks. Candace's begged the question, *Did you tell her?* While Diane's read, *No!* The fact that baby Victory had almost ended Malcolm's marriage was one of those few secrets that hadn't been shared with Mom Etta.

"I watched the way they were with that baby and each other," Marietta explained. "You know if you pay attention, you can get a heap of information off of someone's face." Marietta looked at her daughters-in-law and inwardly chuckled at their tries for blank expressions. Little did they know, but Marietta had been reading their faces like books for years and even now knew that Ace and Diane still screwed like randy teenagers and that when it came to Candace and that man who shot Adam, there was more to the story than she'd been told.

Meanwhile, back at the chat with the cognac, the men, too, continued discussing that story. "I still think one of us needs to put a bullet in him," Marcus grumbled. "That boy shot you, Adam."

"Yeah, Dad, but two wrongs wouldn't make a right."

"How you figure? Fair exchange ain't no robbery!"

Ace chuckled. "Maybe not, Dad, but it would be a crime. Twin, don't let Daddy have any more of that cognac, else we'll be wrestling a shotgun out of his hand."

"Fair exchange is no robbery in business," Malcolm reasoned. "What happened with Quintin is something else."

"Humph. If getting shot in the back isn't business of the most serious kind, then I don't know what is. And after I load him up with buckshot, I'll aim at that punk attorney for helping to get him out."

Adam and Ace shared a look and each took a drink. Neither one of them was going to touch that comment with a ten-foot pole—too much drama either directly or indirectly connected to it: Keisha being Q's half sister (which the parents didn't know), Keisha and Jefferson's cohabitation (another secret), the money she stole and gave to Q (Lord have mercy), and what Cooper surely felt was Bianca's betrayal. No, best to try and divert the subject away from Quintin Bright, shootings, and missing funds before their would-be-outlaw father became the subject of breaking news.

41

Quintin had been seething for almost two weeks, ever since the Livingstons had had the nerve to confront him in front of his crowd at the club. Moments after they'd exited, he'd found one of his partners who was packing, borrowed his gun, and gone after them. But when he got outside, there was no trace of them. *Punks probably burned rubber because they knew I'd come after their asses.* His phone rang. "Yo, dog, what up?"

"You got it," said the man on the other end.

"So you coming up here or what?"

"Man, why are you still bent on this revenge shit?"

"Because those clowns disrespected me, that's why!"

"Q, man, calm down. Look, I talked to Keisha and she told me everything, including a few major details that in all the times we've talked, you've left out of the story."

"Like what?" Q demanded, as if he hadn't been there when the events went down.

"Hmm, let's see. Like the fact that you screwed this chick and then shot her husband, which is why they have a beef with *your* ass! But I know why you didn't feel it necessary to reveal that little piece of information. Because you know I probably wouldn't have helped you if I'd known about your dirt."

"Quit playing, man. You helped me because I paid you hella paper!"

"I helped you because . . . never mind. It don't matter. Because I'm not coming down there, man. I don't have a dog in this fight."

"Oh, so it's like that."

A pause on the other end and then, "Keisha says you're still cool, know what I'm saying, and that you might be relocating."

"Yeah, well, Keisha talks too much."

"Ha! Is it true?"

"Yeah, I got a little island babe waiting for me, and I'm thinking about hanging out down south for a minute. I'm tired of the grind up here."

"You should be tired of the anger too. You've been mad a long time, man. Like your whole life."

"I had my reasons."

"I agree. But you don't have to let your past keep dictating your future. Me? I'm thinking about taking that money you gave me and opening up a nice little car repair and detail shop. Me and the missus are expecting another crumb snatcher."

"Damn, man. Your first one ain't even a year old."

"I look at that girl and she gets pregnant."

Q smiled as the men continued to chat. Maybe the caller was right; maybe it was time for him to stop letting his anger for the Livingstons dictate his actions. They'd been in his blood for the past two years. Maybe it was time for him to get them out of it. He hung up the phone and dialed Jamaica. "Baby girl."

"Black mon," Constance purred.

"How are things?"

"You left me in charge," she said, her lyrical accent clipped, pronounced, and full of attitude. "How do you expect them to be?"

Quintin smiled.

"I've been thinking—"

"Ah, hell—"

"About ways to tap into the tourist market here and earn a lot of money."

"I'm listening."

"Yeah, mon. I thought you would if I mention the green stuff. *Nuh bodda mi.*"

Q smiled as he listened to his girl. She would often leave her school-learned English and slip into patois, as she did now with her statement basically saying that she wouldn't be bothered with his foolishness. "*Nuh bodda mi,* either," he replied. "Now tell me your plan."

She told Quintin about a major business development in Ocho Rios, one that members of her family were heading. "They're going to need a lot of help," she concluded. "And there will be chances to invest and grow your money as well. What do you think about that, Black Mon?"

They talked for a while longer, but when Quintin got off the phone, he'd made up his mind. Fuck the Livingstons. He was going to put the past the behind him, live his life, and be happy. He was going back to Jamaica." *Wait, I've got a much better idea for business than car repairing and detailing.* Quintin actually laughed as he reached for the phone again.

42

It was unseasonably hot this first week in June, but Toussaint walked into the Taste of Soul test kitchen looking as cool as an autumn breeze. That the man had the audacity to be sporting an ivory suit with a black Mandarin-style shirt, something many businessmen wouldn't even attempt, added to his swagger. "Chef, Bobby," he said, rounding the table to give dap to both men. "I have a feeling this summer is going to be a beast!"

"Cool with me," Bobby replied. "That just means more beer and soda sales with the barbeque."

"Spoken like a true businessman. I have a feeling you're going to go a long way with us." Toussaint handed each man a piece of paper. "I just met with Joyce Witherspoon, who is organizing one of the biggest political events of the summer. It's a national democratic fund-raiser on the third of July. Candidates from across the country will be there. There's talk that the president may make an appearance, and if not, Vice President Biden might be there. That," he continued, nodding at the paper, "is the proposed menu. Take a look and tell me what you think."

Toussaint sat back, checking text messages while Bobby and Chef scanned the items.

"Pretty basic stuff," Chef said with a shrug. "We can handle it."

"I like how y'all changed the dish names to match politics: Barack's Baby Backs, the Michelle Mac-N-Cheese—"

"We're going to have to change up the recipe a bit on that," Chef interjected.

Toussaint stopped texting. "Why?"

"Where you been, man?" Chef inquired. "One of her main campaigns has been on healthy eating."

"Hmm, that's a good point." Toussaint looked at his sheet of paper. "Maybe we'll change her selection to a vegetable dish."

Bobby frowned. "What vegetable starts with the letter *M*?"

Silence.

"Good point," Toussaint concluded.

Bobby continued. "Maybe we can have something like 'Michelle's Garden Medley,' a cold mixed vegetable dish topped with some type of red wine vinaigrette."

"Y'all work that out," Toussaint said, and moved on. "What about making it Malia's Mac-N-Cheese to go with Sasha's Potato Salad. Is that cool?"

Chef nodded. "Think so. And the Biden beans—"

"Let's add a little more heat to those baked beans," Bobby interjected.

"Mrs. Robinson Roast Beef Minis?" Chef looked at Toussaint. "Who's that?"

"Michelle's mother."

"Oh."

"We figured everybody wouldn't want pork and some won't want to eat heavy, which is why we've added these mini-sandwiches along with chicken and fish. And we need y'all to figure out some vegetarian offerings. This is a national audience, so we need to adjust."

The men talked for another fifteen minutes before Chef

and Bobby left the Livingston Corporation to return to the Buckhead Taste of Soul. "You've impressed a Livingston," Chef said as he navigated his SUV onto Peachtree and turned on the air conditioner. "We're in a real growth spurt now; there will be many opportunities for good cooks." He glanced over at Bobby. "Have you ever thought about going to chef school?"

"Not really."

"Have you thought about how you want to grow your career?"

"At some point I might open my own restaurant."

Chef nodded. "Been there done that and let me tell you, it's one of the hardest undertakings a man can do. You just may want to consider having a kingdom within a kingdom, perhaps running the kitchen of one of the new Taste of Soul locations. If I didn't have a wife and family bent on staying in the South, I'd think about going there myself."

Bobby listened intently to what Oliver was saying. This was his mentor, and Bobby valued everything that Chef had ever taught him. He had a point about owning one's own restaurant and how difficult that could be. Taste of Soul was already a well-known brand, where the success of new locations was almost assured. *Las Vegas. I wonder how Char would feel about moving there?* Bobby thought back to him and Chardonnay's wedding the previous year and how much fun they'd had on the Strip. Thankfully, they were back to having fun now. After he'd spent almost two weeks of couch sleeping, Chardonnay had forgiven him and let him back in the bedroom. The makeup sex had been incredible, and if Chardonnay hadn't been on the pill, Bobby would have sworn that they made a baby. He was still thanking his lucky stars for the woman he'd married. Of course, he'd known that she'd be his from the moment they'd met, and she'd introduced herself by basically cursing him out for taking "her" space in the first-come-first-served parking lot.

"Chef, you've given me something to think about," Bobby said as they pulled into the restaurant parking lot. "You wouldn't mind it if I relocated to Vegas? Because the restaurant would be losing an assistant manager as well as a cook."

"On the contrary, Bobby. I'd be quite proud, and know at least one place in Sin City where I could get a good meal."

"I'm going to talk to Chardonnay about it," Bobby said as they walked through the back door and into the kitchen. "She's off today, but I'm going to broach the subject with her just as soon as I get home."

Several hours later, Keisha entered Buckhead's Taste of Soul, and after a quick look around, walked directly to the cashier in the bar where takeout orders were placed. "Excuse me, is Bobby working today?"

The woman behind the counter, who looked to be no more than eighteen, maybe nineteen years old, responded with just a hint of attitude. "Yes, he's working."

"Well, could you go get him for me?"

The young woman gave Keisha the once-over. "Who should I say is looking for him?"

Thinking that the cashier might know Chardonnay and tell her about the visit, Keisha decided to stay incogNegro by saying the first name that came into her mind. "Marilyn." Ironically, Marilyn was her mother's name.

A minute or so later, Bobby walked up to the table where Keisha sat, wiping his hands on an apron while wearing a quizzical look on his face. "Marilyn?"

Keisha's smile was dazzling. "Hey, Bobby. Actually, my name is Keisha. I'm sorry to have fooled you, but I didn't like old girl's attitude and didn't want her all up in my business. Remember me?"

"Your face looks familiar." Bobby's face still showed he was slightly confused.

"I met you last year when me and Chardonnay went to a club. You watched my boys, Dorian and Antwan."

"Oh, yeah, Keisha. I remember you now. What's poppin'?" He looked at her midsection. "Besides your stomach."

"Ha! A few more months and I'll be back flat as a pancake."

"Well, congratulations."

"Thank you."

"Ain't seen you here in a while; I didn't think you still lived in Atlanta."

"I was gone for a minute. Had some business to handle back in LA. But I'm back now."

Bobby's eyes narrowed as more facts were recalled. "Right . . . that dude, Q, he's your brother."

Keisha looked up and saw the young woman behind the counter staring so hard that she could count the teeth in Keisha's mouth. "Look, Bobby, I need to talk to you. Can we step outside for a minute?"

Bobby looked at his watch. "I'm working, Keisha. What's this about?"

"It's important and it won't take long." When it looked like Bobby might turn her down, she added, "It's about your family."

"What about my family?" Bobby asked, his tone low and defensive.

"Just a couple minutes, Bobby, that's all I need. And I promise that it will be worth your time."

Bobby looked skeptical but still nodded his head in the direction of a side door. "I'll meet you out in the parking lot in five minutes."

Four minutes and fifty-five seconds later, Bobby stepped out into the restaurant's parking lot. He looked around and spotted Keisha in a sporty Lexus, waving him over. In the time until his break, he'd tried to reach Chardonnay, and then remembered that she was getting a mani / pedi. He also remembered a month or so ago when Chardonnay mentioned running into Keisha at the store, and that their exchange hadn't been too pleasant. So whatever baby girl had to say, it had better not be something about his wife. If so, Bobby knew that he'd shut her down real fast. He walked over to Keisha's sporty luxury car and got in. "Doing all right for yourself, I see."

"I can't complain. How's the restaurant business?"

"Look, I didn't come out here to talk about food. What is this about my family?"

Keisha reached into her purse and handed Bobby a picture. Bobby looked at the photo briefly before asking, "How did you get a picture of my son?"

Keisha sighed and looked away for a moment. "I don't even know if I should be doing this."

"Doing what? Look, I don't know what type of game you're playing, but last time I heard, you and my girl weren't too friendly, so I'm going to ask you again. How in the hell did you get a picture of Bobby?"

Keisha turned and looked Bobby in the eye. "That isn't a picture of your son, Bobby. That's a picture of my brother when he was about your son's age."

A look of confusion and disbelief came over Bobby's face. "Girl, I know you're trippin'," he said, reaching for the door handle.

"I'm not lying!" Keisha said, grabbing Bobby's arm before he could exit. "When I ran into Chardonnay and saw her youngest child, I felt that he looked so familiar to me, but I couldn't figure out why. Then I saw this picture of my brother and I knew why that boy felt like family. Chardonnay's youngest son is not your baby, Bobby. Because that picture you're holding is one of my brother, when he was about a year old. That right there is a picture of Q."

43

Shyla admired the architecture of the Georgia state capital as she walked toward it. At times like these, she was reminded of the state's rich and controversial history and the city's legacy in the annals of civil rights. Today, she felt a part of this history and attached to this legacy, partly because she was entering the halls that had been walked by notables such as Julian Bond, Andrew Young, Joseph Lowery, Vernon Jordan, Dr. King, and so many others, and partly because this was the first time—aside from the 2008 elections—that she'd ever been politically involved. In designing the marketing piece for Jon's private party catering to the elite of Atlanta, which would coincide with the national Democratic gathering on the third of July, she'd researched the political history of Atlanta and the general history of Georgia and had been shocked at how little she knew. Obviously when she'd taken high school history, she'd been flirting instead of listening. How else could she have missed the fact that the place she called home had been one of the original Confederate states and the last to be restored into the Union? Or that there had been four other state capitals before Atlanta and a Georgia gold rush, second only to the one out west? These thoughts accompanied her all the way to

Congressman Jon Abernathy's office but fled as soon as she turned the corner and saw that chocolate, dimpled smile.

"Hello, Jon," she said, offering up a dazzling beam of her own.

"Good afternoon, Shyla," Jon replied, giving her a light kiss. Shyla moved in for a longer hug, which after a moment, Jon politely ended. "I'm excited to see the finished product." He led them over to a round table. "Let's see what you've got. Oh, can I offer you something to drink?"

"No thank you, Jon, I'm fine."

For the next twenty minutes, Jon saw and approved linen invitations, place cards, guest take-home gifts, and a promotional piece that was going into the *Atlanta Inquirer.* "Excellent work," Jon said when they'd concluded. "There's a reason you came highly recommended."

"Oh?"

"Yes. Joyce Witherspoon had nothing but good things to say about your work."

"I'm glad you're pleased." Shyla placed the items into her briefcase. "May I switch the subject to something of a more personal nature?"

"You may, but I may or may not respond." This straightforward answer was tempered with a smile.

"Do you have a date for your party?"

"Yes," was Jon's immediate reply.

Shyla bit back a sigh. "Is it Divine?"

A pause and then, "Yes, we've begun dating."

"Good for you."

"Yes, she is good for me."

"This happened rather fast, didn't it? Seeing how you met her less than a month ago?"

"When it's right, Shyla, things don't have to take long. I'll forever be in Jeff Livingston's debt for that introduction."

Moments later, Shyla headed back down the hallowed halls

of the Georgia state capital. This time she thought nothing of civil rights, gold rushes, capital cities, or the Confederacy. She was thinking of the Livingstons and how it seemed all the heartache she'd experienced over the past several years was somehow tied to them: being fired from her job, overlooked by Toussaint, and now, upstaged by Jefferson with his friend Divine.

"I am so tired of them," she said through clenched teeth as she threw her briefcase in the backseat and started her engine. *What are you going to do about it?* She thought about the upcoming party, an event where their food would be front and center and one that all of them would probably attend. A plan began hatching in her mind, gaining momentum the more she thought about it. By the time she reached the advertising company after her two-hour lunch, she had a foolproof plan in place. She also had a plan for her soon-to-be resignation. She planned to work Jon's event in a way to secure enough clients to resign from a dead-end job she'd never enjoyed. Just thinking about a new life, and her new plan for her nemeses, made her almost dance into the office. It was just too perfect. Let the fireworks begin!

The explosions started just after midnight, when Chardonnay walked in from an evening with Zoe to find Bobby camped out on the couch.

"What are you doing out here?" she asked by way of greeting.

"What's it look like?" Bobby responded before turning his face to the cloth.

"Damn," Chardonnay mumbled. "Who pissed in your cornflakes?" She shook her head as she walked to their bedroom, stopping to throw a last bit of sarcasm over her shoulder. "If you want some of this in the next forty-eight hours, you've got about forty-eight seconds to get in here."

Chardonnay tossed and turned, and when more than an hour passed without hearing a peep from the living room, she figured Bobby had fallen asleep. That may have been why she jumped when he soundlessly walked to the bedroom door before demanding, "Is little Bobby mine?"

"Boy, you scared me. I thought you were asleep."

"I asked you a question and I want an answer. Is Bobby my child or not?"

Not sure where this was coming from, Chardonnay chose to continue being her cynical self. "You have three children, Bobby. Have you forgotten Yak and Ray-Ray?"

Even though the room was fairly large, Bobby reached the bed in two seconds. "I'm going to ask you one more time. Is Bobby my child?"

"Where is this coming from?"

"Uh-huh. I'm going to take that as a no."

When Chardonnay followed Bobby into the closet, she saw him shoving jeans, shirts, and underwear into a duffel bag. "What is the matter with you, Bobby? Where are you going?"

"Away from here."

"Because I wouldn't answer a silly question? You know he's yours, Bobby, damn."

"Mama's baby, daddy's maybe, that's what my grandmother always said."

"Where is this coming from all of a sudden?" The light-bulb flashed on just before she heard his answer.

"Keisha."

"Oh, please, how are you going to trust that skank? She'll say anything to come between us."

Bobby walked over to another bag, the one he always took to work. He reached down and pulled out a picture. "What about this? What is this picture saying?"

Chardonnay looked at the picture and then at Bobby. "I don't know!"

"Look at it closely. What is it saying, Chardonnay?"

"It's just a picture of Bobby. He's—"

"Wrong!" Bobby yelled so loud that Chardonnay jumped. "This is not a picture of Bobby. This is a picture of the man you played me with—Quintin Bright!"

Chardonnay reached up and slowly took the picture. *Dang, girl, you're going to have to think fast.* "I don't care what Keisha told you, Bobby. I should know my own child and I'm telling you without a shadow of a doubt that this is your son!"

Bobby zipped up the duffel bag, reached for his work bag, and walked into the bathroom. Soon, toothpaste, deodorant, razors, and shaving cream were being thrown into it.

"She's just trying to start something, Bobby. She's mad because I don't want to be friends with her and because I told her I didn't want to see Q." Bobby gave Chardonnay a skeptical look. "I did, Bobby, ask her. She told me Q was out and that he might want to see me, and I told her that anything he and I had was over!"

"Yeah, well obviously it ain't over till it's over."

"Bobby, she's lying!"

Bobby whirled around. "You know, I thought this might be your argument, thought that you'd be your usual stubborn self and deny the truth even when it's staring me in the face. So I got on the phone with her mother." Chardonnay's eyes widened. "Yeah, talked to Marilyn in LA. Then I talked to some cousin or something, a dude named Rico, and I asked him to e-mail me a couple more pictures. I told Keisha I had to see more proof before I believed her. And they did. They sent the pictures. You might be confused about it, but I'm as clear right now as I will be when the DNA test comes back."

"You're really going to get Bobby tested?"

"If you're so sure he's mine, why do you have a problem with that?"

"Because, uh, because it doesn't make sense. That shit costs money, Bobby!"

"Better to pay several hundred now than to pay several thousand over eighteen years for a child that ain't mine." Bobby grabbed his keys and headed for the door.

Chardonnay followed behind him, totally out of lies, excuses, and bravado. For all of the ways she disrespected him—yelling, cursing, calling him out of his name—the truth of the matter was she'd never felt so secure in all of her life as she now did as Mrs. Bobby Wilson. He'd stayed when others had left her, accepted her for the crazy woman that she was, took her shit and raised children that were not his. In short, he'd loved her unconditionally. And now that love was walking out the door.

"Bobby, don't leave!"

"I've got to, Char." He walked out the door and to his car.

"Please," she pleaded with tears running down her face. "The kids need you. I need you!"

Bobby reached his car door. "Not too long ago you were ready to kick me out because of doing some shit and keeping it from you. I asked you to forgive me, and then I asked if you had any secrets. You told me no."

"I never said that, Bobby. I just never answered the question."

Bobby took a long look at Chardonnay and opened the car door. "I guess that's all right, ain't it. Because it looks like I've got my answer now."

She stood there until his taillights disappeared around the corner. And then she walked into her house, sat on the couch, and released tears that had been stored up for a very long time.

44

Had Bobby been less angry, he would have noticed the car parked in Jon's driveway. As it was, he stormed up to the front door, rang the bell, and stomped past him as soon as he opened the door. They both talked at once.

"Bobby, hold on!"

"Man, you're not going to believe—" Bobby turned the corner and stopped short—partly from the disbelief that someone so beautiful was in Jon's living room and partly from the fact that this beautiful person was female. "Oh, man, I'm sorry. I didn't know . . ." He turned to walk out the door.

Divine reached for her purse and hurried off the couch.

"Wait, don't go!" Jon had returned to the living room and walked toward Divine. "Baby, I—"

"It's okay," Divine said, placing a hand on Jon's arm. "I can go." Her long legs quickly ate up the distance to the hallway and soon she was in the foyer.

"But I don't want you to."

"I'm not angry," Divine said softly as she caressed Jon's cheek. "I know you had a life before I came into it. He seems very upset," she continued, tilting her head toward the living room. "I think he really needs you."

"Baby, please. Can you just wait for me in another room?

The theater or the great room or"—Jon took a step closer—
"the bedroom?"

Divine smiled. "Do you really want me to stay?"

"More than anything."

Divine took a deep breath. "Okay. I think I'll go watch a
movie on that monster TV."

Jon brushed her lips with his. That he had to tilt his head
slightly to do so mattered not in the least. He'd always loved
tall women and that this one came with a penis was like hitting
the mother lode. He waited until Divine had turned the corner to the theater and then walked back into the living room.

Bobby held up his hands. "I'm sorry, Jon."

"No need to apologize. You look like you could use a
friend, and a drink." Jon walked over to the bar, made a double
Hennessy and Coke, and gave it to Bobby. Bobby drank half
the glass and gave it back to Jon. Jon cocked his brow but said
nothing, just refilled the glass to the top, mostly with Hennessy. He fixed himself a Seven and Seven. "Let's sit down."
They did. "What happened?"

"Chardonnay lied to me."

"About what?"

Silence and then, "Bobby Bicardi is not my child."

More silence and then, "Damn."

"You heard of that dude Quintin Bright, the one on the
news last year for stealing from the Livingstons?" Jon nodded.
"He's the baby daddy."

"Are you sure about this?"

"Ninety-five percent." He told Jon about the visit with
Keisha, and the picture. "Last month when I came clean to
Chardonnay about being unfaithful, I asked her if there was
anything she was hiding from me. All that shit she said to me
about what I had done to her and how she felt . . . and look at
what she was hiding!"

Jon put a hand on Bobby's shoulder. "I'm sorry, Bobby."

Bobby made a sound of disgust. "Yeah, me too."

For a moment, the men drank in silence and then Jon asked, "What are you going to do?"

Bobby stood and paced the room. "I don't know. She came to me with two kids, and I took them into my heart, am raising them like they're my own. Then she goes and gets pregnant again and tells me it's mine when she knew there was a chance that it might not be. That shit's messed up."

"Maybe she truly believed that you were the father."

"She truly hoped I was."

"Do you love the child?"

Bobby whirled around. "What kind of question is that? Of course I do!"

Jon noted the two tears that streamed down Bobby's face. "Then maybe biology doesn't matter. Maybe it's what's in your heart."

"I gave that woman my heart and all she does is stomp on it. How can I ever trust her again? If she'll lie about this, she'll lie about anything."

The men talked a while longer. Bobby drained his drink and stood. "I should go, man. I've interrupted your evening as it is."

"It's okay, Bobby. That's what friends are for."

"Speaking of"—Bobby lowered his voice—"is that for real in there? You changing lanes?"

Jon smiled. "I've changed lanes," he corrected. "It's the real deal, Bobby. I'm in love."

"Here, Char. It's water and an Advil. It'll make you feel better. Here, sit up and take this." Zoe looked at the lump on the couch, her friend curled up in pretty much the same fetal position she'd found her in an hour ago. She placed the water and pill on the table, sat on the couch, and placed her hand on her friend's arm. At this point, she didn't know what to say. All she'd known when Chardonnay called her, talking incoherently, was that she had to come over ASAP. She'd thought her friend was drunk or high and upon entering the house was surprised to find that she was neither. Chardonnay was stone-cold sober and more upset than Zoe had ever seen her. Even now her eyes were puffy from crying, and after revealing that Bobby had left her, she'd said nothing.

Zoe looked at her watch: 2:45. She had to be at work in just over five hours and attend a meeting of the marketing department the very first thing. "Char," she said, this time rubbing her friend's back, "are you sure you don't want to talk about it? At least tell me what happened?"

Chardonnay sniffed loudly, then turned over and sat up. Fresh tears filled her eyes and ran down her face. Zoe reached for a Kleenex and gave it to her. Chardonnay blew her nose, pulled her knees up to her chest, and wrapped her arms around them. "He left me."

Zoe sat back on the couch. "I got that part. What happened?" She watched Chardonnay, who was quiet for so long that Zoe didn't think she'd get an answer.

"He found out that Bobby Bicardi isn't his baby."

Whoa! Zoe's mind went back a couple months to the conversation they'd had in the restaurant bathroom. Then, Chardonnay had told her of the possibility that her youngest might not be Bobby's child, to which Zoe had responded, "oh...my...God." Now, it looked like an intervention by a Higher Power was the only way this situation could be fixed. "Who's baby is it?"

Chardonnay sighed as more tears fell. "Q"

The gasp came out before Zoe could stop it. "Oh, no, Chardonnay."

Chardonnay wiped her eyes, wondering just how many tears one's body could hold, since she'd swear she'd cried a couple gallons of them. She'd cried for everything: being molested as a child, her lost childhood, her hardened mother, the horde of men, but most of all she cried about not realizing until now that she'd never appreciated the good man she had.

"How'd he find out?"

"That bitch Keisha," Chardonnay said softly. "I can't even blame her, though, not really. If it hadn't been true, it wouldn't have been an issue." She paused. "I should have told him, Zoe. I should have told him when I first started to suspect."

"When was that?"

"When Bicardi was about two months old. I was changing him and he made this face and it instantly reminded me of Q. Scared me half to death, and I dismissed the thought immediately. Bobby was so proud to have a son, and I'd never had a father around my newborns, so I just rolled with it and hoped for the best." Chardonnay stopped and blew her nose again. "Then this one time, when he was about six months old, Bobby was feeding him and then Bicardi fell asleep. Bobby just sat there, holding him and staring. He finally said, 'I guess he looks like you, huh, because he don't look like me.' I remember walking over, showing him how their noses looked kinda alike, tried to find some similarities in the forehead. And then Little Man has a big dick like his daddy, and you know Bobby's packin', so he didn't have a problem believing that was from him. I should have told him then. At least I should have warned him of the possibility and let him decide what to do."

"Don't beat yourself up, Char. You did what you thought best at the time."

"I know better. I watch *Maury*. Sooner or later that shit always comes out."

"What are you going to do?"

Chardonnay shrugged. "What can I do? I got three kids to raise, mouths to feed, and nobody to help me." She thought she'd shed them all, but no, here came some more tears. "I'm going to have to get a big-time hustle going."

"Chardonnay, please don't start scheming again, especially against your employers."

"What do you give a damn what I do to them? That don't affect you!"

"But in the long run, it will affect you."

"Them fools owe me."

"I know you don't want to hear this, but it isn't like it's the first time that I've said it. I was there, Chardonnay: when you were dealing with Q, after you found Adam in the parking lot, when you told the Livingstons you'd help bring Q in, when you tried to blackmail Bianca, and when you sold her story to the *Atlanta Inquirer*. Had you not done that, they may have given you more money. You've got enough to deal with without adding more stress to your life. I'm here for you to help in any way that I can. But what goes around comes around, and the more dirt we do, the more dirt comes back at us."

"Oh, so this is just my dirt coming back. Is that what you're saying?"

"No, Chardonnay. This is fucked up; that's what this is. But you can get through this. And I'm going to stay by your side and make sure that happens."

Chardonnay reached over for the water and the pill. "Man, crying is hard work! I haven't had a headache like this since I got hungover."

"It was probably good for you to cry. I don't think I've ever seen you do that before, not even when you were in labor with Bicardi."

Chardonnay took the pill, and then her hand stopped midway between her mouth and the table. She slowly put the glass down on the table. "You know what else I don't think I've ever done, Zoe?"

"What?"

"I don't remember ever telling Bobby that I loved him."

"C'mon now, Char. I'm sure you've told him that."

"If I have," Chardonnay responded, her eyes now bone dry, "I don't remember the last time."

"Then you'll have to do that the next time you see him."

Chardonnay nodded, her eyes filling once again. "Yeah, I will."

45

Adam sat in his office, processing the call he'd just received. There was a plethora of emotions swirling inside him. He didn't know which one to give the lead, so he called backup. "Ace, Adam."

"What's going on, Twin?"

"I just got off the phone with Sterling."

Ace, who'd been over by the sitting area in his office practicing his golf swing, put down the iron and sat on a love seat. "Talk to me."

"He's leaving for Texas, family emergency."

"Is everything all right?"

"He didn't go into detail. Just said that he didn't know how long he'd be there."

"I hope it's nothing too serious."

"Me too. But that's not all he said."

"I'm listening."

"He suggested we suspend the fire investigation."

A pause and then, "Why?"

"Said that right now any trail there was is cold and that looking for the lone possible suspect—the faceless man with the tattoo—has been like looking for a needle in a haystack.

He's checked out several people around Quintin, Cooper, all of the TOSTS and West Coast applicants, even Shyla and Chardonnay, and he's coming up empty. He said that maybe some time away will offer all of us a fresh perspective."

"He said that, huh?"

"Yep."

Ace stroked his freshly trimmed goatee. "Maybe he's right." And then, "How do you feel about that, Adam?"

"That's what I've been sitting here trying to figure out. A part of me wants to nail that son of a bitch Quintin if he had anything to do with it, and another part of me feels like that man has been taking up way too much space in my life. He shot me, and I want him to pay. But maybe that payback is going to come in a way I don't realize and can't orchestrate."

"We can always hire another investigator."

"No, Sterling is the only one I'd trust with this."

"I agree."

The men were silent awhile, each wrapped up in thoughts of all the dramas that had surrounded the man named Quintin Bright.

Ace broke the silence. "Let me conference in baby girl, get her opinion on this. After all, it's her establishment that was bombed."

"Good idea."

Ace dialed Bianca's direct line. "Baby girl, it's Ace."

"Hey, Daddy."

"Your uncle is on the line as well."

"Oh, hello, Uncle Adam."

"Hello, Bianca."

"How's everything going out there?" Ace asked.

"Finally, things are on a roll. In fact, I just came back from a walk-through of what the contractor has done so far. I'm impressed, Ace. The work has gone faster than anyone dared hoped. We don't think we'll get our first wish and open on the

Fourth of July, but we will definitely be back in business by August."

"That's very good news, daughter, very good news. I'm proud of how you've handled this whole thing."

"I've had good teachers."

"I guess you do come from pretty good stock."

"You know how much I love you guys, but my day is crazy. What can I do for you?"

"Adam, you want to tell her?"

"Sure. I talked with Sterling, Bianca, and he wants to suspend the fire investigation."

"Why?"

Adam relayed what he'd told Ace moments before and what he and Ace had concluded. "But this happened to your baby, Bianca, and we wanted to know how you felt about this and what you want to do."

There was only a brief hesitation before Bianca responded. "Honestly, you guys, I'm ready to put the whole thing behind me. The crazy realization is that this has been a blessing in disguise. Because of the exposure it caused, we have a slew of requests for private parties and a couple A-list actors and platinum recording artists have asked us to cater their events."

"A catering arm for the TOSTS establishment? Can you handle all of that?"

"Not by myself. But Xavier has offered to purchase a separate building just for the catering business and to finance all of the personnel."

"That's a pretty generous brothah you married."

"Don't get it twisted, Ace. He's also shrewd. He'll be a partner in the business. Do you guys have a problem with that?"

"I don't," Adam answered. "But Toussaint, Malcolm, or some of the others might have a different opinion. This is something for the whole family to discuss. It could turn into a pretty big deal."

"Speaking of big deals," Bianca continued, "I received an invitation from Jon Abernathy for some swanky party he's having on the Fourth of July."

"Are you coming?"

"Yes. Xavier and I have been working nonstop. We're actually planning to spend four or five days down there. He doesn't really know Mom Etta or GrandMar, and I'd really like them to get to know him."

"Well, you know there's always a big shindig at the estate on the Fourth of July," Ace said. "Jon's party will be no excuse for us not to show up in Lithonia."

"His party doesn't start until nine," Bianca responded. "So we'll be fine."

"All right, then, baby girl. We'll see you in about three weeks."

"See you in three! Bye, Ace. Bye, Uncle."

"Adam, stay on the line." Once Bianca had hung up, Ace continued. "I meant to ask you this earlier. You and Can, y'all okay?"

"We're fine," Adam responded without hesitation. "Why do you ask?"

"The other day I was talking to Mama, and she said she had a feeling that something was going on with y'all."

"Ha! Mama's something else. Me and Can have been placing bets, wondering how long it would take Daddy to talk with her about what I shared, in confidence mind you, and then wondering which one of y'all she'd try and pump for information. Dang! Now I've got to take Candace to a five-star restaurant. That was her prize if she won the bet."

Ace cracked up. "Mama's a trip. But you got to love her."

"With my whole heart," Adam said, laughing as well. "That's my girl."

46

Bobby shoved his apron into the dirty clothes bin at the back of the restaurant. He was dog tired and it couldn't have felt better. Since leaving Chardonnay, he'd buried himself in work and tried to tell himself that it was what he wanted, that Chardonnay didn't deserve him and that it was saving him thousands not to raise someone else's kids. He'd taken double shifts and thrown himself into the planning for the holiday events. His hard work had not gone unnoticed, and Toussaint had all but told him that when the time came, if he wanted to head up the Vegas kitchen, the job was his. Bobby told him that he'd love the chance. There were almost two thousand miles between Atlanta and Vegas. He knew. He'd checked. It would probably take a million miles and even more years before he'd get Chardonnay out of his system. But a new work environment in a new city, two thousand miles away was a good start.

He locked the back door and headed to his car in the parking lot. When he saw the person leaning on his car, he didn't stop, just walked toward the inevitable. "I was going to call you."

"Yeah, right," Zoe said. "And Shaq is three foot five."

"Get in," Bobby said, unlocking his car. "I'm exhausted and need to sit down."

Once they got in the car, Zoe looked closely at him. She noted the tight lips and tired eyes. "How are you doing, Bobby?" she asked with genuine concern.

She was surprised at his honest answer. "I've been better."

"Chardonnay is beside herself. She misses you so much."

"Why doesn't she go to Q for company? I heard he's out."

"Says you won't talk to her here at work or take her calls."

"She should thank me for that. Chardonnay don't want to hear what I've got to tell her."

Zoe turned and stared out at the dark, star-filled night. She had two friends who were hurting like hell. And she didn't know what if anything she could do about it. "I'm so sorry about what happened, Bobby. I know how much you love little Bobby, how much you love all of your children."

"Well, you know what they say. What's love got to do with it?"

"It had to have been horrible to find out."

"I've never hurt so much. It was like somebody reached into my chest and ripped out my heart."

"I'm sorry," Zoe whispered. "Where are you staying?"

"In one of Chef's empty apartments. You know his wife does real estate. They had a studio that hadn't been rented. Said I could have it as long as I wanted."

"That's good. Look, I know that marriage is the last thing you want to think about, but I've got a wedding coming up next week. I want you there."

"Look, Zoe—"

"No, Bobby, you look. I'm getting ready to experience one of the most important days of my life, and I want you there for me, like I've been there for you and Chardonnay. I'm really sorry for what you're going through now, but this is my bridezilla moment and I just can't give a damn. I need a maid of honor and Drake needs some chocolate on his side of the aisle." This elicited the tiniest of smiles. "You and Chardonnay can start hating each other again on July fifth, but on my wedding day? I need smiles and support, and not necessarily in that order."

"You sure you're ready to get married?" Bobby asked. "Do you know Drake as well as you think you do?"

"I've never been surer of anything in my life," Zoe responded. "And I'm not saying that while wearing rose-colored glasses. He and I have worked through some pretty crazy issues, and I'm sure we'll work through some more. One of the things we've both agreed is essential for our marriage to work is honesty. Full disclosure. Another thing is laughter. He and I don't ever want to forget to have fun." Zoe reached over and placed a hand on Bobby's arm. "I was there in the beginning with you and Chardonnay," she said softly. "I know how much love was there and how much probably still is. I can't tell you what to do, or what you should do. I'd totally understand it if you divorce Chardonnay and not look back. She's my best friend and I'll be the first to tell anybody that that chick is a piece of work! However, she'll not only have your back, but she'll also give you the shirt off of hers. She might not be able to say I love you, but she'll show it to you in the craziest of ways, ways that make you warm and fuzzy and maybe even want to kick her ass at the same time." Zoe was quiet a moment. "Remember y'all's engagement? She told me about how you put the ring in her dessert and she thought it was a roach. Was yelling about lawsuits and beat downs while dining in an upscale restaurant?"

Bobby chuckled. "That girl is crazy, I'll give her that."

"At one time you gave her a lot more, Bobby. And no matter what happens, I want you to know that she finally gets it. It took her a while because she'd never seen it before, didn't know what one looked like. But Chardonnay loves your dirty drawers, boy, and she finally realizes that you're a good man."

"I'm one of the best ones, matter of fact."

"I'm glad you said one of, since Drake is the other."

"Oh, really? White boy putting it down like that?"

"Baby boy knows how to make it do what it do."

"Watch out dere now!"

"Ha!" She sobered. "So we'll see you at the rehearsal dinner and then at the wedding?"

Bobby nodded. "You've always been a good friend to me, Zoe, and Drake is cool too," he said, looking at her with affection in his eyes. "I'll be there."

47

Two acres of private property just outside Atlanta had been transformed into a fairyland. Miniature white lights lined cork walkways that led to three large tents. Thousands of flowers added color and fragrance amid draped silks, crystal chandeliers, and a full ninety-piece orchestra. Almost five thousand people kept hundreds of waiters busy serving loads of champagne and signature martinis. And amid it all, Joyce Witherspoon was the not-so-silent conductor, barking orders with a smile and, when she passed them, greeting many of the guests by name. She was more than pleased with the event, and with her new attitude regarding the Livingstons. She'd talked with Jefferson and to his surprise, it was she who suggested that business be their only connection. Right now she was content to grow her business, and if one was interested, let a man chase her for a change.

"You pulled it off," Toussaint said as he and Alexis lifted flutes from a passing waiter. "This is spectacular, Joyce."

"Thanks, but you haven't seen spectacular," Joyce replied. "There's enough TNT in the fireworks we've planned to send a rocket to the moon."

Alexis laughed. "We can't wait."

"You two look amazing. Mix, mingle, and be sure to hit all the buffet tables. The food is off the chain!"

Alexis watched Joyce interact with guests as she directed her workers. "I don't know the last time I've been around so many people," Alexis said, glad to be comfortably dressed in an ankle-length sundress and flats. The stark-white fabric highlighted her dark brown skin, and her locs were piled high on top of her head, giving the illusion that she was a couple inches taller than her true five foot five. "I'm having a ball, honey."

Toussaint reached for a barbequed pulled pork pastry, one of many dishes added to their original menu once the numbers climbed so high. "Girl, you need to get out more."

"Forget you, man!" Alexis said with a laugh. Her eyes twinkled as she gazed at her handsome husband's lips. They looked good enough to kiss . . . which she did.

"All right, lovebirds, break it up!"

"Auntie!" Toussaint said, releasing his hold on Alexis to give Diane a hug. "Ace! We didn't know if we'd see anyone else we knew in this crowd."

"It's quite the spread, isn't it?" Ace asked. And then always the businessman, he added, "I took a look back there in the kitchen. We're making a killing this weekend!"

"Really, darling, must we always think in dollars and cents?"

Ace looked at his nephew. "Is there another way?"

The men gave each other dap while the women rolled their eyes.

"I love that dress, Diane," Alexis said. "It looks dressy and comfortable at the same time."

"I like yours too. Although I stopped being able to wear something that fitting about forty pounds ago."

"You are not overweight, sistah," Alexis countered. "You look good."

Ace looked across the lawn and his eyes narrowed. "There

goes that wimpy Riley son of a bitch." The others turned to look. "And who's that he's with?"

Toussaint looked at the tall, attractive woman walking with Cooper. "I don't know. Last time I saw him, he was with Keisha Miller."

"Oh, Lord, don't get my blood pressure riled." Diane fanned her face with her hand. "I'm trying to relax and have a good time today."

Across the lawn, Cooper was trying to have a good time as well, though his heart wasn't in it. He'd acquiesced to his mother's wishes and agreed not to bring Keisha to this event. She was showing, Evelyn had admonished, and said it simply wouldn't look good for him to squire around an unmarried pregnant woman, even if the baby was his. *Just one more week,* Cooper thought as he walked alongside Dr. Hopkins and nodded at acquaintances. He'd researched and found a noninvasive DNA test for unborn children. They were having the test next week, and if indeed he was the father of Keisha's baby, then they'd either be married in the judge's chambers or in Las Vegas with a black Elvis or drag queen as a witness. At this point, Cooper honestly didn't care which.

"Cooper!" Michelle tapped him playfully on the arm.

"I'm sorry, dear."

"You are a million miles away and haven't heard a word I'm saying."

"I'm sorry, Michelle." He stopped and turned to face her. "What did you say?"

"I said that my colleague had a cancellation in his schedule. He can perform the test tomorrow if you'd like."

"What? On a holiday?"

"Doctors don't get holidays," Michelle said playfully. "At least this one doesn't take them. His wife is also a doctor and is currently doing a Doctors Without Borders run. He's missing her like crazy and working to pass the time."

Cooper was not one to show emotion, but had he been that kind of guy, he would have cried like a bitch right now. Ever since Keisha came into his life, things had been stressful. A large part of this was due to his mother, who he felt had the best of intentions. He also knew that the road to hell was paved with those. Through conversations with the doctor, he'd learned that Evelyn had basically solicited her to try and break up him and Keisha. Being single and searching, Michelle had jumped at the chance to perhaps find love. But after learning about the baby and making the decision to stay with Keisha even if it meant ruining the Riley tableau, he'd shared this news with Michelle who, woman of character that she was, had agreed was the right decision. But out of Evelyn's ministrations had come a great friendship and, ironically, the contact that might place Keisha directly *into* Evelyn's family, instead of out of it.

As if talking her up, Cooper looked up to see his mother subtly waving with a white, lacy hanky. "Come on, dear," Cooper said to Michelle, behind a smile. "Let's let Mother enjoy the last vestiges of her dream that you might actually become her daughter-in-law."

From a partially hidden area near the kitchen, a suspicious-looking person wearing a hat, black slacks, and a stark-white jacket much like the kitchen help, watched the goings-on of the city's elite: Toussaint and Alexis Livingston; Judge and Evelyn Riley and their son, Cooper Jr.; and Congressman Jon Abernathy with an attractive date. The stranger had even recognized the assistant manager of Buckhead's Taste of Soul and then, after seeing that the sous-chef was also there, deduced that the appearance was work related. And speaking of work, the lurker realized it was time to get back to it. There was a job that had to be done and not much time to do it.

After a quick look around, the hat-wearing culprit slipped into the temporary kitchen, easily blending with the waitstaff and line cooks scurrying about. Head down, focus intent, the "worker" walked past the front kitchen to another area where large cauldrons of baked beans, greens, black-eyed peas, and other Southern delicacies bubbled and where long racks of succulent ribs waited to be sauced. Working quickly, whoever this was moved from one end of the room to the other before ducking out of the kitchen and being quickly enveloped in the colorful crowd.

At the exact same time the criminal was making an exit from the event, Joyce was returning from VIP parking, where she'd escorted a potential client as they were leaving the gala. Since founding her company, she'd been trying to snag the annual Jack and Jill event and thanks to being able to introduce the local president to Michelle Obama, her catering of next year's event was assured. She stopped and looked around: at the beautiful day, the tents, the crowd and all of the cars. *You did it, Joyce Witherspoon. You're doing the damn thing!* With a laugh, she again started toward the back tents where the kitchens were housed. That's when she saw something very strange: a worker hurrying away from the area, looking over his shoulder as he ran. Instinctively, Joyce hid behind an SUV, out of sight, but still able to see the person obviously trying to make a quick escape. *Wait, that's not a man, that's a woman. WTH?* Her heart began beating faster as the person made their way to where Joyce was crouched behind the vehicle. *What's someone from the waitstaff doing parked in VIP?* Just as Joyce's knees began protesting their bent position, the woman reached a luxury vehicle and, having already remotely popped the lock, hurriedly peeled off the white jacket before jumping inside the car. Joyce rose up just enough to see through the SUV's glass. Her jaw went slack as the woman took off the hat, snatched off a blond wig, and slammed the hat back down on her head. Looking around once more, she started the car and peeled out of the parking lot like a bat out of hell.

Joyce waited until the car had turned a corner, then slowly came from behind the SUV that had served as her hiding place. Her brows creased in confusion as she tried to wrap her mind around what she'd just seen. *Why was Shyla Martin dressed like the help, and why did she leave in such a hurry?* Joyce's phone beeped with one of the assistants asking for her location. She'd barely answered that question before her second cell phone rang with the program's emcee on the line. Before long, Joyce was back in the thick of making sure her event was a success. But in time, Joyce would come to realize exactly why Shyla had been rolling incog-Negro and why she'd been in such a hurry to leave the scene.

48

It was a holiday, the Fourth of July, but that didn't change Marietta's routine. She still woke up just before six, rolled onto her back, and spent five or ten minutes planning out her day and then slipped out of bed to put on a pot of coffee. Of course, being a family-gathering holiday and all, she was also going to finish the mountain of cooking she'd been doing the last three days. For years her children had tried to talk her out of putting together such a mountainous spread, suggesting that it be catered by one of the restaurants. But the most Marietta could ever allow was what had happened last year: that the women split the menu and prepared various dishes between the four of them. And nothing against her daughters-in-law and their son's wives, but if Marietta ever said any of them cooked as good as her or better, she'd be lying. Especially if it were Malcolm's wife, Victoria, that she was talking about. She was pretty enough, and came from a good family. But Marietta sometimes still wondered how that child got into their family. How are you going to be a Livingston woman when you can't boil an egg?

Humming as she walked into the kitchen, Marietta drew back the blinds and welcomed the day. Within fifteen minutes, the smell of freshly brewing coffee and baking homemade biscuits filled the room. She pulled out eggs and a slab of salt pork for breakfast, and then satisfied that this light fare would be enough, considering the copious amounts of goodness that they'd consume later, she walked over to the wall-mounted television and turned it on to local news. She saw the words *breaking news* but never broke stride as she turned to put on the meat. "According to those folk, news is always breaking," she mumbled and then, "Good morning, partner? Ready for your coffee?"

Marcus grunted, which was the most talking he ever did before his first few sips of coffee. He ambled over to the table and plopped down with a thud. Marietta chuckled. This was the morning Marcus she'd known for over fifty years. She still remembers a conversation they'd had about a week into their new marriage.

"Do you always wake up like this?"

"Like what?"

"Happy."

Marietta had shrugged. "I guess so."

"Then something is wrong with you, woman. Hasn't anything even happened yet for you to be happy about!"

After Marietta had set down his coffee and he'd taken a few sips, Marcus came alive. "How late was it that those kids popped off those datgum firecrackers?"

"Last time I looked at the clock, it was a little before one."

"And you're still over there humming?" Marcus shook his head and took another sip of Joe. "What's that going on there?" he asked with a nod to the television. There was a scene of a large crowd, where several people on stretchers were being carried to waiting ambulances . . .

Marietta could have said, "I don't know, baby. Since I'm over here slicing salt pork and beating eggs, why don't you get off your hind end, turn up the television, and find out?" But that wasn't how this Southern belle got down. So she said, "Beats me, honey." She walked over to where the remote lay on the counter. "Let's see what they're talking about."

The drone of the reporter's appropriately somber voice joined them in the kitchen. "Hundreds of attendees reported feeling slightly nauseous while a dozen people were taken to area hospitals complaining of severe stomach pain. The event was catered by Taste of Soul, a popular and well-known restaurant chain founded in Atlanta and owned by the Livingston Corporation. Members of this family includes Malcolm Livingston, inventor of the popular BBQ Soul Smoker, and Toussaint Livingston, a Food Network star. So far, there is no comment from the Livingston Corporation, but Joyce Witherspoon, owner of the event planning company called Loving Spoonful, had this to say."

There was a cutaway shot to an obviously upset Joyce Witherspoon, who looked as if she'd been up all night. "This is an extremely unfortunate incident. Right now our focus is on making sure all who were affected by the tainted food are being properly treated and that they get well."

"Reports are coming in that those taken away may have experienced food poisoning," the reporter queried. "Can you elaborate?"

Joyce nodded. "When handling food, that's always a possibility. Especially at an outdoor event with the high temperatures we've had. The police are conducting an investigation and beyond that, I'd rather not speculate."

"We know you've been extremely busy and are very tired, so thanks for taking the time to talk with us. Stan, back to you."

Stan's face filled the screen for the wrap-up, and he was obviously reading from a teleprompter or computer off to the side. "Following up on what we just heard from event planner Joyce Witherspoon, an expert has suggested that if the food was not properly stored, with these high temperatures it may have indeed become tainted. She . . . excuse me, folks, but we're live and news is just now coming in. . . . It appears the initial testing of food eaten by some of those hospitalized has found high levels of arsenic. Because of the national and political nature of this event, the FBI has now been called in along with Homeland Security to rule out the possibility of this being an act of terrorism. We will definitely stay on top of this story and give you updates as soon as they come in. And now for the weather, here's . . ."

Marcus had already left his seat and now hit speed dial on his cordless phone. "Adam, it's your dad."

"You've seen the news."

"Of course I've seen the news, boy. Why didn't you call me? Wait, don't tell me. Because you wanted me to stay over here and *chill*."

"No, Dad. It's because we're on our way over there anyway and figured we could all put our heads together once we get there. The PR department has prepared a statement that was just faxed over to CNN and other news outlets a little while ago."

"They're saying something about the food being contaminated?"

"That's bullshit, Dad. We've been catering for twenty years, in weather hotter than this, and have never had an incident."

"And then they said something about arsenic."

A sigh on the other end and then, "Candace is almost ready. We'll be over there within the hour."

"We're here, son. And, Adam?"

"Yes, Dad?"

"Don't worry, son. This, too, shall pass."

A couple hours later, some of the Livingstons and extended family, including Candace's kin, the Longs of Alabama; Diane's relatives and Alexis's mom sat under a large tent on the Livingston Estate. A long table holding more than a dozen warming trays filled with Marietta's good eating lined the back wall, but most of her fare remained uneaten. Inside the residence, Marcus, Adam, Ace, Malcolm, Jefferson, Toussaint, and Bianca sat in the dining room trying to figure out the origins of this latest fire.

"Has Sterling returned your call yet?" Ace asked Adam.

Adam shook his head.

"Damn."

"I talked to Bobby and he swears that there's no way any of the staff he hired would have done this. They all were either Taste of Soul employees or cooks hired through a stellar agency that does extensive background checks."

"Were there cameras in the kitchen?" Toussaint asked.

"Yes," Adam responded. "But not in that back room. At least we'll be able to ID everyone who entered the kitchen; we just won't see anyone actually dumping poison into our dishes."

A frustrated Toussaint abruptly stood up and slammed his fist down on the table. "How in the hell could this have happened? On top of Joyce's security, the Secret Service were all over the place because Joe Biden and Michelle Obama were there! When I find out who did this..." He cracked his knuckles and walked out of the room.

Bianca eyed the guys around the table before going after her cousin to try and calm him down.

"Anybody have any ideas, any clues?"

Jefferson, who'd been twiddling with the spoon in his coffee, spoke up. "Perhaps this was an accident."

"How does arsenic accidently get put into food?" Marcus countered.

Jefferson didn't have an answer for that, so he went back to twiddling his spoon.

"All we can do now is focus on damage control," Ace said. "I'm meeting with the PR and marketing teams later tonight. They're not going to like coming in on a holiday, but we've got our own fireworks going on."

49

There were two members of the Livingston Corporation marketing team who would not make that meeting. Zoe Williams and Drake Benson stood at the altar, exchanging vows that would affect the rest of their lives. Zoe looked radiant in a formfitting, ivory-colored halter gown, adorned with lace flowers and crystal beading. Drake's single-breasted tuxedo had been tailored perfectly, the dark chocolate coloring a perfect complement to his reddish brown hair and green eyes. The maid of honor wore chocolate, the bridesmaids wore tan, and the best man and groomsmen all wore a shade in between. It made for a beautiful vision in front of Zoe's mother's church, the wedding's location. And when Drake kissed his bride, there was no doubt that he was marrying the love of his life.

And Chardonnay was watching the love of her life absolutely ignore her. It had been that way since the day after the argument, when she'd cornered Bobby to tell him she loved him, only to have him say he was working and to walk away, and last night, during rehearsal and the rehearsal dinner, and it was that way afterward, when she'd accosted him on the way to his car.

"Bobby, are you ever going to talk to me?" she'd asked him.

He turned, looked her square in the eye, and responded, "I have nothing to say."

He ignored her now. So much so that she sent Zoe a text message saying that she simply could not come to the reception and sit through another meal trying not to stare at Bobby (who looked better than she ever could have imagined, the tan tux highlighting his deep chocolate skin and fitting him like magic), and she sure as hell didn't want to watch garters being removed with teeth or women scratching for bouquets.

Sorry, girl. Can't do any more of this. Garters, bouquets, Bobby trippin...too much. You looked beautiful today. Enjoy ur honeymoon. Luv ur life. And ur man. White boy cleaned up good, sistah ☺ Char

Chardonnay sent two more text messages before going into the room to change her clothes and call a cab. It was going to cost her a grip, she knew that, but trying to catch buses on a regular day, let alone a holiday in her present state was something she knew she couldn't attempt. The wrong person stepping to her for a seat or a quarter, and somebody could get hurt.

Much later that night, a tired and inebriated Bobby Wilson opened the door to his studio apartment. He hadn't thought he'd have such a good time, but he found out Drake's relatives, especially the Irish side, knew how to get down! Irish whiskey shots were chased with Murphy's Stout, and by the end of the evening, lessons in how to "riverdance" had replaced the electric slide. It was still relatively early, just before nine, but now he was home: alone and lonely. He'd received an invitation to Jon Abernathy's party but after the wedding was in no mood for a crush. Calling any number of the women who'd been blowing up his phone since the separation crossed his mind, and he definitely knew he was overdue for some good sex, but he couldn't seem to drum up the energy for the small talk necessary before getting down.

Taking off his now-wrinkled, sweated-out tuxedo, Bobby headed to the shower. He was just getting ready to step into it when he heard his message indicator beep. He had two messages. The latter one, which had just caused the beep, was from his uncle in New Orleans wishing him a happy Fourth. The first one that he'd missed earlier was from Chardonnay:

Boo, you looked good in that tuxedo. Damn, didn't know u had it like that! All I was thinking about was that big-ass dick behind those trousers and how much I want to feel it in my pussy. I'll be remembering how much I fucked up for the rest of my life. I luv u. White Wine

Just reading Chardonnay's message made Bobby's dick hard, and using the endearing term he used to teasingly call her almost made him smile. It had taken everything he had not to pounce on that round, juicy booty accented by the chocolate gown that made her toffee skin gleam like brown sugar. He read her message again and remembered how good her mouth felt when it was sucking him, how she'd moan deep in her throat and play with his balls. Then he remembered other things. The things he'd do once she'd fired him up beyond all reason. How hard he would hit it and how deep he would go.

"Damn you, Chardonnay!" he growled as he walked to the shower with heavy strides. He thought about the future plans that included running his own kitchen and life on the Strip and who he'd always imagined in that future. He'd talked with the kids, knew how much they'd missed him. He missed them too. He missed...everybody. But how long did you let a woman make a fool of you before you cut your losses and walk away? Bobby had already turned away. *I might as well keep on walking.*

On the other side of town, Shyla sat in her condo pondering her next move. While she'd relished watching the news (and the Livingstons squirm in the process), her dastardly act hadn't brought her the euphoria that she'd thought it might. Especially after watching the news and hearing that the FBI had been called into the investigation. If anyone ever found out what happened, she'd catch a federal case!

"Calm down!" Shyla admonished herself, jumping up from the couch and heading to the kitchen for a glass of wine. She'd replayed yesterday's actions over and over in her head. Her plan had been executed flawlessly. No one had seen her. There was absolutely no way that she'd get caught.

Someone else was pondering also. Yesterday, as the drama was happening, Joyce had hardly been able to think. She'd been questioned by investigators, watched by police and hounded by every news station who'd attended her event. After that, she'd networked at a hip-hop artist's party and had barely gotten any sleep before heading over to Jon Abernathy's to prepare for today's event. After making sure that everything was set up perfectly and that her assistant had the situation under control, Joyce had offered her apologies to Jon for not staying to enjoy his festivities, wearily walked to her car and headed home. Only now, while sitting in her enclosed patio sipping a cup of chamomile tea, was she able to truly get in touch with her thoughts, and replay yesterday's happenings over in her mind.

"Whoa!" The memory came back with such force that the tea sloshed over the side of the cup and burned Joyce's hand. She barely noticed, so fixed was she on the video that was playing in her mind. A wig-wearing woman running from the back tents. Not just any wig-wearing woman, but Shyla Martin, running as though the devil himself were chasing her. "No way," Joyce said aloud, as she stood and paced the length of the room. "That's impossible," she told herself, even as what was coming to her seemed very possible indeed. The force of the revelation almost took her breath away, but Joyce knew that she had to keep it together. After going over several options and scenarios in her head, she reached for the phone.

50

Toussaint looked out the window as a chauffeured town car drove him and Jefferson to the estate hosting Jon Abernathy's Fourth of July event. "Thanks for coming with me, man. I know this isn't really your scene." Toussaint opened a water bottle and took a long swig.

"No, it's cool, cuz. I'd planned on coming."

"Really?"

"Yeah, figured I need to stay in the mix, represent and all."

"Mr. Chief Finance on the scene. Do your thing, son!"

Jefferson nodded.

"You sure you're going to be all right, though, I mean with Divine being there? You know she and Jon are dating."

Jefferson couldn't even hide his smile. No Livingston would ever know how truly all right he was that Jon was dating Divine. "I think that's a good match," he finally said.

"For a while, everybody thought you and Divine might hook up. Y'all were great friends and then all of a sudden, you didn't mention her and we stopped seeing her. What happened?"

"She was interested in taking the situation to the next level and I wasn't. After Keisha, man, I had to regroup."

Toussaint nodded, totally understanding. Getting over the fact that somebody befriended you, had you fall in love with them, move her and her children into your home only to have her steal hundreds of thousands . . . that was a mountain of betrayal not so easy to put out of one's mind. "I never thought I would say this to anyone, but you really should think about getting back in the game. I never thought I could be as happy as I am with Alexis and Tiara."

"Malcolm kept trying to tell you."

"And I wouldn't listen. Never thought that same and steady would beat variety all day long."

"And now you're trying to school a brothah."

"Yes."

"I'll keep that in mind."

Toussaint's phone rang. "Joyce," he said to Jefferson after looking at Caller ID. He answered, placing the call on speaker. "Hey, Joyce. What's up?"

"Hopefully nothing, but I want to share it anyway. It's about what happened yesterday."

"Oh, what you said on the news about food poisoning? Don't worry about that, Joyce. People were coming at you from everywhere. We know that you know how we handle our business. Your comments weren't taken personally."

"I appreciate that, Toussaint, but it's not about what I said yesterday. It's about what I saw."

Toussaint looked at Jefferson. "What did you see?"

Toussaint heard Joyce sigh before answering. "I saw Shyla dressed like one of the waiters, hurrying away from one of the tents . . . the one nearest the kitchen."

"Joyce, this is Jeff. Shyla Martin? Are you sure?"

"Hello, Jeff. I'm pretty sure. I'd say, ninety to ninety-five percent certain."

Jeff shrugged. "So she wasn't rocking designer wear at the event. So what?"

"It's what else she was rocking: a blond wig, baseball cap, and large sunglasses. It was very obvious that she didn't want to be recognized."

"Hum," Toussaint said, rubbing his chin. "Interesting."

"These past twenty-four hours have been so crazy that I'd actually forgotten all about her strange behavior. Not only that, but it doesn't make sense. She helped with the marketing for this, as well as Jon's event. Why would she try and sabotage something of which she was a part?"

Remembering the encounter between Shyla and Alexis, Toussaint could think of at least one reason. "Did she tell you that she'd be attending the function?"

"No," Joyce answered. "I'd just assumed that she was there, and with five thousand folk in attendance, really didn't give not actually seeing her a moment's thought. Until now." The three of them were silent, until Joyce spoke. "What do you guys want me to do?"

Jefferson answered. "Sit tight until we call you. We need to run this past the fam, and decide our course of action."

"Okay."

"And Joyce?"

"Yes, Jeff."

"If it turns out that Shyla was somehow involved in what went down, I'll owe you one."

"You won't owe me anything, Jeff."

"Yes, I will. And I always pay my debts."

Later that night, a man dressed in black from head to toe sifted through Shyla Martin's trash can. The next day, while she shopped at the mall, another man entered her home, broke into her computer, and discovered recent searches for arsenic and its affect. He also found damning evidence in her kitchen, bathroom, and bedroom closet. Through Sterling's connections with the police force, a search warrant was issued. One week later, Shyla Martin was under arrest.

51

Two weeks later the scandal caused by the arsenic-laced food had been replaced by the efforts of a highly paid PR machine. President Obama made an internationally televised stop at the historic Auburn Avenue Taste of Soul, accompanied by his wife, children, and mother-in-law. The president said he'd heard so much about his election year–inspired namesake, Barack's Baby Backs, that he had to personally come down and give them a try. The entire family had met him, and after the president ordered and ate the controversial greens and baked beans, along with Sasha's Potato Salad and Malia's Mac-N-Cheese, Marcus said for the first time in his life he'd almost kissed a man. This is what had the men laughing as the waitress placed down another cognac round.

"So you say it's been what, Daddy, five years or more since we've all been together at FGO?"

"At least," Adam replied, rolling a cigar around on the tips of his fingers, smelling the rich, pungent odor and then reaching for his snipping scissors. "Which is a shame, because when Ace and I first came on board here, we used to meet once a month or more."

"Those times were before the expansion," Ace said, snipping his own cigar and reaching for a gold-plated lighter. "I think time stopped being our own after the fourth store went up."

Marcus sat back and crossed his arms. "Humph, time stopped being my own the day y'all twins were born."

"You know you and Mama were just birthing the help," Ace said with a laugh. "You at least needed another cook and a busboy."

"And a waiter," Malcolm added. "Which is why Daddy snatched Mama up before she walked across the stage."

"Your mama was and still is a catch if there ever was one," Adam corrected. "I married her to take her off the market."

"He did the same thing I did," Marcus said as he puffed a cigar. "Etta had three, four jokers vying for her hand. Your grandmother was a looker, man, a darker-skinned version of Lena Horne. She could have had any man she wanted within a thousand miles."

"Hey, Dad, tell the story about the doctor who'd just finished his residency and thought he was going to swoop in and take Mom off your hands."

"Ace, you always want to hear that story."

"I don't think I've heard it, GrandMar." Toussaint said. "Tell us about how you shut it down back in the day."

"His name was Curtis," Marcus began, taking a puff off his cigar. "Curtis McDaniel. Light-skinned dude, good hair. Had a lot of swagger."

"But not more than you, huh, Dad," Ace said with a wink to Toussaint.

Marcus's deep rumble of a laugh spilled over into the small room. "Truth be told, I knew Etta was the one from the moment I met her. And she knew that I was it for her. We graduated from school, bought the business, had you boys, and never looked back. He looked around the room. "I know I don't say it much, but you'll never know how much I love y'all and how proud you've made me." It was a rare moment for Marcus Leroy Livingston to tear up, but now was one of those times.

At this same moment, Jefferson walked in and took in the scene. *GrandMar is crying? Damn, who died?* He walked into the room, gave silent dap to his cousins, nodded at his dad and uncle, and took a seat.

"I never would have imagined building what we have here," Marcus continued. "Or that the legacy would last through generations. I want to thank you for all your hard work and for forgoing your dreams to latch on to mine." He nodded at the youngest of his grandsons. "Jefferson."

"Evening, everyone."

Subdued greetings echoed around the room before Ace, who'd always been the more sensitive of the twins, showed no shame as he wiped his eyes. "Your dream was always our dream, Daddy. At least for me. I was proud that you had a business I could sink my talent and education into, that I always worked for the family and not other people. So thank you."

"I concur," Adam said. "There was never any doubt about where I'd end up working." He looked at his sons. "You know, come to think of it, I never asked you. Never even considered it. Did you boys ever have a desire to work anywhere other than the family business?"

"Nowhere except the NBA," Toussaint half joked.

"Would it have mattered?" Malcolm asked.

Adam eyed his son as he answered in a somber tone, "Of course, son."

"You mean when I was thirteen I had the choice of whether or not to ride my bike or bus tables? Damn!"

"Well," Adam said with a laugh, "now that you put it that way, the choice would have probably been more tolerable after you moved out of the house and graduated college."

"Seriously, Dad. I've always been a Taste of Soul man. Always will be."

Marcus finished the single two-finger shot of cognac that he'd nursed for well over an hour. "Actually, you're not only a Taste of Soul man, but you're also a BBQ Soul Smoker man, husband, father, and damned good businessman."

Adam nodded toward Toussaint. "Don't forget the TV star we have in the family."

"Hell, he won't stay off the TV long enough for me to forget it!"

"C'mon, now, Pops. I'm not the reason they keep rerunning my shows."

"But the ratings are the reason it's been renewed twice now," Adam said, no small amount of pride in his voice. "And why they've approached you with another show idea for the network."

"With all of these extra shenanigans going on, it's nice to know that there's one of y'all's generation solidly holding it down at the office." Marcus held up his near-empty glass. "To the new chief executive *operating* and finance officer," he said, nodding at Jefferson. Jefferson's impressive first thirty days had convinced them to not wait five years, but to expand his duties and change his title now. "Congratulations, son. We're all very proud of you."

"And to Bianca and Xavier," Jefferson added. "Baby sis got it done and TOSTS is back next week!"

The men toasted Jefferson, and Bianca in absentia, then for the next hour teased, cajoled, and talked smack about the business and each other. It had been the first time they'd hung out this way in a long time, but everyone agreed that it wouldn't be their last. Finally, at 9:00 p.m., Marcus stood. "Y'all boys carry on, but an old man is going to hit the road and get home to the wife before she gets too antsy."

"Are you going to come into the office tomorrow, Daddy?" Adam asked as he stood to hug his father.

"I'll probably be in for an hour or two in the afternoon."

"We'll see you then," Ace said, also standing to give his father a hug.

The boys all followed suit, watching the proud, well-dressed man who was their grandfather walk out of the room, his back still straight and gait still strong.

"That's a hard act to follow right there," Ace said, feeling a tad melancholy as he watched his dad leave the club. "It's sometimes hard for me to remember that he's seventy-five years old."

"Yeah, seventy-five going on forty," Toussaint joked. "Last week on the golf course, he nearly walked me into the ground."

"His birthday is coming up," Malcolm said. "Why don't we do something special, maybe do a boys' night out in Vegas or something."

"Sounds like a plan," Adam said. "We'll leave Mama in charge of the wives, have them get a little instruction while we're away."

A short time later, the remaining Livingston men left the club and headed to their various homes. Before sunrise, all of Atlanta and most of America would know that one of them never made it there.

52

"Why don't we check out that new gym?" Diane asked Candace, shifting the phone from one ear to the other as she finished a cup of tea. "We'll work out as a team, always together, and that way you won't be tempted to get into trouble."

"From what you tell me about the new owner, my getting into trouble won't be a problem."

The women laughed. The owner of the new gym that had replaced Q's Bodybuilding & Workout Center was a trim, fit female named Sport who ran the place with her husband. Her R & B–themed step and Pilates classes were all the rage, and people who followed her simple nutritional tips reported fairly easy weight loss of five to ten pounds over eight weeks.

"Girl, even with the new décor, machines, and owners I'm not sure I can go back into that building. Too many memories. It'd be my luck to go in there and run into Q working out."

"We need to do something. I'm trying to not fall victim to the middle-age spread."

"Girl, I can't even blame the added years. Whatever my waist fell victim to happened a long time before now." The women laughed. "Diane, hold on a minute. Mom Etta is calling." Candace clicked over onto her other line. "Hey, Mama."

"How you doing, Candace?"

"I'm good. Talking to Diane on the other line."

"I guess it's good to get girl time in, since the men are having their moment."

"Yes, Adam said they had a good time tonight and that they're planning to make meeting at the club a regular occurrence. Once a month or so."

"So Adam is home already?"

"No, but he called me. He's on his way."

"Oh, okay. I should expect Marcus home shortly. I'll let you go. Tell Diane hello for me and to call me tomorrow."

"Will do, Mama."

When Candace clicked back over, she heard Diane talking to Ace. "Candace, Ace just walked in, so I'm going to let you go."

"Okay. Mama said to call her tomorrow. Be on the lookout because I don't think she's turned that bone loose, that feeling about me and Adam."

"No worries, girl. We've got that thing locked down! Love ya, girl."

"Love you too." Candace hung up the phone and a few minutes later heard Adam entering from the garage. She walked through the dining room and into the kitchen to greet him. "Hey, baby," she said, giving him a hug and a kiss on the cheek. "Ooh, you smell like cigars."

"Good evening to you, too, baby," Adam replied. "Why don't you join me for a shower and help me get clean?"

Candace sidled up next to the love of her life for more than three decades. "Only if you promise to get dirty with me again right after that shower."

"We might have to get dirty in the water, Candace Livingston. That cognac's got me riled up."

"Boy, stop sounding like your daddy."

While Ace and Candace were in the shower, their phone rang. It was Victoria, who left this message: "Hi, Candace. I was just calling to see if Adam was home. I've tried to reach Malcolm and keep getting voice mail. No worries, I was just going to have him pick up some milk on the way home. I'll talk to you later. Bye."

At the same time Victoria was leaving the message for Candace, Alexis and her mother were putting Tiara to bed. She'd been overjoyed to talk her mom, Jean Barnes, into extending her stay in Atlanta and further bonding with her granddaughter.

Jean, who'd held "Baby Tee" until she'd fallen asleep, now placed her in her crib. "I still can't believe you don't do like the other women in your position and hire a nanny. If I had that option, y'all kids would have never seen me!"

"I never even thought I'd have children," Alexis said, making sure there were no possible air obstructions around her daughter before ushering her mother out of the room. "And I had absolutely no idea that I'd love it so much. But I do, everything about it. Plus, Candace has told me how fast the time passes and to enjoy it while I can."

"Yeah, one minute you and your brothers were all sleeping in the same bed and the next minute y'all were grown and gone."

Alexis nodded but didn't respond. She loved her rather less-than-ambitious brothers, but discussing them with Jean could get tricky. Her mother was a classic enabler who, in Alexis's opinion, had held on to these birdies so closely that they never learned to fly. It probably also explained why she'd married Frank, an alcoholic, who she swore was a good man. "Do you want some dessert, Mama? I have some of that sweet potato ice cream that you love so much."

"That sounds good, Lexy."

The phone rang. "Okay. I'll get it as soon as I take this call." She reached for the home phone. "Hello?"

"Hello, Alexis. Sorry to bother you so late, but it's Diane."

"No bother at all, Dee. Me and Mama were just getting ready to dive in to your sweet potato ice cream. It's her new favorite."

"Tell you mother hello for me."

"I will. Now, what can I do for you?"

"Ace needs to run something by Jefferson before a meeting tomorrow and hasn't been able to reach him. I know that he and Toussaint rode to FGO together and was wondering if he was there yet."

"No, Dee, Toussaint hasn't made it home. Have you tried Jeff's cell?"

"Several times, his home phone too. Can you do me a favor? Call Toussaint and tell him to have Jeff call Ace?" And then, "Girl, what am I thinking? I can call Toussaint myself."

"I don't mind," Alexis responded. "I need to bless him out for hanging out so long with the boys anyway."

"There you go, girl. We've got to train 'em good."

Alexis chuckled. "Exactly. Hey, why don't you and Candace come over for lunch tomorrow? I'll fix something light."

"That sounds like a plan."

They got off the phone and Alexis called Toussaint. But just as happened to Diane and Ace, all she got was voice mail.

About fifteen miles away from all of these ladies, red lights flashed and sirens blared. There had been an accident, a head-on collision on the I-20. One set of paramedics worked frantically to retrieve the mangled body of the man trapped behind the wheel of his smashed-in car, while the other set tended to the injuries of the heavily inebriated man who'd taken the wrong ramp and traveled for more than ten miles in the wrong direction, never realizing that the horns honking and bright lights being flashed at him was a message that he was traveling up the wrong side of the interstate. The drunk driver had sustained a broken leg, broken ribs, and heavy lacerations across his face, but after getting him into the ambulance and stabilizing his vitals, they determined that he would live. Soon, one ambulance sped away with him inside. Two of the police cars that had responded to the scene were right behind the ambulance. The alcohol smell on the man's breath could be cut with a knife. At the very least, the police knew they were getting ready to deal with a felony case of serious injury caused by drunken driving.

"Come on, man, hang on," the paramedic said, working frantically to administer oxygen through the broken window. "The Jaws of Life are on their way, just hang on!"

The eyes of the man inside the car fluttered briefly and then closed. Forever. The paramedic sat back, exhausted. He looked up just as the Jaws of Life pulled up next to the car. Two operators jumped out and raced toward him. He shook his head.

"It's too late," he said wearily. "He's gone."

They extricated the body and reached for the wallet of the man whose face was cut up so badly that it was barely recognizable. The EMT opened it and pulled out the driver's license. He closed his eyes tightly and reopened them, hoping that he'd read incorrectly. He knew this man, or at least the name, had seen him on television, and had eaten at their restaurant just last weekend. They rarely showed emotion, but the EMT covered his face with his hands.

"You all right, buddy?" another paramedic asked after walking up beside him and seeing his distress.

"Not really, man. I know who this is." Anger replaced distress as the EMT added, "Senselessly killed by a drunk driver!"

Just then, two police officers approached them. "How's this one doing?" one of them asked.

The first paramedic just shook his head.

The second officer noticed the wallet in the EMT's hand. "We have a positive ID?"

The paramedic nodded and handed him the driver's license.

"Oh, man," the officer said as he saw the picture and read the name.

His partner looked over. "Who is it?"

"It's a Livingston," he responded. "One of the owners of Taste of Soul."

53

Marietta sat straight up. Just five minutes ago after trying for the umpteenth time to reach Marcus on his cell phone, she'd forced herself to lie down and try to calm down. Even though her stomach rumbled and eye twitched. Even though she felt a foreboding, the likes of which she hadn't experienced since her mother died twenty-five years ago. *Etta.* There it was again, the unmistakable feeling of Marcus whispering in her ear. She threw back the covers and got out of bed. She took two steps and then felt a warm breeze pass over her body. It couldn't have been any more real had a slave been waving a palm frond from mere inches away. This warm breeze was followed by a cold chill, a shiver that literally shook her to the core. The doorbell rang. "Jesus!" She donned her robe and hurried to the door, her heart beating faster with each step. "Marcus, honey, please don't," she whispered in prayer. "I always wanted to go first." Not even bothering to look through the peephole, she threw open the front door. There was absolutely no surprise at the scene of two somber officers that greeted her on the other side. She closed her eyes, took a deep breath, and made a statement, not a question: "Marcus is dead."

Within minutes, shock waves reverberated through the

Livingston family. She called Adam first, the oldest by seventeen minutes. "Adam, it's Mother." She could sense Adam tensing, knew that she only addressed him in this manner when things were serious and seriously wrong.

"What is it, Mama?"

An audible swallow, a sniffle, and silence followed by a resolute tone. "It's your Daddy, Adam."

"What is it?"

"He was in an accident; a drunk driver hit him."

"Oh my God." Marietta could hear rumbling, imagined Adam either rising from bed or rummaging through his closet. "Just stay calm, Mama. I'm on my way to drive you to the hospital. Have you called Ace? Don't worry, I'll call him."

Marietta heard mumbling in the background before her son responded, "It's Daddy. He was in a car accident."

"Bring Candace, son," Marietta interjected. "You'll need your wife here."

Adam, who'd grabbed his keys and now raced for the door, stopped in his tracks. "Mama, what are you not telling me? How's Daddy doing?"

"Baby, everything's going to be all right. Just bring your wife."

Candace was already ahead of the game. She'd jumped out of bed as soon as she heard the word *accident* and was now hastily trading a nightgown for a summer dress and flat sandals.

Meanwhile, Adam was heading to the car, dialing Ace while walking.

"Hey, Twin. I just left you. What's up, man?"

"It's Daddy, Ace. He's been in an accident. We need to get over to Mama's quick."

"We're on our way."

Less than fifteen minutes later, Adam pulled into Marietta's driveway. He and Candace jumped out of the car and ran to the door. It was unlocked, and they burst inside.

"Mama!" Adam turned the corner and stopped short. There in front of him was a woman who seemed to have aged ten years since he last saw her two weeks ago. Tears streamed down her face, and in her eyes was a pain the likes of which he'd never seen. His heart clenched and then began beating rapidly. "Mama," he said again, his own eyes welling before he reached her, before she said a word. His voice was raspy as he spoke. "It's going to be all right, Mama. We'll get you to the hospital. Daddy is going to be fine."

Marietta pulled back and placed a soft hand on Adam's hard jawbone. "We'll get through this, son. But things will never be quite right again."

Adam's eyes searched his mother's, hoping, praying that what he felt isn't what had happened. But seeing a new set of tears stream down his mother's face, he knew. "No," he whispered.

"Yes, baby," Marietta answered, hugging her son. "Your daddy's gone."

They were still hugging when Ace burst through the front door and sped around the corner into the living room. "How is he?" Three pairs of red-rimmed eyes turned toward him. He had his answer and the power of this truth felled him where he stood. He slumped into the nearest chair. "No, man, this can't be. We just left him. I just hugged him! Please tell me something else, anything but this!"

Diane, who'd hugged Candace as soon as she entered the room, now raced over to an openly weeping husband. "Baby, I'm so sorry."

"He came to me clear as day," Marietta said, walking over and sitting down heavily on the couch. "Whispered in my ear." Her voice was soft as her mind's eye took her to another place, where she and Marcus were sitting together laughing and holding hands. "He said my name," she continued, "the way he used to do when he flirted. 'Etta,' in that deep, powerful bass he could use so well. He said my name." She placed a hand over her mouth, lest a primal scream so loud come out that it would wake the dead. "He came to me as he was leaving. Brushed up against me just like a breeze. Lord help me, Jesus. I can't do this. I just can't!"

Candace walked over and placed comforting arms around the mother-in-law who was more like a mother to her than her own. "We're right here with you, Mama. And it's going to be hard, but we can do this. We've *got* to do this. And we're going to get through this. Together, all of us ... we'll ..." Her voice caught in her throat as the tears came and fell. "We'll all get through this together."

Within the hour, all of the Livingstons had gathered at the Lithonia estate, and Xavier had arranged for a private jet to bring him and Bianca in before morning. No one said much. What words could there be? It was the end of an era. Marcus Leroy Livingston, son of Nash and Jane Livingston, founder of Taste of Soul, brother, husband, father, friend, was gone.

54

The scene was impressive: six handsome pallbearers decked out in tailored black suits and designer sunglasses carried a shiny, stainless-steel casket to the waiting limousine. In another circumstance, they would have been the perfect look for a *GQ* ad, but today the Livingston men—Adam, Ace, Malcolm, Toussaint, and Jefferson—and Xavier Marquis were bearing a load that disallowed smiles. They were carrying Marcus Livingston to his final resting place. Their hearts were weighty, but their burden was light. After all, Marcus Livingston wasn't heavy; he was their father, founder, mentor, and friend.

A seemingly endless procession made the journey from the megachurch that had been leased to house the massive crowd to the cemetery and the Livingston mausoleum. The men who'd carried their forefather now sat in a limousine, along with their wives. All were unaware of its luxuriousness or of the pricey bottles of bubbly sitting on ice. The mood was somber, the faces stoic. But soon, a telltale tear slipped past the rim of Ace's sunglasses, causing Adam to grip his brother's shoulder. "It's all right, Twin," he said, his voice hoarse from the handling of his own repressed sob. "We all feel the same way."

"You'd think it would have sunk in by now," Ace said. He took off his glasses and wiped his face with a handkerchief. "But I still can't believe he's gone."

"Pops went out in style," Toussaint offered, his smile appearing bittersweet. "I couldn't believe all of the people who turned out to pay their respects."

"He would have appreciated seeing all of the Atlanta businessmen there," Malcolm offered, taking off his glasses to wipe suddenly wet eyes. "And those in the food and restaurant industries—"

"Not to mention the White House being represented," Candace said softly. "Sending a personally signed bereavement card? Barack Obama is a class act."

"Speaking of classy, what about all of our employees wearing white, with the lone black rose on their dress or lapel? I wonder whose idea that was."

"Zoe Benson," Diane said. "She e-mailed their desires; I thought it a nice touch."

Various affirmative replies or gestures abounded.

"It was nice how the networks came out to support," Jefferson said. "Several CNN news people were there."

"It didn't surprise me to see Roland Martin," Bianca added. "He loves Taste of Soul."

"I wasn't expecting Gayle King," Toussaint said, even though he'd appeared on her TV show.

"She frequented TOSTS," Xavier explained. "I wasn't surprised to see her."

"You saw Sterling, right?" Adam asked.

Ace nodded. "He came over to personally offer his condolences and to let me know that his out-of-town business had been completed. He'll make himself available if we need him."

Toussaint's head shot up. "Why would he say that? Does it have to do with GrandMar?"

"No, Nephew," Ace said with a frown. "Dad's death was an accident, a terrible, unfortunate chain of events."

Toussaint's eyes narrowed behind his dark glasses. "I guess I shouldn't but I can't help but wonder if Pop's death was indeed an accident or something else."

Adam slowly looked over at his son. "The other driver was tested at the scene, son, and was heavily inebriated. He was booked on charges of vehicular manslaughter and is being held without bond. I don't see how anything more sinister could come out of those facts. It's pretty straightforward."

Toussaint sighed and rolled his neck in an attempt to get out the tension-filled kinks. "You're probably right, Dad."

"Of course I am."

The men became silent after that, their thoughts going in a myriad of directions. Toussaint wrestled with feeling somehow responsible for not being able to better shield the family from their recent dramas and tragedies. Malcolm thought of his dad, and how close he and Grandpa Marcus had been. He made a mental note to spend more time with his parents and make sure his dad was okay. Jefferson thought about not wanting to go home to an empty house. Ace's and Adam's thoughts were the most similar—Ace thinking about how he missed his father to the bone, and Adam thinking that and how large were the shoes Marcus Livingston had left to fill.

The graveside service was short but heartfelt. Each Livingston, male and female, threw a single white rose on top of the lowered coffin. Last but not least, a distraught but proud Marietta Livingston walked up to the casket with a bouquet of carnations, very similar to the first bouquet of flowers Marcus had given to her when they first started courting.

"I'm going to miss you, Marcus," she whispered through a veil of tears. "There will never be another one...not in my lifetime. I love..." She couldn't go on and collapsed back onto Adam's chest. Her family immediately surrounded her, and a short time later, everyone headed back to black limos and town cars headed to Lithonia and the Livingston estate.

Someone watched the touching scene from a short distance away. Hidden behind a large oak tree and dark glasses and wearing all black, he was easily inconspicuous among the throng of mourners. As he had been since he arrived in Atlanta—at the wake, at the funeral, and now. He waited and watched until the last car had pulled away from the gravesite and the workers had piled the dirt high before placing the shovels in the back of a truck and driving away. Then and only then did the tall, handsome man venture beyond his hiding place and walk over to what remained of Marcus Livingston.

He reached the mound of dirt, pulled off the white carnation that had been pinned to his lapel, threw it on top of the dirt mound, and whispered two words: "Good-bye, Dad."

55

An hour later and back at the Livingston estate, the post-funeral gathering was in full swing. The mood had lightened amid mouth-watering food, ever-flowing libations, and side-splitting memories of Marcus Livingston.

"So Ace took off and Daddy went to chasing him," Adam continued, wiping tears of laughter from his eyes. " 'I'ma whup you, boy,' he was yelling to Ace's retreating back. 'I'ma whup you good!' "

"And what happened when he caught him?" Toussaint inquired, his eyes twinkling from hearing this story at least half a million times.

"He was so tired he just dropped the switch and asked Ace to fetch him a glass of water!"

The room cracked up. Even Marietta allowed a slight smile to scamper across her face. The table and floor around her were littered with photo albums, and a montage of them featuring her late husband played across a silent TV screen.

"What about the time GrandMar caught that big catfish and ended up in the local paper?" Jefferson asked. "Every time he retold the story, that fish gained five pounds!"

"I still remember you cooking that fish, Mama," Ace said.

"Especially that stew you made out of the head. That was some good eating right there."

"Marcus liked to have hurt himself eating that stew," Marietta said, her eyes staring beyond those in the living room to an afternoon in 1991. She could see her husband as he looked that day: tall, dark, and handsome, wearing overalls and a floppy straw hat. He stood with that twenty-five-pound catfish in one hand and the fishing rod he'd used to reel it in, in the other. Known for being a dapper dresser in his Stacy Adams and tailored suits, anyone taking a glance at this photo would know the truth: that at the heart of the matter, Marcus Livingston was and would always be a country boy from the hills of Alabama who loved good drink, good food, and a good woman.

By early evening, the guests had cleared, leaving only the closest of kin at the house. The hatchet of the past year totally buried, Toussaint and Jefferson talked like old times, reconnecting with their Long cousins who lived in nearby Tennessee and whom they hadn't seen for years. Candace caught up with the sister she rarely saw since she moved to Phoenix ten years earlier, and Diane reminisced with her brother, his wife, and their children.

"Anybody for coffee and cake?" Marietta asked as she wheeled a loaded cart into the great room.

"I can't eat another bite," Candace said, waving away the offer with her hand.

Adam had no such problem. "If that's your German chocolate," he said, already rising, "I'll have a slice."

Various other answers occurred as the remaining men vied for a spot around the cart laden with German chocolate, red velvet, and lemon pound cake masterpieces. They were so boisterous that no one heard the doorbell. And then came the knock.

Marietta cocked her ear toward the front door, a saucer in

one hand and cake server in the other. "Was that a knock I heard?"

The Livingston men were immediately on alert. It had been this way since the fire, heightened after Marcus had been killed. Ace walked to the door. Toussaint fell into step behind him. As they approached, the doorbell rang again. Ace looked through the beveled glass panes that framed the heavy, cherry-wood front door. The image on the other side was a bit blurred, but Ace made out a tall, dark-skinned man wearing a black suit and sunglasses.

"Who is it?" Toussaint asked.

Ace shrugged as he moved to open the door. "Probably a friend of Dad's, come to pay his final respects." He opened the door. "Yes, may I help you?"

The stranger nodded. "Hello. I'm here to see Mrs. Marietta Livingston."

Something about the man bothered Ace. He couldn't put his finger on the wave of discomfort that traveled down his spine. It wasn't fear. The man looked not only nonthreatening, but also refined in his tailored black suit and understated but expensive jewelry. No, it wasn't fear that Ace felt. It was something else. "Who are you?" he finally asked.

The stranger took off his glasses. Ace's eyes widened and Toussaint took a step back. For the younger Livingston, it was as though he were looking at an older, darker version of himself. *WTH?*

"Who are you?" Ace asked again, his voice low, his eyes narrowed in suspicion.

"I'm someone that your mother, Mrs. Marietta Livingston, needs to meet."

Ace moved to block the door. Toussaint was directly over his shoulder, giving the stranger a double-dog-dare-you kind of look. "You're not coming over this threshold until *I'm* satisfied that you're someone my mother needs to meet. Now, I'll ask you for a third and final time. Who the hell are you?"

The stranger sighed and ran a weary hand over his face. "This isn't going the way I'd hoped, but I guess here on the porch is as good a place as any to begin my story. My name is Winston Livingston Meadows. I'm from Winston-Salem, North Carolina. My mother was Dara Buford Meadows and the man who raised me was Carl Meadows."

"What does that have to do with my grandmother?" Toussaint asked, taking a step forward and feeling the restraining touch of his uncle's calm hand.

"Carl Meadows raised me, but he wasn't my biological father. That man," the stranger finished as he squared his shoulders and lifted his chin just a notch, "was Marcus Livingston."

"Who is it?" Marietta's voice rang out as she walked down the hall.

Toussaint wheeled around, walking quickly to meet Marietta before she got to the door. "No one for you to worry about, Grandmother. Just somebody, uh, paying his respects."

"Well, act like you have some brought-upsy and let whoever it is in!"

Ace stepped outside and closed the door. "Man, I don't know who you are or what this is about, but my mother just lost her husband of over fifty years. She don't need whatever bullshit game you're playing!"

Winston met Ace's angry glare with an equally resolute one. "Trust me, this is not a game, and coming here was one of the most difficult things I've ever done. But it was my mother's dying wish that I get to know the other side of where I came from and take my rightful place as a Livingston heir."

"Oh, so now we're getting to the reason you're here. Some long-lost relative of my father impersonating a long-lost son to try and get in on the inheritance. Ha! It shows that you know nothing about my father. You're looking at one of only two children he sired."

"How can you be so sure?"

"Because my father was the type of man who you obviously aren't: trustworthy, loyal, honest, and faithful. He never cheated on my mother in over fifty years. Never!"

"What about before he married your mother?" Winston retorted, his voice low and steady. "Was he a virgin? Or is there a chance that he slept with my mother before marrying yours and spent a lifetime not even knowing that I existed!"

Two sets of eyes, exactly alike, bore into each other. Two jawbones, eerily similar, were locked in anger, and two sets of lips, carbon copies, were clamped into thin lines.

"Look, I don't want you upsetting my mother," Ace finally said through gritted teeth. "Call my office next week. My brother and I will listen to what you've got to say."

Just then there was a rustling at the front door before it was yanked open. "Don't tell me what to do, boy, in my own house!" Marietta marched out onto the porch. "Now who—" She took one look at Winston and stopped short. Her mouth dropped open, her hand flew to her chest, and had it not been for Toussaint directly behind her, she would have crumpled to the ground. It almost took smelling salts to revive her.

56

The ensuing silence of the library where Winston had been hurriedly ushered while Marietta was revived in her master suite was more deafening than when news had been received that Marcus had died. While Ace had gone with Winston to the library (ironically one of Marcus's favorite places in the world), Toussaint had rounded up Adam, Candace, Diane, Malcolm, and Jefferson, who were now either standing or sitting in close proximity to Winston, staring at him as if he were ET needing to phone home. For his part, Winston was the epitome of calm. He hadn't gotten where he was in life—the wealthy owner of a very successful construction company—by letting people see him sweat. Even people as well-heeled as the Livingstons. His mother had always told him that no matter the status of anyone he met, "they put on their pants the same as you, one leg at a time." Aside from that, he'd always carried himself with a calm confidence, even as a child, and that he'd grown up as the only child being doted on by his mother and the man who treated him as well as a dad ever could only helped to make him the self-assured yet humble man that he was.

The door opened and Bianca walked in with a calmer yet

stiff-looking Marietta at her side. They walked into the room and right up to Winston, leaving only a foot or so between them. "I apologize for my improper greeting earlier," Marietta said, her tone filled with Southern politeness. "But you'll understand my shock at seeing someone who so resembles my husband."

Winston stood. "No apologies needed, ma'am, although I most assuredly accept. Please forgive me for this intrusion. I am sorry for your loss, one that I understand since I just lost my mother six months ago and am now carrying out one of her final wishes."

Marietta walked over to the love seat, still eyeing Winston with an indefinable look in her eye. She sat and continued to look at him. Openly and unashamed. The air in the room was palpable. Those inside it barely breathed.

"Did anyone offer you something to drink?" Marietta asked, seemingly the only one besides Winston with working faculties. "Some coffee or tea, or perhaps a splash of...something stronger."

A slight smile scurried across Winston's face, causing familiar-looking crinkles at the sides of his eyes. The kind that Marcus had, as did Ace, Adam, and Toussaint. "It's kind of you to ask," he replied, "and honestly, I could use a bit of libation. Cognac if you have it."

At the mention of their father's favorite drink, a look passed between Adam and Ace and Malcolm and Toussaint. Jefferson, who hadn't touched a drop of alcohol since his visit to Chicago, was tempted to join this familiar-looking stranger in a finger or two but on second thought changed his mind.

Adam rose and poured four snifters for himself, Ace, Malcolm, and Winston. Toussaint, who'd declined, stood with arms crossed, still ready for battle. He didn't give a damn about the brother's story. He just knew that he'd do whatever it took for his grandmother to not be hurt.

After he'd received his drink and taken two healthy swallows, Marietta said softly, "Son, tell us why you're here."

Winston put down his drink, reached inside his jacket, and pulled out an envelope. "This is why I'm here," he said, turning the stark-white paper over in his hand. "And believe me, I was as shocked when I read it as all of you are now. As I tried to tell your son, there." Winston cocked his head toward Ace.

"That's Abram," Marietta offered. "But everyone calls him Ace." A slight frown marred her face. "Wait, y'all haven't introduced yourselves?" An embarrassed cough accompanied a snort and a sigh. "Boys . . . ," she drawled in a voice that brooked no argument but rather strongly suggested that those addressed get with her program and get with it quick.

"I'm Adam."

"Malcolm."

"Jefferson."

The women introduced themselves as well.

When everyone looked at Toussaint, he said, "I'm the brother wanting to know what the hell you're doing here before I tell you my name or anything else."

"Please," Winston said, holding up his hand to cut off Marietta's would-be comment.

"He's here with his hand out," Ace offered. "Daddy's barely in the ground and this fool thinks he's going to get a slice of the inheritance pie."

"This isn't about money," Winston explained.

Ace exploded. "That's not what you said outside!"

"I say we hear the guy out," Jefferson calmly offered. "This arguing isn't going to get us anywhere."

Winston took a breath, knocked back the remainder of his cognac, and began again. "I was born Winston Livingston fifty-six years ago and was raised in Winston-Salem, where my parents lived until their deaths. I say born a Livingston because that is what's on my original birth certificate. The only father I ever knew, Carl Meadows, adopted me when I was a year old. I only found out these facts six months ago, after my mother died and I had retrieved her will and other items from a safe-deposit box. This"—again he held up the envelope—"was one of the items in the box along with her will. I think this would be a good time for you to read the letter before I continue, Mrs. Livingston. It will give you a more proper perspective of why I'm here."

Marietta's nod was almost imperceptible, but Bianca saw it. She walked over, took (okay, snatched really, but tempers were running high) the envelope from Winston, and walked it over to her grandmother. "My glasses, child," she said to Bianca as she reached inside the envelope and pulled out two pieces of paper filled with elegant cursive strokes. She put on her glasses, unfolded the paper, and read aloud:

" 'My dearest Winston: Since you are reading this, I have done what I never, ever wanted to do—leave you. From the time of your birth, you've been the apple of my eye and the joy of my life. There are simply no words for how much I love you. But as Red Skelton once said, no one gets out of here alive. So I am now happily joined with your father as your angel in paradise.

" 'For my entire adult life, I've grappled with what I'm about to share. At one time, I said I'd go to my grave with this secret, but later, as you got older and began asking questions, I felt it unfair to deny truths of which you should know. Still, I had too much love and respect for your father—God rest his soul—to share this earlier and, quite frankly, too little courage. How would you respond to this revelation? Would you hate me? Despise me for not telling you sooner, or feel ashamed because of what I'm about to share?

" 'When your dad died, I almost told you. But you grieved so for his loss that I didn't want to compound it with what I'm sure will be unsettling news: that while he loved you like his most adored son, Carl Meadows is not your biological father. Please don't feel bad, son, or hate me for relaying this information at this time in your life. It doesn't change the past of what you shared with my darling Carl. But I believe it will impact your future.

" 'Your biological father is a man named Marcus Livingston. Yes, son, as in the Livingston Corporation, the barbeque sauce kings and the Taste of Soul chain owners. He is a fine, upstanding man, always has been, which is why he never knew of your existence.

" 'I met Marcus when we were both very young. I'd gone to Atlanta to visit a cousin and met him at a party. For me, son, it was love at first sight. Your father cut a handsome swath across the room and my heart was at once captivated. I was seventeen, and a virgin. As I recall, he was about the same age. I wanted to be with him so badly it hurt, and even though he was reluctant, he finally came with me back to my cousin's house. It's a bit embarrassing to share this, but you need to know: I am glad that I was able to give something so precious as my virginity to a man like Marcus Livingston. I came back to Winston the following week and two months later discovered that your father had given me more than fond memories—he'd given me you. I was overjoyed at being pregnant, but also frightened. Why? Because shortly after I learned this news, I learned something else. Marcus had gotten married to a woman named Marietta. My cousin told me they were madly in love with each other, that their wedding had been held at a large church and attended by hundreds. Throughout my pregnancy, I wrestled with whether or not to tell Marcus about you, but then, again, fate seemed to intervene. Shortly after you were born, I found out that Marietta had become pregnant. And I met your real father, Carl.

" 'From the start, Carl adored you. You see, he was unable to sire children and felt that you and I were an answer to his prayers for a family. He asked to adopt you right away. Out of respect for his kindness, I closed the door on the wonderful weekend I'd shared with Marcus Livingston and out of respect for his new wife and family, chose to never tell him that he had another son. But now, my dearest Winston, as I enter the winter of my life and am filled with reflection, I believe it best that you know. God makes no mistakes. There was a reason that I conceived you during my first experiences with intimacy. And

there is a reason that you are who you are—a Livingston. Please for-
give an overprotective mother for my methods of revelation and for
what I now ask. That upon my death, you seek out your father and his
family. Let them know that you exist. What happens after that is up
to you, up to them, and up to God.

" '*With all my love, your mother,*

" '*Dara*' "

As she slowly folded the paper and placed it back in the
envelope, Marietta observed Winston try and surreptitiously
wipe a tear from his face. In that instant, the way his shoulders
curved and his chin jutted, it was as if she were looking at a
younger version of the man that she'd married. In this moment, she knew without a doubt that this was indeed her late
husband's son.

She stood, walked over to Winston, and handed him the
envelope. "She sounds like she was a wonderful woman," Marietta said, her voice soft, her tone sincere. "I'm sorry for your
loss."

"Thank you," Winston said, his voice soft and eyes glassy as
he took the envelope and stood. "I think it best that I leave
you now. I've fulfilled my mother's wishes." He pulled a card
out of his breast pocket and laid it on the table beside where
he'd sat. "I have a lot of questions about my biological father.
Perhaps someday, after the shock has worn off, I could visit
with you again."

Marietta placed a soft hand on the jaw that reminded her
of her husband. "You look like him," she whispered, unshed
tears glistening in her kind eyes. "In my heart, I know you're a
Livingston." Then she did something that only a Southern
born and bred, confident, selfless, practical, loving woman
named Marietta Lucinda Livingston would do. She opened
her arms, smiled, and said, "Any child of Marcus's is a child of
mine. Welcome to the family, son. Welcome."

57

"I don't believe him," Toussaint said, pacing the floor of his father's study. Since last night and Winston's surprise visit, there'd been little sleep gotten by the Livingston clan, and this morning, the sun had barely nodded its good morning before he was entering his parents' home.

"I won't be totally convinced until I see a DNA test," Adam said, nodding as Candace silently asked if he wanted a coffee refill. "But I have no reason to doubt the man's story. After all, he does look like us. There's no denying that."

"But didn't GrandMar talk about some distant Livingston relatives he'd known as a child and then lost touch with when they moved to Detroit?" Malcolm reached for a freshly made cinnamon roll and took a large bite.

"Yes," Toussaint said. "And one of them might have done some searching on the Internet, stirred with curiosity brought on by GrandMar's passing, did the math, and decided to pay us a little visit."

Adam turned and looked at his brother, who'd arrived with Diane shortly after Toussaint and before Malcolm. "Ace, what exactly did he say last night about wanting some of our money?"

"He didn't use the word *money*, just said something about his rightful place as a Livingston heir."

"If that isn't about money," Candace interjected, "I don't know what is."

Ace put down his half-eaten cinnamon roll and reached for a napkin. "Now that I've calmed down, I'd like to talk to him. I understand why he chose to leave, to give us a chance to absorb all of this. But now, I definitely think we need to talk."

"Oh, we're going to talk all right," Toussaint said with the same amount of attitude he'd had ever since opening his grandmother's door and seeing a near mirror image. "Because the way he stepped to us was foul."

"How would you have proposed he do it, son?" Ace asked. "It could have been worse. He could have made a big deal at the funeral or the gravesite. Or he could have sold his story to a tabloid, went to the TV stations. He didn't do any of those things. And he was very respectful of Mama. I appreciated that."

"I Googled the guy," Malcolm said, rearing back in his chair. "He's the owner of Meadows Construction, one of the largest such companies in the South."

"So at least he's not broke," Diane said, having walked in as her husband was sharing his perspective.

"Far from it, according to the figures posted online. His company pulled in around twenty-five mill last year. That's not chump change."

"What kind of construction?" Adam asked.

"Business, mainly," Malcolm answered. "I saw a link for residence construction on the Web site, which looked to focus on traditional Southern colonials, but the home page touted their success of blending traditional with modern for their office designs."

"'Meadows Construction and Design. Connecting the past with the future, one brick at a time,'" Toussaint read the iPad screen that was never far from his reach. He snorted. "Guess that slogan is about more than buildings."

"On the other hand, there are his feelings to consider," Candace said, her look thoughtful as she gazed out on a sunny Saturday in late July. "It must have been traumatic for him to learn that the man who'd raised him was not his real dad."

"You could tell that from the look in his eye," Diane said. "I watched him while Mama was reading that letter. He's conflicted to say the least."

Toussaint, who'd never stopped moving his fingers across his pad, continued. " 'Providing general contracting and construction management services to leading businesses and organizations throughout the South and southeast since 1971.' "

"And he's fifty-six?" Ace queried. "That means he started the company at what, twenty-five or six years old."

Adam nodded. "Yes. About that."

Ace took a sip of coffee. "I wondered how he got into that business and made his money."

As if on cue, Toussaint read from the Web site's history page. " 'Founder Carl Meadows set a high bar when he founded the company and constructed its first site, the award-winning office building in the suburbs of Winston-Salem, and since then, the standards of excellence in design and craftsmanship have only increased. A team of highly educated and talented individuals work to carry on the legacy that Carl created, and the success that he achieved.' "

He scrolled down to a picture of the founder. A tiny piece of the ice melted that was around Toussaint's heart where Winston was concerned. "No wonder that as he got older, the brothah had questions," he said into the silence.

"Malcolm walked over to where Toussaint sat. "What do you mean?"

Toussaint held up the image on the iPad. "This is Carl Meadows."

Everyone in the room took in the light-skinned, mild-mannered-looking man with thin lips and kind eyes. "Oh, goodness," Diane softly uttered.

"Jesus," Candace quietly exclaimed.

Ace put the situation in a simple perspective. "I don't know what his mama looked like, but he sure doesn't favor his daddy."

Malcolm took the pad from Toussaint and studied it closely. "Last night Mama saw what we didn't want to acknowledge— the truth. We'll get the DNA test done as soon as possible. But I'm almost as sure right now as she was last night. That man we met last night is my uncle."

"I think so too," Jefferson said.

"Oh, Lord," Candace lamented. "What are we going to do?"

Diane looked over and without missing a beat said, "Set another place at the table."

58

Chardonnay had just set another plate at her dining room table, glad to have the seat occupied by another grown-up. With Bobby gone, that rarely happened.

"This smells good, Char," Zoe said as she pulled out her chair.

"This came out of a box, sistah. Instead of Chef Bobby this is Chef Boyardee, so slow your gourmet roll." She opened the bottle of her namesake before sitting down.

Zoe laughed but immediately dug into the pasta dish. She'd not had a chance to eat lunch, and since Drake was working late, she had jumped at the chance to catch up with her friend. They'd talked on the phone a few times, but this was the first time they'd seen each other since the wedding. And so much had happened.

"Where are the kids?" she asked.

"Over at Bobby's sister's house."

Zoe's brow rose. "Oh?"

"Yeah, she started being able to stand me after Bobby left. I take the kids over there so that he can see them."

"Oh." Another bite and then, "So you guys still haven't talked at all?"

"Not unless you count me telling him to hold the sauce for a customer's rib order or put extra butter on somebody's baker to go."

"It's been what, almost two months?"

Chardonnay nodded.

"Dang, and he won't even let you explain?"

"No, but you have to admit that that DNA test spoke pretty loud. At least I haven't been served papers yet, so until that happens I'm going to keep hope alive."

"Have you tried calling Q?"

"Hell, no! What would I want to call him for? So little Bobby can have a crazy aunt named Keisha?"

"So the child can know his father. Bottom line, that is Q's child. He deserves to know about him."

"With Keisha's big-ass mouth, I'm sure he already does. And he hasn't called me, so there."

Zoe didn't have an answer for that, so she sopped up some of the tomato sauce with the Texas toast that Chardonnay had heated and took a healthy bite.

"So how is it being married to the boss?"

"Amazing. I can tell people that I'm sleeping with him and it's okay. The office is still pretty quiet, though. Mr. Livingston's death is mostly what everybody is talking about."

"That tripped me out when I heard it," Chardonnay said. "I was just sitting here chillin', watching the news, and when I saw why his face was on TV, I almost passed out."

"So sad. He'd just started coming back into the office. He may have been seventy-five, but he didn't look it and he definitely didn't act it. We haven't seen them too much. We think for the most part they're working from home."

A knock at the door interrupted the flow of conversation.

"I wonder who the hell that is?" Chardonnay said, rising from the table. She walked over, looked out the peephole, and turned around with wide eyes. *Bobby,* she mouthed. She opened the door, then looked behind him. "Where are the kids?" she asked. And then realizing that that probably wasn't the best thing to say to a man—excuse me, husband—who was darkening the door of the home front for the first time in two months, she added, "Hey, Bobby."

"Hey," Bobby said without looking in her direction. Instead he continued through the living room to where Zoe sat. "Hey, Zoe, what's up, girl?"

"Nothing much," Zoe said, rising. "Just came over here for a quick minute, waiting for Drake to tell me he was ready to meet me. I just got his text." Later, Zoe would wonder how in the world she'd made up that lie so fast. She walked into the living room, reached for her purse on the coffee table, and gave Chardonnay a hug. "Thanks for dinner, sistah. It was better than a drive-through. Bye, Bobby."

After Zoe left, an awkward silence descended on the room. Bobby stared at Chardonnay, who began straightening up a basically clean house. "I figured you were bringing the kids back home," she said, stacking up a pile of DVDs and placing them in the cabinet. "Are they still at your sister's house?"

Bobby's eyes smoldered as he answered her. "I didn't come over here to talk about the kids."

"Oh, okay." *Damn, I spoke too soon.* Chardonnay wondered where the divorce papers were. Had he folded them up and placed them in his pocket? "Uh, why'd you come over, then?"

"Because I'm tired of getting those nasty texts you keep sending me all day every single day."

Knowing Bobby's sexual appetite, Chardonnay had been texting him constantly with what she wanted to do to him and what she wanted done. So many that if she strung them together, she probably would have had a novel worthy of Zane Presents. She'd thought that if she could make him horny enough, he'd come back for the sex if nothing else. *Obviously, I thought wrong.*

"I know I should move on, Bobby. But every time I think of being with somebody else . . . it's just not the same."

Bobby almost nodded. It had been the same for him too. He'd had plenty of opportunities since separating, but none of them had ended up in his bed. Because none of them was White Wine. "Take off your clothes and get over here."

The command was so sudden and so unexpected that Chardonnay thought she was hearing things. "What?"

"You heard me. Get naked, woman. I'm going to answer those texts that you sent me, and I figured that I could show you better than I could tell you."

You didn't have to tell a woman like Chardonnay twice. Pants went one way, thong the other; bra and top stayed wherever they landed.

And still Bobby stood there, his only reaction a large, thick imprint in the front of his slacks that hadn't been there earlier. Finally, he spoke. "I thought I told you to get over here."

This command was like a starter gun. She ran across the room and into his arms, pulling tee and jeans and belt and buttons until he, too, was naked. The first throw down was right there on the living room floor: hot, fast, amazingly intense. They grunted, moaned, cried, screamed. It was a good thing Bobby's sister had agreed to keep the kids, or else even hardened Cognac may have been traumatized. The second time was slower, and on the couch. The third time was in the bathroom: before, during, and after their shower. A statistician may have technically called that six times, but the lovers weren't counting. In between loving, they warmed up Chardonnay's dinner. Bobby's comment while eating: "No wonder the kids have lost weight."

After the fifth set of fireworks (or eight for the statistician), Chardonnay and Bobby lay in the middle of their king-sized bed, arm in arm. "I love you, Bobby," Chardonnay said, cuddling closer against him.

"You finally realize that, huh?"

She nodded.

Bobby felt something wet on his chest. He looked down. "You crying?"

She shook her head.

Bobby smiled. "Yes, you are."

Several moments of silence and then Chardonnay whispered, "I'm sorry, Bobby."

"I know."

"I fucked up everything."

"Yes, you did."

"I wish there was something I could do to get you to come back here. The kids miss you. And I do too."

At this comment, Bobby abruptly got out of bed. He walked into the living room and began pulling on the clothes he'd discarded there earlier.

"Wait, Bobby, why are you leaving? What did I do?"

"You didn't do anything, Chardonnay. I came over here to answer your text messages." He glanced at her. "I think I did that."

"You just came over here to fuck me?"

Bobby reached for his shoes. "Pretty much."

Chardonnay crossed her arms. "Well, you know what, Bobby? Fuck you! I've spent the last two months on my knees, kissing your ass, telling you I'm sorry and I love you until my black face is blue. I've done for you what I haven't done for any other nucka, any other human being for that matter—in my entire life. I've let you know how I really feel, risked being hurt, humiliated, rejected. And you've done it all. Yes, I fucked up. Yes, I have three kids by three different fathers, even when I thought the last one belonged to the man I married. Newsflash, nucka. I'm not perfect. But guess what? Neither are you. Because after everything I've done, all you can do is come over here and shove all my feelings right back in my face. So you know what? You can kiss my black ass!"

The sound in the living room now probably resembled that of the quiet after a hurricane had struck. Then Bobby calmly put on his other shoe. "There you are," he said once he stood. "The Chardonnay that I remember." He walked to the door.

"Yeah, this is me and I'ma always be me. And as fucked up as I am, I still love you, Bobby Wilson. I still love you!" She ran after him but instead of trying to stop him, she slammed the door after him so hard that it shook on its hinges. She turned off the lights, stomped back into the bedroom, threw herself on the crumpled sheets, and dared herself to cry.

Several moments later, she heard a noise. *WTH?* Without turning on the lights, she tiptoed to her bedroom door and cautiously peeked her head around it. There, in the middle of the floor, stood Bobby. The duffel bag he'd left with and other belongings were at his feet.

Chardonnay stared at Bobby.

Bobby stared back. "The Chardonnay I remember is the one I want," he said simply.

Chardonnay ran into his arms. "Ooh, nucka, I'm going to kill you! But first let's fuck again."

59

Adam and Ace sat in Percillius Phelps's office, the same attorney who'd represented them during their trial against Quintin, and who upon Shyla Martin's arrest, had been called upon again. They were joined by the sons: Malcolm, Toussaint, and Jefferson. Bianca and Xavier had returned to LA.

"Gentlemen," Percillius began, in an authoritative tone. "I have news." Five sets of determined brown eyes stared him down. "Shyla Martin is being released."

Reactions? Instant:

"What the hell?"

"Why?"

"You've got to be kidding!"

Percillius held up his hands. "Guys, please. I understand your anger but let me explain."

Toussaint let out an expletive.

Adam added, "Please do."

Percillius clasped his hands together, and placed them on his large mahogany desk as he leaned forward. "You know she did it. I know she did it. We just can't prove it."

"Joyce saw her!" Jefferson shouted, his raised voice a rare show of anger.

"I believe you," Percillius replied. "But it won't hold up in a court of law."

"You saw the tape!" Toussaint persisted. "We could tell it was her!"

"The evidence is not conclusive," Percillius explained. "We can't definitively connect the person seen entering the kitchen area at the event with the woman Joyce saw running to her car and racing out of the parking lot. And there is no tape of whoever entered the kitchen pouring anything into the food. There was no camera in that back kitchen."

Adam thought back to an eerily similar incident: Quintin caught on tape in the Livingston Corporation parking lot—his image not conclusively identifiable. "Were there no cameras in the parking lot?"

Percillius shook his head. "Only near the entrances and exits, not in the area where Shyla parked."

"But that will at least show her being in the vicinity," Ace implored. "Those tapes will put her squarely at the scene of the crime."

"There were five thousand plus people at the scene of the crime that day, gentlemen. I'm sorry, but there was absolutely nothing I could produce that could keep Shyla locked up."

Adam leaned back against his chair. "What do we do now?"

Percillius looked Adam in the eye. "Put this incident behind you. Go on with your lives." He continued to eye each man in the room and knew there was no way in hell what he'd just suggested was going to happen.

Ten minutes later, the Livingston men stood near their cars in the Phelps Law Firm parking lot. "There's nothing more for us to do," Adam said with resignation. "At least we know what happened. Now, like Percillius said, we can put it behind us and move on."

Toussaint exploded. "That's bullshit! I'm tired of muthafuckas fucking with us without retribution!" And then, remembering the company he kept added, "Sorry, Dad, Ace."

"No need to apologize," Ace quickly countered. "I'm upset, too." He looked over at Malcolm who was using his finger to scroll down the screen on his cell phone. "I can see the wheels turning inside your head, man. Who are you calling?"

"Jon Abernathy," Malcolm said without hesitation. "Shyla may not be guilty in the court of law. But by the time we get finished with her reputation, she may think that going to prison would have been the lesser punishment."

The men standing in the parking lot nodded, and Toussaint smiled for the first time that day.

60

It must have been the week for reunions, retribution and res-
olutions because shortly after Bobby and Chardonnay got
back together and the Livingston's plans for Shyla Martin had
been put into place, another dramatic event occurred. Evelyn
Maureen Riley stood in her husband's chambers, joined by her
son, Cooper, and a very pregnant Keisha who despite her pro-
truding belly made a stunningly beautiful bride. She wore a
white chiffon A-line dress that dropped just below the knees,
and at seven months she still rocked five-inch heels. Evelyn
had suggested she choose a different color attire: pink, yellow,
or ivory at best. Keisha had patently ignored her, reasoning that
she may not have been a virgin, but it was her first marriage.

The ceremony was short, less than ten minutes, and witnessed—at Keisha's insistence—by a courthouse clerk. She
trusted Evelyn about as far as she could throw her and didn't
think it above her to later claim the marriage was counterfeit.
Sitting down, Keisha placed her hand on top of her insurance
marker—the baby that DNA had proved was a Riley offspring
with 99.9999998 percent accuracy.

And ten minutes after the ceremony, the judge, Evelyn,
Cooper, and Keisha entered a waiting limousine. "That was . . .
pleasant," Evelyn offered, trying to honor her wedding prom-

ise to be cordial. After seeing the tests results (discussed with her by none other than Dr. Michelle Hopkins, and how could she question that?), she'd resigned herself to the inevitable and begun planning for how to make the best of a bad situation. She knew she'd have to use finesse in how they were introduced, but already she'd hired speech and etiquette coaches and in short order would set up weekly lunches less for conversation and more for manners practice. It would take a Herculean effort, but Evelyn hadn't gotten where she was by backing down from challenges. She may display hers differently, but when it came to balls and being bodacious, she could roll with the best of them.

"I'm just glad it's over," Keisha said, squirming in her seat.

"It's only just begun, my dear," Cooper Sr. intoned in his usually dry fashion. As usual these days, his mind was elsewhere. Having lost his boy toy, Bobby, he was experiencing dick withdrawal. He had a couple people discreetly looking for a replacement, including Jon, but so far, a trustworthy substitute had not been found. And when it came to Jon, all the judge could do was roll his eyes. He may be the only person in Atlanta who didn't believe that Jon was as in love as he claimed in his interviews. But unless that woman had a dick, Jon would not be satisfied. A woman with a dick. Now *that* was a concept. He chuckled immensely at the thought.

"What's funny, dear?" Evelyn asked as they neared the five-star hotel's private entrance where a penthouse suite had been transformed into a summer wonderland.

"A funny thought is all, Evelyn. Let's go inside."

They were met at the door by a personal butler who whisked them to their personal elevator and shooed them inside. Seconds later, they entered the French-style living room with ornate brocade furniture, high ceilings, marble floors, and sparkling chandeliers. Sitting there was Cooper's sister, Kathy, and her husband, Charles. Keisha's shoulders slumped, but just slightly. The pregnancy preventing her from drinking was a serious hitch in the giddyup to hanging with this stuffy crowd, but at least she could get these clothes off and put on her custom-made silk sweats. She was heading for the master suite when she heard muffled voices. She stopped, listened more closely, and then heard a laugh. With a look of incredulity, she walked toward a closed door that led to a second living room in the penthouse suite. The voices were louder now, the laughter more pronounced. She thought she was dreaming but . . .

"Q!" Keisha flung open the door and raced in to hug her brother. Only after that did she realize the other people in the room, including her mother, Marilyn, with whiter eyes than she'd ever witnessed on this alcoholic's face, and even crazy Rico was in the room. "I can't believe it! How'd y'all get here?" Keisha was laughing and crying at the same time.

"Your *husband* did it, baby girl," Q explained. "And his bougie mama called ours personally and asked her to come."

Keisha was so shocked that she forgot that her feet were hurting. "Well, what are y'all doing in here?"

"Where else were we supposed to go?" Keisha's mother asked. "Out there with the folks sitting like statues in their chairs?"

Keisha knew exactly what her mother meant. At all times, the Riley clan was a study in perfected poise. "C'mon, y'all." Keisha reached for Q's hand and led the party of Millers and Brights into the room of Rileys. "Excuse me," she said, although she didn't have to. As soon as the motley crew entered, all talking ceased. "Thank you, baby," Keisha looked at Cooper, "Mrs. Riley," she looked at Evelyn, "for doing this, bringing my family here. I really appreciate it." Keisha reached for Marilyn's hand and with tears in her eyes, walked them over to where Evelyn stood. "I never thought I'd see y'all in the same room, let alone say these words but. . . . Mama, meet my mother-in-law, Evelyn Riley. Mrs. Riley . . . this is . . . my mother."

61

Q looked around his now near-empty apartment. He'd made a life-changing decision and he felt good about it. In fact, all of life felt pretty good right now. After more than ten months, his mother was still clean and sober, Keisha was married to Mr. Cooper, and the only man he loved more than himself was coming with him to Jamaica. He broke into a smile as he picked up the phone.

"You ready to rock and roll, my brothah?"

"Pretty much."

"You don't sound too excited."

"I am, man. Just tired. The wife and kids are beside themselves, though, and that makes me happy."

"I'm so glad you decided to move your family down and go into partnership with me, man. You're going to love Jamaica: beautiful, laid back, and the weed is tantamount, man, I'm telling you!"

"It's going to be a good change I think."

"It's going to be off the charts, man!" Q was fairly bouncing around he was so excited. And he was experiencing another rather foreign emotion: happiness. "Listen, my plane arrives just after six. What about you?"

"We land in Miami at eight thirty."

"Then it sounds like we'll be boarding the plane for Jamaica in twenty-four, and in forty-eight I'll be chilling with my girl. Man, I'm so glad we're doing this. We're going to be living a whole new life."

Quinn ended the call with a smile on his face. He may have been angry for a very long time, but now he felt that true happiness was within his reach.

Across town, there were at least two other people trying to exorcise Q out of their lives: Adam and Ace. "He's going to messenger over the stuff from his files," Ace said to Adam as he placed down the phone. "Not all of it, mind you, just some pictures and newspaper clippings."

"Why would you want to hang on to that?"

"Why wouldn't I? Looking at that will remind me to never, ever let down my guard."

Adam rose with a sigh and walked over to the window. "You ready for what's getting ready to happen, Twin?"

Ace walked over to the bar and poured a drink. "Ready as I'll ever be."

It had been all the brothers had talked about since getting the news that Winston Livingston Meadows was indeed their half brother. They'd felt a variety of emotions, from the loss of being Marcus Livingston's only seed to the excitement of having something they'd never experienced—another sibling.

"From the couple times I've spoken with him, he seems like a cool dude. He even sounds kinda like Daddy when he pronounces certain words." Adam walked from the window and sat back down on the couch. Then, because nerves wouldn't let him sit still, he walked over to the bar to refresh his drink as well. He'd just started to pour when the doorbell rang.

Ace and Adam exchanged a look before Ace walked to his front door and opened it. He still couldn't get over how much

Winston looked like his nephew, how he could have said he was Toussaint's father and no one would have questioned the claim. "Winston," Ace said with hand outstretched. The men shook hands. "Come on in."

"Nice neighborhood," Winston said as he followed Ace back to the den where Adam sat. "I appreciate the architecture."

"We've been here about fifteen years," Ace responded. "The wife keeps bugging me for us to upgrade, but I like it here."

Adam stood when the men entered. "Winston, how you doing, man?"

"Can't complain," Winston said, shaking the hand that Adam offered before doing the shoulder bump.

"Two fingers, right?" Ace asked, holding up the decanter filled with premium cognac.

"This has been the most interesting, trying time of my life," Winston countered. "Better make it three."

After making drinks, the men gathered around the game table in a corner of the room. Ace went into the kitchen and retrieved a large tray that Diane had prepared before she and Candace went shopping. It contained buffalo wings, thinly sliced roast beef, blue cheese dressing, and coleslaw. She'd left the rolls and chips in plain sight on the kitchen island, and a pitcher of tea chilled in the fridge as well. They shared small talk while they ate, themes common among most men: sports, politics, the rising cost of living.

Then Winston finished off his drink, sat back, and stared at his brothers. "I want y'all to know that your mother is amazing. Not many women would have done what she did—welcome me into the family like that, even before the tests came back."

Adam's smile was wistful, his voice tinged with pride. "Marietta Livingston isn't your ordinary woman."

"Yeah," Ace added. "After they made her, they broke the mold." He looked at Winston. "It's crazy how much you look like Daddy. We saw a picture of Carl Meadows and you look nothing like him. You were never curious about that? Never wondered why that was?"

"Of course, but when you got as much love as I did, you didn't dwell on it. Mama was dark-skinned, and a couple of her brothers were tall. So it wasn't inconceivable that what she told me was true: that I'd pulled my looks from her side of the family and my brains from my dad's. Carl Meadows was a genius: built a multimillion-dollar company without graduating high school."

Ace whistled. "That's impressive."

"Yes, it is. He built Meadows Construction from the ground up, started out as a laborer and ended up owning it all. He was a good man. I think that's why Mama planned it so that they'd both be gone before I found out the truth."

"How do you feel about that?" Adam asked.

"I understand it. But considering what's happened since then, your father's death, I wish she'd told me sooner. I always felt a connection with your family, would follow your progress in the news. I thought it was because I shared my middle name with your last one. Little did I know that I shared much more." Winston looked from Adam to Ace before asking, "Would you guys tell me about him? Would you share with me what Marcus Livingston was like?"

For the next hour that's exactly what they did, shared stories and pictures and memories that served as a catharsis for the twins and as info for their newly found brother. They laughed and cried as they remembered, a slow yet undeniable bonding occurring between the three of its own volition. By the time the doorbell rang again, all traces of discomfort and strangeness were gone.

Ace went to the door and this time returned with a box.

"Sterling is nothing if not efficient," Adam said as he watched Ace set the box down on the table. "If this is just a small portion of what he gathered, I don't want to see the whole file."

"We can go through it later," Ace said, taking a knife and splitting the tape. "But I just want a quick peek and see what type of stuff he gathered." He opened the box and pulled back the flaps. On the very top of the pile of papers was a mug shot of Quintin, the one taken when he was arrested in Jamaica more than a year ago. Ace looked at it a moment and then quietly handed it to his twin.

"Who's that?" Winston asked, unable to see the picture. "If you don't mind me asking."

"A man who was a pain in our ass for a long time," Adam answered. "But we finally closed the chapter on that part of our lives. Someone who was helping us resolve the situation had this sent over." Adam held out the picture to Winston. "Just so you can see what trouble with a capital T looks like."

Winston took the picture. "You're having trouble with this man?" There was no denying the incredulity in his voice.

"Don't let the good looks fool you. That man would sell his mama down the river if the price was right."

Winston continued to stare at the photo. "And what's with this name . . . Quintin?"

"He went by his first initial, Q," Adam all but spat. "He's a hustler and a scammer. I wouldn't be surprised if he has aliases." When Winston continued to stare intently, Adam's frown increased. "You're staring at that picture pretty hard, Winston. Do you know him?"

"I know someone who if not him could be his spitting image, a man who I've employed several times over the years. Good worker. Family man. But this man's name is Denton, not Quintin. And his last name is Williams."

"Wow, that is strange," Ace agreed.

"Well, you know what they say," Adam interjected in an effort to lighten the mood. "We all look alike."

"They say we all have a twin," Winston said, tossing the picture on the table. "Except for someone to look exactly like Denton, they'd have to have a large cross tattoo on their left arm."

Ace sat straight up. Time stood still. "What did you just say?"

"I said that Denton has a tattoo from his motorcycle-riding days. It's a Celtic cross. It really stands out because he didn't know when he got it that he had sensitive skin, causing the area to make a keloid scar. For Denton, though, it just made what he had more unique."

Ace jumped up and dumped out the contents of the box, and Adam reached for the phone. Winston sensed the atmosphere had changed, but he didn't know why. "What's going on, fellas? What did I say?"

"You just may have answered a million-dollar question, Winston," Adam said as he waited for his call to be answered. "Sterling, it's Adam. I'm over at Ace's house. You need to get here, quick!"

62

By the time Sterling arrived at Ace's house, Toussaint, Malcolm, and Jefferson had already arrived. Candace and Diane had cut short their shopping trip and come back as well. As these people were en route, Adam and Ace gave Winston the short version of their history with Quintin Bright, the TOSTS fire, and the critical answer to a clue that his information provided. Little had Winston known how much such a casual observation would impact his newfound family.

"Incredible," was Sterling's one-word response after Winston shared with him what he'd told the twins. "Now everything makes sense: the North Carolina connection, the continued activity even though Bright was behind bars, and the couple times we thought he'd been spotted before he got out."

"A twin brother, imagine that. Denton," Toussaint said reflectively as he looked at his father and then at Ace.

Adam added, "I always thought his actions were those with twice the asshole quotient."

"I can't ignore the irony of the havoc one set of twins has had on another set," Diane said, setting a tray of coffee and condiments on the sofa table.

"Double the trouble," Ace said, shaking his head.

"That's the interesting part of this," Winston said, reaching for the cup of coffee that Diane presented and nodding his head in thanks. "During the time he worked for Meadows Construction, Denton was one of my best workers—quiet, focused, always delivering excellent workmanship. He got along well with the rest of the guys, and one time, when a fellow worker's house caught on fire, Denton started the fund among the workers to help the brother out. And there's something else." Winston leaned forward in concentration as he recalled past conversations. "I remember him mentioning that he grew up in a poor, violent neighborhood and that his brother had served as the head of the family, taking care of him and his sister when they were young. I wonder if Quintin is the brother that Denton was talking about?"

The room was quiet, realizing just how little they knew about this man named Quintin Bright who'd so affected their lives.

Sterling made a note, asked Winston a few additional questions, and made more notes.

Ace thoughtfully sipped his coffee. "So what happens now?"

"I'm going to alert the authorities in Winston-Salem," Sterling replied, "and take the first available flight out in the morning. In the meantime, I'm going to try and locate Quintin Bright . . . and have a chat."

At about this same time and just over eight hundred miles away, two tall, dark, and handsome men made quite the statement as they strolled through Miami's International Airport. Their height was equal and their build almost the same, but where one sported a close-cropped style that was expertly cut, the other man's head was perfectly bald. Both men wore jeans, nice shirts, and dark glasses. Just behind them was an attractive woman pushing a stroller as she talked on the phone.

"I'm glad you're here, bro," Quintin said as they approached the gate for their American Airlines flight.

"Me too," Denton acknowledged. "Although I still don't know what was the rush, why you were so bent on us leaving now, instead of in a month or two.

"I told you, dog. We have to strike while the iron is hot. The planning for this two-billion-dollar revitalization project is going down, and waiting even a week to become residents might be too late for us to get in on what her family is doing. I told you that her uncles have portions of that on lock. One of them is the minister of tourism, another heads up law enforcement, and a third one is involved in construction and real estate. That's the one she thinks you'll be able to work with, get a project manager job or something, make some good money so that we can live like the other half for a minute."

"As I recall, you got to taste a little of the good life before you got locked down."

Quintin smiled. "Yeah, and thanks to our sister, I'm still living off of the Livingston's unsuspecting generosity."

"I don't know, man. I kinda feel bad about what I did, burning down that nice restaurant. You already had their money. Why did you ask me to do what I did?"

Quintin shrugged. "Maybe I shouldn't have burned old girl's spot. But really, that was more a nod for our brother-in-law than for me."

"Cooper?"

"Yeah. During one of his many jail visits, we talked about Bianca, the Livingston sibling who runs the joint out west. She hurt him bad, man, stringing him on for two years and then dogging him out and marrying that white dude."

"So he asked you to, what, get payback or something?"

"He didn't ask me outright, but he made it known that he wouldn't mind having her know how it felt to have something that you loved taken away from you. People like the Livingstons always get what they want, play by their own rules, and don't know what it's like to suffer. I was just helping out a brothah who'd helped me by doing what he'd never have the nerve to do."

Denton shook his head. "I don't get you, man. Wait, yes, I do. You're a gangsta with a heart."

"Ha!"

They settled into their seats to await their flight to Ocho Rios. "So, is it over?" Denton asked.

"Is what over?"

"The feud, this beef you have with your boys back in Atlanta. Is it over?"

Quintin was quiet for so long that Denton didn't think that he'd answer. But then Quintin's phone rang, bringing a slow and easy smile to his face. "Hey, baby," he said into the phone.

"Black mon, when you getting back here so I can get some of that loving?" Constance's sternly spoken question was music to Quintin's ears. He knew the kind heart behind the frown she often wore and the passion that was between her legs. "Woman, I was just there a few days ago. Can't a brothah have a minute to come back and grab his family? Hold on a minute." He turned to Denton. "Yeah, brothah, about what you asked me? It's over. Quintin Bright is getting ready to turn over a new leaf."

Late that night, Ace and Adam sat in their mother's kitchen. Since Marcus's death, they often came over two to three nights a week, and the wives visited as well. She tried to maintain a brave face, but the brothers knew how much she missed her husband. One couldn't spend almost six decades waking up to someone and not feel immense pain once they were gone.

"It's getting late, boys," Marietta said, taking away the saucers where crumbs were all that remained of her sock-it-to-me cake. "Y'all need to go on home. I'll be all right."

"We know you'll be all right," Ace said. "But we're over here so that we'll be all right. Somehow being in this house makes me feel closer to Dad."

"Uh-huh, and y'all think I'm going to leave this place and move back to Atlanta. No sirree. When I close my eyes for the last time, it's going to be here, in the last home Marcus and I shared."

"Okay, Mama," Adam began, "you're about to start something. I don't want you to even think about you closing your eyes like that until Tee turns forty."

"Toussaint's child? How old is she, one?"

Adam smiled as he nodded.

"So you expect me to live until I'm one hundred and twenty?"

Again, Adam nodded, trying to fight away a smile.

"Honey, my name is Marietta, not Methuselah. You'd better recognize."

Adam's phone rang. "Evening, Sterling. Any news?"

"Yes," Sterling said, "and I don't think you'll like it."

"Talk to me."

"Both Quintin and his brother, Denton, have moved out of their respective houses. Denton quit the job where he was working and his wife resigned from her teaching gig."

"What does that mean?"

"My guess is they've left the country. But don't worry. We caught them once; we'll do it again."

Adam hung up the phone and gave Ace a look.

"Problems?" Ace asked.

"We'll talk later," Adam replied.

"Don't think you're hiding anything from me by not talking," Marietta said, joining her sons at the table. "Sterling is that detective y'all hired, right? The one who helped capture the man who shot you?"

Adam gave a reluctant nod.

"And the one who just got out of jail?"

"Yes, Mama," Ace answered. "But there's nothing for you to worry about. Anything come up to do with him, we'll handle it."

"Uh-huh, that's what I'm afraid of. I've been hearing about y'all handling this situation off and on for over two, three years now. I know y'all don't want me to know about the troubles that have happened and the dramas going on. But I know more than y'all think I do and more than Marcus has told me. Things just come to me. It's always been that way. Now, that Quintin fellow has done us wrong, and he's been punished. Y'all may not agree with the reasons, but whatever they are, he's free. But what about you, Abram?" She looked at Ace. "And what about you?" She looked at Adam. "Because as long as y'all go chasing after that boy and have him crowding up your gray matter, he's still winning and you're the one in prison—a jail called revenge and retribution. Y'all are so much like your father, God rest his soul, who didn't take nothing off nobody and never backed down from a fight. So I wouldn't dare tell you to back down. But I am asking you to back away. Even though I was with your father for over fifty years, they went by in a flash. In other words, life is too short to spend it upset and angry. Let that boy go on about his business, and let's put our focus back on this family, on the Livingston legacy, and on continuing to honor your father's name."

63

Toussaint stepped into a dim, quiet home, and as always, it was as if the cares of the world faded away. Alexis said it was the feng shui touches she'd created throughout the home, but Toussaint knew that the peace he felt couldn't be delivered through a correctly placed plant, mirror, or water feature. The complete serenity he felt was due to what he had waiting upstairs or, more specifically, who. He took the stairs two at a time, and after a quick peek into the nursery and a kiss to Tee's forehead, he proceeded to the master suite. He opened the door, surprised to see that the room was dark and totally quiet. *Alexis is asleep? At ten o'clock?*

After a quick shower, Toussaint slid into bed and up against Alexis's back the way he always did—hard and naked. He lay an arm over her middle and nuzzled her neck until she stirred.

"Hey, baby," Alexis whispered.

"Hey." He nudged her. "Did I wake you?"

Alexis chuckled. "Didn't you mean to?" And then, "How was the evening?"

"Good, I guess."

Alexis turned to face Toussaint. "You're still hesitant, even after the DNA test?"

"No, I believe the test. And even if I didn't believe that, Marcus Livingston is written all over the brothah's face."

"He looks as much like your father as Adam."

"I don't know about all that, now."

"He does! But that's because you look so much like your grandfather."

"Yeah, and so does he."

"Do you think he'll become a part of the family for real?"

"After how he helped the family today, I'm sure of it."

"Really? How did he help you?"

Toussaint began placing kisses along Alexis's jaw. He'd spent a good part of the day talking about Quintin Bright and really didn't feel like bringing the brothah into his nighttime. "Why don't we talk about that tomorrow," he said, easing a hand over Alexis's thigh and squeezing her butt. "I have something else I'd rather do right now."

They began kissing, slow and leisurely, arousal coming in an instant. Alexis stroked Toussaint's long, thick, hard dick, her inner walls clenching at the mere thought that soon he'd be inside her.

And then a cry pierced the night.

"Oh, no!" Toussaint groaned as Alexis rolled out of bed.

"She's been cranky all afternoon," Alexis said with a chuckle when she returned to their suite. "She's teething again."

Toussaint took a still-whimpering daughter in his arms. "Quiet down, Tee," he commanded as he walked them to the sitting room. As soon as he sat down, the crying began anew.

"Just walk her for a bit," Alexis said, once again crawling into bed. "Maybe she'll go back to sleep."

He did, and she did, and after about twenty minutes Toussaint was back in the bed, ready to take up where they'd left off. "Now," he said, nipping a nipple with his teeth, "where were we?"

"You were just about to put this"—Alexis grabbed his rapidly hardening shaft—"right here." She straddled him, seconds away from sinking down on his manhood.

And a cry pierced the night again.

"Tiara!" This time Toussaint threw back the covers and stormed out of the room.

Alexis laughed as she, too, got up and this time reached for her gown. She knew the way that Tiara was crying that nooky would not come quickly tonight. Moments later, they lay in bed once again—Toussaint, Alexis, and Tee.

"Uh-huh, why aren't you crying now?" Toussaint asked when Tiara began cooing and playing with his finger. "I see that I'm going to have to teach you exactly who the boss is around here." But as the three of them went to sleep in the king-sized bed, all of them already knew that answer. Toussaint wouldn't get to make love to Alexis this night, but going to sleep with their child in between them was a different kind of affection—and perhaps the greatest love of all.

"Bianca, it's Ace." Xavier walked into the bedroom where Bianca was dressing for their nine o'clock dinner reservations and handed her the phone.

"Hey, Daddy."

"Hey, baby girl."

"We're headed out, Daddy."

"No problem. I'll make this quick. It looks as if Quintin and his brother have fled the country."

"What?" Bianca sat on a chair in her dressing room, intently listening to Ace recount what Sterling had told them. "Oh, it's on now. We're going to nail them," Bianca vowed, a fierce scowl marring her blemish-free skin. "Put both of them in jail where they belong and throw away the key! What's the plan of action, Ace? Do I need to fly down there?"

"That's why I'm calling you, baby girl." A short pause and then, "There's no plan of action."

"What do you mean there's no plan of action? Are we going to let him get away with destroying my business?"

"Mama had a long talk with Adam and me about this whole Quintin situation. She wants us to drop it, to put the past behind us and move on. She has a point, Bianca. Insurance covered the fire, no one was injured, and with all of the publicity the fire generated, Quintin actually did us a favor."

Bianca looked at the phone. "Okay, what have you done with my father and who is this imposter on the phone?"

Ace chuckled.

"What do you think GrandMar would say, Ace, if he heard that we were letting someone get away with what Quintin did?"

"Oh, I'd say his reaction would about match yours. But that's the thing, baby girl. He isn't here. So after more than fifty-five years of doing things his way, Mama has asked us to do this one thing her way for a change. And we've agreed."

"So he's just going to get off scot-free?"

"Mama said that he might get by, but he wouldn't get away."

They talked a bit longer and after getting off the phone, Bianca shared with Xavier what Ace had said. "I will go after him and get him, *cherie*," was Xavier's immediate response. "If that is what you want."

Bianca thought for a long moment as she slipped on her earrings, dress, and shoes. As she did a last spritz of perfume and reached for her purse, she thought some more. Finally, as they settled into Xavier's sports car for the ride to their favorite restaurant by the ocean, Bianca answered him. "Thank you, baby, but I'm going to acquiesce to Mom Etta's wishes."

Xavier looked at his fighter of a wife in surprise. "Why?"

"Because like she says: those assholes might get by, but they won't get away."

Jefferson entered his house and threw his keys on the table. It had been an interesting and full day, and he was more than ready to wind down. After leaving Ace and Diane's, he'd put on his uncle hat, stopped by Malcolm's house, and volunteered to take five children to the mall. "Time for uncle bonding," he'd told his startled cousin. Ten minutes into the trip and he knew why Malcolm and Victoria had looked at him like he was crazy. Because if you hadn't already lost your mind by picking up five children between the ages of one and ten, then by the time the trip was over, you were sure to have gone stone crazy. But it had been a good day, full of family, which had Jefferson—the only remaining single sibling—thinking of a family of his own.

He'd just started up the stairs when the doorbell rang. "I wonder who that could be," he mumbled, looking at his watch. It was a little after 10:00 p.m., and he thought that it might be Toussaint wanting to have a drink at the club. He looked through the pane and smiled as he opened the door.

"Joyce."

"Hello, Jefferson. I could say that I was in the neighborhood and just decided to drop by, but I'd be lying. I just heard it through the grapevine that Quintin had left Atlanta and considering what recently went down with Shyla, thought you could use some company and a listening ear."

"You came over here to talk business?"

Joyce laughed. "Believe it or not, I really did. Jefferson, you may not believe this but when I brought you home that night, it really wasn't with the plan to seduce you." Jefferson cocked a brow. "It wasn't! Not until I helped you undress did that thought cross my mind."

"Ha!"

"I know with our history that that might sound messed up. But hey, you're single, I'm single, I figured . . . why not? But that was then, this is now. And now," she pulled a bottle of pricey champagne out of her tote bag, "I'm here offering friendship and a drink. No more or less."

Jefferson blessed Joyce with his lopsided smile as he widened the door so that she could enter. As she walked fully into the room and over to the bar counter, he took his time appreciating her luscious, round booty, thick thighs, and generous hips. She turned and caught him staring. His smile widened.

He walked over to a china cabinet, pulled out two crystal flutes, then walked over to where Joyce stood. He took the bottle, opened it, and filled their glasses. "So you're here offering friendship, huh?"

"Yes. Friendship."

"I see." He looked her over, his chocolaty bedroom eyes darkening as they browsed. "Is that a friendship with benefits?"

What? Joyce had come over prepared to, at best, initiate a potential friendship or, at worst, get booted out on her romp. The last thing she came over for were benefits. But while this sistah was born at night, it wasn't last night. When it came to answering him, she didn't hesitate. "Definitely with benefits if that's what you want. But for me, having your friendship is what's most important."

"You know that I still owe you, right?" Joyce nodded. "Then let's toast to friendship and whatever else happens."

"To friendship," Joyce said, clinking her glass with Jefferson's. "And whatever else."

64

Six Months Later

Keisha sat on the couch in her living room, watching Cooper's pitiful attempt at trying to feed his daughter. "Hold her head back, Cooper. And stop acting like she's china. She won't break!"

If there was any truth to the proverb that a little child shall lead them, then Serenity Maureen Riley was that child and the Rileys were her loyal subjects. From the moment that Serenity was delivered into her father's arms—all eight pounds of butterscotch goodness, with a head full of thick black hair, half-moon dimples, and a spray of freckles across her nose— Keisha's life had changed. She lost her baby weight in just six weeks, in time for the mammoth baby shower that Kathy had belatedly decided to throw. And what a breath of fresh air her sister-in-law turned out to be. Around her family, she was a replica of her mother, but when Keisha turned sister-girl onto Patrón shots with Moscato backs? She went buck wild!

Keisha's phone rang. She fished for it beneath a mound of pillows. "Ooh, this is the call I've been waiting for. Hey, brother!"

"Hey, baby sis. How are you doing?"

"Fine."

"How's my beautiful niece?"

"So you got the pictures."

"Yeah," Q drawled. "All dozen of them."

Keisha laughed. "I didn't send that many. Okay, maybe I did. How's Constance?"

"As evil as ever."

"Ha! That must mean she's keeping you in line." Keisha watched as more applesauce landed on Serenity's bib than in her mouth. " Look, I have to go but I just wanted you to know that Cooper made the reservations. We'll be coming there for New Year's."

"That's what I'm talking about! Mama is coming too."

"So are the Rileys."

"Word?"

"As in my sister-in-law, Kathy, and her family."

"All right, then, bet."

"I'll call you later. Give Denton a hug for me. We'll see y'all soon." Keisha ended the call and took the baby.

"We've got to go, dear," Cooper said, reaching for the diaper bag. "Mother is a stickler at Sunday dinner. It's aperitifs at three and we can't be late."

Bobby and Chardonnay relaxed on the couch, Chardonnay in a reclined position, Bobby rubbing her feet. "All right, that's enough. Your rough-ass heels are about to cut my hands!"

"You're lying! I just got a pedicure last week!"

"You should have gotten a massage, too," Bobby said, shifting Chardonnay's legs off of his lap and reaching for the beer that rested on the table. "Because I'm done."

"When is your sister bringing the kid's back?"

"I don't know."

"Do we have time to do the nasty?"

"Damn, girl. Don't you ever get enough?"

"Oh, no, you did not just say that." Chardonnay watched as

Bobby flipped through the channels. He stopped on a news channel showing a photo of current senators. Jon Abernathy stood proudly among them.

"What's up with your boy, Senator Abernathy?"

"What do you mean what's up?"

"He was in town the other day and came into the restaurant. You would think him and that woman Divine are glued at the hip. I've never seen a man so goo-goo eyed."

"Are you sure about that, woman? Have you ever seen me staring at you?"

"Whatever, nucka." But Chardonnay was grinning from ear to ear. She repositioned the pillow and reached for the remote next to Bobby's leg, sometimes still needing to pinch herself to know this—Bobby back in their lives—was real and not a dream. When he moved back home, they'd had a long talk . . . about everything. Two months later, they'd gone to visit an attorney and were now in the beginning stages of Bobby adopting all of the children. They'd contacted Quintin through Keisha, and while he still hadn't met Bobby Jr. and seemed to be cool with Bobby, who he'd spoken to on the phone, he was still the last holdout on signing away his parental rights. In time, however, Chardonnay and her family would truly be united under one father and one name. And then there was the icing on the proverbial cake.

"Bobby, I'm hungry."

"Hungry? Girl, we just ate not more than an hour ago!"

"But you didn't fix that much."

"What? Steak, mashed potatoes and gravy, corn, green beans, biscuits, and a salad to start? And you're hungry again? What the hell is wrong with you?"

Chardonnay smiled. "You'll see what's wrong with me in about seven months."

"What the hell is going to happen in seven months, besides our getting ready to move to Las Vegas?"

"It's happening right now . . . me, uh, eating for two."

"What, you schizophrenic now? Trying to be, what's her name . . . Sybil, and shit?" Bobby looked at Chardonnay, laughed and shook his head. "Are you sure it's just two of you in there because . . ." The sentence died on his lips as reality dawned. His face was an unreadable mask as he looked at his wife. "What are you telling me, Chardonnay?"

Chardonnay swallowed her nervousness. She knew it was another mouth to feed but he just had to be happy. He had to! "I'm pregnant. And this time I know that the baby is yours."

It felt that minutes passed when in reality only seconds had gone by. The only sound heard was from the television, its low volume now serving as a distraction. Bobby reached over for the remote and turned off the TV. "What did you say?"

"I didn't mean for it to happen. But I bought a test from the .99 Cents Store. We're getting ready to have another mouth to feed."

Chardonnay stared at Bobby's stone face, not knowing whether he was getting ready to celebrate or curse her out. Then a lone, single tear dropped from the corner of his eye, followed by another. "You're getting ready to have my child, for real?" Chardonnay nodded. "Come here, woman!"

Bobby hugged her so hard, Chardonnay couldn't breathe. But she didn't care. This was the reaction she'd dared to hope for . . . that Bobby would want her to have this child.

"Okay," Bobby said, pulling back and looking at Chardonnay with a very serious expression. "I'm going to tell you how it's going down from here on out. No more alcohol. No more weed. No scheming, lying, and conniving trying to get over on the Livingstons or anyone else. When we get to Vegas, we're turning the page on all that shit. You're a wife, and a mother, and it's time you move on from that hoodrat mentality. Got it?" Chardonnay didn't answer. Bobby grabbed her arm. "Chardonnay, I said do you got it? If not, tell me and I'll bounce right now!"

Now it was time for Chardonnay to tear up. She could get used to this new Bobby, the one who didn't let her walk all over him, didn't take her shit. "I got it." She scooted over to close the distance between them and fell into his arms. "I love you, Bobby," she said, amid kisses.

"I know," Bobby replied, when he came up for air. "I love you, too . . . with your crazy ass."

Shyla Martin heard her aunt knock on the bedroom door. Knowing that she wouldn't be left alone until she answered, she sat up and cleared her throat. "Yes, Aunt Jackie?"

"Are you okay, dear?"

"I'm fine."

"Will you be joining us for dinner?"

"I'm really not hungry."

"Dear, we're worried about you."

"I said I'm fine!" And then because she knew it wasn't her aunt's fault added, "I'll join you and Uncle Morris for dessert."

"Okay, sweetheart. See you in about half an hour."

Shyla rolled her eyes and lay back on the bed in the room where she'd spent childhood summers. Even with all the time that had passed, she still couldn't believe everything that had happened, still couldn't believe what had happened to her life.

For starters, she now had an arrest record. Shyla Martin in handcuffs? The thought of that alone made her shudder, the weeks she'd spent behind bars made her cry. The other prisoners had hated her, threatened her from the very start. If it hadn't been for the fact that a guard had befriended her, and had her placed in a solitary cell away from the general population, who knows what would have happened.

Once she was released from prison, she thought her troubles were over. Sadly, they'd only just begun. The advertising company had fired her, paying her attorney had left her broke and after two months of not paying rent, the ritzy apartment complex had thrown her out on her behind. Going to her parents was not an option. Having them all up in her business would have been worse than being locked up. After exhausting every contact she had in Atlanta, and being denied entry into FGO, Shyla had finally admitted defeat, boxed up her belongings, concocted a story about "an exciting job opportunity in Cleveland" for her parents, and fled to relatives in Ohio.

Rolling over and crushing a pillow beneath her, Shyla thought back to her last interaction with the Livingstons. It was a phone call, from Toussaint. And it was a conversation that she'd never forget.

"We know you did it, Shyla."

"Toussaint, I have no idea what you're talking about."

"Really? Well, we have no idea why you can't get a job, a loan, entry into the club, or have a single soul in this city pay you the time of day." Shyla's heart had clenched at this pronouncement. Suddenly all of the closed doors made sense. "You might want to think about leaving Atlanta. I hear that this place is getting more unsafe by the minute. Crime is rising. Living alone, no one to watch your back . . . you never know what might happen."

Later that night, Shyla had returned home to find her apartment door standing ajar. Though nothing was taken, her place had been ransacked. Shyla left Atlanta two days later. And the way things looked right now . . . she would never go back.

It was a beautiful day in Los Angeles and Bianca was beside herself with joy. Since opening the West Coast locations, it was the first time that her entire family had joined her here. Even Marietta, who swore that flying was for animals born with wings, had faced her fears and braved the journey. They sat in Bianca's dining room, where she'd removed her smaller table and set up two round tables instead, enough to accommodate Adam; Candace; Ace; Diane; Malcolm; Victoria; Toussaint; Alexis; Jefferson, Joyce (yes, really); Winston; his wife, Roslyn;

and Xavier Marquis. The children were in another part of the house with the nannies. This was grown-folk time.

Once everyone had been served, Marietta stood. "This is the first time we've all been together like this since Marcus left. I still..." She faltered, and her eyes filled with tears. "I still miss him so much, still can't believe he's gone. But you children have helped me get through what I didn't think I'd survive, and I thank you. I know he said it to your face, but y'all have no idea how often he said it to me, how proud he was of each and every one of you. How you've worked and persevered and come through all kinds of trials and tribulations. You took his dream and went further than he ever imagined. And now here I am at my granddaughter's house, having eaten that finger food mess she calls tap us—"

"Tapas, Mama," Ace corrected, hiding a grin.

"Whatever. I'm just glad that what I see on the table today has some grease in it."

Everyone laughed.

"I don't want the food to get cold, so let me propose this toast. It's to my husband, y'all's daddy, who's still with us in spirit, and to the business that the Livingstons built, one rib at a time. That's what Marcus loved the most, that y'all know how to take care of business. But you know what means the most to me? That y'all take care of each other. When it comes to this Livingston family, there's no business more important than that."

TAKING CARE OF BUSINESS

Lutishia Lovely

ABOUT THIS GUIDE

The suggested questions that follow
are included to enhance your group's
reading of this book.

Discussion Questions

1. Now that you've met most of them, which is your favorite Livingston (male or female) and why?

2. I found it a pleasure to tell the story of Marcus and Marietta Livingston, the couple through which the dynasty began. Did this historical perspective enhance your understanding of and love for all that the Livingstons achieved?

3. The Livingstons were faced with one challenge after the next, from plotting ex-mates to vengeful business personnel. Why do you think this happened? Did the family bring on any of what happened through their own actions, or do challenges and haters simply come with the territory called success?

4. In this novel, the business that Bianca managed was targeted by Quintin for retribution. Do you think this was fair, and do you buy Quintin's explanation of why he continued to have a beef against the Livingstons?

5. In this novel, secondary characters such as Chardonnay, Bobby, Keisha, and Cooper received major parts of the story line. Did this enrich the story for you? Why or why not?

6. Do you think Cooper would have stayed with Keisha had she not gotten pregnant?

7. Do you think Bobby should have come back to Chardonnay? Were you surprised that he did?

8. If you found out your man had experienced same-sex intimacy, would you stay with him the way that Chardonnay did Bobby? Did learning about Bobby's prison

experience change how you felt about his double lifestyle? Do you know men friends with this same experience?

9. What are your thoughts about Jon and Divine? About homosexuality and transgender roles in general, and about the continued presence of the "down low" male in particular?

10. Were you surprised that Jefferson and Joyce got together? How do you think his family feels about that? How do you feel? Do you think that they'll stay together? Why or why not?

11. Winston was an unexpected addition to the Livingston family drama. What are your thoughts about him? Should he have done what he did in seeking out the family? Do you think he will continue a productive relationship with the family?

12. Who would have ever imagined that Quintin Bright had a twin? What are your thoughts on Denton Williams?

13. *Taking Care of Business* was filled with several different themes. What are your thoughts on love? Greed? Family ties? Social status? Betrayal? Mixing business with pleasure?

14. Of all of the couples—Adam and Candace, Ace and Diane, Malcolm and Victoria, Toussaint and Alexis, Bianca and Xavier, Jefferson and Joyce, Chardonnay and Bobby, Jon and Divine, Quintin and Constance, and Keisha and Cooper—which one's journey would you like to know more about. Why?

15. Marietta Livingston has decreed that the beef between Quintin Bright and the Livingstons be put to an end. As of this moment, her sons Adam and Ace have acquiesced to her wishes. Do you think this impasse will last?

All Up in My Business

Seven months earlier...

"Y ou've come up, my brothah! This place is off the charts!" Toussaint Livingston moved around the new "man cave" in his brother's house.

"I was hoping to have it done last weekend and invite y'all over for Memorial Day."

"That's all right. The NBA championship game is coming up. I know where I'll be watching."

What had formerly been a seldom-used, garden-level family room now resembled a gentlemanly sports club: Dark-stained walls offset by white marble floors surrounded a pool table, a poker table, oversized chairs, and well-placed ottomans, and a wall-length, fully stocked bar anchored the room. Framed, autographed photos of some of Malcolm Livingston's favorite athletes lined the walls, along with a few famous jerseys, foot-balls, basketballs, and a Hank Aaron—autographed baseball bat. Anyone seeing the man who now stood before a signed Michael Jordan basketball, which was encased in Plexiglas and sitting on a pedestal, may have mistaken him for a professional athlete. A tautly muscled six foot two and two hundred pounds, Toussaint looked ready to catch a pass and then run for fifty yards, or hit a baseball out of the park. "Man," he said, continuing to scope the room. "You make me want to fix up my place."

"What's stopping you?" Thirty-four-year-old Malcolm Livingston, Toussaint's older brother by eighteen months, proudly walked over to the bar that had been made to resemble the one in his favorite gentlemen's club. Aside from stocking almost every liquor known to man, the bar housed four beer taps and the necessities for serious drink-making: shakers, strainers, muddlers, slicing boards, and glasses of every shape and size. A full-sized refrigerator, with the front made out of the same wood as that on the walls, blended seamlessly into the well-appointed space. Malcolm couldn't wait until the next Super Bowl. "Huh? What's stopping you?" he asked again, pouring him and his brother mugs of ice-cold beer.

"You have a wife to handle the details. I don't have one of those or the time to do it myself." He accepted the beer from his brother and took a swig. "Ah. This is on point!"

"First of all," Malcolm said after he, too, had taken a long swallow, "you don't have a wife because you don't want one, and secondly, everything you're looking at was my idea— well, mine and the designer's. All Victoria did was let the woman in."

Toussaint's ears perked up. *Woman?*

"Yeah, I thought that would get your attention. Unlike the past two months when I've tried to tell you about the renovation and you were too busy to listen."

"I don't remember you mentioning a female."

"That's because I was trying to tell you about the design, not the designer, brother. Uh-huh, you wished you'd listened now, don't you? And she's fine too. . . ."

"What's her name?"

"Don't matter," Malcolm answered, purposely messing with his skirt-chasing sibling. "This one isn't your type, Toussaint. You like 'em tall and light, all polished and refined. Like Shyla. Alexis is a dark, bohemian-style chick."

"C'mon now, Malcolm. You know I like dark meat. Alexis? That's her name?"

Malcolm sighed and walked over to a rectangular coffee table. He reached down and pulled out a folder. "I know you won't stop until you've satisfied your curiosity, so here you go. This is her marketing material. And I'll tell you now—she's good, but she don't come cheap!"

"In designing or dating?"

"Ha! Definitely the designing but probably both."

Toussaint took the folder and sat on the dark leather love seat. DESIGNS BY ST. CLAIR was emblazoned across the front of the pocketed folder. He sipped his beer as he opened it and was immediately drawn to the photo of a woman on the folder's bottom left side. Toussaint's eyes widened as he hurriedly set down his beer. "I know her!" he exclaimed.

There she was, looking just the way Toussaint remembered—like a bar of dark chocolate. And, he imagined, probably tasting as sweet.

"What do you mean, you know her?" Malcolm asked.

Toussaint chuckled and sat back, his eyes still glued to her picture. "She got into a fight over me," he began. . . .

"Wait, wait!" Long locs flew behind the compact, curvy woman as she ran up to the parking meter attendant. "I've got a quarter." She hurriedly dug into her purse and pulled out a wallet.

The attendant, who'd just flipped open his pad, began punching in numbers.

"Don't tell me you're going to stand there and write up a ticket. I told you, I have the quarter."

"Look, when I got here, the meter was expired."

"We got here at the same time! Why are you going to charge a ridiculous fine when I'm standing here telling you that I've got it?"

"You should have thought about that before you came back late to your car."

"This isn't my car, but that's not the point!"

"What? This isn't your car? Then why are you yelling at me? You can't pay for someone else's meter time."

"Are you kidding me? How do you know who's paying for what?"

"I know that you aren't paying for this. This vehicle is being ticketed."

Alexis St. Clair knew she was being totally irrational, but she was livid. Recently, she'd received a citation for being parked in a nine-to-five no-parking zone. She'd been to a business meeting breakfast and had reached her car at 9:01. After finding out the amount of the fine—over one hundred dollars with court costs—Alexis had become incensed and decided to fight the charge. She showed up in court, but her very logical argument of why one minute should not equal one hundred dollars—with a timed and dated camera shot provided as evidence—was soundly shot down. She learned from a couple other citizens who were also fighting their tickets that a new company had taken over monitoring the streets of Atlanta. The number of tickets issued had gone through the roof. She'd been angry ever since, which is why when she saw yet another hapless Atlanta citizen about to get jacked (because in her mind it was straight-out robbery), she took matters into her own hands.

Hands on hips, the usually calm Alexis brushed aside the attendant and placed a quarter in the slot. "You cannot put a ticket on a car that is parked legally, and this car is now parked legally. So your ticket is null and void!" When she was really angry, a slight accent from summertimes spent with her St.

Croix paternal grandparents surfaced. Now was one of those times. Her words were clipped and precise, her voice raised.

"Look, I've had just about enough of you," the short, slightly overweight officer said with a huff. "If you don't leave now, I'll have you arrested!"

Toussaint, who'd been observing this exchange in rapt amusement, hurried to the scene. He'd enjoyed seeing a complete stranger come to his, or rather his Mercedes's, defense—had enjoyed watching her give attitude. Not to mention he'd appreciated watching her ample breasts heave with her movements, loved how her thick booty filled the back of her jeans. Yes, he'd enjoyed the show and the scenery but didn't want to see the sistah get arrested.

"Officer, there's no need for that. If you'll give me the ticket, I'll be on my way." Toussaint's comment was directed toward the officer, but his dazzling smile was on Alexis. "Thanks for defending me. That was impressive."

"Toussaint?" For the first time since the encounter began, the officer stopped punching his pad.

Toussaint turned to look at the officer. "Greg?"

"Man, how are you doing?"

The two men did a soul brother's handshake.

"I can't complain." Toussaint looked at the ticket machine. "At least not too much."

The parking meter officer looked embarrassed. "Aw, man, I wish I'd known. I've already processed it so, you know... maybe call the office."

"Oh, so if you'd known it was *him*"—Alexis whirled on Toussaint—"whoever you are"—and then back to the officer—"you wouldn't have written the ticket? Is that how things work? Not what you know but who you know? So Mr. Mercedes gets off scott-free if he *knows* somebody, but Ms. Infiniti here has to pay?" Alexis was now as angry that the officer might *not* give the ticket as she was when he was determined to give it.

"My goodness, we're feisty," Toussaint said, his flirty eyes scanning Alexis's body with admiration. "If it makes you feel better, baby, I'll pay the ticket. And I want to thank you for defending my honor by taking you to dinner." He reached out his hand. "I'm Toussaint Livingston. And you are?"

"Out of here," Alexis said as she turned to walk away. The man was obviously some muckety-muck who got life handed to him on a silver platter. People who got passes like that got on her nerves. His deep-set brown eyes, long curly eyelashes, wink of a dimple, and thick juicy lips had gotten on her nerves as well. She didn't have time for . . . none of that.

"But wait." Toussaint hurried after her. "What's your name?"

"I'm not interested."

"But it's just dinner!"

"I'm not hungry." With that, Alexis crossed the street and disappeared into downtown Atlanta's morning rush crowd.

Malcolm laughed as Toussaint finished his story. "She left you hanging, just like that? Alexis is a smart, talented designer, but that feisty filly you described doesn't sound like the woman I know."

"You haven't seen her fire, my married brother, but I have. And I want to fan that flame. This is the same woman. I'd know her anywhere."

"You mean you *want* to know her. But it doesn't sound like that feeling is mutual." Malcolm laughed again at the thought of his Don Juan brother being rejected. That didn't happen often. No wonder he was curious.

"Can I hang on to this?" Toussaint said, placing the folder under his arm as he stood and drained his glass. "I think it's about time for me to redo my house."

After Toussaint left, Malcolm poured himself another brewski and then settled himself into one of the room's over-sized recliners. He opened up the arm, revealing an array of buttons that operated every electronic feature in the room. Smiling, he pushed the first button. A smooth pulley system began retracting a deep navy curtain along one wall, revealing a 125-inch screen. Malcolm popped the remote control out of its recessed cradle, also in the arm, and turned on the set. The television was set on ESPN2, and tennis was playing. It didn't matter to Malcolm. Aside from polo and maybe swimming, he'd never met a sport he didn't like.

Ah, yeah, that Nadal dude is bad. He watched the tall, mus-cled Spaniard race across the baseline and backhand a volley across the net. The crowd went wild, and the player clenched his fence. Malcolm noted Nadal's opponent was the equally talented Roger Federer. Malcolm reached for a bowl of salty pretzels, ready to enjoy a quiet Sunday afternoon watching the Wimbledon final. He turned up the volume, smiling. *This is going to be good.*

"Daddy! Daddy!" Brittany, Malcolm's rambunctious six-year-old, came bounding down the stairs. On her heels were his three-year-old twins. "We want to go shopping, get some ice cream. Can you take us? Please!"

"Where's your mama?" Malcolm asked, his eyes not leav-ing the screen. God knew that he loved his children, but he'd be lying if he said there weren't times when he didn't long for the good ole bachelor days. Like now, when he wanted to chill and watch TV—alone.

"She said she's tired. She told us to ask you!"

Malcolm fought to not show his irritation. Britt saw everything. One hint of a frown and she'd turn into the *En-quirer,* asking why he was mad at her or her mother. He swore the child was psychic, because as quiet as he and Victoria tried to keep their ever-increasing disagreements, Britt always seemed to sense their discontent.

"Look, Daddy's tired too. Let me rest awhile, finish watching this game, and then I'll take y'all out somewhere."

The twins begged to stay downstairs with him, but he bribed them into returning upstairs. Now he had to get ice cream *and* toys. Malcolm thought about his wife and this time didn't try to hide his frown. *What's really going on with you, Victoria? You've been acting strange for the past couple months. Ever since . . .* Malcolm abruptly turned off the set, poured the almost-full mug of draft beer down the bar sink's drain, and walked up the steps. Thinking about his marital situation had darkened his mood, especially as he thought of his footloose and fancy-free single brother. He imagined that even now Toussaint was making a date with the sexy interior designer at whom Malcolm could only look and not touch.

I love being married with children, Malcolm concluded as Brittany, the twins, and the oldest son, Justin, piled into his SUV and they headed to Lenox Square. *But I don't like it all of the time.*

Mind Your Own Business

"Why can't a woman be on top?" Bianca Livingston demanded, tossing shoulder-length, straightened hair over her shoulder. She stood over her older brother as if ready to strike, looking totally capable of kicking butts and taking names. Her quick smile, short stature, and girly frame had caused many men to underestimate her—to their peril. But anyone seeing her now—shoulders back, hands on hips, her perfectly tailored black suit and four-inch heels adding to her aura of power—would believe her capable of running almost anything. "I'm as qualified to run the West Coast division as you are, even more so, matter of fact."

"You're qualified to run the kitchen, *maybe*," her older brother retorted. Jefferson suppressed a smile. He'd taunted his sister from birth, and he did so now. Her fiery personality was the perfect foil for his laid-back teasing. But even with his ongoing provocations, this time Jefferson's antics masked the seriousness of his quest. He had every intention of being the Livingston who moved to LA to establish the Taste of Soul restaurants both there and in Nevada. But unlike most Livingstons, he didn't like confrontation or competition. He'd quietly made his bid to step away from his cushy position in the finance department to run the West the same way he cooked his ribs: low and slow. "Isn't that why you spent the last nine months in Paris?" he queried to underscore his point. "Learning the fine art of cooking so that you could give our soul food some class?"

Actually, Bianca had fled to Paris to get away from the chain around her neck otherwise known as fiancé Cooper Riley, Jr. But only one other person knew this truth—her cousin, Toussaint Livingston. Initially, forestalling the marriage everyone else believed was a *fait accompli* was also why she'd expressed interest in running the West Coast locations. But now, after months of talking with Toussaint, who, besides being her confidant and a Food Network star, was also the ambitious brainchild behind their company expanding out West, Bianca wanted to relocate to put her mark on the Livingston dynasty and make the West Coast Taste of Soul restaurants shine.

Bianca replied, "Need I remind you that I have not only a culinary certificate from Le Cordon Bleu, but also an undergrad and a graduate degree in business administration?"

"No, little sis, you don't need to remind me." Jefferson's smirk highlighted the dimple on his casually handsome face, his sienna skin further darkened by the November sun. His deep-set brown eyes twinkled with merriment. "But do I have to remind you that I have double masters in business administration and finance?" Jefferson had been the first Livingston in two decades to follow up his stint at Morehouse with two years at Wharton's School of Business.

Bianca, knowing that she couldn't go toe to toe when it came to her brother's education, tried a different route. She walked away from Jefferson and sat in one of the tan leather chairs in the artistically appointed office. Reaching for a ballpoint pen that lay on his large and messy mahogany desk, she adopted a calmer tone, yet couldn't totally lose the petulance in her voice. "Jefferson, the only reason Dad is promoting the idea of your heading up the location is because you're the oldest."

"And the son, don't forget about that. You know Dad doesn't want to see his baby girl fly too far from the nest."

"Okay, probably that, too," Bianca conceded. It was no secret that when it came to her father, Abram "Ace" Livingston, she was the apple of his all-seeing eye.

"Besides, how are you even considering relocation when you've got a fiancé champing at the bit to get married? Cooper has been more than patient with you, Bianca. Not many men would let the woman they love move to the other side of the world, even if it was, as you successfully argued, for the union's greater good. What did you call it? Increasing your company value and the marriage's bottom line? As if being a Livingston isn't value enough? No, Bianca, Cooper allowed the wedding to be pushed back once already. He's not going to delay it a second time. And you know he isn't moving to LA."

Tears unexpectedly came to Bianca's eyes. She abruptly rose from the chair where she'd been sitting and walked to the window. The glory of the day, boasting colorful autumn leaves framed by a sunny blue sky, was lost on her. "You're probably right," she said, quickly wiping her eyes. "If everyone has their way, in six months I'll be married and in nine have a baby on the way." *But how can I marry Cooper after what happened in Paris?*

"Hey, sister, are you all right?"

Bianca jumped. She hadn't heard Jefferson rise, hadn't been aware that he'd walked from his desk and joined her at the window. "Actually, no, if you want to know the truth. Jeff, I—"

"Hey man, oh, Bianca, I'm glad you're both here." Toussaint Livingston burst into Jefferson's office, and now rushed toward his cousins on the other side of the room. The seriousness of his countenance took nothing away from a face that models would envy, along with six feet, two inches and almost two hundred pounds of delectable dark chocolate. "We need to roll to y'all parents' house right now. Emergency family meeting."

Their conversation forgotten, both Jefferson and Bianca turned at once, talking simultaneously.

"What's the matter?"

"What's going on?"

Bianca's heart raced with concern. "Why are we meeting at Mom and Dad's house, Toussaint, and not in the conference room?"

Toussaint turned and headed for the door. "That's what we're getting ready to find out. I'll meet y'all there."

Fifteen minutes later Toussaint, Jefferson, and Bianca joined their family members in the living room of Ace and Diane's sprawling Cascade residence. Toussaint's parents, Adam and Candace, and his brother, Malcolm, were already there. The trio from the office was the last to arrive and as soon as they sat down, Ace began speaking.

"We've got a situation," he said without preamble. "Some-body's stealing company funds."

Reactions were mixed, with bewilderment and anger vying for equal time.

"Who is it?" Bianca demanded, ready for battle though the culprit remained unnamed.

"We don't know," Ace replied. "But it's definitely an inside job."

The family members looked from one to the other, a myr-iad of thoughts in each mind. *Who could it be? How did this happen? Is the guilty party somehow connected to someone in the room?* One family member even pondered the impossible: *Is the thief one of us?*

"What kind of money are we talking about?" Toussaint asked. "Hundreds, thousands . . . more?"

"A couple hundred thousand," Ace replied, his tone somber and curt.

Again, responses were symphonic.

"What the hell?"

"Who could do such a thing?"

"Oh, hell to the *N-O*. We're not going to take this lying down."

"You're absolutely right, baby girl," Ace said to Bianca. "We're not going to stand for this, not at all. Nobody steals from our company without feeling the wrath of a Livingston payback."